DANCER'S FLAME

ALSO BY JASMINE SILVERA

Lenore
Dance like
no one's
watching!

DANCER'S FLAME

GRACE BLOODS BOOK TWO

JASMINE SILVERA

Published by No Inside Voice, Seattle, WA 2018

ISBN: 978-0997658217

Cover design by Damon Freeman

Book Design by No Inside Voice

Printed in the United States

✿ Created with Vellum

For the OG
Weißt du eigentlich, wie lieb ich dich hab?

PROLOGUE

The timing couldn't have been worse, but so it went with death. As a principal ballerina of the Praha Dance Academy, Yana's schedule was overbooked with rehearsals, performances, workshops, a photo shoot, and interviews. And now this—her grandfather was dying, and she was due at his bedside. She postponed everything that could wait, gave her performances to her understudy, and booked a flight to Moscow and a car to the airport.

A car that was nowhere to be seen.

She peered out of the expansive three-bedroom apartment over-looking the Vltava on the Malá Strana side of the river. It was a ridiculous expense, this place. But her father insisted on the best. He had a reputation to uphold.

She also knew that she was under surveillance most days from a team of discreet but professional bodyguards. Begging her father not to hire security had been useless.

Much like the man on his deathbed waiting for her arrival, her father was not to be denied much.

A black cat with a white star on its chest bounded onto the windowsill beside her.

"It's only a few days, Mischa," she reminded them both absently as he batted her hand with one dainty paw.

She obliged, rubbing his petite ears. A purr too big for the small body vibrated into her arm. Her phone buzzed.

The name on the screen made her smile. Of all her former dancing partners, only one had become a friend. She read the text. *Course I'll look after the little hellcat while ur gone. Even tho he will probably eat me 4 dinner.*

She smiled. *He's a pussycat, Blondie. Toughen up. Door code is same. IOU.*

The phone screen flashed with his reply. *At the airport yet?*

She glared out the window again, willing the car into appearance. *I should have been on my way 5 minutes ago.*

Where 2 again?

Moscow, grandfather ill. Back in a few days.

The intercom for her door buzzed. She glanced to the curb to see a black Mercedes double-parked where it should have been twenty minutes ago.

Car's here. TY again for Mischa.

She flung open the door for the valet, gesturing to the stack of luggage, then checked her purse for her essentials. The doorman stood inside the held elevator.

"Paní Petrova." He waved her in before trundling the bags in behind.

Her phone buzzed.

Anytime, babe. Be safe. Text me when u get there.

Always do. XOXO.

XxOO.

She smiled as she slipped the phone back into her bag.

In her memory, Kyle and the Academy were indelibly intertwined. She might not have otherwise paid attention to Isela Vogel no matter how gifted everyone claimed the refugee handpicked by Director Sauvageau was. But Isela and Kyle were a package. Now she could not imagine her life without them, and godsdancers did make life interesting.

Of course, things had gone too far when Issy had been hired by the Necromancer of Europe. Not that anyone listened to Yana. Necromancers did the devil's work, summoning the dead and creating their zombies out of anyone who defied them. Yana had known no good would come of it. She'd been right. Issy had come back changed, even if Yana couldn't figure out how.

According to the press and PR machine, Isela Vogel retired from dance after accepting a position as a special consultant to the Necromancer Azrael. Voluntarily, they were careful to add. She'd even done an interview tour, demonstrating that she had not been made a zombie. Smiling in that pasted-on American way, she'd claimed to find the work with the necromancer challenging and rewarding. She was looking forward to this new phase in her career.

Yana, Kyle, and a few others knew the truth. Isela had taken Azrael as a lover. It was as unimaginable as it was preposterous. Yana loved Isela like a sister, but sometimes the girl lacked sense where it ought to be.

It was the godsdancing; Yana knew it. Godsdancers were always a bit off.

The driver waited, offering a litany of apologies for his tardiness.

"Only fools give excuses," Yana muttered in Russian under her breath. She slid into the back seat.

With growing alarm, she glanced outside as they left the city behind. Did this imbecile need directions? She spoke in Czech. "Where are we going?"

"Private plane, miss."

"My father?"

"He insisted, miss."

Yana fought the urge to stamp her foot against the lushly carpeted floorboard. Her father must have found out she had booked a seat on a commercial plane and changed her itinerary. Even first class would not be enough. The family business had kept him absent during her childhood, and he'd replaced his physical presence with financial support. She'd wanted for nothing. Though she'd gotten money from her father, Yana had inherited her superstitions about necromancers from her mother. Her father had no such qualms about doing business with Azrael's many companies just as his own father had in Russia.

He had done well in Prague as his father's scion. Yana, an only child, had earned her grandfather's notice first through her father's accomplishments.

Their first meeting was impressed on her memory, though she could have been only seven. The short flight had been her first, followed by a long car ride afterward to a sprawling estate outside the city. In spite of her mother's attempts to make her wear suitable clothing before the patriarch, Yana had insisted on her dancing leotard and tights, flat ballet slippers, and a much-loved gauzy pink tutu.

Because her father could forbid her nothing, he overrode her mother's demands and allowed her to go as she was.

"My father appreciates passion," he chided. "Plus she is adorable. Like a little prima already."

There were armed guards in fatigues at the gates. They circled the car with large tan-and-black dogs on tight leads. She pitied their dense, shaggy coats in the sweltering heat.

At the end of the horseshoe drive, suited men with serious mouths and eyes hidden by reflective lenses stood sentinel. Inside, the enormous, cool marble halls swarmed with more suited men, these moving through the house on unknown missions. They were shown into a waiting room more elegant than anything she had ever seen. She could picture the walls hung with tapestries of folktales.

While they waited, her mother walked her around the room, telling her of the heroic figures and beautiful heroines. A servant delivered cold beverages on a tray. For her, a pink confection so sweet and cold it stung her nose and made her flinch even as she sucked at the neon bendy straw. At last the summons. She walked between her parents, one hand in her father's while the other clutched the almost-empty glass sticky with sugary condensation.

Her grandfather was vibrant and boisterous. He praised her father, kissed her mother's pale cheeks wetly. Then he locked eyes with the small creature looking back at him. She remembered the touch of shock at the sensation of looking into a distorted mirror—his eyes were the same color as her own, but in every other way he and she were opposites. Yet she stood still as he lowered himself to one knee before her. She smelled the faintest whiff of eucalyptus, like her father after *venik*.

He grinned. "Not afraid of much, are you, little one?" He looked up at her parents. "She speaks only Czech then?"

Yana spoke Russian in clear, confident voice. "What is there to fear from an old bear?"

He threw back his head and howled with laughter until he was red in the face. Enchanted, Yana stared. She tugged her hand out of her father's and handed her glass to her stunned mother.

"I would like to show you my dance now, Grandfather."

Her father paled. "Not now, Yana—"

The blue eyes that had been so bright with amusement at once went icy as they cut to his son's face. She shivered, but when they returned to her, the ice was gone.

"It would please me," he said, bowing to her.

No one had ever bowed to her. But Yana curtsied as Madame LeFey had instructed, forgetting she should not grab the edges of her tutu until she was midway through. He stepped back, leaning on the massive desk with his hands clasped before him. She did the firefly dance for the part she had played in the spring recital. In hindsight, she was both puzzled and embarrassed that the simple performance had inexplicably charmed the big man. It was barely ballet.

The rest of the visit passed by in a blur. She spent most of the trip with her mother, aunts, and a horde of cousins while her father and grandfather did business. And on the final day as he walked them to the limo, he knelt again before her and bade her kiss his cheek. She breathed in strong aftershave and cigar smoke. His whiskers tickled her mouth.

"You'll begin next term at the Praha Dance Academy," he said, ignoring her parents' objections that the waiting list was years long and that she was too young. "You'd like that, yes?"

The whole ride home, Yana ignored her parents arguing. Her mother pleading, her father shrugging. All she could think about was becoming a dancer. She would be the envy of Madame LeFey's other students.

Twenty years later, as the car pulled up at the airplane hangar, the first stirrings of grief rose in her throat. She'd had little more than the occasional phone conversation with her grandfather over the subsequent years, but after every performance a bouquet waited in her dressing room with the card signed An Old Bear.

The steward waited at the bottom of the stairs to the plane. "Welcome, Miss Petrova. It's an honor to have you on board today."

Yana couldn't speak through the lump forming in her throat. She nodded as she climbed the stairs. Inside the small cabin, two of the more senior members of her bodyguard team lounged in the rear with glasses of champagne and relaxed faces. She fought annoyance; they were just doing their jobs. She took her seat as the steward delivered a glass sparkling with bubbles.

"Just tea, please." Yana shook her head.

The steward looked dismayed for a moment. When she returned, she bore an elegant single-service pot-and-cup combo. Yana recognized the brand as one that her grandfather owned. So this was his plane.

She rifled through her purse for her eye mask as the cabin doors were secured and the plane came to life with a subtle tremble.

"How is your tea?" The steward seemed more urgent than the simple question implied.

Yana looked at the teapot and then the steward. The woman's eyes flickered to the rear seats, and Yana sat up a little straighter.

"I'm sure it's fine," she said. "Thank you."

Her hand in the purse abandoned her eye mask in favor of her phone.

The steward clasped her hands and moved to the crew area. As the plane taxied down the runway, Yana buckled in and opened a text.

Something wrong. Call my father.

She was being paranoid. She recognized the guards. This was her family's plane. And yet.

As the steward passed, Yana slipped her phone down her side and made a show of pouring her tea. She took a sip. It was delicious but left a bitter film on the back of her tongue. Perhaps it had brewed too long. She set the cup down.

The captain's voice announced over the intercom, "Estimated flight time to Saint Petersburg one hour and forty-five minutes."

Yana reached for her phone but managed to miss it. A growing fog dulled her senses. "Saint Petersburg?"

The steward smiled. "Yes, miss. There's been a change of plans. Someone important wants a word with you."

She's a zombie, Yana realized. She'd never seen one so normal-looking. But she had... at Azrael's castle. The one assigned to Isela looked like an ordinary man except for one thing. Like him, this woman wasn't breathing.

It took an enormous effort to look at her guards.

One set aside his glass, she assumed to come to her aid, but his eyes went to the steward. "Is there a problem?"

The steward peered into Yana's face. Yana tried to recoil, but her body was too heavy.

"I think we're fine," the steward said. "That's right, Miss Petrova. Just relax. We'll take superb care of you."

Yana's fingers connected with her phone, and her eyes went to the screen. The notification showed her last message had not been sent.

The steward plucked the phone from her hand and deleted the message.

"I'll hold this for you," she said, slipping it into her pocket.

Yana opened her mouth to protest but nothing came out.

And then, darkness.

PART I

CHAPTER ONE

A goddess tilted her face up to the sky, drinking in the sight of the stars and the distant moon and her own thin breath and wondering what greater magic there was than this. Her skin prickled in the cold. She relished the sensation of gooseflesh and the tickling of hair on her shoulder blades and breasts.

The other stirred fitfully in the back of her mind. *Sleep, little one,* she bade, stroking it tenderly. *Tonight is for me.*

Then she lifted her arms, bathed in the moonlight, and began to dance.

* * *

AZRAEL WOKE ALONE in the dark. His fingers stretched out, reaching for Isela without thought. The sheets where she should be were rumpled but cool. He sat up in the bed.

Father?

Lysippe, he responded after a quick scan of the room determined Isela was gone.

The garden. Her telepathic voice was terse, worried.

Azrael leaped from the bed, tugging on the pair of pants he'd discarded hours ago when Isela showed him her own version of the dance of seven veils. He had lost his head, in a manner of speaking, in the best way. Returning arousal at the memory was immediately dampened by concern. He might not be able to read Isela's mind any longer, but even when she turned restlessly in her dreams he had awareness of her. That she had slipped out, unnoticed, was wrong somehow.

Barefoot, he jogged down the stairs into the main room of his quarters. The door to the garden was wide open. He hadn't heard that either. Rory stood on the other side, scowling.

Azrael frowned. "Where is she?"

"Thought it best for Lysippe to keep an eye on her until you got here," Rory grunted, thrusting a bit of fabric at him.

He took a moment to recognize the heavy silk in his hand. Isela's robe. He looked at Rory again. The bigger man shrugged, articulating his opinion without words. *Your choice, your problem, mate.*

Azrael followed tracks through the snow-dusted garden. He recognized Lysippe's but not Isela's. Something with the placement was wrong. He stepped over a crumpled length of familiar cotton jersey. Isela's nightshirt. How many times had he teased it off her, amused that she clung to the old thin fabric instead the more obviously seductive items he'd filled her wardrobe with.

He emerged beside Lysippe where the trees circled an enormous fountain. The shadow of the old winter palace, long ago closed up, loomed in the background. Without a word, he followed her gaze.

Isela danced in the moonlight, clothed only in the spill of her sleep-tousled hair. She'd been in the fountain; water curled the ends of her hair into tighter spirals and dappled over the velvet expanse of her brown skin. The pale moonlight caught in droplets and glittered like jewels. Her muscles bunched and lengthened as she swept through wild, uncoordinated movements.

Arousal jetted through him even as the hair on his arms stood on end.

Rory was on patrol, Lysippe said. *She said nothing on her way out, refused to respond to him at all. He called me when she started—*

Her brow rose. Isela cartwheeled, missed the landing, and tumbled into the snow, laughing. Snow clumped in her hair, mud on her elbows and knees. He'd seen her perform more acrobatic maneuvers—she was as sure on her hands as her feet. She didn't *fall.* Something was not right.

Thank you, he said.

Lysippe dropped back into the shadow of the trees. Azrael turned his attention to his consort.

"Little wolf," he called softly.

She didn't respond. He stepped forward. She was on her feet again, dancing. The movements were uncontrolled and uncoordinated, like a child's.

"Isela."

She froze, deerlike, and turned to him. He shivered. He'd followed the contours of her face a hundred times with his fingertips. Fast asleep or in the throes of passion, he knew it. Whatever was looking out at him wore her features like a mask.

He switched to the oldest tongue, the one he used to summon the dead and command the pure strength of his powers. It was said gods had no language before humans danced for them, but that wasn't entirely true. Most humans had just forgotten it by then.

"Goddess," he said.

Eyes the color of molten gold fixed on him. "Begone, death dealer. This night is mine."

"Where is she?"

"Her heart was heavy; I offered to lighten it." The goddess curled around herself as if cradling a baby to her breasts. "She sleeps. Safe as a babe."

"This was not the agreement you made."

The goddess flung out her arms as she stalked toward him. Her mouth curved, teasing. "How do you know what bargain was made between her and me, O lord of death?"

She slid against him. Her nipples, pebbled with cold, brushed his chest as her frozen arms wrapped around his neck. His body responded and she smiled knowingly.

"I know Isela," he said into the brilliant gilded pools of her eyes. "She would not want this."

"She wanted you so badly she would have agreed to anything." Her mouth brushed his, tongue darting out to lick his lips. "Now I know why." She ground her hips into his.

His arousal throbbed, painful. She danced her fingertips down his chest, nails leaving tracks as they went.

"Come, death dealer," she whispered. "Let this night be ours. Do you think you can bring a goddess to her knees?"

He trapped her wrist before she reached his waistband. "Ah, but that's where you're wrong, goddess. It was she who brought me to mine."

Her eyes flicked up at him again, startled. He twisted her wrist behind her back, drawing her against his chest.

"*She* chose you." He sent his breath directly into her mouth, imbuing the words with power enough that Isela, wherever she was inside, would hear him. "I chose her. And I will always choose her."

She shuddered in his arms, eyes narrowed. "You would rather have…"

"A hundred thousand times," he affirmed. "Make your choice. But know you are nothing to me without her."

She pursed her lips, and he felt the power building in her. Even weakened by being bound to mortal flesh, she was still a god. While necromancers commanded individual elements, the gods could over-rule the laws of nature. He had no way of knowing exactly what Isela could do. With the goddess in control, he was afraid to find out.

He sent a warning to the Aegis, the elite warriors that served him. He felt Lysippe respond in the affirmative, but she refused to stand down. Gregor, too, kept coming. The best chance he had of keeping them all safe was getting through to Isela. He wrapped his arms around her, locking her to him.

"She is my consort." He hissed the words into Isela's ear. "You are a guest. Now honor your vow, and wake her up."

Isela's body stiffened in his arms, and for a moment he prepared to battle with the divine. Abruptly, she sagged in his arms and he soft-ened his knees to catch her.

"Azrael?" Isela's teeth chattered.

He slipped the robe over her shoulders and swept her off her feet, sending a wave of heat into her body. She clutched at him, fingers scrabbling.

The clouds covered the moon, and it began to snow. She shivered.

"I wasn't dreaming?" She glanced around them.

"No, love," he murmured, nodding to Lysippe as he passed.

"Oh gods." Isela flushed as the Amazon retreated. "I'm so cold."

"In the oldest days," he murmured, "women danced under the moon to pray for fertility or to thank the goddess in abundant years or because they'd had a bit too much to drink and it was a good time."

She rested her head against his shoulder, her cheek warmer now. Even her breath came in a rhythm as familiar as his own heartbeat.

"Naked?"

"It was more effective that way," he said with a grin.

"I'll bet."

"The gods, attracted by the beauty of their dancing, came into the bodies of men and danced with them," he said. "And that is how necromancers and witches came into the world."

Her eyes sought his in the dark. No longer pools of gold but stormy gray, and he sighed in relief.

"Truly?"

They'd reached the building. Rory and Gregor stood guard at the door. When Azrael appeared, both men slid into the darkness. Isela flushed at Rory's disapproving glare.

"They must think I'm a lunatic," she muttered as Azrael closed the door behind them.

"If one believes the moon causes intermittent insanity," Azrael whispered against the shell of her ear. "Perhaps."

Isela smiled.

"They've seen—we've all seen—much stranger things," he said. "You only suffer from a mild case of possession—a voluntary case, I might add."

She was laughing by the time he mounted the stairs. He set her on her feet by the hearth, then stoked the fire. She dusted bits of decayed leaves and dirt from her palms, and he brushed a smear of mud from her hip. She shivered. When he looked up, she was watching him. He knew the contours of her face again and the emotion her eyes contained—the question in her brows, the doubt turning her mouth down.

"I should take a shower."

He heard the need for distance in her voice and let her go.

When she emerged, robed with velvety fawn skin pinked about the edges from the hot water, he waited with an old T-shirt and a plate piled high from their recently stocked refrigerator.

The smile that creased her mouth didn't lift the shadows from her eyes. "What is this?"

He beckoned to the ottoman by the fire and the place he'd made for her between his thighs. She settled, lightly bracing on her right hip. It was old habit from her human life, where a degenerative hip joint had threatened her career as a dancer. The goddess had taken care of that, and she was growing stronger and faster, closer to immortality every day. But old habits died hard. Gradually she relaxed with a little sigh.

"Close your eyes," he instructed, handing off the T-shirt.

This time the smile quirked her mouth with more strength.

"Bossy." She sighed, squeezing the moisture out of her hair and dramatically closing her eyes.

He chose an olive, the shiny, deep purple skin plump against his fingers. Lifted it. He didn't even need to get it close to her nose.

"Kalamata."

Her lips parted in anticipation. He followed the olive with the tip of his finger, the pad of her lip pushing against him as she chewed.

"Salty," she said, opening one eye.

"Eyes closed," he rumbled.

Obediently she closed her eyes, but this time her lips remained parted.

He swiped pita in hummus.

She nibbled. "Red peppers, cilantro, and garlic. Are you sure about that?"

He wiped a fleck of hummus from the corner of her mouth. Arousal flared again, held at bay. He tamped it down and ate the rest of the slice himself. "We're even."

He didn't touch her other than to steer food into her mouth or clean it up. She leaned into him, the tight lines of her face softening, the smile infusing her cheeks and the corners of her eyes. Once he had been able to read her mind. Now he relied on her body to tell him what he needed to know.

"What is this?" she asked after chewing roasted cashews, pistachios, and a few salty almonds.

"A reminder," he said, plucking the last of his selections. It was room temperature now, softening and growing shiny in the heat of his fingertips. "This body is yours. Its desire and tastes are yours."

Her inhale was deep and slow, and the smile that curled her mouth would have reached her eyes if they'd been open. "How did you know?"

She bit into the date, chewing.

"I have my ways," he said.

She opened one eye. "Did you read someone's mind?"

"I spoke with your mother. She mentioned that dates were your favorite."

Both eyes popped open. "You what?"

"Eyes closed," he ordered. "Taste is richer without sight. You never wondered why you lost weight after you started dancing with your 'golden shadow'?"

She finished the date, swallowed. "I thought it was the stress. Running from demons takes a lot out of a girl."

He huffed laughter, and when her fingers crooked in invitation, he pressed another date between her lips. "It takes an extraordinary amount of physical energy to communicate with the gods. Most possessions that go on too long simply burn out the human body. Something different is happening with you. You're able to contain her without extraordinary cost, and you're getting stronger and faster. You will need to consume more—at least until whatever you are becoming stabilizes. And you haven't been."

Grief was a strange companion. It showed up without warning and lingered long past its expected departure. If it wasn't given its due, it took in other ways. Already thinner from the burden of the god, he'd watched her open and close the refrigerator without making a selection and pick at the meals sent up from the kitchen.

"But *these* dates…" Her voice drifted, hesitating. Her breath caught, and she struggled with the words. The tip of her nose flushed bright pink. "My dad."

"Used to take you on Sunday afternoons to a little shop in Žižkov owned by a Tunisian family," he finished, brushing the tear from her cheek before it could reach her chin. His fingers left a sticky trail. "A well-kept secret—they import the finest Deglet Noor dates in the city. You would play with their children, and your father would practice his Darja. He had a passion for languages."

She covered her mouth with her hand to contain the sob. He trapped her fingers.

"You try to run from your sadness," he said. "It is part of you. Any part you reject is an opening for her. Own your grief, Isela."

She crumpled and he collected her, mouth moving over the sticky marks on her cheeks.

"What did he smell like?" Azrael asked. Isela's legendary sense of smell was one of the few traits granted by her father's were genes. Isela had inherited a complex sense of smell that was both specific and associative. He waited for her to collect the memories within.

"Hazelnuts," she said, and her voice broke. "He kept them in his desk as a snack when he was working." She paused. "And sand. When we lived in California, he would take us to the beach every chance he got. I was too young to remember much. But he always smelled like warm beach sand."

His lips moved over the damp waves of her hair, scenting only her conditioner and the faintest hint of soap beneath. "Memories are anchors. I've been thinking this is what necromancers lost. We made it easy to behave inhumanly because we try to forget we once were, that once we may have loved someone. It's not always easy. To remember. Memories can mean loss; loss means pain."

At last she tilted her head up, her eyes ringed with red but dry again. She dabbed at her nose. "Who do you remember?"

The tongue of his birth came easily to him now. He translated. "Copper. My first horse."

She laughed, drawing back to dab at her nose. But this time the laughter went all the way to the stormy gray of her eyes, and he slid his fingertips along her jawline, watching the heat build in them in answer to his own.

"My sisters," he said. "They were my constant. My mother was... absent often, my grandmother too old and well known to be more than a legend. My brothers were much older, one had a left to follow a woman from another band. My sisters— were always there."

"Your father?"

"I did not know my father." Age had given him distance from the emotion. "It was not uncommon. In my bala, lineage was determined by the mother."

"But that wasn't it for you, was it," she said. "Your mother danced with a god one night, under the moon."

"Perhaps."

He'd asked once. Most of the others his age had some indication of their father from looks or habits. A few of their mothers even maintained their partnerships. The presence of his siblings confirmed his mother's occasional dalliances, but she had named no man as the equal in her tent. She spent little time among the bala. One sunny afternoon he found her crouched beside the front hooves of her favorite mount, a blade of long grass in her teeth as she watched the herds move along the river. Her horse lifted its head and blew out a greeting to his as he swung down, humbled and embarrassed as she took him in without turning her head. But she did not move. So he crouched beside her, glancing out over the backs of grazing horses.

Side by side, he noted their differences. The way the skin on her arms had burned and freckled with sun while his grew dark gold like the tall grasses in fall. The fine rippled strands of her hair bleached sun bright at the end of the long tangled plaits trailing down her back, his heavy in thick waves over his collar. He was scrawny for his age and dirty from an afternoon of playing with the other boys. She was long limbed and strong.

They spoke of many things. His chores. His education. His role in the family. He answered, and she seemed pleased. Emboldened at last, he asked. After a long moment, his mother rose, her joints creaking as she moved to her horse's saddle.

The sleek animal, the color of hammered steel, pinned her ears at his little chestnut gelding and showed teeth. By the time Azrael had calmed his gelding, his mother was mounted.

"I had much regard for your father though he was not of our world," she said. *"We will not speak of it again."*

Azrael spoke to Isela. "It was a story I was never told."

"Does it bother you?" Isela asked.

Azrael shook his head. "I left my home when I was twelve. Losing my sisters, even my mother, caused more pain than the absence of a man I had never known. But that is a story for another night."

He pressed his lips to her brow as she tried to bite down on a yawn. "Sleep now." Her frown creased the skin beneath his lips. "No geas. I promise. I will call you back. I will always call you back."

He sat up for a long time by the fire after she had succumbed to exhaustion. The memories had come haltingly at first, buried by time. But as he forced himself to recall them, they became clearer and more complete.

We protect always the vulnerable, she'd said that day among the scent of horses and fresh grass on the windswept rise. *What good is your strength if not for that service? What other purpose for your anger than righteous cause?*

Two thousand years later, far from the steppes of his home, the words were clear as springwater in winter.

I will be your shield. Isn't that what he'd promised Isela?

* * *

Azrael, the immortal necromancer who controlled all of Europe, poured his own coffee.

Isela watched, amused at the sight of him stirring in enough sugar to make the caffeine negligible. Her lover. If she stopped to think about it, it was a terrifying prospect. She'd seen him rip a man's spine from his body, and still she'd taken him to her bed. She'd become his consort in part for her own protection against the rest of the Allegiance of Necromancers that ruled the world. Chasing down a supernatural killer bent on revenge had brought them together. But she could not deny her attraction to him or the way he responded in kind. Somewhere along the way, they'd chosen one another. As he'd said once, she was his and she was home.

For a moment, standing in the kitchen of his expansive quarters on the grounds of the Prague castle, overlooking gardens and the summer palace, life seemed refreshingly mundane. She imagined one of the many ordinary mornings they might have together. Sugar with coffee for Azrael, tea for her. A discussion about their day.

"You told Divya, I presume."

The director of the Praha Dance Academy was on a first-name basis with few of her students. She counted Isela among her own children. She had seen Isela's potential as a child. Potential Isela had fulfilled in ways no one, not even Divya, had expected. Isela no longer danced for gods. But if she could teach... "Divya's been holding the position for me since New Year's. Classes have already started."

"Channeling a god was not an accident. You are special, Isela, different from the others."

No matter how nice he made it sound, dread built in her.

"I believe you would have connected with a god on your own," he said. "The Allegiance warned me when we began searching for the killer—"

"Your mentor," she said of Necromancer Róisín. "The one *they* set us against, hoping we'd fail."

"Paolo knew, yes. Perhaps Vanka, but I doubt the others had any idea."

In her quest for vengeance, Róisín had tried to raise an angel and unleash an apocalypse on the world. Isela died in the fighting. Agreeing to become a vessel for a god had been the only way back.

"They wanted you to put me down."

She watched him trying to sort out her flair for idiom. With two

thousand years and a dozen languages—living and dead—to his repertoire, it amazed her that she could stump him.

She clarified. "The same way they talked Róisín into killing her
consort." She pressed on. "Believe me, I am grateful that you saw past
that. But god or not, it's still my life. I have to dance, Azrael, and not
just for you."

The issue had lain unspoken between them for weeks. Hired by
the Allegiance to help him find Róisín, Isela had learned to act as a
conduit for the power of a god, boosting his own. She would be lying
to say some cynical part of her did not wonder if making her his
consort had not only been for her protection. As a vessel, she had
access to unknown power. It was an advantage that had brought the
Allegiance to their door to challenge him after they'd defeated Róisín.
United with her god, he'd overwhelmed them, sending them fleeing
back to their territories with the promise to leave them be if they did
the same.

They had won. Róisín was dead; what remained of the artificial
heart that powered her occupied a special case in Azrael's aedis. And
somewhere in the castle, under security so tight even Gregor would
not speak of it, was the grimoire containing the spell to raise an angel.

The temperature in the room dropped a few degrees. All necromancers manifested their powers in the form of classical elements. His
was fire. When he lost control, things burned to the ground. They'd
lost a bed that way. Restraint worked the opposite way.

"We don't yet understand what makes you different," he said. "The
PR people want a meeting. The human resistance is restless, and they
don't know the danger they put themselves in. You can keep them
from acting on their plans—and hurting anyone."

She could not stand his coldness. She preferred the inferno.

Her eyes burned with unshed tears. "Now I'm a poster child for
the necromancer public-outreach campaign? I have given up everything, Azrael. My home, my freedom, my life—"

It was his turn to look away. She bit the inside of her lip hard
enough to taste blood, wishing she could take it back. Since they'd
emerged from the tomb, Azrael had barred her from any further
summoning work, left her out of his affairs. He hadn't suggested she
so much lift a finger for him.

Bound by their word, the Allegiance had paid her fee on the
completed job. She was wealthy beyond belief. The degenerative hip

condition that had once threatened to end her career was healed. It was a luxurious retirement by any standard.

But her death had done something to him. Sometimes she woke with his arms so tight around her she clutched for breath. She'd learned to stay calm, to reassure him that she was there and would not leave, until his hold loosened. It was fear she understood. It had driven her to take a deal with a god.

Azrael was unlike any other in the Allegiance. He loved when others would—or could—not. That knowledge usually made her heart begin soaring acrobatics in her chest. But now it sank like a stone. He loved her. And that love was poised to crush the life she'd built for herself.

"Advanced seminars are where all the theory comes in," she said. "I'll teach technique or balance work. Anything."

"We can't take the chance."

"I *need* to dance."

"And I need you safe," he barked.

Isela snapped. "I am not a thing to be locked away in a glass case and kept under guard and key until you need me next!"

The mug splintered in his grip. Steaming coffee sprayed over his hand and onto the counter.

"That was— I shouldn't have said it." Guilt squeezed her throat.

She went for a cloth, but Azrael was already moving away, shaking his fingers over the sink, not in pain but irritation. His skin wasn't even red.

"The Allegiance is at our door, slavering for an excuse to challenge me for my right to rule," he said. "Your god is sneaking out in the middle of the night to play while you sleep. There is too much at stake. You will not dance. Not until we know it's safe. That is all."

CHAPTER TWO

Tyler pulled up in front of the Praha Dance Academy and Isela opened the passenger door. Niles, the director's personal assistant, was bundled up for a wait, cheeks red from cold, but he greeted Isela with a rare smile as she slid out of the car. There was a surprising lack of paparazzi out front as he herded her to the front doors of the art nouveau building the Academy called home.

"It's been quiet since you've taken up residence at the castle, Miss Vogel," Niles said, catching the door. "A little too quiet if I'm honest."

"How is she?" Isela asked.

"She's survived worse things than losing her premiere godsdancer," Niles said with an air of joviality that faded fast. "Several families pulled their children from the school. Apparently they prefer the necromancer as a distant patron."

Isela understood. Learning to communicate with the gods via dance had led to an international conflict as countries used their powers against one another. Necromancers had saved humanity, but at a high price. They enforced a ruthless brand of peace by dividing the world among themselves and ruling over it all. They barred humanity from direct contact with the gods. Now all requests had to be approved. Necromancers might have prevented chaos after the godswar, but they still engendered terror in the human population. Isela knew the feeling. She'd stood among their most powerful members, the Allegiance.

"It will recover," Niles said as he escorted her through the halls. "Always does. She's concerned about you."

A few students moving between classes slowed their pace or paused to stare as she passed. Isela smiled, but few met her eyes.

Her mentor seemed older than Isela remembered, and more tired. But the strength of her gaze was undiminished. She rose from her desk and greeted Isela with a hug.

"Tea, Niles," Divya said, not taking her hands from Isela's arm.

Already in motion, he raised a brow conspiratorially at Isela. She almost laughed. Divya glanced between them, missing nothing.

"You two," she chided. "Sit, Issy. We have to talk about when you'll start with us."

Isela slid into the chair with a sigh.

"Oh," Divya said, settling opposite her. "Is it your hip?"

Isela nodded, hating that she had to keep this secret. Niles served the tea and made a discreet exit. He brushed Divya's shoulder as he passed, a movement so small Isela would not have noticed it except that in all her years at the Academy, she'd never seen them touch. Divya's variegated eyes followed her assistant for just a moment before returning to her former student.

Isela cleared her throat. "I wouldn't be doing the Academy any favors. I know what they say about me... and Azrael."

She tried to ignore the gossip. Depending on the day, she was a grasping seductress who'd bounced from the head of the necromancer's security detail to his master, or the victim of a Machiavellian scheme of seduction by proxy. Most suspected she was a zombie or otherwise under the thrall of one man or the other.

"What better way to dispel those ridiculous rumors than having you here?" Divya asked. "Some on the board think it might be a draw for students."

Isela stirred her tea. Divya slid the plate of small cookies closer, but Isela shook her head once. She forced herself to swallow a sip in the hope it might help loosen the lump forming in her throat.

"Azrael and I decided it's just best." Isela swallowed. "For the time being..."

"Did you?" Divya's brow rose. "And Azrael?"

Isela flushed. Divya had always seen right through her. She was as much a surrogate mother as a teacher. "It's just right now is a bad time, Divya. We have to figure out how to make this work."

Isela waited for her suggest a way to work around Azrael. But when her teacher met her eyes, Isela read shrewd calculation in them.

"He doesn't want you calling down another god," Divya said, surprising Isela. "Or teaching another dancer how. I see."

"How did you know?"

Divya smiled. "I suspected at the wedding, but seeing you now— I'm certain. May I ask?"

Isela blinked hard. "In the cemetery. I died. This was the only way to come back. I just wanted... him."

Divya's mouth curved, suggesting a smile. "Love forces our hand, does it not?"

Isela sat back in her chair and contemplated her tea.

"It's something I hadn't considered," Divya said at last, frowning. "And perhaps, for the time being..."

Isela's throat closed on her next breath. She was being forced out of the one place she truly belonged. She stared at the fire to avoid her teacher's gaze.

The director leaned forward, reaching out to rest her fingers on Isela's jawbone. Isela gave in to the pressure and met her teacher's eyes.

"You are family," Divya finished. "The Academy will always be your home."

She let Isela go, slipping a tissue into her hand as she took a sip from her cup. Isela clenched her teeth and struggled for control of her emotions.

"Your apartment door has been fixed." Divya changed the subject. "And we had everything boxed after the... break-in. I can have the boxes sent to the castle."

The dam of emotion broke in Isela, and she set her cup down with a rattle. "Throw it away. I don't care."

Divya sat upright. "Isela Vogel. It is unseemly for a dancer of your status to pout."

Isela laughed against her will. Her mentor's serene gaze was a challenge.

"I am not pouting," Isela confessed. "I'm just... adjusting poorly."

Divya sighed. Her cheeks softened and the line between her eyebrows melted away.

"No one is clamoring for a drafty attic apartment in this old building," Divya said casually. "We'll hold your belongings until you decide what to do with them. There must be room for a few boxes in that enormous castle."

Isela tried again to be surly. "You might as well just dump it."

Divya squeezed her arm, rising. "Call your sisters, see if they can use any of it first. We'll take care of the rest."

* * *

TYLER HELD the car door as Isela stepped back out of the Academy and into the weak winter sunshine. She paused, as she always did, to admire the colored glass archway. Leaving the elaborate art nouveau building for the weight of the enormous castle on the hill made her glum. She hadn't even gone up to her apartment. She didn't think she could bear it.

"Issy?"

"Go home, Ty," she murmured. "I'll walk."

"But…"

Let me.

Isela felt the words leave her mouth and the geas that interlaced them. They emerged musically, with the unmistakable cadence of a command. Tyler paled, but he closed her door. With jerky limbs, he returned to the driver's side.

"I'll be fine," Isela said when she had control of her voice again. "Promise. I'll go straight home. Just need to stretch my legs."

He looked like he wanted to protest. Still, he climbed inside and closed the door. The car pulled away from the curb. She shivered against the cold seeping up from the cobblestones beneath her boots.

How did you do that? she asked the god.

Words are power. All this time I've been borrowing from you, but we had language once. I'd forgotten. Azrael reminded me.

Alone, Isela snugged her coat and tugged her wool cap over her ears. Aside from the few glances she attracted for standing still in the middle of the walkway, no one seemed inclined to acknowledge her in the least.

You're welcome, the god said. *They don't recognize you. I tweaked the one Bebe taught you to hide your eyes.*

Nice trick. And thanks for Tyler.

My pleasure. I am sorry about last night.

Sorry for trying to seduce my lover or for considering destroying him?

Isela grumbled. *Or wait, how about for sneaking out and making me dance around the fountain... naked.*

The god was silent, and Isela had the impression she wasn't the only one in a sulk. She crossed the road between cars and started down the long avenue that ran through the west edge of Old Town Prague. The pedestrian thoroughfare lined with international luxury stores and dotted with food and cigarette stands connected the Obecní Dům, or Municipal House, home of the Praha Dance Academy, with Wenceslas Square and the National Theatre beside the river. She could catch a tram back toward the castle—

I just wanted time to feel *again,* the god admitted reluctantly. *It's so glorious—all that flesh. I am a passenger.*

Isela snorted. *You want to drive? That's fine. Let's talk. But you can't just take over... and Azrael is off-limits.*

Don't be such a prude, Issy. There was a definite note of teasing in the god's voice. *It wouldn't even be cheating. After all, I am you.*

No, you're not. Isela stopped in her tracks.

Someone bumped into her from behind, and she muttered an apology and kept walking. Isela's sense of the god retreated to the back of her mind. She burrowed there, in whatever corner she'd designated for herself, and did not speak again.

* * *

THE THING that grabbed Isela's wrist on the packed tram was not human. She'd missed it as she'd hurried on with the rest of the passengers to the standing-room-only tram; she saw now that it only looked human. Torn between avoiding the overpowering stench of it and growing curiosity, she remained still.

The hand locked around her wrist was skin stretched over bones and tendons. The stringy muscles stood out in relief on clenched fingers, the thick palm coarse on her healed scar tissue. For a moment she wondered if she'd made a mistake in advocating that a half-formed angel go free. Maybe now it had returned for vengeance.

All around her, humanity pressed in, forcing her closer to her captor.

"A word," it hissed, head bowed against the plastic seat as its fingers locked.

She felt the bones in her wrist grind against one another an instant before the cool of healing spread through the breaks. It had to be tall, but hunched over itself, it seemed vulnerable. He, she amended. The height and the hand and the shape of its broad shoulders made it seem male enough. Isela was getting used to things being more than they appeared. She racked her brain through the supernatural creatures she'd encountered. Incubus? Necromancer? Witch? Were?

The rags of his clothes contributed to an overall stench of cheap vodka and unwashed flesh. She wasn't sure what color his hair was— grease and dirt made it a shiny, stringy auburn. Ratty tennis shoes with mismatched laces thumped as he tapped the floor spastically. He hadn't shaved in weeks. She didn't know it was possible for a person to be so filthy. With his head bowed, neck vertebra jutted against the skin. She wondered when he'd last eaten.

Thanks to Lysippe, she knew half a dozen ways to break a hold, but none of them would allow her to avoid excess attention or risking human lives. Innocent lives, she reminded herself. Lives that should not be aware that the world around them was darker and full of scarier creatures than appeared in their nightmares.

The world that had become hers.

Goddess. She turned her attention inward. *Need a little help right now.*

"A word," it said again, mournful.

Nonhumans obeyed a strict code of secrecy enforced by the Allegiance. The human population would know as little about them as possible, to keep them from the panic that had almost brought the world to the brink of apocalypse during the godswar. Showing itself on a tram full of humans would violate that code. Whatever it was, the message was important enough to risk revealing itself to her.

The voice was rusty from lack of use—or overuse—and trembled. "A word."

Three times, she thought. Saying something three times—thrice— was more than a request. It was power. It was geas.

Isela felt a small shifting against her skull as the god stirred. *What's a phoenix doing dressed like a man?*

A phoenix?

She glanced down as the creature looked up. When their eyes met, she forgot to breathe shallowly.

Beneath the layers of dirt over freckles and skin cracked and dried by the elements, it was beautiful. Enormous, hooded green eyes fissured with gold belonged to something inhuman. Shaded by a broad forehead and sunken above prominent cheekbones, they spoke of being captured and broken but never tamed.

His mouth—no mistaking its maleness now—pulled in a rictus of pain as it glanced at her, then away.

Isela, something is super wrong with this guy, the god said.

That is your great insight?

The god sighed. *Well, let's see what he wants.*

"Okay," she heard herself saying. "You can have your word."

The tram jerked as the overhead buzzed an announcement of the next stop. The press of passengers shuffled against her. A few cast curious glances her direction.

"But we have to get off this tram. Come on. Next round's on me," she said, coaxing him.

The narrow cabin shifted as people began the process of exiting and entering the tram. The doors closed, warning lights flashing with the incomprehensible recorded warning to clear the entryway as the last passengers crammed in.

Her captor leaped. It was follow or be dragged. In spite of his thinness and alcohol reek, his grip was a vise on her wrist.

On the cobblestone island dividing the tram tracks from traffic, she thought of her opening to break away. His eyes lit on her again, wild and afraid and unbowed. She ran with him.

"Where are we going?"

They followed the twisting streets narrowing into one-lane passageways between centuries-old buildings, deep into the oldest part of the city.

Fleetingly, she remembered stories of how the Czechs had resisted military invasion by removing all the street signs. It wasn't hard to see how effective that would be as she found herself disoriented by their pace. Now would be the moment. She should break his hold.

Yet she stayed. The memory of his eyes made her wonder how much pain a being could stand—how much he had stood—before he'd made his life forfeit by grabbing her. The moment she became Azrael's consort, she was marked as being under his protection. It had been a way to safeguard her from the rest of the Allegiance, but every nonhuman in his territory would know it as soon as they were in her presence.

Once Azrael found out, and he would, this creature would pay the price for his transgression. Not because Azrael took pleasure in it but because the seven most powerful necromancers in the world would see any sign of weakness in him as an opening.

Isela hadn't thought her situation could get any worse. Then they emerged in the heart of Old Town, on the square ringed by the Astronomical Clock and the spires of Our Lady of Týn. At this hour people packed the open area from the monument to Jan Hus to the ring of restaurants and gelato stands bordering the opposite side of the plaza. Lined up on the curb, horse-drawn carriages waited to give scenic trips in the city. Tour guides moved groups like flocks of flightless, graceless birds from building to building, waving colored umbrellas to distinguish them from one another for their patrons.

"What is it?" she hissed, impatient now.

People were staring. Across the plaza, the pairs of horses threw up their heads and called out in panic. Animals always honored their sense of the supernatural.

Her guide staggered sideways, for all appearances a drunk. She knew better. The skin on her wrist was hot. He pointed at the clock, grunting.

"We don't have time for charades," she snapped. "What is it?"

"Time," he said. "No time. No time. No time. You will not be the only one."

"No shit." Isela glanced about. More than a few devices were aimed at them, recording the entire scene.

"Listen to the time," her abductor muttered.

Enormous beads of sweat pooled and raced down his cheeks and neck. Waves of heat rolled off him. The color leached from his face. He swayed on his feet.

Isela slowed his fall, and the impact on the cobblestones bruised her knees.

The sound of a throat clearing caught her attention. An older black man, dapper in a three-piece suit and wool coat, emerged from the crowd. He folded a newspaper and tucked it under one arm to hold out his gloved hands in a gesture of peace.

"Pardon me, lady." His voice had the smoke-and-whiskey-soaked lilt of an old blues song. "May I be of some assistance?"

Necromancer, the god filled in.

Isela's guard went up. The god doubled her vision, showing her broad, curling strokes of navy blue that rose from his exposed skin.

He was old and powerful. Dizziness swept her, and the god switched the overlay off.

"I mean you no harm, lady," he said, sweeping the battered fedora to his chest and revealing a mahogany-colored pate fringed with groomed, curly white hair. "Dante Abraham, at your service. We have a mutual friend up on the hill."

He tilted his head toward the castle but kept his eyes on her. They were an ordinary, loamy brown. No metallic shine. He wasn't Allegiance level.

The filthy man muttered, "A word, a word, a word. I need a word."

Dante's eyes switched to him. He laid his paper down and came to one knee on top of it, addressing the man. "I'm sure you do, my friend, but now is not the time or the place."

The man groaned. Intense heat rolled off his body, turning the slush-covered gray cobblestones muddy. When he opened his eyes, the red gold of fresh flame had overtaken the green.

Isela forgot her alarm at the look of concern on Dante's face. "I met him on the tram. He wanted to show me something important."

"I'm sure he did," Dante murmured, checking the man's pulse. "But he's in no condition now."

Dante looked up at the crowd. He smiled, and his voice took on that singsong quality she recognized as geas.

"That's all there is, y'all," he said, his accent growing deeper with the command. "Just a man needing some medical attention. And I am a doctor. Move along and give us some space, ya hear?"

The crowd drifted, though they did not disperse. Across the square, the horses screamed, rearing in their traces.

"I'm not strong enough to clear this place," Dante said. "And that's what needs to happen. In a moment he's going to combust. Judging by the eyes, he's been holding it back, so instead of the usual self-immolation, he'll take half the square with him."

Isela shook her head, clearing her questions. There was no way they could empty the area in time. "What can I do?"

Dante frowned, wrinkled his brow. "Imagine that little friend of yours might help. But I'd start by thinking this man into a container. Wrap him up in cold blankets in your head and draw that heat off him. Easy does it. Just a trickle or you could hurt yourself."

Oh, he's good, the god said. *The intention is what counts, but visualization is a nice trick.*

The unconscious man's eyes rolled up and his body shook, a thin line of foam trickling from between his lips. Isela turned inward. *We have to do this.*

That much power will attract attention. Are you sure, Isela?

So will destroying a plaza full of people, Isela said.

The god took over. Isela's body jerked to the man sprawled on the cobblestones. She placed her hands on either side of his face. Heat flared but didn't touch her. The man arched, mouth falling open and a gibberish wail escaped him. The wave of power that emanated from her knocked Dante back. People fled, screaming.

Her eyes closed. A few words of the singsong god tongue left her lips, and then the heat abated.

Isela shivered in the sudden cold as the god retreated. Her body was her own again. The man was still unconscious, but his tremors had ceased. He appeared to be sleeping. She checked his pulse, just in case. Still thrumming. The power inside him had been subverted.

She'd done it.

Whatever "it" was.

Devices and curious eyes turned to the scene before them, a few not only curious. The man on the ground twitched, and Isela pressed a palm to his head in comfort.

A shout drew her attention.

"Die, necromancer whore." A rock hurtled out of the crowd.

Isela flung up her arm, hunching to block the impact. It never came. When she looked up, the rock hovered inches from her face.

Little ingrate, the god snarled.

Isela felt a wild pressure building up inside her, straining against her skin. *No. Don't—*

A gust of air brushed her cheek as a massive bronze hand snatched the rock out of the air before her face. Dory, her favorite of Azrael's ageless guardsmen, flashed a grin down at Isela. The mountain of his shoulders cast a shadow over them. Then he squeezed, and when his palm opened, crumbled stone and grit trickled out. The crowd broke in fear. A group of young men lingered. Thin and pale, their cheeks red with cold or fury, their eyes shone with animosity. Dory turned. They fled.

Dory cocked his head with a wily grin. "If you'll excuse me, Issy."

Tear them limb from limb, big man.

"No," Isela whispered, but with enough force to stop Dory in his tracks. "If you start punishing them for things like that, it will never end. Let them go."

"Issy, you're no fun," he said, but his fists loosened and he smiled at her again. "What have we here?"

"He found me on the tram," Isela said. "He has a message, but then he almost killed us all."

She sat back on her heels. A sharp ache grew behind her right eye; she fought the urge to rub at it. A side effect of possession, she thought humorlessly.

"Perhaps we should resume this conversation in another location," Dante suggested, troubled. He picked up his paper, frowning at the soggy, unreadable contents.

Dory lifted the unconscious man as easily as a small child, leading them toward the Range Rover parked on the edge of the square. Isela followed, scanning the crowd that was eyeing her with mistrust.

"Dory, how did you know I was here," she asked.

"The *Matai* sees all," he said loftily.

Isela's groan ended in a laugh. "Now you sound like your brother."

"Made you laugh though, didn't I?" He grinned back at her as he swung the tailgate open and deposited the sleeping phoenix inside. He closed the hatch and stood for a moment.

She rested a hand on his arm. "Thank you."

"Anytime, Issy," he said, bumping her chin with his knuckle. "Gregor got a call from your attaché. Whatever your little friend did wore off when Tyler got to the castle."

Isela groaned and flung herself into the back seat, ignoring Dante at the passenger door.

Dory climbed in, grinning at the necromancer. "She hates it when you hold the door."

CHAPTER THREE

Near the west bank of the Vltava river, the sliver of an island named Střelecký ostrov was connected to the city by the Legion Bridge. Once a royal garden, Shooters Island earned its name as a popular location to practice archery, and later firearm skills. In heavy flood years, the entire island had been submerged. These days it was a city park.

It was also, tactically, an excellent location to avoid an ambush.

Azrael descended the stone stairs from the bridge to the island. The offer of information that would be useful to him made him risk a face-to-face meeting.

He was no fool. At worst, it was a trap. It could be just an attempt to gauge his strength, to measure his ability to defend his territory from attack. He was not going in unprepared. Rory had dropped him off at the entrance to the island halfway across the bridge and now waited on the west side. Gregor held the east side, no doubt enjoying a tiny espresso in a café within sight of his latest automobile. Other members of Azrael's Aegis held unobtrusive posts close enough to step in if required.

He found himself hopeful that he wouldn't need the strategic advantage provided by the island.

A deep cold settled in the city this time of year, and close to the water he felt it acutely. It hadn't snowed in days. Most of the accumulation had softened, leaving the ground sticky with mud where grimy snow hadn't frozen in slick chunks. But the clouds hung weighted above him; it would snow again overnight and coat the world in the soft white glow that removed edges and softened the sharpness.

The island was empty of all but the most determined: old men sat on the few sunny benches, bundled up mothers pushed prams along the paths, and the ever-present swans, moving in graceless, waddling strides, picked at the grass beneath the snow.

Isela would not approve of this. Too many civilians in proximity. But also, he considered, out of a concern for his safety that he still found amusing. His fierce dancer, so mortal still in spite of the fact that she had only ever been superficially human. With a witch for a mother and three werewolf brothers, her blood was never more than passing for human.

On the northern tip of the island, sitting before the most stunning view of the snow-shrouded castle, was a man Azrael was not quite ready to call an ally. One had to start somewhere. But a few matters must be settled first.

Raymond Nightfeather lounged on the bench in jeans and motorcycle boots, as oblivious to the cold as the swans that squabbled over the bits of bread he tossed at regular intervals. A collarless black jacket stretched over his broad shoulders; his braided hair was so long and dark it blended into the beaten leather folds.

Leaning against a nearby tree, the captain of his Aegis did not disguise her presence or the two slim swords at her hip and waist. At least not from Azrael. He detected a low level shielding that made human eyes skitter away. Unable to focus on her, they would be drawn to the castle, or the river, or the scenic buildings on the opposite bank. The slight tilt of her head showed awareness of his approach, a courtesy and warning to him. Like Gregor, she managed well the balance between fearless duty to protect her own master and a healthy respect for his equals in the Allegiance.

She stood guard, not over Raymond but two hunched figures huddled on the next bench. A quick scan revealed no life, though they were still animated. Undead. He hadn't thought traveling with servants was Raymond's modus operandi.

A bitter wind whipped up as he approached, sending broken leaves dancing over the frostbitten earth. Azrael didn't take offense— the elements could be impossible to control near another necromancer of similar strength, especially when the terms were uncertain. The heat radiating off his own skin betrayed that.

"How is Lysippe?" Raymond asked as Azrael joined him on the bench.

Azrael bristled, feeling his teeth snug together. *So much for diplomacy.* "You should know better than to mention her name in my presence, Ray."

"Fair," Nightfeather said without smiling. His face was as sharp and unforgiving as the sheer cliffs of the Pacific Northwest coastline. Dark eyes, obsidian sheen recalling his indigenous heritage, stared back at Azrael. "But best to get out what lies between us, isn't it? I don't sense her among your shield today. Thought there might be a reason."

"Lysippe is away on business."

Ray shrugged in feigned carelessness, but his eyes drifted out over the water. Gregor confirmed Ray had come alone except for his second.

"Word is Paolo and Vanka are teaming up on something big," Ray said without further preamble. "They're making the rounds, but so far no one will bite. Seems you're a force to be reckoned with these days."

Azrael said nothing. He wasn't surprised, but it was good to know they were the only ones he had to contend with.

"Paolo paid me a visit," Ray said. "Under the auspices of studio contracts with several Suramérican locations. Wanted to take my temperature about your *transgression.*" The word was snarled with disdain. "I told him you'd made your rules understood. I wasn't interested in overreaching my bounds."

"How did he take that?"

For the first time, emotion flickered across Ray's expression: humor. "Like a hound with a nose full of porcupine quills. He's never had much of a poker face."

"Didn't know you and Paolo were so close."

"Can't stand the guy," Ray admitted. "All quickstep and a greasy smile." Ray focused on the nearest swans, tossing a few chunks of bread.

"You stood with them against me in my home."

"I've gone along with his fearmongering twice." Ray nodded. "Now he's playing the bogeyman with rumors you will use the god at your command to take control. Far as I can see, you've kept your word about staying out of everyone else's business. That's more than I can say for him." Ray snorted, bracing his elbows on his knees and casting Azrael a plain, unguarded look. "I'm damn tired of being trotted out like a bull by the nose every time he needs extra muscle, all while he weasels into my territory."

Azrael had no idea that Paolo had been so aggressive. He sat back against the bench. The enemy of your enemy might be an ally, but that didn't make them a friend. "Why come here?"

"As a gesture of good faith." Ray dusted his hands of breadcrumbs and spread his palms. "I come bearing gifts."

He glanced over his shoulder. The swordswoman strode forward and gave the nearest undead a sharp push. He tumbled off the bench into the mud, limbs askew.

"Up, worm," she barked at the other.

The second, also male, rose from his place, weaving a little, but did not fall. The first levered himself off the ground with the low sound of a beaten animal. Layers of fresh mud increased the already mottled appearance of his bruised face. The second seemed untouched, but his limbs jerked and twitched as the two shambled forward. Face muscles slack and unseeing, both looked vaguely familiar, though he couldn't place them. Raymond made Los Angeles his home and heavily influenced the film industry. These two had the square-jawed, generic handsomeness of leading men. When Isela couldn't sleep, he often found her on the couch downstairs, curled up watching an implausible action movie starring men like these.

He wondered if that's why they looked familiar but for the way they jerked and stumbled, moving with mechanical unnaturalness. Had they been recently converted? Sometimes if there was a gap between death and conversion, their motor skills suffered. He could see no reason why Raymond would choose these two to accompany him.

"What are these?"

Raymond did not look away from the two when he answered, and his gaze hardened. "Spies."

Azrael was careful not to let his confusion show. All undead bore the unique imprint of their maker; it was obvious that Raymond had turned them.

"That's right." Raymond agreed with his unspoken assumption. "I made them, but it appears someone got to them before me. Sleepers, planted in *my* home. Ana caught them trying to steal an alchemical spell of great power from my library. They were also transmitting information. I've had to downgrade them to what you see now. It's been the only way to ensure their security."

"Paolo," Azrael said.

Raymond shrugged, addressing the undead. "On your knees."

Both men dropped, heads hanging. One of the two moaned softly. He must have bitten his tongue with the abrupt fall; blood ran down his chin.

"My gift to you," Raymond said.

"Does he know they've been discovered?" Azrael asked, unable to look at them.

Raymond's smile tightened with malice. "I assigned them work on a production at a studio. A situation comedy known for being somewhat repetitive, and I created a loop to replace their transmissions. They are wired to destruct on discovery. You'll have a few days before he realizes they've been compromised to get whatever information you can from them about why they were sent and what plans their progenitor intends."

A long line of saliva dripped from the muddy one's mouth, glittering silver and wet as it settled on his chest. There were two ways for humans to become undead. Converting a human by force required wiping their minds and leaving them blanks. They were blunt objects, not suitable for a mission of some nuance like this. That meant these had a contract, bargaining their free will in exchange for longer-than-human lives. Contracts were the most useful, because they could retain some of their personality and past skills. But few mortals bargained well with immortals who had had centuries to perfect the terms to give themselves the ultimate advantage. These two might not have volunteered for this specific task, but without properly defining the promise to serve, they had opened themselves up to be used in whatever way the necromancer saw fit.

"The angel of death is disgusted," Raymond said, as if with dawning awareness of something he'd missed before. "To see them treated this way."

Azrael shrugged uneasily. "It has never served my purpose to use undead as cannon fodder."

"How humane." When he looked at Azrael next, a smile turned

his sharp face handsome. "I like you, Azrael. You succeeded where Róisín failed."

Azrael let his confusion show.

"Your dancer," Ray clarified, rising. "She must be special. Perhaps, when conditions are better and I have earned your trust, you will introduce us."

Azrael stood with him. Raymond didn't acknowledge his silence as they walked toward the steps. Ray's second fell in, herding the shamblers behind. The wind had died down but picked up again as Ray moved. For a while companionable silence lingered. He would have to talk with Lysippe again when she returned. She knew Ray best.

Morning sun cast deep shadows beneath the bridge.

Azrael stopped by the steps and Ray faced him.

"I suggest when you've gathered all you can, you dispose of them quickly. Who knows what traps that snake has laid?"

"Paolo will not be happy if he finds that you've come here."

It was Ray's turn to bare his teeth in the feral approximation of a smile. It made him truly frightening. "When. Let him sulk."

Azrael offered his hand. Ray's grip was firm, cool, and when their energies met, it was without agitation. "If I learn anything that would be of use to you, I'll send it along."

"In their minds you broke the laws, allowing your dancer to live," Ray said, and his smile faded. "Words are tricky things, twisted easily enough when you're looking for a way. Don't get comfortable."

"Understood," Azrael said, "thank you."

Raymond touched each undead man's forehead with his thumb, sketching a quick symbol that left a trail of cerulean sparks fading fast in his wake. Azrael recognized a geas for control in the sequence.

"All yours."

Azrael watched the other necromancer go. Ray ascended the steps first. He paused for a moment and looked back at Azrael with something akin to regret on his face. "Tell Lysippe... Send her my regard."

He continued on. Behind him, the swordswoman hesitated at the bottom of the stairs and gazed into the darkness beneath the bridge. Even Azrael had not known Ito was there until the head of intelligence made himself visible by stepping into the lighter shadows. Dressed in slate, his cropped black hair a spiky assemblage over his narrow face, he palmed his fist and gave a deep bow.

Azrael didn't know the woman well enough to be sure, but her stiffened posture suggested surprise. A hand settled on the hilt of her top sword as she folded at the waist in response. She turned and trotted up the stairs after her master.

Follow Ray and his companion out of our territory, Azrael ordered his Aegis. One could not be too careful.

When he finished, Ito waited at his side, having crossed the distance so silently he startled Azrael.

"You know her?" Azrael asked, his eyes on the figures retreating from the bridge.

"Of her," Ito said. "I believe she calls herself Ana these days. She is a formidable fighter, even without the Gift."

It was how his Aegis referred to their exchange. The necromancer created protections around their soul, giving them almost immortality, increased strength and physical prowess, accelerated healing, and a symbol of their ability. Some, like Gregor, claimed physical weapons. Others had more subtle gifts.

Like all contracts, time periods of service were clear. When it was complete, they could remain or seek another necromancer to serve. Most never left.

Ito had departed Japan and service of the necromancer there, having completed the terms of his original contract as a guard. There he had been a second. The new retinue Azrael assembled offered an opportunity he would have never had in his home.

Azrael understood the gamble in taking on a ranking intelligence agent from another court. He'd taken the chance.

With a network of connections and ways of accessing information that mystified even Azrael, Ito had gained strategic advantages for him time and again. Azrael didn't bother to ask him who or where he'd gotten it from. The young shinobi had proved his worth a thousand times in the past century of service. Of all the Aegis, he was the most self-contained. Yet Lysippe trusted him. That meant the most to Azrael.

Azrael waited.

"He's telling the truth," Ito said. "Both Vanka and Paolo have been campaigning. I'll continue to look into the other claims. As for these?"

Azrael sighed as two pairs of blank eyes fixed on him. He lifted a hand, hesitating for just a moment. Claiming them would create a connection. He would feel whatever awareness of their situation they retained. Another reason he resisted using humans this way. What did it do over time, to feel another's fear and suffering and simply ignore it? But he could not waste an opportunity to gain information on Paolo's workings.

He formed his geas with a susurrus of words, minimizing the amount of physical contact he must have with either man. He passed his thumbs over the eyes of each man and they sank carefully to the ground, curling up around each other like littermates. He sighed. In sleep, their minds would be quieter, less fearful.

Master, it appears your consort is in some trouble. Gregor's voice broke his thoughts. *She's headed to the square.*

Azrael ground his back teeth. What could Isela have gotten into between breakfast and—he checked his watch—noon? He opened his mouth to give instructions for preparing his aedis to house the two spies, but Ito spoke first. "Sire, your progeny have arrived."

Azrael swore as his glance ricocheted from the two men to the castle on the hill and the east-bank side of the river toward Old Town. *Dory, get Isela.*

On it, Matai.

"If you will allow me." Ito nodded before Azrael could speak. Azrael had the sense that his head of intelligence found the entire scene amusing, though he was careful to keep his face impassive. "I'll secure these two."

"Go ahead," Azrael called over his shoulder as he took the stairs in threes. "Laugh."

CHAPTER FOUR

G regor stood sentry by the doors to the aedis as they unloaded the phoenix. Tyler shifted from foot to foot in his shadow. When he saw Isela, he started forward.

"Dr. Sato." Gregor cut him off. "Perhaps it's best if you ensure the welfare of our visitor. Isela, your presence is requested in the Old Royal Palace."

Tyler scraped a bow, a high flush in his pale cheeks.

Little stooge, the god snapped.

Gregor advanced, leaning in so his words were for her ears alone. "Careful, dancer, you forget who are your allies and who is your guest."

Isela stepped back, surprised. Smug, Gregor resumed his full height.

"The eyes," he mock whispered as if sharing a secret. "They're still giving you away."

He lifted a hand, flaring his fingertips below his cheekbone. He had, she noted, perfectly groomed cuticles and the nails were short and buffed. She wondered who was brave enough to give Gregor his manicures.

I'll give him something, the god hissed.

Why are you so angry today? Isela sighed.

Why aren't you tired of being treated like baggage?

"What will you do with him?" Isela asked, concerned.

As the gurney passed, Gregor did a cursory inspection of the man's pockets and extracted an old battered wallet. He wrinkled his nose at the smell.

Gregor rifled through the wallet—no ID, no money—and tossed it back as Azrael's undead wheeled the phoenix away from them. "He'll be contained until Azrael can determine why he is like this."

He crossed her path, blocking her lingering view.

Isela flexed her fingers. The second heartbeat, merging with her own, sent waves tingling through her system as power raced to her extremities.

"You are due in the sparring ring in one hour," he reminded her. "Put it to good use."

He turned his back on her, striding down the hall. She stood for a moment looking after him, wishing she knew some geas to make him trip and fall on his perfect face.

"Come on, Issy," Dory said gently behind her. "Save it for the ring."

What was it about Gregor that set her off, she wondered. And why did he seem to enjoy it so much? As head of castle security and chief enforcer in Azrael's Aegis, Gregor answered to no one save Azrael. Gregor was Azrael's sword. Or gun. Or bare-handed executioner. Whatever the situation required.

From the moment they'd met, their exchanges had been barbed. She'd picked fight after fight with Azrael's captain, and he seemed to like provoking her.

And then there was the night she'd been confronted by the scattered remains of a murdered necromancer. She had lost her stomach and her senses in the basement turned abattoir. The words he'd whispered in their shared tongue—German—were the ones that would be used with a beloved child taken ill. There was no disguising the tenderness in that tone.

A few hours later he was back to tormenting her. Azrael claimed he hated her for reminding him of his lost humanity.

Now that she was Azrael's consort, he would lay down his life for her. Such was the bargain he had made when he traded his soul for Azrael's gift. Not that it stopped him from treating her as an extra—unwanted—responsibility. And with Lysippe gone on one of Azrael's interminable missions, he was in charge of her training.

She turned a smile on Dory. "Why is it again you can't train me?"

He laughed. They left the aedis, emerging in the narrowest part of the old castle buildings. Here the walls and the cobblestones sloped upward toward the main courtyard. The spires of Saint Vitus, the cathedral housed within, rose over all. One of these days she would check out those Mucha stained glass windows.

Dory shortened his stride to match hers without comment. It was nice to not feel like a small dog chasing someone for the first time all day. A mountainous man with an easy smile and dancing dark eyes, Dory was an easy favorite among Azrael's Aegis.

"As consort, you will be closer to Azrael than any of us," he said. "Your willingness to fight at his side is admirable. But without proper training, it's suicidal. And he can't afford to lose you. Not now."

Isela made a rough sound in the back of her throat. She wiggled her fingertips and sent gold sparks dancing, but her eyes were on the cobblestones at their feet. "I get it. He needs the god—"

"Not because of a god, Issy." Dory shook his head. "They say necromancers do not love. That they cannot."

She looked at him. His broad hand almost spanned her back from shoulder to shoulder.

"I have never seen Azrael like this," Dory said. "If Gregor is hard on you, it's because he knows what's at stake."

"Your brother likes to remind me that I'm Azrael's weak link," she said, gritting her teeth against emotion. "I didn't think you—"

Dory squeezed her gently. "A woman like you is once in a lifetime. And he's lived a long time."

Isela's chest constricted. She smiled, and Dory wavered in her shining eyes. "Gods, you're a romantic!"

His laugh boomed, echoing against the walls. The narrow passage opened up, and the sight of the grand cathedral, rising in the afternoon light, stole her breath. She hoped she never got used to it.

Never is a long time, the god chimed. *It's a big old building. Now, the Hanging Gardens in Babylon—*

"How come none of you have girlfriends... or boyfriends," Isela asked to distract herself from the temptation to argue with the god. "I bet getting laid once in a while would take Gregor's edge off."

"Gregor's something of an ascetic."

"Surprise, surprise."

"Still waiting for the right one, I suppose," Dory said.

"You can't win if you don't play."

They'd arrived. Rory stood outside the Old Royal Palace, in the same position she had first seen him. Unlike Dory, his brother, who was casual in cargo shorts and a short-sleeved button-down shirt patterned with hibiscus blossoms, Rory wore a wide swath of thick fabric around his hips, a dress shirt tucked in above the knot below his waist. On the other side of the door, stood a Nordic bruiser with impressive facial hair. Except—

"Aleifr, you didn't!" She gasped.

She leaped the distance, chased by Dory's laughter, and stretched up on her toes to put a hand on his cheek. The long bound plait bearing trinkets that caught the light when he moved had been trimmed to hug his cheeks and jawline in a neat sandy-blond shadow. He had a generous mouth, she noted. And with his hair pulled back in a tidy bun to reveal the shaved underside of his head, she could see the strong lines of his face. He might have even groomed his brows. Beneath, eyes the color of a northern sea in summer were fringed with platinum-tipped lashes.

"Speaking of girlfriends." Dory chuckled.

Aleifr was the height of the brothers, but his strength was lean and wiry. "Handsome, eh?"

She had to tilt her chin up to glare at him.

"Talking and now dating," she said, a speculative element of teasing entering her voice. "Careful, Thor Odinson, you're going to be a modern man before you know it. Next thing I know, you'll be asking for car keys."

He grunted, but the laughter brightened his eyes.

"Who is it?" Isela asked.

Aleifr smirked with a shrug.

"Apparently she likes the strong silent type." Dory rolled his eyes. "Witches."

She mentally reviewed the witches who had trickled in since Azrael made his territory a sanctuary.

"A foolish man speaks much and says nothing," Rory said. "Mistress, you should enter."

Isela glared at Aleifr before settling on her heels. "We'll take this up later."

* * *

SHE'D WALKED in on a gathering of necromancers. Again.

Only the surprising lack of tension kept her from turning around and walking right back out of the room.

Light streamed into the Old Royal Palace from the broad windows, casting shafts against the square-patterned wood of the main floor. The lit chandeliers chased the last of shadows from the arched stone ceiling above.

Her eyes settled on three figures at the far end.

For a moment, everything in the room fell away but Azrael. She would have known him without sight. The solid beat in her chest engaged in familiar acrobatics. Born when the rigors of daily life demanded soundness of body, he dressed as a solider might, but with the studied elegance of a diplomat. Modern styles favored him, and he wore them well. Slim-cut trousers defined long, lean legs, and a button-down shirt hugged the width of his shoulders before nipping in at the waist. Dark hair curled just past his collar, a touch of the wildness of a predator in otherwise measured restraint. He was a collection of classical lines and sharp edges. Even his face reflected humanity at a younger age: skin touched with gold, full lips, and heavy brows shading upturned eyes of minted silver. Once, she had found them strange and inhuman. Now they were the most beautiful thing she had ever seen.

Gaining power interrupted the aging of necromancers, the essentialness of their natures coming to the surface in a way that was both inhuman and magnetic. Only the strongest went without some layer of disguise in public, allowing the final and most visible transformation—their eyes—to be revealed. Once a necromancer reached what she thought of as "Allegiance level," the irises mutated from a normal human shade to the iridescent shine.

Of the two standing before Azrael now, only the male's eyes held the beginning of a telltale glow. A thin circle of metallic sheen around vibrant hazel. The interior of his irises picked up flecks of bronze that reflected the light, making them appear to flicker as they fixed on her. He was shades of the desert, from the tan designer jeans to the ochre racing jacket over an artfully faded T-shirt. A dark line of neatly trimmed hair outlined his angular chin, the line of a goatee defining full lips a shade more pink than his burnished amber skin.

At a glance, Isela would have mistaken the female for any of the young corps dancers at the Academy. She stood with one hip cocked as a resting place for her long, delicate fingers, wearing the dismissive expression of a bored adolescent like a second skin. Nails painted a carnal red and filed to points drummed at the hipbone over her fitted leather pants. Her hair, shaved above one ear, fell to the small of her back in a tight braid. The hint of a tattoo curled around her neckline and down the back of her hand to her wrist below the cuff of a black chunky-knit sweater with an asymmetrical toggle close.

Isela felt the weight of her gaze across the room. The god reared up against Isela's consciousness, revealing an overlay of strength emanating from the female that belied her apparent youth.

Dory made a sound between a breath and grunt, placing Isela on his left. The female broke eye contact first.

Isela glanced between the newcomers and Azrael. They were all impeccably dressed; most necromancers seemed to have a keen sense for dressing well in the fashion of whatever era they chose. She had walked in on a ceremony of sorts. And in spite of Azrael's adoption of modern conveniences, there was an ageless formality about him when it was time to do magical business.

She fought the urge to look down at herself. She had stumbled in off the street. Her jeans, wet from the slushy ground, clung to her calves. Wisps of hair floated in an untidy mess around her shoulders.

"Ah, my heart." Though Azrael's expression didn't change, she heard the suggestion of a smile in his voice. "Meet my progeny. They will... staying with us for the immediate future."

Heat curled languorously from her core to her fingertips and toes. He slipped one hand from the pocket of his slacks and offered it to her.

She didn't hesitate. Nor would she slink to his side. She knew where she belonged. Chin up, she crossed the room as elegantly as she had ever navigated a stage.

When his fingers closed over hers, the lights in the room flared. The corner of his mouth quirked as the flush returned to her cheeks. It made a simple touch as intimate as a kiss. He clasped their fingers and brought her knuckles to his lips. His scent, agar and molasses, banished the phoenix from her mind.

The door opened again, and Dante crossed the distance briskly, his hat in his hand as he took his place beside the female necromancer. "Forgive my tardiness. Got caught up in your new visitor."

This should be an interesting story. Azrael's voice was even richer inside her head; it also held the dry humor his face lacked.

Her eyebrow twitched as she fought the edges of a smile from curling her lips. *Later.*

After a shower and a change of clothes, preferably.

Aloud, he turned to their guests as he spoke. "Isela Vogel, my consort and the god vessel."

But she liked the way he gave her name first. He would not define her by their relationship, yet he put it between her and the vast unknown of what she had become. Once she had been a loose end, even among her own large and complicated family.

Azrael had changed that.

You necromancers have a fancy title for everything.

Your mouth distracts me.

Think that's a distraction—imagine it wrapped around your co—

Enough, Isela. A distinct pause in which the heat from his body flared and was swiftly contained. *Please.*

She bit down on a smile as she returned her gaze to the visitors.

At the introduction, all three had swept to one knee. But Isela didn't miss the skepticism in the girl's eyes before her head lowered. Isela shivered, and a curl of heat rolled up her spine. Azrael's attempt to reassure her fell flat. Being disliked on sight, without provocation, had that effect on her.

"Please," Isela said to them, looking to Azrael for help. She understood formality, but this was just ridiculous. "You don't need to do that."

"Dauntless," Azrael said.

Summoned, the male with the bronzing eyes rose at Azrael's introduction and offered his hand. "Tariq Yilmaz."

Isela took a half step forward, but Azrael's hand on hers kept her from leaving his side. Tariq closed the distance and brought her knuckles to his forehead with a second bow. She resisted the urge to lean closer and sample the scent of sandalwood and freshly peeled tangerines.

He looked into her eyes when he spoke. "Consort of my master, I offer you my sword and my shield." After a moment of awkward silence, he leaned in with a murmur. "Do you accept?"

What exactly am I accepting? Isela asked Azrael.

Protection, physical and otherwise, from our enemies.

But the Aegis…

It will be good to have one who is not bound to obey you among them.
The last was said dryly.

The god chimed in so that only Isela could hear. *A keeper?*

Isela didn't like it either, but she had put her life in Azrael's hands the moment she'd come back with a god. She would not gain the almost invincible immortality that he took for granted for hundreds of years. She remembered the rock flying at her. If she lived that long.

It is appropriate to extend them our hospitality, Azrael instructed. *As consort.*

"I accept," she said. "Thank you, Tariq. I offer you the hospitality of our home."

She took Azrael's silence to mean she'd done it properly. Tariq stepped away with a wink.

Dante filled the space. "Dante Abraham. I lend you my wisdom of mysteries great and small."

"He is a walking library," Tariq added, earning a fleeting smile.

Dante had once been tall, but age stooped him in ways that made her think of her own father. The comparison brought a rush of tight heat to her chest that was neither the god nor Azrael. Is that all she was without them, she wondered, an endless well of grief and loss? Her father would only be the beginning. As she remained unchanged, everyone she knew and loved would walk slowly toward death. She thought of her mother, who had seemed to age years in the weeks since her father's passing. Powerful witches might live longer than most mortals, but it was not immortality. Her throat ached with the pressure of rising emotion. Azrael's fingers tightened on hers, bringing her back to the here and now.

"Thank you for your help today, in the square," she said, her voice huskier than before. "Please accept the hospitality of our home."

"My pleasure." He winked before stepping aside with a nod for Azrael. "Long time, no see, old man."

Azrael clasped his hand, drawing him close. "My friend."

Isela cleared her throat, lifting her chin. The spot behind her eye throbbed.

"Nitiu Nandipame Diaz Estrella." The girl spoke next, rising. "My sword and shield are yours, señora."

Woman, Isela thought. Perhaps there was one part of necromancers that aged: the voice. She might look nineteen, but there was no hiding the knowledge of centuries in that voice. Up close, Isela was startled to find herself taller. The woman cupped her hand, palm facing her face and rested it beneath the hook of Isela's fingers. The charge between them snapped painfully. It took all of Isela's determination not to flinch when thick dark brows brushed her knuckles.

"She is called Gus," Tariq clarified.

Both women frowned at him.

I don't care for this one, the god chimed in unhelpfully. *She has no respect for her betters.*

"Thank you," Isela said.

The female necromancer's head jerked up, and her lashes tightened around eyes so dark it was impossible to distinguish between pupil and iris. Azrael squeezed Isela's fingers again.

She blurted out, "I accept and offer the hospitality of our home."

Gus nodded and rejoined her companions. The ease and familiarity between them and their mentor was obvious as conversation resumed around her with less formality. Clouds scuttled across the sun, interrupting the flow of sunlight into the room. Isela shivered.

She stepped back, misjudged the distance, and bumped into Azrael. Trapped, she thought. I'm trapped in all this; I don't even know what I am anymore. The lights flickered, dimming and brightening before settling.

Steady, Isela, the god said as Azrael asked: *Little wolf?*

"Excuse me," Isela muttered. The light bulbs popped.

All four necromancers looked at her in question. Azrael still had a firm grip of her hand.

She forced herself to form the words louder. "It's been a pleasure —meeting you—but I have to go."

Tariq swept another low bow her direction. Gus's eyes narrowed in suspicion. Dante smiled gently enough to break her heart. Azrael brought her knuckles to the center of his chest, over his heart, and then he let her go.

Isela fled.

CHAPTER FIVE

I sela dragged herself back to Azrael's quarters from the sparring ring. She poured half a bottle of wine into one of the fishbowl-sized glasses and limped to the bath.

Her clothes brushed patches of skin scraped raw by sand and pressed against bruises on the way to the floor. Her cargos fluttered where sliced. She inspected her calf. At least the cut had stopped bleeding.

The first rounds with Tyler had earned nothing but sharp criticism from Gregor, finding fault with her technique, her speed and her focus. Life as a professional dancer had toughened her. She knew how to turn her own anger into determination. But she could not withhold her compassion, and Gregor overheard her apology as she helped Tyler to stand. His fury had been complete.

"No apology, no remorse." Gregor picked up his own staff.

The noise in the room vanished.

"You want to slit my throat, little god," he said with a homicidal grin. *"Come."*

Her fingers ached as she turned on the water. When steam rose from the spray, she hesitated. The pain would be exquisite, but the desire to be rid of sand and defeat overwhelmed her. She stepped into the shower, unable to swallow a cry.

As a teacher, Lysippe was tough but fair. She took what Trinh had started at the Academy while Isela was still just human and shaped it into something more deadly. She recognized Isela's natural gifts: speed, grace, balance. The god presence had amplified them; she must learn to use them again. At first they had been a hindrance. She moved faster and farther than she intended. Her spins had more momentum than necessary. She could catch herself but not recover enough to meet her opponent.

When Azrael sent Lysippe to see to his shipping interests in Barcelona, Isela's hell began. Gregor delighted in showing her exactly how not good enough she was.

The god rose in her several times but offered nothing more than rage at Gregor.

I can't yet, the god admitted as Isela lifted her staff up to fend off his blows. *Not this one. Not after the square. But the first chance I get, Issy…*

The god helped her absorb the blow that dropped her to one knee, dampening the pain. Isela swung, but Gregor was out of range, and when she lost her balance, he struck. She hit the sand hard and tasted blood.

Can't you do something? Isela pleaded near the last. *Róisín—*

That was the In Between. Frustration tightened the god's voice. *You weren't in your body.*

"You are dead," Gregor pronounced. He didn't even look at her as she braced her elbow beneath her and staggered to her feet. "Twenty-five, no, twenty-seven times. If you are lucky, Azrael will incinerate your remains. If not, you may well find yourself serving another necromancer."

The worst part was her audience. Rory wouldn't meet her eyes. Tyler looked sick and pale. Gus's expression was one of icy calculation. Gregor turned his back, dismissing her.

Showering, she turned her face up to wash away tears. Hatred rose with the senseless rage that made her muscles tremble. She slammed her hands into the walls and screamed. Tile cracked and fractures rippled out in concentric circles from the imprints of her hands. At the sharp pain, she flipped her palms up. Blood welled up where broken tile had sliced skin.

The rumble of Azrael's voice rolled through her. "Do I need to kill Gregor again?"

"Not unless you're interested in testing how strong his vow to protect your consort is," she said, proud that her voice did not shake.

She fought the urge to open her eyes, letting her ears take in the sound of clothing falling to the tiles. The sight of him would overwhelm her as it always did. She wanted the clarity brought by the hot burn of anger to linger a moment longer. The scent of him—agar and molasses with the hint of cinnamon—curled into her with every inhale, drowning out her own blood and sweat.

He captured her wrist in one hand, cradling it as he inspected the new bruises over skin twisted and blackened by an angel's touch. His gaze climbed her arm. She tried to pull away, but he went still until she let herself be held.

"I will break his hands," Azrael said as though he were contemplating what color tie to wear.

Though she doubted Azrael even owned a tie. It was Gregor who belonged on the cover of a man's luxury magazine, collection of expensive watches and all. Yet for two hundred years, they'd fought back-to-back. Nothing had come between them until her. She was Azrael's weakness. She suspected Gregor would kill her himself before he let her become a big enough chink in Azrael's armor. Vow or not.

"I don't think he needs another reason to hate me," she murmured.

* * *

HER WORDS WERE LIGHT, but he heard the anguish in them. He regretted losing the ability to read her.

"No one challenges Gregor the way you do," he said. "It's good for him."

He compartmentalized his need to deal with Gregor. A rough sparring session wasn't the only thing weighing on her. Her departure from the palace had been more like flight.

Once, he would have pushed, baited, and cornered her like the wolf she was descended from. Now he had other tactics at his disposal. He brought the bruised wrist to his mouth, flicking his tongue over the damp, soapy skin below her palm. Her gasp was music to his ears. When he brought his eyes up to hers, the heat building in them was unmistakable. The gold had almost faded from her irises, returning them to the smoke-before-fire he knew best.

He pressed his lips to flesh again, sucking until tremors wracked her. Her whole body revealed layers of sensitivity to the slightest contact. The difference between a gasp and a tremble, a sigh and a scream, kept him coming back to her bed night after night, determined to seek, discover, and elicit every ounce of pleasure she held.

Her spine arched when his mouth moved higher.

"I understand you had a busy day," he murmured against the flesh inside her elbow, letting his words thrum against the pulse in her arm. "Brought home a new pet?"

"Phoenix."

His brows rose. His mouth moved in a long line up the inside of her arm, taking in her scent and then moving toward her collarbones. "Truly?"

She made a sound of affirmation, or a moan. "He'd delayed his transition. Almost took out half of Old Town."

He drew back, and this time she moaned. Her eyes fluttered open. Desire and confusion warred in their depths.

"You stopped him," he said, his voice cooling as his mind turned over the possibilities. Phoenixes never postponed their transitions.

"Something's wrong with him." She sighed, dipping under the spray one more time. "Besides the transition. He's human, or he looks like one."

Who had transformed a phoenix? One necromancer in his territory might be capable of that level of alchemy—the satrap over southern Europe, holed up among a harem of godsdancers in Seville. He was an ally, or at least not an enemy. Maybe his meeting with Raymond had made him paranoid, but this couldn't be a coincidence.

She forced her lips closed against a yawn. "It must be the Allegiance, to cast a spell that strong, right?"

"It would take a great power," Azrael admitted, shutting off the water.

"The phoenix is reborn from its own ashes," Isela said dreamily. "The cycle of creation and destruction is essential to their nature."

"You've been spending time in the library." Azrael smiled at last.

The sight of her in the shower when he arrived, back bowed in defeat, had affected him more than he expected. A yawn escaped, making her jaw pop. He scooped her up. Her body healed faster than any human's, but even watching the bruises fade didn't ease his mind.

He would figure out what to do about Gregor tomorrow. Tonight he would give her the gentle pleasure of a worshipful lover, to bring her back to herself.

She was asleep before he reached the bed.

CHAPTER SIX

I sela woke alone in the big bed. She examined the previous day's injuries, but even the faded bruises and pale, healing lines on her palms were no comfort. Her head throbbed faintly; the god she'd nicknamed Gold mercifully maintained silence. She spent a long time on her mat beside the window overlooking the garden. The repetitive sequence of sun salutations served as a moving meditation. Her muscles warmed through the practiced motion, strengthened as she bore her own weight through the transition between postures, and softened as she breathed into each space where worry had created tension in her body.

The mat, like the sequence that followed, had been a gift from her mother. She had never known a time when one like it hadn't occupied a corner in whatever space they lived. Her mother went there every day, moving through her sequence with single-minded intensity. When they were young, the siblings all tumbled around her hands and feet as she moved, imitating her with childlike enthusiasm. Only Isela stayed until she was old enough to need her own mat, placed beside the first. Moving together, breathing as one, connected them.

You are your mother's daughter, her father liked to say when she was small and unable to sit still for more than a few moments at a time. *But you are also my child: when you choose, you do nothing without purpose.*

Azrael might have barred her from dance, but that didn't mean she had to sit still. By the time she reached the double digits, her limbs shook and her breath came harder than she was used to. She found herself more tired than she should have been and remembered she hadn't eaten anything the night before. Grief, taking its senseless toll, had stolen her appetite again. But that was no excuse. She was going to have to be more careful about fueling her body, especially after the god tapped it for anything. It would do no good to burn herself out. She showered, dressed, and then stood in the kitchen. She took a deep breath and filled a plate.

She sat down at the table, poking at the delicacies that had a moment before seemed palatable. Resolutely she took a bite of toast. It tasted like sawdust and reminded her of the crumbs her father always left on the countertop. Tears choked her, fighting against the half-chewed lump of bread making its way down her throat. She took a breath, focusing on the feeling of the sun coming in the window from the snow-dusted garden and the hum of the appliances and the sensation of her seat in the chair and her hands on the table. She swallowed.

By the third bite, it was no longer a struggle. She found thinly sliced meats and cheeses. The scent of bread drew her to a basket of *brotchen* freshly baked and fleetingly warm. Cherry tomatoes and pickles and olives followed. She took a break with a cup of tea, then attacked the honey jar with a spoon. A hurried ransacking of the cabinets turned up a jar of peanut butter—a luxury she infrequently treated herself to before—and she spread it on toast, and carrot sticks and celery.

At last she sat back on her stool and loosed a long belch. The giggle that escaped after startled her. For the first time in weeks, her head felt clear and as though it was her own again.

Now it was time to interrogate a phoenix.

In a fireproof room deep in the aedis below the castle, Dante sat beside the phoenix on a bed, scribbling in a little notebook.

"My lady Isela," he said, a smile in his voice.

She fixed her eyes on the figure in the bed. He looked thinner and softer around the edges somehow, as though he were a photo out of focus.

Gold?

He's coming apart—the body can't contain him like this.
Can you talk to him?

Gold's presence prickled against the inside of her skull. The sensation was just shy of painful. *Distract the necromancer.*

Isela cleared her throat. "Have you ever seen anything like this?"

"There are few creatures of both life and death. The blood—grace blood—tends to split and leave us to one or the other. Most of them died out after the godswall was cast. And this phoenix is—was—one of the last of its kind." He sighed, shaking his head. "I'm not as old as the others, and there are so few of us sometimes everything feels new."

"So you must be what, three, four thousand?" Isela said, trying to make a joke of it.

He gave her a brief stare. "I was born in Baton Rouge, shortly after emancipation." He paused. "Of the slaves."

"But you…?"

Now he laughed. "Azrael found my talents worth his considerable effort to train. For that I am forever indebted to him. I'll never be as powerful as the others. My aging simply slowed when theirs halted."

His voice lacked bitterness or regret. His lips moved silently as he studied the phoenix for a moment. He made an observation in his notebook in small, precise print. His gaze flickered back to her, and Isela remembered her job. "And the others?"

Dante closed his notebook on his pen and crossed his arms, leaning back in his chair as he contemplated her. Isela fought the urge to squirm, afraid to reach out to Gold for fear of betraying her.

"Tariq was Azrael's first," he said. "He was mostly gone by the time Gus came along—out of the nest, so to speak. Gus found me. She's always been a little overprotective."

Isela bit her tongue against a less charitable description.

Dante said after a long pause, "You have to forgive Gus."

"She's definitely strong willed." Isela kept her voice even.

Dante laughed. "She's not the only one."

Isela ignored the pointed expression he aimed over wire-rimmed glasses. "Did she have a rough time, becoming a necromancer?"

"Didn't we all." He sighed. "But Gus's problems started well after she came into her powers. She spent a long time running from Paolo's attempts to seduce her into becoming his consort or destroy her."

Isela couldn't wrap her brain around that enough to form a question.

Dante opened his journal again and added something to his notes. "She's a threat to Paolo as long as she stays in his territory," he said without looking up. "But it's her home too. She won't give it up even if it kills her. Whole situation makes her a bit... temperamental."

He's in there somewhere. The bird, Gold said, frustrated and drawing back. *Isela, what do you know about sanctuary?*

CHAPTER SEVEN

Someone—Tyler, most likely—had tried to make the undead spies comfortable in Azrael's aedis, providing water and food. But these two fit the shambling-zombie image better than most. Ray had bound any of their higher functioning, a precaution Azrael understood given the circumstances, but it left them utterly devoid of any traits that would have qualified them as living.

They stood, shuffling from foot to foot, with vacant gazes and sagging, slack expressions. They would not eat, or drink or sleep, unless commanded. Left to their own devices, they would simply waste away. Dehydration would take them before starvation, though in the end neither would be pretty.

He tried to see them as they had been, tall and strikingly handsome. One square jawed and sandy haired. The other with ethnically ambiguous olive skin and impossible-to-distinguish eyes. A leading man for any starlet. A casting director's dream.

They were also work of master craft—the command to spy had been impressed while they were still human but had been masked so well Raymond would not discover it when he took them on and turned them as his own servants. The undead were bound to obey the necromancer who created them, though Raymond had relinquished his claim. Now they were Azrael's problem. And his responsibility.

"Drink," Azrael murmured, testing his control. "Eat."

The two shuffled obediently to the table. One groaned when the bread touched his tongue, a low, desperate sound of mingled relief and torment. The other spilled half the water down his shirt guzzling from his cup and dissolved into fits of wet hacking.

Azrael cursed himself for assuming Ray would have subdued their appetites as well.

It was undead like these that the necromancers had displayed during the takeover to cow the human population into submission. Each member made undead to stand behind them, silent witness and visible promise to anyone who dared to resist or defy them. Azrael had been careful to choose from the worst criminals Gregor could find, but watching the others that day, he doubted many had bothered that much. Some of the Allegiance had been particularly illustrative in their descriptions, warning that their victims would feel the urges of their body even as they were unable to meet them. Living torment.

Apt, he thought, considering the two now weeping silently as they choked in their hurry to acquire simple bread and water. When had they last eaten? It would end today, he vowed. He would get whatever information he could and then release them.

Would he have done any less if he'd discovered another necromancer's spies in his territory? Raymond said the one had been found in his map room. The other had attempted to break a ward guarding his potions locker. Raymond's collection of elixirs knew no equal. Azrael could only imagine the protections Raymond had erected to safeguard it. Yet the zombie had dared. What had he been looking for?

He turned his attention inward, searching for the knot of spellwork that tasked and bound them. He identified the wards first. Used to create the boundary of their awareness and exclusion of other commands, the wards had been reworked recently to allow Azrael to take control. With delicately wrought interlacing, they connected to geas: the command of the necromancer they served. Together they formed the spell that bound the soul to the body and their creator.

Next, he pried deeper for their true purpose.

He began cautiously, scanning for carefully disguised geas and finding them knotted in the base of the skull, the reptilian portion of the brain. After a moment, his natural ability took over with deft confidence built over centuries and a natural inclination to untangle and defeat opposition. It was his talent, after all, the one Róisín had taught him to hone by making him her scout. When they would come upon a failed necromancer or a supernatural creature, it fell to him to discover and define any threat.

"The danger will teach you surer than any book or lesson." She overrode his objection. "And if you survive, the knowledge will be embedded in your bones. Such is the value of experience."

He'd had a few near misses, and she'd had to save him once when he underestimated a soul-stealing ward and nearly spent an eternity trapped in a bottle like a *djinn*.

"You've expended your grace, goat boy," she'd chided after. "You'll see to yourself from here on out. Don't make such a stupid mistake again."

Satisfied, he withdrew carefully, leaving the base-level geas intact for now.

Neither reacted as he strode to them. Unlike an untouched mortal, they wouldn't be able to flinch away, though the nearest's eyes widened in alarm. Azrael sketched the geas for obedience and truth on his forehead. He anticipated that once he got too close to the truth, their built-in wards would act in one of two ways: defense or self-destruction.

"What is your purpose?" he asked it, his voice activating the geas he'd instilled.

Its voice was rusty from dehydration and lack of use. "To be famous."

That would have been true enough when they joined Raymond's service.

"Who is your true master?"

It hesitated, and he could see the defensive wards struggling against his geas. He watched it flare, then unravel, and whispered words of a binding to keep it from triggering the secondary wards that would cause the undead to self-destruct.

"Bran," Azrael said softly, worming the geas deeper into the man's consciousness. "You have a story to tell me, don't you?"

The square chin dipped once, and the undead's Adam's apple bobbed convulsively. It took a breath, and its eyes widened in panic. Its mouth clamped shut. A muted, shrieking moan sounded between its locked jaws as blood trickled from the corner of its mouth. It gurgled behind closed lips, gagging.

Azrael spat out a command to block the latent ward from continuing to take effect. "Open, you fool!"

Its jaw fell open. With a soft pop it unhinged, swinging loose from the joint like a snake. Blood coated its chin, and a wet lump of meat fell out, landing on Azrael's toe. It coughed, and Azrael sidestepped the spray of crimson before shaking off his boot. He nudged the lump with his toe.

Tongue. It'd bitten off its own tongue.

Azrael swore in three languages. How had he missed that ward? The undead stared at him in mute horror and pain, unable to lift a hand to its bloody mouth. It gagged, trying to respond now that the ward had been defeated, but the words were unintelligible. Azrael silenced him with a quick gesture.

He had been so focused on the condition of the undead, not wanting to inflict any more harm on them than necessary. His concern—this compassion—was a distraction. And he was weak for not wanting to go into the man's memories out of a desire not to feel the undead's emotions as he tried to follow the trail back to the beginning. In the end, both only made things worse.

Now he would have to invade the man's mind anyway, and whatever sensations—pain, terror, despair—he felt would be stronger with this newest injury. From across the room, the other undead began to moan and rock unsteadily, its eyes on the bloody pool forming at Azrael's feet.

"Sleep now." Azrael waved a hand, and the second undead sank into a huddle on the floor, chin to chest.

He commanded the first onto one of two gurneys and gave him the command to sleep, laced with a geas for remembrance. Then he closed his eyes and slipped into the man's thoughts.

For a moment it was all he could do to breathe and be calm, assailed by the storm of emotion that had taken over the undead's mind. He focused on his own breath, drawing his wards around him piece by piece until the gale battered the edges of his walls but did not touch him.

Show me what you would say, he commanded.

The image spun around him, a blur of impressions at first until the night he tried to break into Raymond's elixir vault. They became clearer, more cohesive. Arriving in Los Angeles. Stepping off the plane and staring into the sun and crystalline blue sky with awe and a bit of terror. Azrael encountered resistance as he urged the undead further back. There was a gap and then a familiar face. Paolo.

Stop, Azrael commanded. He felt the human mind around him recoil in terror, but he could not afford mercy. Not now. He pressed, forcing it into the blackness it had created to block the memory. Paolo's smiling face and easy promises to care for the man's family and eventually to free him to enjoy the rest of his unnaturally long life if he was successful.

Become my vessel and be rewarded beyond value.

The scene wavered, trembling, as the mind crumpled around him, taking the memories with it. He pushed harder, reliving the memory of what Paolo had done next and the agony that had followed. That only sped up the process of degradation. Azrael pulled back the moment before the mind collapsed into a permanent gray blankness. He stared at the figure on the table, unhinged jaw frozen open in a rictus of pain. He touched its forehead with his thumb.

"Release."

The corpse loosed its soul in one long exhale. Azrael stared at the empty shell on the table for a long moment. Then he snapped his fingers and the body went up in a burst of white-hot flame, contained by the force of Azrael's fury. The last ash drifted to the stainless steel, and fragments of rib cage crumbled into dust. He rolled the second gurney forward and sighed.

The second undead had served Paolo much longer, a human servant who craved nothing but to become one of Paolo's undead. Its willingness made the process by which Paolo inserted his secret geas tolerable, if not less painful. But even better, it had been present during a call from Vanka, a forgotten set of eyes and ears that Azrael accessed now with surgical proficiency.

It's gone. Vanka's rage was only dampened by the distance of memory. *While I was securing the dancer, it overpowered my guards. They're tracking it now, but...*

Paolo tsked lightly, his brow furrowing. *It has served its purpose— we know it can be done. We no longer need it.*

Your spies...

Leave in the morning, Paolo finished smoothly. *If Ray has the elixir—*

We don't have time to wait, Vanka said.

Calm yourself. Paolo rose from his chair. Azrael was aware of the intensity of his host's response to Paolo's movements, the well of desire rising at the sight of his broad shoulders and the sun from the window on his curling tawny hair. He was suddenly aware of his host's own position, sprawled in the sheets of a messy bed. This one had been Paolo's lover then. Not that it meant much to Paolo. Human life was almost valueless among some of the Allegiance. Had Azrael been one of them once? Of course he had. He considered how willing he had been to use Isela for his purposes—including seduction—and then release her, or kill her, if need be.

She was one; his territory protected many humans just as vulnerable, or more so than she was. That was his rationale. And now? Now he would let the entire city burn to prevent harm from coming to her. Which was better?

Paolo spoke again, and Azrael forced himself to pay attention to the words as the first tremors began to shake the edges of his vision. This mind was beginning to break down. Time raced toward the edge.

…headed to Stary in the morning, Vanka said, and centuries' worth of place names and locations flashed in his mind until he identified the small town on the sea. *It's there, and I'll find it.*

Paolo shrugged carelessly. *If the destination is achieved, what does it matter by whose road it is reached?*

It matters if you are caught, Vanka snapped. *If Raymond suspects…*

They will destroy themselves before revealing anything. I've seen to it, and whatever intel they've gained about the workings of Raymond's house will be worth the loss. Paolo cut her off. *And you? It's disputed territory. Azrael—*

Will be too busy enforcing the vow he made over his human pet to notice, Vanka said. *I've taken care of it.*

Paolo sucked his teeth and returned to the bed. Azrael had to fight the urge to recoil as the necromancer reached out to him, caressing the cheek of his host body. It leaned into Paolo's touch, eager.

Not human anymore, Paolo said, as if an afterthought. *And not the only one soon.*

Azrael snapped back just as the mind around him crumpled to a blank point. He came back into his own body, staggering backward with the effort. Even sapped of energy as the work had left him, he felt invigorated. He had a name. *Stary.* And a purpose. His eyes flicked back to the corpse on the table. The blank, vacant stare was at odds with the serene smile beneath.

"I release you," Azrael said as pity welled up in him.

What had the human thought, taking a necromancer for a lover?

Had he feared at all, even at the end? Azrael thought of Isela and the way she curled against him in sleep, a smile on her face. Contentment, safety. For the first time he was grateful she was the vessel of a god. What other chance did she stand in a world such as this, with humans as fodder for the intrigues of necromancers? The god would protect her, out of nothing more than a selfish concern for its own survival, but nonetheless. Everything else he would provide.

He left the smoldering remains of the second corpse and sent a mental summons to Gregor. *Call Lysippe. Find out what she knows about Stary.*

Master?

And pack an overnight bag, Azrael said before cycling through his other mental connections. *Tyler. Have the plane fueled and on the tarmac.*

My lord, Tyler replied.

Azrael headed to his study to wait.

✶ ✶ ✶

"I WANT to offer the phoenix sanctuary," Isela began, rounding the corner.

The room was meant to be a study, but the books that lined the wall and the enormous tables made her think of a library. One wall was all grimoires, part of an enormous collection amassed over centuries. The others were filled with manuals and reference books that Isela had never seen or heard of before. She'd dedicated a few hours a day to that side, trying to expand her understanding of this new world. She most often ended with a headache. Academics had never been her strength. Unlike Tobias, who came by his family-book-worm status via their father, studying had been a painful ordeal for her. She could memorize choreography after watching it once, but she'd struggled to get even passing grades in her classes.

Gold helped, allowing her to focus, and helping with translations, but there was only so long she could sit with dusty old books, struggling with archaic sentences, before her body itched to get up and move.

Unlike Azrael, who stood as still and certain as an oak at one of the tables, hands braced on either side of an open book. It was one of a stack he had built up around him. There was no indication of how long he'd been in that position, but his head rose with leonine grace at her entry.

Isela waited for his eyes to come back from whatever deep focus he'd gained. Instead he dipped his head again.

Isela advanced to the table opposite him. She braced her hands, bending down and angling her head so that she fell into his line of vision. She glanced down at the book before him. The page was illustrated with colorful drawings of plants and rocks, tiny expert lettering in a language she didn't recognize. "Is that an elf?"

"No such thing," Azrael said with a sigh, closing the book. Isela leaned back to avoid getting her nose caught in the pages. At her expression, he clarified. "Elves."

Isela gaped. "You mean there are zombies and shape-shifters and phoenixes, and gods only knows what else roaming the planet. But no elves?"

His brows rose. Azrael cocked his head in that absent way she'd learned to associate with his telepathic connections to his Aegis. He straightened his spine, banking the fire in the hearth with a wave of one hand.

"And to the question about sanctuary, no."

Isela followed him out of the room. She caught up in the long hallway toward the elevators. "Excuse me... Did you even hear what I said?"

"I heard." Azrael waited until she was inside before pressing the button that took them to the passage leading to his quarters. "If it wanted sanctuary, it should have presented itself here, to me. Instead, it kidnapped you on the tram."

Isela frowned. "Kidnapping? I could have broken the hold anytime. I just didn't want to draw attention—"

"Like what happened in the center of Old Town Square?" Azrael's brows rose. "It's going to take days to make every last video of that disappear, and I have my entire team scrubbing the feeds."

Isela was silent all the way to the kitchen. He sniffed at the remaining coffee, poured a cup, and heated it in his hand on the way up to the bedroom. Frowning, Isela followed. She watched him disappear into the closet.

"The phoenix had a message for me," she called after him. "Maybe he knows more—"

Azrael emerged with a small travel bag. He shook his head. "Phoenixes cannot be made to easily cooperate."

"Yes, but it sought me out," she said. "It wants to tell me something. Maybe I could meet it halfway."

He folded his arms over his chest and his eyes narrowed.

"Gold," Isela began. "That is, the god, she spoke with him." Silence. She cleared her throat. "Well, she tried to. Whatever has happened to him, he's coming apart. She doesn't think his body is going to hold. So I was thinking she could help us."

"No."

Isela paused. "Dante knows your library like the back of his hand. Maybe he and I could work together—"

"I want you nowhere near the creature."

Isela felt Gold crackle to her skin as she struggled for words. "You what?"

"Did you hear what I just said?" He cocked his head, sipping at his coffee over a little smile.

Isela fought the urge to throw something at him. This was the same argument all over again. Would he let her do nothing?

"I can sit in the library all day trying to learn, but wouldn't it be more practical if I had something to work on? Like a project."

Azrael shook his head. "Whatever it's been through has changed it. I do not trust it."

"We don't have to trust it to help it," Isela began. "Especially if it could help us."

"I forbid it."

"But I want to help," Isela said. "And Gold will protect me. After all, my skin is her skin now, so she won't let anything… What?"

He had gone absolutely still again, but this time without the calm intensity of focus. His distant eyes seemed turned inward, and she watched tension crawl his shoulders as his lips pressed into a tight line. He shook his head once in response to something unheard, and when his eyes returned to her, something unfamiliar lingered in their depths. His eyes roved her, hot and possessive. She had seen him burn with rage and go icy with control. But this was neither.

"This abomination of a phoenix accosts you in the middle of *my* city," Azrael said, a new edge in his voice. "In broad daylight."

She shivered. "He was trying to warn—"

"In the heart of *my* territory," he roared. "*My* consort."

When she paused, the part of her that had once responded to him as prey to a predator quailed, but she refused to back down. *Gold, I might need you in a minute.*

"*Our* city, Azrael." She imbued his name with all that lay between them: love and longing and loyalty. "You're not alone anymore."

Azrael's quiet returned like a wave. The sense of any emotion in him died away. His eyes caught the light from the window and shone as he looked out over the gardens.

He sighed. "Covens are trickling into the city, seeking protection I have guaranteed as part of my alliance with the high priestess. Others will be next: shifters like your brothers and broken things like that phoenix. Never mind the human population."

Isela's eyes stung. In another necromancer's territory, her mother and her sisters-in-law would be hunted for revealing themselves as they had. And her own brothers. Their ability to become wolves at will put them among the creatures living in the shadows at the whim of the necromancers.

"And you will have to protect all of us," she said. "But you don't have to do it alone. I can help. The god—"

The door chimed.

"Go away," Isela barked as Azrael called, "Come."

"This isn't over." She followed Azrael down the stairs to the kitchen.

Tyler paused in the living room, glancing between them. "My lord, Gregor is on his way in the chopper, and the plane is ready."

"Fine." Azrael dismissed his report with a wave of one hand.

Isela recognized the bag in his hand. "You're leaving."

"Dr. Sato," Azrael said. "A moment."

Tyler did not look at her as he departed. Isela braced her hands on the counter and forced a deep breath into her lungs.

"I have to go away for a few days." Azrael moved toward her, and she could read the longing in his face.

She swallowed hard, putting the island between them. "Where?"

"A small town near the Black Sea." He sighed. "It's disputed territory between Vanka and me. I've never been able to keep a proper hold on it. I've had reports that she's been there, searching for something. I need to know what it is and if she found it."

"What if she's still there?" she said. "Isn't that dangerous?"

"I'm taking Gregor with me." He smiled faintly. "Consider it a gift. Lysippe is already on the ground."

Isela crossed her arms over her chest. "And the city?"

"Rory and the others will look after it," Azrael said. "And you. Tariq will see to your training. You'll find him a more forgiving teacher."

No longer sharp with the weight of decisions, his voice made her think of his touch in the night, his arms sliding around her when she tossed in a nightmare or woke brokenhearted with grief. She closed her eyes. She was to be handed off in his absence like a child. She had chosen him, and in doing so she had chosen this life.

He would enter disputed territory where he might run into that homicidal redheaded necromancer. The injustice burned in her throat. Now she would worry about him—and Gregor and Lysippe—alone against gods only knew who, doing what gods only knew what. While she was safe in her gilded prison. She wished she could hate him or feel grateful. Either would have been easier. The sound of footsteps bringing him closer drove her backward. She bumped into the L-shaped counter by the sink and rebounded away, toward the dining room.

Azrael stopped. "I must go."

She faced the windows overlooking the garden and focused on the buds appearing at the edges of long, dark branches of trees. She didn't hear him leave.

PART II

CHAPTER EIGHT

Azrael stepped off the plane on a forgotten runway north of the Black Sea. This time of year close to the water, the wind found all the seams in his clothing and sent icy tendrils to his skin. He banished them with a single flare of heat, jogging down the stairs as the plane's engines began to whine again in preparation for departure.

Azrael didn't blame the pilot for her hurry— based on the clouds boiling across the horizon, she didn't have a lot of time. It didn't help that this was disputed territory with Vanka—technically his after Róisín had descended into madness and abdicated her holdings, but his ability to manage the borders was less than complete. He and Vanka simply turned a blind eye to each other's presence here until a final reckoning could be taken. He knew he had, at most, a few days until she found out about his arrival. Depending on what she had found and her remaining interest in the area, he would either be allowed to depart uncontested, or he'd have to fight his way out.

At least he wouldn't be alone. Never that. The metal stairs clanged behind him as Gregor disembarked, shouldering a black carryall and tossing down a second bag of gear.

A decade after the war for American Independence ended, Gregor had the unfortunate luck to be taken when his ship was captured by pirates en route to Europe. The captain, a necromancer whose rivalry with Azrael had reached a fever pitch, turned his crew of undead loose on the prisoners. Gregor succeeded in bashing in the skulls of three before the necromancer called his men off and threw the young soldier in the brig.

"I am dead twice now to everyone who knew me." Gregor told the darkness of the hold, chained beside the cage holding Azrael by iron and geas. "And it seems I am now to become something unholy. Or food for it." He kicked a bare skull across the hold.

It was that simple forthrightness, tinged with wry humor, that lifted Azrael's focus from his own predicament. His rival was stronger than he'd anticipated, and his bonds were firm. His own crew waited for his call. He could feel Lysippe's anxiety growing, but he urged her to have patience. After 2,000 years, he could bear much it seemed.

Until Gregor. His time as soldier was obvious in his economy of movement and speech. Though it wasn't unheard of to find a minor noble serving in the more elite jäger units, this one held none of the pretensions Azrael expected of his breeding. He was no gentleman— though he was dressed in the latest fashions, his skin was tanned and wind roughed, his hands scarred with labor and shoulders broad with work. Most of the Hessian mercenaries serving under the British had gone back immediately; a few remained to carve out new lives in the young country. This one was something of an enigma. And then there were his eyes. Haunted and blue like the sky over a battlefield. What had happened to him in the New World was a story that roused Azrael from his ennui. Humans like Gregor always had that effect on him.

"Do you play?" the young nobleman asked, his gaze falling to the forgotten chessboard and its broken pieces in the corner of Azrael's cell. "If I am to remain until it's my turn to be fodder, I'd like to keep my mind occupied."

No question of how Azrael had come to be caged, or why caged when the others were chained, or how he had remained alive, bearded and thin as he was, for so long. Gregor repeated his inquiry in three languages. At last, he reached fearlessly through the bars.

"Don't touch it." The words were forced from Azrael's throat as if dragged across gravel. "The only thing more dangerous than the crew is friendship with me."

Gregor sat back on his haunches but didn't withdraw completely. He assessed Azrael's tattered clothing and filthy skin.

"You are the pearl trapped in this hellish oyster. Does he hope to wear you down, with all of this... carnage?" He gestured around them.

Azrael almost smiled. Almost.

Gregor withdrew. He sat in silence, eyes closed for a long time.

Azrael leaned against the bars nearest the rough-hewn wall, feeling the pounding of the waves the other side. He could burn the ship down with a thought. And drown himself in the process.

"I shall be dark, and you play the light," Azrael said finally, waving his fingers.

A ghost image identical to the board in the corner materialized between them. Gregor's eyes widened, but he did not flinch away or make religious symbols against evil. Curious. Even nobles were superstitious.

Azrael called out his first move, and the ghost image of the piece slid across the board. Gregor got the hang of it quickly. After several days, Azrael stopped materializing the board entirely. They called out pieces and positions, each holding the game move by move in their minds until one declared checkmate and the other sighed ruefully. Conversation came later, stories, haltingly.

The board never moved from its forgotten corner, but it didn't take long for the captain to discover the companionship between them. Suddenly Azrael found he could no longer watch and wait.

With preternatural insight, Gregor woke the following morning, resolved. "I'd take my chances with your lot if you would have me, sir."

Azrael grinned. He couldn't help himself. "What makes you think I have any chance at all?"

Gregor lifted a pin from one of the hinges of Azrael's cell, flipping it in his palm. Azrael blinked. When had he managed that?

"During your last"—Gregor glanced at him—"interrogation."

A day before.

"I've discerned that you are not able to touch the bars," Gregor explained. "So I took the liberty."

"And yet you waited?" Azrael mused.

"For the word to be forthcoming."

Azrael assessed the wall. The cell had been assembled from hinged panels attached top and bottom with identical pins. "One pin."

"Actually..." Gregor pulled back the old scraps of fabric that made up his bedding and revealed more. "I'd thought to take the last today, but perhaps we are out of time."

"Perhaps."

Gregor held Azrael's stare. If anything, his shoulders straightened and he cleared his throat lightly as if preparing to present himself to a superior officer. There were footsteps on the deck overhead.

"You'd best attend to that last pin," Azrael said, settling in his cell.

When the captain came for his daily round of brutality, Gregor fought just enough to pull the captain's thugs close to the cell wall. When they yanked him away, he had a grip on the bars and simply pulled the walls apart. Azrael stepped through the gap as the wards bound to the cell dissolved. It ended quickly. Gregor stood unflinching as Azrael rose from the ruined corpse of his rival.

He'd displayed only marginally more surprise when Azrael's people had boarded the ship and subdued the crew. Lysippe was at their head. Rory and Dory cleaned up anything left moving in her wake. They broke into the hold, taking in the stench of rotted remains.

"He comes with us." Azrael greeted his crew with a gesture toward Gregor.

Lysippe jingled keys, stepping lightly over the remains of the captain. "Your hands."

Emaciated and broken, Gregor had not lowered his eyes to their liberators, nor did his gaze hold the disdain many men of his time held for her sex or the color of her skin. Instead, he had looked curious as he offered his wrists. "Thank you, lady."

Lysippe rolled her eyes, but a little grin tugged her mouth as she shook the rusted shackles free, being careful of his bloodied wrists. Dory carried him out of the hold. Eyes the color of a battlefield sky paused briefly on Aleifr beheading the last of the undead. The rest of Azrael's crew piled the bodies and doused them for burning. There was no horror or fear in Gregor's gaze, only a greedy, squinting joy at the sunlight on his face and the fresh salt air.

"You will stay with us until you've made a recovery," Azrael informed Gregor as they boarded a smaller vessel and the first torches were cast onto the abandoned ship. "Then we will drop you at whatever port you require. I owe you that much at least."

"I have nothing to return to," Gregor said, looking around at the small and unusual crew. "If it suits, I should like to travel with you a while."

Gregor accepted Azrael's explanation of being a gentleman of fortune and leisure with an interest in pursuing the occult from all over the world but kept his own counsel. He didn't ask questions about how Azrael traveled with such an unusual accompaniment or the mysterious things he witnessed in their presence. Even years later, when they had abandoned the ship in search of an ancient grimoire made of human flesh, he proved a fearless companion and made himself useful at every turn. And he was the only member of the party who ever bested Azrael in chess.

One afternoon, camped in a desert basin shadowed by the Altai Mountains, Lysippe brought the last bottle of claret to Azrael where he waited out the glare of sun and heat. After pouring two generous servings in battered cups and pausing for a toast, she announced, "Give him the Gift."

Azrael shook his head but took a drink. "Eight is a good number. Perfection beyond that which nature is capable of."

"Nine is three triads," she countered. "There is power of threes."

They drank in companionable silence. Descended from Amazons, Lysippe's way reminded him most of her mother when she hunted, sitting in perfect stillness for hours and waiting for the moment to strike. As the sun descended and the others began packing camp for their departure, he sighed, drained his cup, and extended it for a refill. As she poured, he realized it had been exactly the moment she waited for.

"He's been tested," she said. "And broken. If you don't take him, he won't live long. That would be a loss."

"This isn't exactly living, Lys," Azrael said, his own brows raised.

"Then let him be useful while it lasts. He's handy with a blade and a damn good shot."

Azrael had noticed. More than one of the Aegis had taken to training with him, ostensibly to help him recover his strength. And, for all his dislike of horses, the man could drive a team better than anyone but Lysippe.

"Doesn't ask questions, but he watches and learns. He takes orders and the others listen when he gives them. It's in his blood."

Azrael sighed. "You remember how hard it was to break Aleifr of his damned Nordic prince-ness once he left Róisín?"

"I don't have a mind to break him of it," Lysippe said. "Rather the opposite."

Azrael stilled, studying her carefully. "My Aegis already has a first."

She didn't flinch from the frankness of his gaze, but after a long moment her eyes slid to the cooling desert over his shoulder. With the heat of the day behind them, it began to stir with life. "I have done as you asked, Father. There is no Aegis that will rival yours."

"A Herculean task," he admitted with a laugh. "Admirably conducted. Now the bill comes due?"

She canted an eyebrow at him.

"If you want release from your vow," he began.

It was her turn to laugh.

"You earned it centuries ago," Azrael finished. "Of all my Aegis, your presence is by your will only. I'd have it no other way. Your freedom is yours to take—"

"Why is it all or nothing with men, eh?" She put down her cup, stretching her arms over her head and rolling her head on her neck in the familiar gesture that signaled the end of a battle well fought. "My freedom? What greater freedom is there than this life? I only want to let go of the reins. Enjoy the ride and let someone else fight for the bit."

Something Azrael hadn't realized was clenched in him released. For a moment he had been certain she would walk away from him, and he wasn't sure how he would honor his vow if she did. He raised his cup. "You train him."

She lifted her own. "I always do."

"Only when I am satisfied will he lead," he said as their cups met with a solid thunk. "And then you can drop your reins."

Two centuries later and a thousand miles away, Azrael and Gregor stood side by side on the tarmac. Waiting on the ice-crusted ground beside the runway, a Land Cruiser idled with headlights shining a beacon against the coming dark.

"Is all this necessary?" Azrael hefted the second bag. Knowing Gregor, it contained a small armory.

"She said to come prepared." Gregor bared his teeth and shivered, hunching his shoulders in the cold. "At least she didn't bring horses."

Azrael laughed. He couldn't help himself. Their diametrically opposed opinions on transportation remained one of the many areas in which his eldest and youngest were polar opposites. And yet.

He clapped Gregor on the shoulder. "Remember that bay mare? The toothy one?"

"As if I could forget." Gregor shuddered with recollection and allowed himself to be drawn toward the vehicle. "She nearly broke my arm with those teeth. If she hadn't carried me halfway across Morocco on a skin of water and a prayer, I would have fed her to the dogs myself."

The mare had spent the rest of her life as the pampered princess in a stable of the fleetest Arabians for her feat. Gregor had seen her buried among the legends of the stable. He might have even shed a tear.

A lean figure in a fur-lined parka and tall boots strode past the illuminated headlights to meet them. She finished a call that sounded terse and impatient as only Slavic tongues could and pocketed her phone with a wild grin. "Father."

"Lys," Azrael said. "You made it."

"As if I would miss this." Lysippe grinned. She always looked more herself after she'd had a few good weeks of strong sun. In that respect, the mission in Crete had been good to her. Short black curls escaped from her woolen cap when her furred hood slid down as she grabbed the bag. She opened the tailgate.

"Good thing you got in when you did," she said, glancing at the departing plane. "Storm's coming—you would have had to jump."

"My jumping-from-plane days are over," Gregor drawled from the front bumper.

Azrael's eyebrows canted. "Tempting fate?"

Gregor popped the hood and peered inside the battered Toyota. "What is this piece of shit?"

Azrael appraised the stocked vehicle—gas, food, camping gear. This *was* going to be an expedition.

"Crete's a dead end," she said before he could ask. "Whatever information was there is gone now. We're not the only ones looking, not anymore. I was headed to London when you called."

Something in her voice made him pause. Beneath the fresh color and the dangerous grin, she looked weary. Most of his businesses could run themselves, and few required Lysippe's direct intervention. Sending her to Barcelona to attend to shipping enterprises had provided good cover for her real mission.

Contrary to the speculations of the human resistance, there was no conspiracy between gods and necromancers. The necromancers and witches knew about as much about their history as humanity understood of their own DNA. He'd been searching for their origin before he'd been called to help Róisín align the Allegiance, then to take over her territory when she'd disappeared. Since then he'd been kept busy—and grounded—in Prague. He'd let the search die. Until Isela did what was thought impossible for a mortal after Luther Voss.

Lysippe had eagerly taken up the search again at his request, following a lead to the Greek islands. Like all of his Aegis, he felt her presence like a phantom limb. She'd had to fight her way out of a few tight scrapes. Not for the first time he wondered if he should have insisted on sending Aleifr or Ito as support. But she'd fought him tooth and nail for the right to go it alone.

"It's not too late," he said anyway.

Her eyes on him were fierce.

"We need Ito where he is." Gregor stepped between them as he finished his inspection. "And Aleifr stands out like a big blond sore thumb. Lysippe's assignment stands." He patted the Cruiser's chassis with satisfaction approaching approval. "Good rig, Lys."

As she climbed in the driver's seat, she called, "The horses are waiting at the village."

His groan became a laugh. "Of course."

Alone with Azrael on the tarmac, Gregor's next words were as blunt and unforgiving as a sheet of Baltic ice. "Lysippe is not the one who needs your protection."

Lysippe had trained him well, too well it seemed. Not for the first time, Azrael wondered what Gregor's history with the Vogel family was. Isela was wrong. Not everyone in his Aegis was an open book. When Azrael offered near immortality to Gregor, the young nobleman had been around long enough to understand that Azrael did not read Lysippe's mind as he did the others and to ask for the same freedom in his Gift. Azrael granted it willingly.

He had seen the inside of Gregor's head in their watery prison and used it to keep him alive in the darkest hours. The names Gregor had spoken—Heinrich, Rob, Lark—brought the young man back from the brink of despair. He'd seen the faces of those who meant the most to him. A woman's face. He'd been wrong to accuse Gregor of having never known love. Whatever had become of it had cost him everything.

When he took his oath to Azrael, Gregor admitted he left no one living to mourn him. Azrael hoped that leadership would root him.

But the Gift only honed both his skill as a fighter and the knife-edge of sanity he clung to. Gregor didn't seem to concern himself with much of anything not immortal, or nearly so. Until Isela. Now there was a new edge and intensity in his demeanor, and the timing of its arrival could not be a coincidence.

The Land Cruiser might have seen better days, but the engine sounded as strong as the day it had rolled off the production line. Azrael climbed in the passenger side. Gregor closed the back door. Lysippe put the car in gear.

Azrael glanced at the closest members of his Aegis. Lysippe's face fixed in concentration as she navigated the rough terrain in the coming storm, and Gregor pensive as he stared out the window into the growing darkness. He'd missed hunting with them. It would be good to spend a few days together.

It would give him a chance to assess how much danger Lys was truly in and whether or not he could trust Gregor anymore.

CHAPTER NINE

I sela dressed warmly, sweats over leotard and tights, a thick wrap over her arms and shoulders, and fingerless gloves that rose nearly to her elbows. She packed a small speaker in her dance bag and an extra pair of shoes with a knit cap.

She'd spent all week being as unremarkable as possible. She clung to a routine, stretching in the morning, visiting the unconscious phoenix, spending time with Tyler or Dante in the lab, before heading to the ballroom to dance. The afternoons were for sparring with Tariq, who was a more forgiving instructor. It worked, and as the Aegis was busy on whatever mission Azrael had them on in his absence, she saw only Dory or Aleifr periodically. She could travel around the castle grounds without a constant companion. And she planned on staying on the grounds. Technically.

She warmed up at the barre, letting the repetitive sequence of movements calm her mind. When she was warm, she stretched, contemplating her choice in location. It would be a good spot, close enough but secluded. As far as she knew, no one went there but her. Next, her mind went to wondering about the intelligence of what she planned to do. And what Azrael would say if he found out, which he most certainly would if anything went wrong. She grit her teeth. She'd have to pay that piper later.

It was time she stopped being idle in all this, relying on everyone around her. She had to know what she could bring to the table. She switched off the music and swapped her dance shoes for thick socks and an ancient pair of Converse. She laced them tight and slung her bag over her shoulder. Her heart raced against the bones of her rib cage.

What's this? Gold roused from the stillness she always assumed while Isela danced. That was when she was the most quiet, a gentle buzz in the back of Isela's mind that never interrupted.

Something that's going to get me in big trouble if we mess this up, she said. *Can you tell if anyone is between us and the Powder Tower?*

Gold was quiet, but Isela could sense her working.

I can, Gold said finally, a note of satisfaction in her voice, *and now so can you.*

The words came with knowledge. Isela did know. She could feel Azrael's Aegis and the absence of life that were his undead servants— all linked in greens. Azrael's progeny were all necromancers, and since their power was not bound to Azrael, bloomed in colors of their own —amber for Tariq, turquoise for Gus, and a deeper blue for Dante. The phoenix was a bright orange glow in the depths of the building. It was a dizzying sensation, and nausea swept her.

Okay, enough, she said. *I think you'd better keep an eye on that, or I won't be able to get us out of here.*

Out of here?

Isela opened the ballroom door. The hall was as empty as the preview had shown. She tightened her bag on her shoulder and moved as fast as she could without running, ignoring any servants she passed. Except one. The tall, gaunt man who was the head of Azrael's household. She knew him only as Azrael's valet, but he seemed to be everywhere.

Now he appeared to be waiting for her at the external door. She paused.

Want me to zap him?

Not if we can help it, Isela said. *I don't know what kind of alarms that would trigger.*

She contemplated what to say to him, but he swept aside as he opened the door, offering a long scarf.

"Thank you," she said, plucking it swiftly from his fingers.

He closed the door behind her.

Outside, the crisp air stung her nostrils. She wrapped the scarf around her mouth and nose, tucking the ends under the strap of her bag. She wished she'd brought a bigger coat, but that might have called attention to her plan.

I can help with that, Gold said.

Instantly she warmed from within. Isela moved at a quick half jog along the north wall to the gates. She slipped between the gates and moved east along the path that led down to the stag moat.

Originally part of the castle's defense, the moat stretched along the northern side of the fortress, bridged by a stone archway leading to the royal gardens and the winter palace. It had gained its name from King Rudolph's herd of deer, kept for his private hunts. Once bears were kept as amusement for the royalty. Now it was a quiet, empty place, blanketed in snow along the long path that ran down the side into the ravine. She could hear the stream at the bottom, sluggish now in the cold. She moved along the trail, and birds and small animals stirred in the brush as she passed.

The soft light cast long gray shadows, filtering pale oranges and yellows in the treetops. She found a clearing and dropped her bag, unpacking her speaker. Her breath came in big gouts of steam, betraying her nerves. She turned on the music.

"Music and dance go hand in hand," she said, pushing back her gloves and beginning to clap in time. "Rhythm and movement are thought to be the earliest human arts. Now it's your turn. These are the rules. I stay conscious the whole time. And when I say it's done, we're done. You hand back the wheel. Agreed?"

What are you doing? Gold's voice was hushed with eagerness.

"Letting you drive," Isela said grimly. "Though it may be the biggest mistake I've made this week. We are going to have to share this body. And that means working together. Not trying to sneak off with my body and seduce my man."

I'm sorry—

"Just skip it," Isela muttered. "You've kept your word so far—mostly—and I want to give you this."

The god was silent for so long Isela thought she'd changed her mind.

"Plus, if we can figure this thing out, maybe we can wipe that stupid smirk off Gregor's face for once."

I'm ready.

Isela softened her awareness of her body as she focused on her breath and the beat of her own heart. She became aware of a second beat, merging in time with hers. Her fingers rose without her control. They hovered in front of her face. Her hands turned this way and that, curling and uncurling, twitching. She heard her own laugh at a distance, pealing with delight. Now was the moment she'd feared most. Would the god participate or decide to go rogue? And if she did the latter, was Isela's vow specific enough to stop her or would she find a way around it?

Her hands spread, fingers wide, and then came together. Once. Twice. After a few strikes, the god found the beat, and they were clapping in time with the music.

"What now?"

Now we dance, Isela said. *Close your eyes. Feel the music. Now move, small, slow, side to side. Catch the beat again.*

Her body swayed, jerkily at first, as Gold took over more of it from Isela's control.

Good, Isela said. *Now step-clap. Right leg first. Step, together, clap; step, together, clap*

Gold was a quick student, Isela gave her that. She had them spinning, stamping, and clapping. Isela could no longer tell who was laughing. She taught her basic steps from a half dozen dances and let her experiment with each until she'd gained comfort. Then she called out corrections.

Step-ball-change, Isela called. *Step-ball-change! Don't transfer your weight!*

They careened around the clearing, kicking up snow and spinning until even Isela was dizzy.

Gotta teach you to spot next, she said, hands braced on her knees as they waited for the dizziness to pass.

Gold didn't speak, but Isela felt the delight race through her system as if it were her own. She remembered the first time she'd felt that way dancing. The first time she'd hit her grand jeté or executed a flawless pirouette. The first handstand.

Gradually she felt the weight of her own body again as the god retreated.

Don't stop now! Isela laughed. *You're making progress.*

"This body… It's heavy," Gold admitted. "I think it's going to be a while before I can take on Gregor for you in the ring."

I was afraid of that. Even after an hour, Gold's coordination was rudimentary at best.

Isela couldn't deny the relief she felt as her limbs once again came under her control. She was aware of the physical sensation of her body in a way she hadn't been before. She'd taken it for granted, feeling the strength in her limbs rather than their weight. What she didn't expect was the sadness.

Thank you, Isela. You're a good teacher. We have to convince Azrael that it's safe for you to dance again.

Isela swallowed against the hot scratch in her throat. "Maybe it's for the best at the moment."

You can't believe that, Gold said firmly. *I don't. Will you dance, just a little bit? I miss feeling you move. You're much better at it than I am.*

Isela nodded, wiping her cheeks. She swept through large, easy movements, becoming settled in her body again. The air burned her lungs. She jumped, then crouched, rolling her shoulders and shaking her hips and arching her fingertips to the sky. The cold faded and the dim light, leaving only her breath and her heartbeat and the sensation of her limbs moving through space. And when she was done, she sank to her knees in the snow, great billows of steam rising from her body.

Someone's coming, Gold said.

Isela struggled to one knee, alarmed to find her body spent. She glanced at her bag and the knives tucked just inside. *Shit shit shit.*

Gold light crackled down her fingertips, dancing onto the snow.

Gus materialized from the trees like shadows taking shape. Her depthless black eyes narrowed, and a smile quirked the corner of her mouth.

"Nothing better to do but follow me?" Isela said in challenge.

"*Pardón, señora.*" She folded at the waist. "I'm told you have a propensity to wander. Given the last episode, the others thought it best if I do the honors."

Isela rose, reaching for her bag, but Gus was faster. She shouldered Isela's bag easily and offered a sealed stainless steel bottle.

"It is tea." Gus sniffed. "Ginger with lemon. The kitchen sent it."

Isela accepted after a moment.

"Did you learn anything?" Gus asked as they walked. "About your companion?"

Isela had never thought of Gold like that, but after today's experience, she thought they might be a step closer. A sense of new loyalty formed the answer before she could even consider. "No."

Gus made a thoughtful sound. At the door of Azrael's quarters,

Gus deposited the bag. Isela made her way into the kitchen slowly. She'd forgotten Gus was there until the woman spoke.

"Gregor is right; you are not a fighter," Gus said. "But I have never seen anyone dance like that. Learn to dance with your blades, and he will eat his words."

She might have a point, Gold murmured when she was gone.

"Ugh, not you too." Isela groaned.

In any case, are you ready?

"For what?"

I need to take you out of your body, Gold said. *I thought it best to wait until you were someplace warm. But we have to go soon. I have to show you something.*

Chill raced through Isela though the room was warm enough. "I don't think—"

You need to see this, Gold insisted, *and we don't have time to argue.*

Isela staggered backward, but there was nowhere to escape to. She felt herself sinking into the chair behind her, the sensation already distant.

Close your eyes; it will be easier.

* * *

WHEN SHE OPENED THEM AGAIN, she found her senses wholly inadequate for orienting herself in the space. She'd been in the In Between before, the night Azrael fought Róisín to stop her from raising an angel. The space had taken on the shape of the underground tomb around them, grounding her. This time vast emptiness closed in on her. Her stomach dropped at the sense of being suspended without the weight of her body. She thrashed, trying to right herself, but every direction was simultaneously right and wrong. Her vision began to go dark.

Strong hands closed on hers, grounding her.

"Open your eyes, Issy," Gold said. "It's safe now. I'm sorry. I forgot."

Isela opened her eyes again, and this time the In Between was grounded over Azrael's quarters. She recognized familiar shapes of furniture and fixtures in the overlay, and her stomach righted itself. Before her stood a woman washed in gold. Her features were as indistinguishable as those of an old sculpture, worn by time, but her wings, the black and orange of a monarch butterfly and folded around her shoulders like a cloak, were too vivid to be real.

"You like it," Gold asked, and Isela had the sense of her smiling shyly. "It's my avatar, for when I appear to humans. I have a male version too. Would you prefer—"

"No." Isela cut her off. "No, this is… which god? That is…"

"I am only a small god," Gold admitted. "I helped ferry the dead on to the next plane. I got to know humans and, I suppose, love them in my way. But I know what the gods know, and when they wanted to watch you destroy yourselves, I knew I had to act…"

"You betrayed your kind to help us."

Gold nodded solemnly. "Others overlooked me because I am not as old or powerful. I chose. We had our turn. We gave up the physical world to evolve. It belonged to your kind."

Questions crowded Isela's mind, fighting for precedence and rendering her speechless.

"We can't stay long," Gold said, tugging on her urgently. "The others will be alerted to the opening of a portal. But this can't wait. Something's happened. Come."

Gold led her from the apartment, through the gardens. They moved through walls and trees with only the slightest tug of resistance as she passed.

"What did you just do?" Isela breathed.

"You're a physical creature," Gold explained as they ran toward the edge of the garden. "Your mind depends on the sensations of your body to stay grounded. We have none, so we dispense with the boundaries created by your natural laws. Necromancers try, some of them get quite good at it, but most are still human enough to need a recognizable place."

"Human enough," Isela breathed. "Does that mean they *are* part gods, like Azrael said?"

"Azrael is wise." Gold smiled mysteriously. "But he only has pieces of the puzzle. And now we have more pressing matters than looking backward. Ready?"

"For what?"

"To jump!" Gold said, and her cloak unfurled itself as she sprang off the turf.

Isela moved without thinking, her body flying into the grand jetè that it knew from years of performing.

Gold grasped her hands from above. When she looked up, all she could see were wings, magnificently impossible wings beating impossibly fast.

They landed in a tumble in a place that was dark and colder than any human space. Gold was a bright glow against the blackness as she landed beside Isela. Her enormous wings folded, becoming as draping cloth once again over her shoulders and cascading to the ground. Isela could not look at her directly. The god dimmed.

"I am sorry, Isela," she said. "I am bad at this. But I will learn, I promise."

The tremor in her voice made Isela uneasy. Gold was a god. If she was afraid, what chance did they have? They were in a deep canyon, the walls rising black and jagged around them. She shuddered in the cold wind, and flakes of something like snow began to fall. In spite of the dark, each flake held the vivid tones of a multifaceted jewel. She held out her palm and collected a ruby, a sapphire, and an opal. They weighed nothing and did not melt at the touch of her skin. Instead, her skin began to glow as colored threads in each shade raced down along her veins and disappeared into her body. Isela felt them as they reached her heart, pumped out with each beat to the rest of her body. Each burned with a cool tingle.

When she looked up, Gold watched her with a knowing smile on her featureless face. "I knew you were special. It's called to you."

"What is this place?" Isela turned a circle as more jewel flakes gathered, swirling around her like her own miniature whirlwind.

"It is nowhere and everywhere," Gold said, glancing around them. "It is a representation of what is real but also the reality. This is the only way I could think of to show you what you need to see."

At last Isela had absorbed so much of the jewel glow she began to glow around the edges. She felt stronger, and the nausea of disorientation faded. Whatever the flakes were, they made her feel as though she belonged here as opposed to intruding. Gold took her hand, lacing their fingers together.

"This will be easier now." She smiled, and this time when she brightened it didn't hurt Isela's eyes at all. "See."

Before them rippled a reflective surface, a still pond rather than a mirror. Gold light poured from her features, framing her in illumination.

"Now look." Gold turned her around. Isela gasped.

Beyond them, the canyon was blocked by a wall. It reminded her of cobblestones snugged against one another, but it lacked the substance of stone. With a rhythm that reminded her of breath, it swelled and released. As she and Gold brightened, shining light on it, it reflected back all the colors of the rainbow and the shades between.

"This is the covenant," Gold said. "When the necromancers allied with one another against the gods, this is what they built."

Isela moved forward, her sense of something restless moving beyond startling her back a step before she approached again. "How is this possible?"

"It shouldn't have been," Gold said sensibly. "Necromancers have powers that come to them from the gods. And when they learned that humans could lure us through dance, they used it. Róisín called for a great parlay. Your allegiance and ours. There was much dissension on our side. Some wanted to be done with humans once and for all. The eldest of us chose to leave this world altogether, and only the squabbling, greedy ones bent on destruction remained. Then Róisín tricked them. She lured them to the In Between. And she and the others created the wall, barring them from the physical world."

"So the wall doesn't keep the gods out?"

"The shepherd has two ways to protect the flock," Gold said. "Guard them or fence them in. Róisín chose the second."

"And you," Isela asked.

"I chose to remain with the sheep," Gold said, the tone in her voice suggesting retreat, or fear, "rather than take my chances among the wolves." She flinched, dimming. "I'm sorry, that was a terrible analogy. I don't think of you as—"

"It's okay, go on." Isela glanced at the breathing, pulsing wall, wanting suddenly to be very far away from it.

Gold confirmed her instinctive fear with her next words. "It is safer for me here. When they learned what I'd done... Well, even gods can be killed, Isela."

"And when Róisín killed Luther?"

"I didn't count on that." Gold sighed. "I had to hide so that necromancers couldn't find me. And then you came." She brightened. "And you were something different. There has never been another quite like you, Isela Vogel. Many dancers have the blood of witches in their veins. But you also contain that which enables transformation. Change."

"The wolf blood," Isela breathed.

"That is one way it manifests." Gold nodded. "And perhaps because I am only a small god, you and I are compatible."

Isela looked to the wall again. She recognized Azrael's power when she looked, the threads of emerald running along the sapphire of his mentor, Róisín. So she had used his power too to create this wall. He was part of it. Was this the beginnings of his becoming a monster? Something about the wall tugged at her; she scanned it more closely, squinting her eyes though it wasn't necessary to see in the end.

"What is that?"

"You can see it," Gold breathed. Relief and dread warred in her sigh.

A blight formed a ragged tear near one edge. "What happened?"

"Can't tell what side it started on," Gold said, edging closer to Isela. "But something's trying to get through."

The wall buckled and the tear widened for a moment. A flash of something large and scaled brushed against the gap. She jumped back, bumping into Gold, and for a moment they just stood together, leaning on one another. Gold trembled, and the light of her face had dimmed.

"What do you mean, what side it started on?" Isela murmured.

"Do you remember what the phoenix said in the square?" Gold whispered, though Isela sensed her gaze was still fixed on the tear. Her voice assumed a perfect mimicry of the transformed creature. "'You will not be the only one.' Why transform a phoenix to a human, stripping it of its magic, if not as some kind of test?"

"You think a necromancer is doing this."

"Perhaps not all were satisfied with Azrael's threats about their interference," Gold said. "And what better way to fight one god than with another?"

Isela, too, dimmed as the fear set in her bones. For the first time she felt the cold. She shook her head. "But it's impossible, right? No one even knows why I can contain you without being burned out, never mind how we joined in the first place."

"Many things were judged impossible before they happened," Gold said grimly. "But Isela, gods don't obey or submit. And if they come, it won't be to answer the whim of a necromancer. It will be for revenge."

CHAPTER TEN

They drove all night and into the next day, stopping to refill the tank from the drums strapped to the Rover's flanks.

"It's best if we approach the village in the morning." Lysippe pulled up to what could barely be called a shed. In the vast wasteland of white and brown, it was a change in elevation.

She parked the Land Cruiser in a lean-to beside the shed, and they all helped drag the thatch doors closed.

"Traders and nomads use this as a waypoint," she said, grunting as she dumped the two black bags on the ground to dig out kindling for a fire and a small camp. "Mary. What did you pack, a bazooka?"

Azrael canted his brow at Gregor. "My question exactly."

Gregor took them both in with an expression of ferocious boredom before stalking into the shed. The look Azrael gave his first brought to mind the night of the French wine and the conversation, as if laying the fault for Gregor exactly where it was owed.

"You said yes." She shrugged, gesturing him to precede her inside. "Clothes are in there."

Gregor's voice came right on cue. "What the fuck is this?"

* * *

Azrael remained inside the small building, which reeked of grease smoke, sheep, and human funk, only long enough to change before retreating outside. Gregor and Lysippe, passing a bottle of something that had already killed their olfactory senses, made room for him around the campfire. Their cover was that of university professor and students doing an ethnography study of the remote villages. It was the same story they'd been using for a hundred years, alternating roles as appropriate. Their cots had been laid out with credentials and clothes —dressing like an academic doing fieldwork did not appeal to Gregor.

Gregor hunched in his parka and fur hood, sipping petulantly from the earthenware bottle when it came back to him. Azrael made himself comfortable and stoked the fire, his brow furrowed. Gregor swung the bottle his direction.

Azrael took it and gritted his teeth at the bitter tang that filled his mouth before passing it on to Lysippe. She chuckled.

"We've drunk worse rotgut than this," she said, taking a pull. "And you rather enjoyed it at the time."

"What can I say." He grimaced as the liquid burned a path down his esophagus. "I was young and foolish. Tell me about Stary."

"It's a thin place," Lysippe said, the human word for a place gods had crossed over many times, weakening the barrier between worlds. "Otherwise unremarkable, though it was once a major stop on the overland trade routes and suffered a mining disaster before the godswar."

"The mine collapsed?" Gregor said.

She nodded. "The company blamed it on poor tunneling, but the villagers swore they had angered the guardian of the mountain and caused the collapse. The company tried again, but they found no new veins. And the expense of importing workers was too great. Operations shut down—until two months ago."

The fine hairs rose on the back of Azrael's neck.

"A company started exploring the mining site," Lysippe said. "I had my team track it down. It's a shell company—"

"Vanka's?" he asked.

They both looked at Gregor. He seemed to be occupied in making a dense study of the wood cracking in the pit before them. His gaze rose lazily. "Too good to be a coincidence."

"Too good," Azrael mused. "Gregor—"

"Are you going offer to relieve me too?" he said sharply. "The dancer's made you soft, Azrael. Two hundred years ago you never would have asked—"

The dancer. Had he ever referred to Isela by name?

"I'm not offering," Azrael said quietly, but he noted that all the droll humor and vague disinterest that was Gregor's way had vanished, replaced by an iron focus. "But she has made me understand that the well-being of those you care for must be seen to, regularly."

Gregor looked away, his jaw tight. Lysippe busied herself with locating another clay jug.

"I am not afraid of that redheaded termagant," Gregor snarled finally, rising.

Lysippe offered the jug as he passed. Gregor stalked off into the night, Azrael's eyes following the shape of his hunched shoulders until he vanished into the darkness.

"There's a word I haven't heard in a hundred years." Lysippe shook the jar in Azrael's direction with a sigh. "He's not a child anymore."

"I am aware."

"We are the shield you raise against the world, necromancer," she said, her eyes meeting his in challenge as she spoke the ancient words of their covenant. "We absorb the blows meant for you and hold off the sword that you may make a killing strike."

He stared into the fire, willing it higher, as though he could somehow reach Gregor with warmth, wherever he'd disappeared to.

"You are also my family, of a kind," he said at last. "And a shield that takes a blow it cannot hold will break."

* * *

AT DAWN, Azrael stood on the far side of their camp and watched the sun creep up over the frostbitten plain.

Home.

He tried to remember if the migrations would have taken his people this far west, but the memory escaped him. So much had changed. Even the land itself had been altered by time. It had been two thousand years after all. The tricky part about eternity—the details started to slip.

But his body remembered. If he squinted, he could see the herds moving in the distance. When he closed his eyes, the sensation cut clean through to his core. He could almost smell it—cold wind bearing the musk of animals and the smoke of cook fires. The combination of grasses and distant trees, even the scent of the frozen earth, sang to him.

He crouched, using a combination of heat and strength to pull a handful of earth away from the hard ground. It steamed and crumbled in his grip, sifting through his fingers and leaving runnels of mud behind as the water vaporized. He brought it to his nose, inhaled. Touched it to his tongue.

The memories came back.

* * *

HE REMEMBERED the story of his mother's parentage—his grandmother had been taken defending the elders and children from foreign raiders. Generations later, they still told stories about those invaders— tall, pale men with deep, rough voices and dense, unkempt hair on their faces and arms—intending to scare children into behaving.

She was assumed dead or worse, a captive. She returned months later, swollen with child and leading a string of fine horses, carrying the spear of her captor. Some of her rivals muttered of magic and demon's bargains.

The rumors worsened for her final child. Azrael's mother had been taller than most women, the pale skin and eyes a contrast to those of her people. Some said it was the influence of her mixed blood that caused her wandering. She would disappear for weeks at a time, leaving her children among her relatives.

Some said she returned to her father's lands. Others that she performed strange magic in an unknown lair in the hills. They advised the elders to find her another mate, but she would look on no man. Still, there must have been someone—she had been alone for three years with five children by the time he thickened her body.

Azrael had grown under the shadow of their doubt. In spite of the fact that he looked more like his people than his mother did, they studiously avoided eye contact with him, muttering ancient phrases against evil and possession as he passed. He knew they thought he had been got on his mother by something not entirely human. It was why the dogs came before he called them, the horses shied from his presence, and even the birds fell silent at his approach.

The honesty of children was a comfort by comparison. They threw stones from the protection of packs until they found other diversions.

It was not the supernatural that came to his defense but one of his sisters. All older, all the image of his mother, as though their fathers had played no part in their creation. They faced bullies, delivered black eyes, and bruised shins. They insulated him from the mutterings of the adults and would not permit him to entertain the whispers. Instead, they doted on him—treating him like a beloved little baby until he really did earn the nickname Terror.

He was thirteen when he stumbled on a group of children poking a dead bird with sticks. Furious at the sight of the fragile, feathered body under attack, he charged them, swinging his fists and kicking. He put his body over the thing, feeling the tiny, thin bones and itchy feathers press against the ragged assault of his heart. A breath later, he felt the sharp pecking and the scratching of tiny claws.

When he flung himself backward in alarm, the bird—*a small, gray thing... a dove, perhaps?*—launched itself from the dust to land dull eyed and staring a few feet away on the rocks.

The children fled. The dead bird—*because it could never really be anything but dead; somehow he knew that even then*—followed him all the way home.

For the first time even his siblings shied away from him.

Only his mother approached, capturing the bird gently in her long-fingered hands. With a quick twist, she snapped its neck. She gave the corpse to one of the camp dogs and made Azrael warm mare's milk and buttered bread.

When he was finished filling his belly, she met him at the front door of the spacious, felt-wall tent that was the only home he'd ever known. She'd saddled her best horse—a young mare the color of old nickel. The mare's saddlebags were packed for a long journey. One of the many family hounds—the one he'd always thought of as his—stood close with head and tail low. The sleek, silky-coated body trembled with eagerness or fear, but tawny eyes met Azrael's, and his tasseled ears perked expectantly.

"He's a good companion." His mother touched the dog's slender head gently. "The mare will get you far from this trouble, but not willingly. Ride hard, but don't wind her. Sell her as soon as you are able. The money will get you much farther than her legs will."

The muddle of his closest siblings stood by, sweating in the heat. They must have moved industriously fast to carry out their mother's commands.

"When can I come back, Mother?" he'd asked naively as his closest sister buckled her blade around his waist. Even on the smallest hole, the belt dipped low around his hips. His eldest sister moved her aside, unbuckled it, and tied a fast knot to snug it against his waist in the silence that was his answer.

"Don't forget us, little terror." His mother brushed aside the forelock of hair that always seemed to be in his eyes. "And don't look back."

She gave him a leg up onto the mare. The horse skittered sideways as soon as he was alight. Her eyes rolled back at him, and her skin twitched with the desire to flee. Every child rode without stirrups around camp and on herd duty; only as an adult on long rides or in battle did the stirrups come in handy for bracing the rider. His eldest sister adjusted them to fit his short legs with the same effortless efficiency with which she'd knotted the knife belt.

Over the beating of his own heart he could hear them now—the first of many mobs that would assemble when he displayed the smallest show of the power that came in tantalizing and dangerous flickers throughout his adolescence.

His mother reached up, touched his knee and then his hand, then her own heart. "Remember, you are what you make of yourself," she said. "Give that power to no one."

Then she turned the mare's head south, toward the distant villages on the sea. As she stepped away, she whistled sharply and the mare launched herself into a dead run. He clapped his heels to her side and gripped two handfuls of mane just to stay astride. When the mare faltered, the quick snap of jaws from the silky-coated hound at her hocks drove her on.

Through the blur of his eyes, he glimpsed his fingers, clenched in the shaggy, slate-gray mane of the horse beneath him. What had they done, his hands? What was he?

* * *

"MY MOTHERS USED to tell the stories of the times before Troy," Lysippe said behind him. "I can hear hoofbeats when I close my eyes."

Azrael squeezed his palm, capturing the last of the earth in a fist. He pumped heat into the fist. When he opened his hand again it was just dirt, the last bits of moisture and smoke rising in the cold dawn. Lysippe laughed.

Azrael's brow rose. "Expecting diamonds?"

"From horse shit?" She snorted.

He dusted his palms off and stood.

"This is closer to home than either of us has been for a thousand years," he said, taking her in from the corner of his eyes.

She looked pensive and tired. They'd had longer nights of drinking. This was something else.

"What do you think Vanka is after?" Lysippe asked finally.

Azrael accepted the topic change without comment. He briefed her on his meeting with Raymond. "I don't know. But I don't trust her or Paolo to accept my terms. Holding my territory—keeping it safe—means being ready for whatever they will try."

Lysippe made a thoughtful sound. "And when do we decide to stop waiting and take the fight to them?"

Azrael's brows rose. "You're talking war, Lys."

"You said once that a world ruled by necromancers is not balanced. That it will end someday. Yet you persist in believing you can create an island of safety in a sea of sharks."

Azrael shook his head. "There is too much at stake. Isela—is not ready—to go up against the Allegiance as we are would be suicide."

"Living under siege isn't pretty, Azrael," she said. "I don't need to tell you that."

CHAPTER ELEVEN

Tariq called it quits when Isela managed to graze his neck. The iron tang of blood in the air made the newly born warrior in her howl with glee. She flexed her knees and showed teeth.

"I think I've taken enough of a beating for one day," Tariq muttered, dabbing at the blood.

Isela retrieved her fallen blade and met him outside the ring. Tariq had been a much more generous teacher, pausing to slow things down to show or repeat a move. He seemed to understand what she was capable of healing that wouldn't impede her sparring. He had an easy smile at the ready and never snapped at her for missing an opportunity. Not for the first time, she wondered if Gregor's objective really was to teach her. If she couldn't fight, she would be dependent on Azrael and his Aegis.

"So, Gregor and the Aegis see to your combat training," Tariq said lightly, swiping his sword clean with a long cloth.

He inspected his weapons carefully, using motions as practiced and automatic as she did to brush her teeth.

"Gregor beats me to a pulp on a regular basis," she said. "I've learned a few things. But when Lysippe is here, she teaches me."

A furrow appeared between his brows, but he kept his eyes on his task.

She handed over the borrowed blades, hefting them lightly. "I like these. Light but effective. And beautiful."

They were not twins. The longer, curved blade was her primary weapon. The second, shorter blade was made to stick and deflect. They required being closer to her opponent, but because she'd already been training with dual blades, they were her preferred weapon. Not that Gregor had skipped an introduction to the long blade. And the firing range. Also the hand-to-hand combat that always ended with her on her face and his knee digging into her spine.

"True Damascus steel," he said. "I commissioned them from a metalworker who had studied with a guy from Nepal—about fourth century, perhaps. I've forgotten. What's not to like?"

Isela stared at him as he gave the blades the same cursory but thorough inspection. When he looked up, his full mouth pulled sideways in an attempt to repress a smile. "What?"

"You've forgotten more than I'll ever know."

He laughed, a generous sound that made her face itch with a smile. Unlike the others, he didn't seem to hold it against her that she had, up until very recently, been human.

"Don't worry," he said. "You'll have your turn at being the oldest guy in the room soon enough."

"I hope not. I kind of like being a woman."

Tariq laughed again, and the bronze in his eyes danced.

He contemplated the blades in his hands. This time Gold's sight settled delicately over her own vision with only a moment of dizziness to show her the wards that marked the metal. Delicate lines of power shaped into geas clung to the rippled steel pattern. From her research, she knew some were common, known among necromancers and others who commanded power. But necromancers could also create new ones with combinations of power and effect. These were warded to evade normal sight so they could be carried openly and also defensively.

"You fight well with them." He slid both blades into their sheaths. He flipped the hilts toward her. "They're yours."

Isela's smile died. "I can't take these."

He lifted his hands, an offering. "Humor me. My people give gifts. It's just how we are. So take them or risk offending me mortally. And given that I am effectively immortal, that's a grudge that won't die soon."

She swallowed hard.

"Plus, what man doesn't like the idea of a beautiful woman

fighting with his knives?" He winked, destroying the weight of the moment. "You are even more lovely when you blush, light of my lord's eye."

She took the larger blade, shaking her head at his relentless charm. He hesitated with the second blade, capturing her hand with his. He slid the blade free enough for her to see the geas.

"They are partners," he said, fingertip caressing the imperceptible mark. "Like the best partnerships, they complement one another. You hold Catsfoot, the force, the power, but not the most deadly." He hefted the smaller blade, light and needle fine. "*She* is."

"She?" Isela raised a brow.

"When you are in need, Peerless will be with you. Here or in the In Between."

"The In Between," Isela said, remembering the place where Azrael had battled Róisín. "Where you go when you summon?"

Tariq's troubled look returned at the hesitant question. His hand still cradled hers beneath the blade. She was acutely aware of the contact. "Your combat training is well attended. Who sees to the development of your power?"

Isela looked away, remembering Azrael's prohibition against her interacting with the phoenix or dancing. At her lack of response, Tariq's expression darkened. He said something in an old language, shaking his head.

"How come you aren't so formal?" At his blank look, she elaborated. "You sound like you actually learned to talk in this century."

"I've always been a man of words." He cupped his elbows behind his back. "My first lover was language. In the caress of her sentences, I found ecstasy."

She paused, one eyebrow rising. "A poet and you didn't even know it."

"Oh, but I am a poet, lady," he said. "My columns once filled royal libraries. More than one prince has wooed his match with my words. Many a royal heir was conceived after his mother's ear bent to my verse."

"Seriously?"

"My word is my vow, lady." He placed his hand over his heart without an ounce of humility.

Against all reason and despite her present mood, a genuine smile twitched at the corner of her mouth. "Does that line work for you?"

Tariq laughed. "The greatest gift of immortality is watching language evolve. I may be an old man, but I don't have to sound like one. Your words are a great compliment."

"You're welcome."

Across the room, a throat cleared. Tariq released the blade into her hand in no particular hurry, looking up. She realized how close they stood when she stepped back.

Tyler hesitated in the doorway. "Sorry to interrupt. Issy, did you still want to go?"

Tariq snapped to attention, his bronze eyes no longer warm. "Go?"

Isela hesitated, fighting the urge to scowl at Tyler. Her attaché seemed happy enough to rat her out to anyone who happened to be in a position to put the kibosh on her plans. She considered lying to him.

There are many ways reduce suspicion, Gold murmured against the base of her skull. *Perhaps keeping Tariq close would be most effective.*

"I was going to visit my family after training." She focused on arranging both blades in the holster Gregor had commissioned for her and kept her voice light.

Tariq helped after a moment, but bronze eyes flecked with metallic sheen did not leave her face. "Azrael suggested it would be best if you remained on the grounds."

"I haven't seen my mom since the wedding." She shrugged. "She gets fussy if I don't show my face once in a while. Ask Gregor."

"The high priestess of Prague?" Tariq said, and interest crept into his voice.

"The very one, apparently." Isela paused for effect. "Why don't you go with me?"

Tariq hesitated.

"I'm not sure how she'd take to a necromancer showing up on her doorstep unannounced," he said. "There's a certain protocol to these things, Issy."

"You are an ally. She's my mom. It would be good for you to meet her if you plan on staying in the area for a while. Anyway, I need you."

His eyes widened.

"To drive," she said quickly. "Gregor still hasn't forgiven me for wrecking the Schwarzmobile."

"The Schwarzmobile?" Tariq laughed. "What was it, a Bimmer? Porsche?"

"Audi, I think. The logo with the rings, right?"

"He *is* loyal. You wrecked it?"

"In my defense, there were demons involved," she said. "But he kind of lost his mind."

"He does love his automobiles." He ducked his head, dragging a towel across the back of his neck.

Isela pushed. "I mean, they gave me what I think is Azrael's idea of a beater, and I should probably stay off public transportation for a while." When she looked up, Tariq was watching her with those inscrutable bronze eyes. She gave what she hoped was an encouraging smile.

"I am a humble servant," he said, making a courtly bow. "O shining jewel that crowns my master's brow."

She stuck out her tongue. "Give it a rest."

He laughed. "Twenty minutes—meet you in the garage."

* * *

BERYL GILMAN-VOGEL, the high priestess of the Prague witch community, set down the phone, resting her hands on the sink and bowing her head.

"Mom, are you okay?" Bebe said from the doorway.

The kitchen was quiet, breakfast dishes cleaned and the kettle on the stove for tea. It was Tuesday, Toby's day to take the older kids to school. Bebe hoped he remembered to bring his own wallet. He always forgot something, and then she would have to hop on a tram to meet him for lunch. Which wouldn't be terrible. Maybe they would grab a doner kebab and walk around the Jewish quarter before she opened the store in the afternoon. She hadn't been to the Kafka statue in ages.

Those little moments stolen between the routine were the ones she treasured. She loved her children and her store and her place in the coven, but it was Tobias that brought it all together in her mind and her heart. The thought of being without him brought her back to the kitchen and the sight of her mother-in-law's bowed shoulders. Shared loss clenched painfully in Bebe's rib cage, and the air in the room felt too thin. She wondered if she would have the strength to get out of bed every day in Tobias's absence.

And yet Beryl insisted on keeping the same routine they had before Lukas's death, in spite of her family's desire to give her space to grieve his loss. "Children need routine," she'd said. "And I need my grandchildren."

As they always had, every morning a tumble of Vogel children made it up the stairs, trailed by their parents, to where a pot of oatmeal simmered on the stove and the scent of hot coffee filled the air. Beryl presided over it all, the littlest ones on her lap.

"Go back to bed," she had said more than once to her daughters-in-law after colic or a new tooth or just plain sleeplessness had kept them up most of the night. "I'll take care of it."

Evie arrived with lunches for school-aged ones. Bebe checked off coats, gloves, hats, and scarves. Since Markus left before dawn to whatever site he was working on, Tobias and Chris did most of the drop-offs. Bebe got the little ones who weren't ready to go to school sorted in the living room with games and art supplies, or down to Mrs. Simpson's on the fourth floor if she had to see a client or spend time in the shop. It was a familiar routine; sharing tasks made everyone's job lighter.

But now, after the barely controlled morning chaos had wound down, Beryl retreated to the kitchen. She would stand at the sink and look out the window into the view of the park behind their building, sometimes for as long as an hour.

Bebe was grateful that they could keep the routine after her father-in-law's death, but she also felt an abstract sense of guilt, that she should be doing more, or Beryl doing less, under the strain of grief. Today, without Evie to stop her, Bebe entered the kitchen.

"Can I do anything for you?"

The older woman drew on a boundless well of strength and her chin rose, shoulders dropping back as she turned to face her daughter-in-law. "I'm just fine, Barbara. Thank you."

Bebe smiled faintly, leaning against the refrigerator and crossing her arms. "Who called?"

"Isela," Evie said, her soundless entry into the kitchen making Bebe jump. "What trouble has she managed to get into now?"

Bebe always felt like toadstool, caught between Evie's ethereal beauty and Isela's athletic grace. She stood up a little straighter. Evie poured another cup of tea, a line forming between her brows. The note of affection was unusually absent from Evie's voice. Beryl frowned.

"There's so much at stake," Evie said. "I just worry about what she's gotten us all into. And what with the new witches coming into the city…"

"Our sisters deserve their freedom to practice, to *exist* in peace," Bebe said stubbornly. "We're safe here—"

"Are we?" Evie sighed before Bebe could respond to the anxious challenge in her voice, waving a hand. "Just ignore me. Someone has to be the voice of doom, right?"

Beryl crossed the kitchen to rest a hand on her shoulder. She squeezed gently, and Bebe watched all the resistance go out of Evie in a breath. She softened, and Beryl slid an arm around her as they rested temple to temple.

"No, Evelia," Beryl said. "You are no Cassandra. Your concern is heard. But we must keep moving toward the world we want to live in. There is no other way."

She opened her other arm, and Bebe went gratefully, finding her place. "Isela is bringing a new ally. A necromancer, one of Azrael's progeny. They need our assistance, and we are going to give it to them."

Evie bit her lip.

"It would be good for you take the little ones out for a few hours," Beryl said before she could argue.

"I'll pack the car," Bebe began.

"I need you here, Barbara," Beryl cut her off. "Call Ofelia. She's bound to need a break from Chris."

Bebe could hear the relief in their newest sister-in-law's voice as Evie held the phone away from her ear, wincing. A few moments later, Ofelia tromped up the stairs from the flat two floors below. She and Chris, the youngest Vogel brother, were hurrying to finish renovations before the baby came. Fifi's beauty was eclipsed only by her vibrant personality. She freed her tightly wrapped hair from the bun on the top of her head, fluffing the strands to form a round ball of dark brown coils.

"So, Issy's in trouble again eh?" Ofelia avoided Evie's glare as she poured herself a cup of coffee while rubbing her low back with her knuckles. "It's my first cup today. I promise."

"She's found a phoenix," Beryl said.

Ofelia's eyes widened, and she paused midswallow.

"It found her," Evie said, uncannily certain. "It has a message for her, but it's been— Something is wrong with it."

Bebe looked at her, dumbfounded. "How did you know all that?"

"I dreamed of a firebird at Issy's feet last night." Evie shrugged. "I thought it was a metaphor. You know—transformation. It didn't occur to me that it was actually literal."

Precognition wasn't common among witches. Evie's ability was stronger than most. Bebe didn't envy her sight. It was the kind of gift that too often brought pain.

On instinct, she hugged Evie. Evie stiffened at first—she always did—but Bebe knew she had the woman's trust. Witches needed physical contact often. Especially after any use of their power. It was comfort but also restoration. That need had been difficult for Evie because after losing her family, her life had gotten brutally hard, and touch became something she learned to fear. She had been isolated for so long her power had begun to corrupt. Only Beryl and Markus had been strong enough to pull her back. Now she trusted them all to serve that purpose.

She held on until Evie softened and returned the hug with a long sigh. "Thank you."

"My pleasure," Bebe said, drawing away only when Evie let her go.

Beryl smiled at them all. Impulsively, Bebe took her hand and Ofelia's. Ofelia grabbed Evie. Beryl completed the circle. The energy sparked between them immediately. It was as if the past few weeks had brought them all to new power. Now that they no longer had to practice in secret, it felt more solid and grew stronger with exercise.

"Guide, protect, love," Bebe said quietly. "Defend. These are our vows."

"Let none stand against us." Ofelia was firm.

When they released one another, Beryl looked lighter and happier than she had in weeks.

"Boy or girl?" Ofelia asked, furrowed brow and rubbed the rounding mound of her own belly.

Beryl shook her head with a little smile. "You wanted a surprise, and I promised I would not tell you."

Ofelia sucked her teeth. "Can't a girl have a change of heart? I gotta pee, Evie. I'll be ready in two minutes."

When she was gone, Evie and Beryl's eyes met with shared humor. Bebe looked between them. "What?"

Evie began to laugh, pressing her fingers to her lips. Beryl shook her head, chuckling to herself.

"Do we tell her?" Evie asked when she could catch her breath.

Beryl's hands rose as she backed away. "I made my promise."

"What!" Bebe hissed, stomping her foot.

Beryl had always accurately predicted the sexes of their babies. But if Evie also had a precognition, it was certain. Beryl went about refilling the water kettle, ignoring Bebe's plea.

As Evie turned, she flashed two fingers.

Bebe gasped. "No!"

"Not a word." Evie glared at her. Then she admitted, "One of each."

"Boy and girl?" Bebe hissed.

Evie favored her with a superior glare. "Wolf and witch."

* * *

"I THOUGHT you said it was a beater," Tariq said, sweeping his fingers through still-damp hair.

He'd showered, shaved, and trimmed his mustache and goatee. She'd never seen him look so formal in rust-colored slacks and a matching asymmetrical button waistcoat over a trim, collarless ivory shirt. Even the well-worn chukkas and open wool coat could not make him look less polished. She spent a moment trying to figure out if the tangerine scent was a cologne or just the way he smelled.

Isela tossed him the keys and stalked to the passenger's door. "I said Azrael's *idea* of a beater. He told me to break it. I don't think he was joking."

Tariq rested his hand on the roof of a coupe so deep green it was almost black. He whistled. "Have they even released these yet?"

Isela looked at him blankly, shivering in the cold of the underground garage and pulling the oversized hood of her sweater onto her head. She tapped her foot impatiently as he admired the vehicle. The electric coupe was low-slung on a wide wheelbase and just under ten feet from nose to tail. It was also, Isela discovered, ridiculously maneuverable and stupid fast.

"I'd imagined Azrael's investment in national technologies had perks," Tariq said, "like getting the new models before they are released to the public."

"He said they need some real-world data." She slid her hands into her pockets before her fingers froze stiff.

Tariq's mouth curled upward. "Then get over here."

She puffed out her cheeks but slid in when he opened the driver-side door. When Tariq climbed in the passenger side, he ran a hand over the charcoal dashboard appreciatively. The computer came to life with a pleasant chime and a personalized greeting.

"Welcome, consort," it said. "How may I assist?"

"Start eco mode, Libby."

The car came to life with a barely audible tremble. The lights switched on, and an illuminated map of the city appeared in the dash.

"Libby?"

"Liberty. It has an autodrive function," she growled. "But it's disabled. And it's a stick."

She looked balefully at the gearshift.

"Well, let's see what she's got."

Isela put the car in gear and eased onto the accelerator. The car shifted but didn't move. She swore.

Tariq cleared his throat. "Parking brake."

They pulled out from beneath the gate of the castle, leaving the battling Titans in the rearview as she thundered up the damp cobblestone street to the main road.

His hand crept toward the molded grip on the door. "How is it you don't drive? I thought you were American."

Isela shrugged, downshifting with a flinch as the gears grumbled in protest. "I was born in the US. My parents moved us here when I was little."

"Ah," Tariq murmured. "Watch out!"

Isela swung into traffic and hit the gas. The car accelerated to a high scream before she shifted and gained more speed. "What?"

"Nothing." He shook his head, unable to take his eyes off the road.

"My older brothers remember it better than I do. It's Mark, Toby, then me. Chris was born here."

"Your brothers, the pack?"

"The Vogel boys," Isela agreed loftily, weaving through traffic. "Young wolves all."

Tariq's gaze darted out the window, then back to her, then out the window again.

"What's wrong?"

"Nothing," he said, wincing as they thundered through a yellow light. Tariq tugged at his collar. "The Allegiance had to stabilize civilization after the war. Getting people working and fed went a long way to avoid total anarchy. Azrael invested heavily in technology." He gestured at the center of the steering wheel where the emblem of a lightning bolt pierced a stylized *T*. "Azrael lured engineers and designers into contracts and formed a conglomerate of a bunch of languishing state-owned companies. They named it Tesla—after the inventor—hired anyone with experience, and founded a school to teach others. Transportation has been their big success; they make the trams and the buses and shipping vehicles. And luxury electric cars."

He glanced at the road once, then away again, fingertips dancing on his knees. "Ray tried something similar in the US, but it was harder for him with the loss of the financial centers on the East Coast. He had better luck beefing up the entertainment industry. Bread and circuses."

"Ray?"

"Raymond, the North American necromancer," Tariq said. "Calls himself the Nightfeather. Big guy—long hair. Face like a knife."

Isela remembered him from the night in Azrael's study. Dressed simply in jeans and a T-shirt, motorcycle boots, and the sheet of black hair that fell down his back like midnight rain. Quite a looker. And scary as hell.

"Careful," Tariq breathed.

Isela braked hard, swerving around the car stopped in front of her. When she looked at her passenger, his knuckles were white.

"I warned you," she muttered. "Tell me about Ray."

Tariq tore his eyes away from the road. "He's almost as old as Azrael. They were friends for a while. But they had a falling-out."

"Over what?"

Tariq laughed. "A woman, of course."

Isela looked at him sharply and the car swerved into the neighboring lane.

"Eyes on the road!" Tariq cried. "It's not like that. It was Lysippe."

Isela frowned. The Amazon was the oldest member of Azrael's Aegis and his surrogate daughter. She ran much of his business endeavors. She had a cooler head and a mind for corporate warfare. Isela supposed anyone who had grown up shooting arrows while riding a horse at full speed on an arid plain could handle a roomful of egomaniacs in thousand-dollar suits.

"Ray broke her heart," Tariq said bluntly. "Lysippe hasn't been the same since. I don't think Azrael ever forgave him."

Whoa. Isela hadn't seen that one coming. The Amazon had a persona of iron. She embraced her immortality with open arms, like a true conqueror. The image of her heartbroken made Isela incalculably sad. It also made her want to kick Ray where it counted.

"I suggest if you want the replay, you bring her a bottle of bourbon on American Independence Day. She always gets maudlin around then."

Fascinating. The downside of immortality—getting over a broken heart could take a while. She imagined losing Azrael. What would happen if he turned away from her? Could she spend an eternity without him? She made an illegal left turn onto a street beside the river, just south of the Vyšehrad fortress ruins that had been converted into a city park.

Tariq spoke as she pulled up in front of the building she grew up in. "You are the consort."

"Reading my mind now?" she said, shutting off the grateful car.

"No, your face." Tariq covered her hand on the gearshift with his own. "I can only imagine— No. He would be a fool to walk away from you."

The car seemed too small. Isela gently withdrew her hand.

"Forgive me," Tariq said. "I have been too forward."

"It's okay." She smiled. "It's very nice of you to say that. It's just— he's everything to me, Tariq, and I belong with him."

He nodded, and his eyes fell away. A breath later he smiled again, all harmless flirtation. "I know why Gregor's angry with you—you're the only person who drives more recklessly than he does. Get me out of this car."

*   *   *

"BEBE." Isela jogged up the steps to embrace her sister-in-law.

The petite brunette squeezed her tightly. "We've missed you, stranger. Come in."

Isela's mother appeared in the doorway behind her.

"Mom." Isela slipped an arm around the woman crowned with a pile of neatly coiled silver dreadlocks.

Beryl looked over Isela's shoulder.

"Come on in, son," Beryl Gilman-Vogel said, raising her voice. "I leave the biting to my boys."

Isela was heartened by the little laugh in her voice. Tariq came up the steps and sank to one knee. "Forgive me, mistress, for arriving unannounced. I am Tariq Yilmaz, ally to Azrael of Prague and the consort."

"Honey, Isela told me you were coming," Beryl said gently at his look of surprise.

Isela held her thumb and pinkie finger to the side of her head and stuck out her tongue. "It's called a phone, old school."

Beryl glared at her daughter before addressing her guest. "I thank you for your consideration. You are a friend here, according to the code of the alliance."

"I will comply," Tariq said, bowing his head as he rose. "Your home is my temple, mistress. I will do no spell nor interfere in yours."

"And you will be granted safe passage," Beryl agreed.

"Code of alliance?" Isela looked between them.

Beryl addressed Tariq. "Forgive my daughter's ignorance. Without my power or her father's gift, I didn't anticipate she would ever need the knowledge."

"That's me, plain old ordinary Isela. Did I mention I have a god living *inside me?*"

Beryl's lips pursed in a tight line. Tariq coughed to conceal a laugh. Bebe tugged her arm as they followed Beryl inside.

"You still have to learn the codes, Isela," Bebe hissed at her as they followed Beryl and Tariq up the stairs. "It's *très importante.*"

Isela stuck out her tongue.

Bebe wagged her eyebrows at Tariq. *Who is his royal hotness?*

Azrael's progeny, Isela returned.

Bebe opened her mouth and pantomimed fanning her cheeks. Tariq took that moment to glance back at them both. Bebe coughed and focused on the step under her feet.

"Tariq, my sister, Barbara," Isela said.

He slowed a step, took her hand, and brought her knuckles to his lips. Bebe almost swooned.

"Sister-in-law," Isela growled at him. "My brother's *wife*."

"I understand the relations created by human marriage very well, my lady," Tariq grinned, winking at Bebe.

"Human marriage?" Bebe asked, a little breathless.

"Marriage is a human ritual," Tariq explained. "A gift from your kind, I believe."

Ahead, Beryl nodded approvingly. "Corrupted over time by a patriarchal need for possession, originally the binding of lives was our gift to humanity, as death rites were yours. Marriage is just one such ritual; there are many ways to make family."

"So necromancers don't..." Bebe abandoned her sentence, and Isela felt the woman's fingers wrap around hers.

Isela squeezed. She knew how much her family valued the bonds created by marriage. To the witches, creating life and union by blood and bond was an ultimate priority. Necromancers could do neither.

"The consort vow is the equivalent among our kind," Tariq said sagely. "And your sister is the consort to the most powerful necromancer in the world."

"One of—" Beryl said.

"No, mistress." Tariq corrected her gently. "My master is unmatched. In part due to his union with your daughter. Goddess or not, she gives him something the rest of the Allegiance lacks. Heart."

The family's top-floor flat was surprisingly empty, not just because of her father's absence. Isela immediately noticed the missing scents of her brothers, nieces, and nephews. She touched a small jacket that hung from a hook beside the door with her fingertips, the little cuffs a few fingers wide.

"Evie and Fifi took them to the zoo," Bebe said as she lingered. "Mom thought it best." She let her words fall away, but her eyes followed Tariq.

Isela nodded, understanding, but the knot in her throat did not ease.

"The twins made you something though." Bebe herded her to the kitchen. A necklace constructed of painted wood and glass beads threaded with satiny, colorful ribbons sat on the counter.

Beside it was a card, Isela's name spelled in careful rakish crayon letters, tented over a miniature wooden knife.

"Philip." Bebe grinned ruefully. "He read a book on Japanese sword schools and now he wants to be a ninja. Chris has been teaching him how to carve things. I can't even watch. I'm terrified he's going to lose a finger."

"Not bad." Tariq hefted the "blade" before Isela plucked it from his hand.

"Mine." She gathered her gifts, bringing the card to her nose. If she strained, she swore she could still smell the trace of macaroni and cheese that had clung to tiny hands as it was drawn. When she opened her eyes, she had to blink to force back tears. She twisted the necklace carefully around her wrist and slipped the card and knife into her bag.

Isela felt sadness in Bebe's gaze not connected to her own grief. "Come, let's have tea."

Tariq tried not to gawk at the room around them. Isela wondered what he made of the ordinariness of it all—scattered colored pencils and paper on the coffee table, building blocks tangled in the long strands of the throw rug, the pile of laundry folded in the easy chair that had been her father's. He paused at the wall papered in children's drawings to stare at one of a family. Even a child's young hand made clear the father figure's pointed, furry ears and the peaked witch's hat on the mother. Between them were three smaller figures. Two wore pointed hats. One had a tail.

"Do they know already?" Isela murmured as Bebe returned with cups and a tray.

Bebe shrugged. "Won't know for sure until they're a little older. But Octavia did this one, and she's got a bit of the eye about her already."

Tariq looked between the women, naked surprise on his face.

"My granddaughter sees things as they are," Beryl said proudly, appearing with the tea. "A good gift in a world like this, wouldn't you say?"

As they settled on the couch, Bebe leaned in to Isela with a raised brow. "We're having to talk to her about the drawings she does at school though. It didn't help that she told that boy he was an ogre."

"He does have a fair bit of troll in his veins," Beryl said sagely, pouring.

Tariq accepted his cup, his long lashes fluttering as he dipped his head in gratitude. He sipped and then closed his eyes. He sat back, a look a pure delight on his face. Beryl eased back in her own chair, holding her cup like a queen as she waited for her due.

"Madame Vogel," he said finally, opening his eyes. "It has been centuries since I have tasted anything so sublime."

Beryl bowed her head and lifted her cup in salute.

"Mom's got a thing for tea," Isela added wryly.

Beryl gave her long look. Isela explained quickly about finding the phoenix, and what had been done to it.

Bebe shook her head. "Unbelievable. The cajones of some necromancers. Do you have any idea who may have done it?"

"Azrael forbade me from talking to it," Isela said. "Before he took off to tangle with Vanka."

Bebe's brows rose. "So you're here—"

"I don't know what all being his consort entails yet," Isela said. "But I'm positive there's nothing about obedience in it."

Bebe laughed. "You are more wolf than any of us gave you credit for. Issy, this is dangerous, dabbling in other people's magics."

Isela nodded. "And I won't ask you all to help me beyond this. I'd never endanger you. I just need to know if there are any resources that you have that might help. He's suffered enough, and he came here—risking everything—to give me a warning. The least I can do is help him stay alive."

"And what say you in all this?" Beryl addressed Tariq.

Isela paused, teeth sinking into her lower lip in anticipation of protest. He shrugged, spreading his palms. "I swore to protect the consort from threats even she cannot see. But the jewel in my master's crown has a good point."

Isela sat back. Tariq gave her the hint of a smile.

"Then you need an alchemist," Beryl said finally. "Someone who understands the workings of transformation. That's never been my strength. Barbara, you will go with them."

"Me?" Bebe sat up in her chair.

Beryl smiled. "You are always asking for more adventure. And you have a good knowledge of the codes. Someone has to keep Isela from opening her mouth and inviting trouble to dinner."

It was a lighthearted remark, meant to be a tease, but it still left a barb. Isela bit her mouth closed over the retort that she hadn't ignored the codes. She'd never known anything about them because they'd hidden everything from her. She ignored the bitter sting that her mother trusted her grandchildren with their secrets more than she had her own daughter. She blinked hard and felt Bebe's hand on her arm.

Even that stung. Her sisters-in-law had a bond with her mother that she could never have, because she wasn't a witch. No one could tell her what she was, but everyone knew she wasn't like *them*.

Tariq's hawk eyes were on her. He cleared his throat to speak, but she rose first, setting down her cup. "Excuse me. I need to use the facilities. Is there some ritual I must undertake?"

"Don't be smart, Isela." Beryl frowned.

"I'm not," Isela said. "Apparently."

She left before her mother could reply. She went down the hall to her father's study. One hand on the door, she cupped the handle, twisting it slowly. She eased it open, careful to stop before the squeak that her father had never fixed. He called it his early-warning system, and it kept the boys from springing one of their many practical jokes in his sanctuary.

She slipped inside, fingers curled to her mouth to silence her gasp at the sight of the room her father had spent so many hours in. It looked almost exactly the way it had for as long as she remembered. A fine layer of dust told her no one had disturbed a thing. The only new addition was the stack of boxes in the corner. She went to her knees, lifting the lid from one to reveal his clothes. This one was full of old sweaters, neatly folded and tucked in like sleeping children.

She lifted the first one, pressed her face into the wool, and inhaled deeply. Tears sprang fresh to her eyes as his scent saturated her nose. Dry and warm, like beach sand and polished wood with the hint of hazelnuts he always snacked on while he worked.

A warm hand settled at the base of her neck, and for the sheerest moment she thought— But it couldn't be. She'd released him at Ofelia and Chris's wedding weeks ago. She wouldn't wish her father's spirit to linger, not even for her own longing.

When she looked up, it was Bebe, fingers threading through the small hairs at the base of Isela's skull. Isela let her forehead rest against Bebe's hip. She gave in to the gentle hands that stroked her back and let Bebe's smell—baby wipes and maple syrup—soothe her. Of her sisters-in-law, it was Bebe who remained the most generous with her love. Isela suspected it was Bebe who'd started the campaign to reach out to her when she had felt isolated from her family by the rigorous demands the Academy placed on her life. The patience of a saint and the ability to forgive like one was the family platitude given to Bebe.

After all, she'd picked Tobias, the most cerebral of the brothers.

He loved her with every inch of his soul. He was also prone to drop down one scholarly rabbit hole or another in his work. The kind that meant he would forget to eat all day, or birthdays and anniversaries. It was Bebe who took up the slack, cheerily, and without seeming to take it personally when she was the one on the receiving end of his absent mind.

"Thought I'd find you here," Bebe said, affection and loss roughening her voice. "We're hanging on to everything, but Mom needed it out of the closet, you know."

Isela nodded, drawing back. "I'm sorry, I didn't mean to leave you."

"What, with Istanbul's sexiest lord of death?" Bebe laughed with a little shrug. "He keeps up with those eyes and I'm gonna forget I have three kids and a husband."

"You would not." Isela laughed against her will, and the grief lightened just a bit.

"There, that's better." Bebe smiled, wiping at her face. She plucked at an imagined hair on the sweater in Isela's arms before clearing her throat. "I have to remind myself he's probably older than all of us put together."

Isela said, "By a millennia, give or take."

They rose.

Bebe sighed unhappily. "You know we'll help you, but I don't like this, Issy. I can't believe I'm saying this, but maybe taking Azrael's word for it isn't a bad idea."

Isela scowled. Bebe hugged her.

"Here, I brought you a bag. I thought maybe you'd want to take something home with you."

"Home," Isela mused, touched as Bebe presented a large zippered plastic bag.

"Yeah, you know, that enormous castle on the hill," Bebe joked, helping her sort through the sweaters.

Isela picked one of her father's old favorites, the one Beryl had begged him to get rid of for almost a decade. Pilled and faded, it smelled so strongly of him it stole her breath.

"Doesn't quite feel like that yet," Isela confessed. "I mean, I love Azrael…"

"But it's new, I get it," Bebe said, helping her carefully bag the sweater. "I didn't feel like this building was home until Philip was born, even though I couldn't imagine life without Toby. Don't worry. It will grow on you. Home is where he is. The rest is just rooms. Lots of rooms, in your case. Big rooms full of fancy artwork that belongs in a museum, or several."

She slipped the sealed bag into a larger paper satchel.

"Come on, Mom's giving Turkish delight directions, and we should get going."

CHAPTER TWELVE

"Pull in here." Bebe leaned forward from the cramped space between the front seats, pointing at a thicket beside the road.

Isela pointed at the GPS in the dash. "The directions say keep going almost a mile."

She'd insisted on plugging in the address when they'd gotten in the car after catching the tail end of her mother's directions. After all, what was GPS for?

"That's not how this works, Issy." Bebe smiled as Tariq put on the turn signal and slowed down.

"So what's the point of giving us an address?" Isela asked.

"*You* asked for the address, O light of my lord's eye," Tariq said. "Your mother provided the *directions.*"

Bebe unbuckled her seat belt, tapping the back of Isela's seat impatiently. "Let's go."

Outside, the growing afternoon sent long light into the trees and the thicket they'd stopped alongside. The shafts of light piercing the overhang seemed solid enough to draw blood. The deep loamy scent of fresh earth reached her beneath frost and rotting leaves. Tariq's casual air was gone, replaced by something watchful and dangerous.

Isela stood restlessly by the car door, waiting for Bebe to unfold herself from the back seat. "I am missing the difference."

"Hiding something in plain sight is an old trick used by both witches and necromancers," Tariq said, watching Bebe approach the thicket. "You should know that. We learned from the gods."

It looked to be a solid wall of brambles and thick, shiny leaves. Bebe held out her hands, pressing her palms to the wall. She hissed, and Isela picked up the metallic tang of blood. Bebe yanked her palm back, wiping at the smear of red.

"I would have given it willingly," she snapped at the glossy leaves.

A crack formed in the wall, leaves and branches rolling in and away to clear a human-sized opening. Bebe and Isela slipped inside easily; Tariq had to duck his head and hunch his shoulders and still his shirt caught on brambles.

"She doesn't like necromancers," Bebe said, half apologetically.

The remaining light fell away under the dense canopy of trees and walls of bushes. Isela peered around Tariq to the path behind them to find it gone altogether. No sign that they had passed. In the distance she could hear male voices in conversational Czech, and farm machinery. A tractor? But the sound carried in such a way that it was impossible to tell how close or far it was. Bebe led the way fearlessly, so Isela put her effort into keeping up.

The branches fell away at the crest of a small clearing. Their path joined an old, unused farming road and ran down into the clearing, crossing over a brook still burbling in spite of its frame of frost. The road led to an old farmhouse converted from a mill once run by the stream. The building overlooked a field of shaggy black sheep. Behind the clearing, the old wooden structure of a railroad bridge hung like a protective ward over this perfect, untouched little respite.

At their appearance, a low, unhurried woofing went up. One of the black mounds she had thought was a sheep rose from the snow and trotted along the fence line. It was a dog the size of one of her brothers in wolf form, with a dense, curly coat and eyes like black diamonds beneath a heavy forelock. It kept its distance but followed their progress.

"Hey, Černá," Bebe greeted the dog without affection.

The dog woofed again. The hoarse sound reminded Isela of a bird rather than a dog.

A pretty piece. Gold spoke up. *Masterful.*

When Isela blinked, it was as if the dog shape was superimposed on another, or perhaps the other way around. A great blackbird existed beneath the wild, matted tangle of dog hair.

It knows what it is, she said. *Both of it.*

A column of smoke rose from the main building, and as they grew closer, Isela could see it was not the only structure. An enormous greenhouse stretched out behind it, glass-paneled walls made opaque by age and condensation. The dog skirted the fence and paced them. Bebe knocked on the door to the main building, but there was no answer. She sucked her teeth, stamping impatiently in the growing cold, and checked her watch.

"What time do the kids come home?" Isela said.

Bebe waved. "Evie and Mom will take care of them. It's your brother who will freak when he finds out. He doesn't trust her. Come on. Let's go around back."

She led them, stomping a little in her tall rain boots, and Isela wished she had thought to bring a sturdier pair of shoes as she skirted the worst of the muddy puddles and a suspicious-smelling pile or two. Bebe banged on the greenhouse door, rattling it. From inside, Isela picked up the faint strains of music. Édith Piaf, she thought. Bebe grumbled something uncharitable and opened the door.

"I'm coming in," Bebe said. "Beryl warned you we were on our way, so don't spring any of your booby traps on me, or I swear…"

At the mention of traps, Tariq stepped swiftly in front of Isela, shaking his head once when she opened her mouth to protest. All she saw as they entered was his back. But the heat hit her like a wave— damp, humid air almost physically thick with that loamy smell. And where his broad ended, green began.

"You're letting out my heat!" An ancient female voice cackled as the music faded.

Isela turned, but Bebe grabbed her hand and hissed, "Don't touch it."

"Close the door yourself, old hag," she bellowed, making Isela jump.

The door slammed shut.

"How you speak to your elders," the voice called, amused. Isela tried to identify the accent of the speaker but couldn't pin it down.

They followed the voice into the rich green heart of the world around them. The sound of burbling water and chirping of birds— birds!—seemed to come from nowhere and everywhere all at once.

Past the outer ring of heavy elephant's ear and ivy and banana trees were flowers. Orchids of all kinds and sizes hung from the ceiling to the floor. In one row, each bloom carried variegated colors that looked like paint thrown haphazardly on canvas, or splashes of blood. Plants with smaller blossoms cascading like fireworks in pastel colors also hung from the ceiling.

In the innermost circle was a master gardener's dream, with big wooden tables covered in tools, soil and empty pots. In the background, the old record player spun on, the needle lifted and poised in waiting. Standing in a dirty apron covering a pair of faded jodhpurs and shirtwaist like something out of a nineteenth-century advertisement for a modern woman was a female Isela would have placed in her midforties. She dusted her soiled hands off on her apron, resting one palm on her hip as she narrowed her eyes at them.

"Brought one of death's hounds along for the ride?" she said in that ancient-woman voice that made Isela double take. "Didn't warn me about that."

"Forgive me, grande dame." Tariq folded at the waist, never dropping his eyes from her. "I serve only as my lady's guard. I mean you no harm."

"That's what they say," she said, "until they try to get a little too friendly. Isn't it?"

Her oversized features broke into a wild, terrifying grin as she strode forward. Isela leaned back a bit. Bebe didn't flinch. She took the dirt-covered hand offered to her and curtseyed deeply, bringing it to her forehead. The woman's other hand rested on the back of her head briefly. Isela felt a moment of fury that the woman would touch Bebe so intimately with such filthy hands, but Bebe rose, looking a little awed.

"And what are you?" The woman nudged Bebe aside to gaze at Isela.

Tariq drew in automatically as she approached, putting Isela behind his shoulder. The woman came up against his chest, gazing up at him along her nose like a teacher with a defiant student. Silver streaked the hair tied hastily at the top of her head, but in the humidity bits of the ends curled free in dark, ropy waves. Lines creased her eyes and her mouth, pulling down to a frown.

"May I present the lady Isela, Consort of the Necromancer Azrael of Prague," Tariq said formally without moving.

The woman reared back, clapping her hands together and cackling in delight. "Indeed! A necromancer's consort. And *the* Azrael no less. The humans wrote him into their holy books—or left him out—out of terror. To some a gentle monster, to others an untold horror. To this day nothing grows at the site of Iram, and nothing will."

Tariq laughed. "The city of pillars is a fable told by the desert tribes to scare children."

Not so. Gold stirred. *Even the gods know it was a necromancer who turned a city of stone and sand to melted glass.*

"All fables begin with the seed of truth," the Alchemist echoed.

A chill raced up Isela. Wouldn't fire heat sand to glass? She remembered Azrael's promise, that he would be a monster to keep others at bay. He'd walked the earth for two thousand years, give or take, he'd said. Had Azrael wiped out an entire city full of people? Surely all of them couldn't have been guilty. Her stomach swayed unsteadily.

The Alchemist cocked her head. "But no necromancer, this one. What are you hiding then, little *matryoshka*?"

She leaned in, ignoring Tariq. He moved his shoulder more firmly between them.

"Madame," he said resolutely, and his hand went to a sword Isela hadn't seen until that moment.

Had he been armed this whole time? How had she missed it? She thought of his words about the hidden nature of the blades. For a moment, they all froze in a tableau.

The woman relented, both hands on her hips this time as she turned her gaze up to Tariq. She smiled beguilingly, and the years fell away from her face before Isela's eyes. She blinked at him, thinned lashes replaced with full, mink-colored ones. Her lips plumped, top and bottom, cheeks filling out again as the lines disappeared from her face. A dimple appeared in her chin.

"I promise you no harm here, though it is you who intrudes in my sanctuary," she said. "I will do no magic against you; you have my protection here against all my defenses."

"And your curiosity," Tariq insisted, seemingly impervious to the breasts blooming under the apron and the way her hips rounded.

"Will remain satisfied by questions you are willing to answer," she said, aiming the last at Isela in Tariq's shadow. It still raised goose bumps on her arms to hear that ancient voice coming from the face of a woman who now looked no more than twenty-five. "Happy now, Turk?"

Tariq bowed his head. "As can be, given the circumstances, dame."

"Dame sounds like someone's grandmother." She blinked at him, her skin smooth and colored like fresh caramel now.

Tariq inclined his head.

"Just remember it was you who came to me," she snapped. "You needed my help, remember."

"Advice," Bebe clarified.

The woman's mouth turned down in amused displeasure. "Fine. You won't even let me see it, will you?"

"Not unless it wishes to be seen by you," Bebe said. "If it survives. So we have a common interest in that outcome."

The woman crossed her arms over her chest but nodded. Isela took the softening in Tariq's stance as a sign that accord had been achieved and laid a hand on his arm. He slid sideways the tiniest bit, but now she could see the woman full-on.

"We haven't been properly introduced," Isela said.

The woman brightened. "Finally, someone with manners. But the accord had to be reached first, so all the verbal sparring. It's for the best, truly. But it does set a bit of a mood, doesn't it?"

Isela felt the smile itching at her face. "It does. I'm Isela, or Issy. I mean you no harm if you will do none to me."

She offered her hand. Tariq looked as though he were going to choke on his tongue. Even Bebe opened her mouth in surprise.

"I have been many names in many times, but what I am never changes. You can call me Alchemist." The woman smiled back and took the hand in a firm grip. "See how much easier that was? Have to say one thing for these moderns, they do favor simplicity, don't they?"

When Isela glanced back, Tariq rubbed his upper lip with one hand, trying very hard not to laugh as he cast his gaze upward. Bebe still looked stunned. The woman's grip was firm and warm. Isela felt a tingling of power in their connection.

Ah ah ah, Gold chided, sending sparks down Isela's palm. The woman withdrew her hand, shaking it, but didn't look upset. *She promised not to take liberties with her curiosity. But I don't think she can help herself trying to unpack us, really, it's what she is.*

"You are something unusual," the woman said, her tone hovering somewhere between admiring and covetous. "Is that how you tamed the angel of death?"

"Why is everyone so bent on trying to figure out why Azrael wants to be with me?" The words escaped before Isela caught herself.

The Alchemist watched her with somber eyes. She waved her hand and her age reappeared with a long inhale. "Youth is wasted on the young, and beauty untested is no prize. Eh, Turk?"

"I'll keep my pretty face," Tariq said. "And you look more beautiful now than ever."

She smiled at him slyly before returning to her plants with a sway of her hips. Her strides slowed, and the smoothness went out of them. By the time she reached the table, she moved at an aged hobble, leaning heavily on the thick plank for support.

"What say you now, silver tongue?"

Now the face matched the voice as it turned back to them. Bare scalp under a few strands of hair caught the light from above. Mottled skin like faded petals clung as delicately to the hollows of her face as old blossoms held to the stem. One eye, a marble of gray and blue, floated beneath the lid. The other, still amber, bulged out at them.

"Your necromancer will never suffer waking to this," she said to Isela in gravel tones with a wicked smile. "What man would not claim a blossom that did not fade? How they do hate age, those cowards who call themselves masters of death."

Isela swallowed hard, but her chin lifted and she slid her shoulders back defiantly. "I was mortal when I became his consort. He chose me, not the god. I don't want to waste your time, Alchemist. You seem... busy."

For a moment the old woman just stared at her, bushy brows lowered over her eyes as though she wasn't sure what to make of what she saw. "I'm a lonely old woman. I'll spend my time with visitors however I wish." She exhaled. "You look for keys everywhere but around your own waist, consort."

Isela frowned. She knew nothing about the kind of magic that would transform a boundless magical thing capable of moving between worlds into something human.

"A god then," the Alchemist said resolutely, returning to repotting a crimson orchid. Her hands moved about the task with rote familiarity in spite of their heavy tremble that sent bark chips shaking to the tabletop. "And yet you are still whole and sane. Such a thing is not possible. Nor is your phoenix."

"Nonetheless, both are true," Tariq suggested gently.

"How they speak in reserved, respectful tones before age!" The old woman cackled at Isela. "It is the maiden they chase but the crone they respect. Typical."

"You did it before," Bebe interrupted. "The pigs—"

"Slow and stupid and dull, not very good pigs at all." The Alchemist waved her off and carried the newly potted orchid to the shelf by the gramophone. With her back to them, her next words were muffled. "And after a diet of saltwater and hardtack, terrible eating as well."

"The alchemy of living things is an impossible art," she roared suddenly, facing them. "And a cruel one. Even I've given up on it after old Černá out there. Even some of those who carry the shifter gene don't have the ability, isn't that so, lady? Although no doubt you could now, if you willed it so. You and your little god. It might not even cost you much."

Could she? She hadn't even considered it. And what would she be, a wolf like her brothers, or something else?

"But you, Alchemist," Isela said, "have transformed before us three times."

The Alchemist shook her head. "I have only become what I was, what I am, and what I will be. I could not turn myself into the flower in my hands. Though I would if I could and not be bothered by infants questioning the impossible."

"But there's a man lying in a bed that used to be a phoenix," Isela said, frustrated.

"And he's dying, isn't he," the Alchemist snapped.

She returned to her work. Her hands steadied, and the mottled marks of age faded. Her hair sprang out and thickened. She swore as a hank of it fell in her face and brushed it impatiently behind her ear, leaving bits of bark and moss tangled in the ropy curls.

"A few days he'll cling to life." She sighed. "Living things always do, but alchemy by force takes a toll on both creatures."

Isela paused. Force, that was it. Was that why she survived and others had not?

You accepted me, Gold reminded her. *And I gave up some of myself to fit inside you.*

The Alchemist smiled knowingly. "The keys have jingled, and she chases the sound."

"What can we do," Bebe asked, impatient, "to fix it? Can we change them back? Odysseus's pigs—"

The Alchemist slammed her hand down on the table as she roared, "Do not speak that name in my presence!"

A new scent crept into the room. Warm, earthy loam gave way to a gasp of brimstone and sulfur that made Isela cough. The lights dimmed and flickered, and the leaves around them trembled. The gold raced to the surface of Isela's skin in response, sparks rippling to her fingertips.

Tariq planted Bebe firmly behind Isela. "Protect your sister, and stay out of it."

He put himself between the women and the Alchemist.

"Your favor," he said, hand again on the hilt of his sword, "O blossom that cannot fade. We beg your forgiveness. Is the phoenix not revered by your kind more than all others? You must understand the urgency that makes us careless. We crave the wise hand of your guidance. Are we not allies in preserving this creature?"

The Alchemist pressed her palms into the table, her head bowed as her shoulders trembled. The flowers on her table began to smoke, popping into flame. Tariq dropped his left hand, flashing his palm at Bebe and Isela in an unmistakable command—go. Bebe grabbed her arm, tugging her backward, but Isela resisted.

The sulfur faded from the air. The Alchemist faced them with an enormous sigh. Her wry grin did not reach her eyes. "I see your mother's wisdom in sending this silver-tongued devil, Barbara. Return, child, I will not harm you. Of all your witch kin, you are my favorite. You know that."

Isela stared at Bebe in surprise. Bebe flushed a little but obediently returned to her place.

"You don't consider yourself a witch?" Isela asked before she could think about the wisdom of asking.

The Alchemist's eyes fell on her, and Isela fought the urge to step backward. The woman ignored the question and shook her head at Bebe like a mother chiding a stubborn child. "I told you once, they made terrible swine, those men, and so I gladly turned them back to something resembling what they were before. At least they were useful then. Though a few never forgot the pleasure of lying around in the sun or bathing in mud. But a thing changed can never return to what it was, truly." Her eyes returned to Isela. "Surely you know that."

"We would try," Isela said, stepping around Tariq again.

The Alchemist dusted off her hands and set her them on her hips. "What is the obsession with those damned pigs?"

Bebe shrugged lightly. "You showed men what they were in their hearts, and they never forgot it. Or forgave it. I'm sure there are many other more remarkable things you've done that have been forgotten by history. A phoenix needs you."

"He's not the only silver tongue in the room, it appears." The Alchemist narrowed her eyes at Bebe, but they were bright with humor. Her face stilled as she considered Isela like an unexpected bug in her garden. "I am no witch. Nor necromancer. The world is not divided as easily as they wish, and not all power comes from gods. I refused to choose sides in their little spat. As I refuse to bow to this new high priestess of Prague and join their fold."

Isela's spine stiffened. "My mother only wishes to protect the witches of Prague as part of her alliance with Azrael."

A satisfied little smile lifted the Alchemist's lips. "Does she? Witches form communities, but they do not have overlords. Did she not tell you that?"

"Well, you are not a witch," Isela snapped.

"And it would be wise of her not to forget it," the Alchemist retorted, her eyes going pointedly to Bebe, "when she calls on me demanding favors for her new allies."

"Daughter," Isela said, correcting her.

"Is that what you are to her?" the Alchemist said wryly. "She didn't mention it."

Isela sealed her lips shut and tried to pretend the words hadn't struck a blow in her rib cage.

She's baiting you, Gold warned.

No shit.

So quit playing into it.

Isela took a breath. She met the Alchemist's eyes. "I accepted what I became. And the price I paid. The phoenix did not. What can I give you for knowledge that might help us?"

Isela heard Tariq's sharp intake of breath and she squeezed his forearm, willing him to be silent. Bebe's dark eyes seemed too shiny and wet. She mouthed something Isela could not understand.

"Let me see you." The Alchemist held out her hands. "As you are now, both of you."

She learns by touch, Gold said. *She wants to know what we are. But there's something else, Isela. Something about you.*

Me personally?

Gold paused. *Your line. I don't understand fully, but I don't trust her.*

Can you limit her?

She's right, Gold said. *Whatever she is, it's a power not of gods. I don't know what she's capable of...*

I trust you.

The god was silent for a long moment. *I will do my best.*

Isela looked at Bebe. "You might have to close your eyes, Beebs."

"A kindness," the Alchemist agreed. "And stand behind your escort."

Bebe passed close to Isela, her eyes too wide. "Be careful, Issy. She—"

"I know." Isela squeezed her hands reassuringly and looked at Tariq. "Protect her."

"As you wish." He nodded, his eyes never leaving the Alchemist.

Isela moved forward. *Protect what you can, give her only what you must.*

She felt Gold's assent. Hesitating, she laid her hands in the Alchemist's. The other woman's palms were warm and gritty with the soil of her task. Strong too. Her fingers locked around Isela's hard enough for her to gasp. The Alchemist's smile widened, predatory now.

"Show me," she commanded.

Gold sniffed. *At my pleasure.*

The Alchemist laughed, and Isela knew she had heard the god's words. "Indeed."

Isela felt the layers of the geas leaving her skin, drawing away like the petals of a flower. She knew what she would see if she looked at her own hands—brown giving way to gold as the god came to the surface. It had started slowly after her transition with a few threads of gold in her hair. Then, healing from a sparring wound, the skin had been replaced by a layer of gold. One morning Tyler had winced and squinted, unable to look at her fully. After that it had happened quickly. Every time she showered, flakes of brown skin fell away like the skin of a snake, shedding. Her hair began to fall out in her hands, replaced quickly with strands of gold until it flowed thicker and more curly than ever and shining like a sunset on water.

Azrael taught her how to build the geas to disguise herself. Piece by piece—skin, hair, nails. She learned to paint herself with power and illusion to cover the fact that she no longer resembled something human. The eyes were the hardest part, and they still slipped when the god was active in her, a giveaway that she was something *else*.

The Alchemist stripped away the geas like the peel of ripe fruit. Isela felt naked. No one but Azrael had ever seen her like this; he was the only one powerful enough to withstand it. Even then the damage to his eyes had taken hours to heal.

The Alchemist recoiled a bit but did not look away. Nor did her grip relax. A thousand tiny touches crawled over Isela's skin. It was not painful, but the hairs rose on the back of her neck and arms. She felt the memories of her encounters with the phoenix pawed through as the Alchemist scrutinized the withered creature.

Force, choice, freedom. Choice. It all came down to choice.

She's looking at your bloodline, Gold said warily. *She's not even interested in us. Not really.*

What is she looking for?

Don't know. Gold grumbled. *She's found something—something she needs. OH. Oh.*

Stop it, Isela said out loud and to Gold. "Stop."

I can't, Gold cried, suddenly panicked. *She has—she's done something to me. I'm stuck. Isela.*

Isela felt the god inside her, buzzing angrily against her skull. The more she fought and buzzed, the more erratic she became, pieces of her shattering and bouncing around Isela's mind until the pain became blinding.

Help, Isela! She's trying to unbind us. She wants to steal me.

"Stop!" Isela screamed.

"Enough, sorceress." Tariq's voice cut through the buzz. Isela opened her eyes.

They were in the In Between. And the edge of Tariq's blade rested at the Alchemist's jugular. She glared at him, eyes bulging as the metal tasted flesh. It should have been impossible for his physical blade to exist here, but Isela remembered what he'd told her about the blades he'd given her. Whatever geas he'd marked them with allowed them to travel with him into the In Between.

"How is this possible?" the Alchemist asked.

"I've picked up a few tricks in my time," he said. "Same as you, I suppose. Now it's time to end this. I suspect you've taken what you needed. And more, given my lady's protestations. Now it's time to withdraw, or I will assist you."

The blade bit, parting skin, and a line of red rolled down her neck.

The Alchemist let Isela go abruptly, and they were all dropped back into their real-world bodies. Isela hurried to restore the illusion geas, but the struggle had cost her dearly. Bebe helped her step back from the Alchemist when her own strength failed her. The headache was back, pounding a hammer against the nail behind her right eye.

The god was silent—not just quiet, but absent. *Gold?*

There was no response. Isela didn't have the strength to search for her, and fear rooted out a deep place in the pit of her stomach. She didn't think it possible for anything to harm the god. Was it? But certainly if the Alchemist had succeeded… Her knees buckled.

"I've got you," Bebe whispered, sliding Isela's arm around her neck. "Easy."

Tariq covered them, waiting until they were across the room before lowering his blade. He withdrew a handkerchief from his coat and offered it. "Your pardon, madame."

The Alchemist snatched it from his fingers, dabbed her neck, and withdrew to her potting bench, leaning heavily on the wood. Whatever she had done had drained her too. She looked older, not yet the crone but no longer the vibrant woman of middle age. Still, she smiled at Isela. It lacked any warmth or familiarity.

"There is nothing that can be done for your phoenix or the man," she said. "The body is dead in one, and the soul in another. They cannot exist without each other. Much like you and your parasite god."

"You lied then!" Bebe shouted.

"I did not lie," the Alchemist said, and for the first time her expression took on an emotion, regret. "I promised what advice I could give. And there it is. What was done was not alchemy. If you try to separate them, you will lose both."

It was Isela's turn to draw Bebe away. Bebe shook with fury, her face mottled with an uneven flush. Isela leaned her weight on her sister-in-law, more to hold her back. Isela had never seen her in a rage.

"You will find cold hearths among the witches for what you've done here."

The Alchemist's mouth strained downward. "You think that hurts me, witch? I have never been welcome at any hearth. And yet I survive."

Tariq met Isela's eyes over Bebe. His expression was clear. Time to make their exit. Isela bodily pulled Bebe toward the door.

"Beryl gave you her friendship and alliance," Bebe shouted.

"Your *high priestess* was the first to dare my friendship in years," the Alchemist agreed. "And then she demanded favors of me as though I were one of hers." She waved at Tariq. "Tell her she is no longer welcome here. She *nor* her coven."

Bebe sucked in hard breath, and Isela felt her tremble. She blinked furiously for a moment. Bebe who loved so freely and joyfully, with no reserve, had loved this woman in whatever way they had known each other.

Then it was as if grief fell away and left only cold anger in its wake. "All will know that you are not to be trusted. Die alone and cold in your greenhouse."

"So be it, witchling." The Alchemist bowed her head. "Now leave me to my fate. And I give you to yours. Attempt to unravel what was done to that phoenix, and more than it will die."

Outside the greenhouse, the cold struck Isela, robbing her of scent and stability for a moment. The thicket was gone. Now a pitted farm road led from the greenhouse down to long fields. The rumble of an old tractor came from a barn, the voices of the farmworkers rising and falling around the noise. Tariq took a good look at both women, assessing them for visible damage and, finding none, led the way. Arms around each other, Bebe and Isela followed.

The late sunlight cast long shadows, but it seemed not enough time had elapsed between when they entered the greenhouse and their departure.

"How is that possible?"

"She has a peculiar effect on time." Bebe gave her a squeeze in reassurance. "I'm okay. Thank you for holding me back. I don't know what I would have done—or tried to do—but it wouldn't have ended well for me. She's too powerful to take on alone."

Isela hugged her back. "Thank you for standing up for me."

"Always," Bebe said fiercely. "We weren't born sisters, Isela. But we're family. Are *you* okay?"

"She was looking for something in my bloodline. Gold seemed to think she found it. You have to warn Mom."

Bebe nodded. "She won't be pleased about how today went. It's not true, Isela. Your mom asked for nothing without offering a favor in return—an enormous debt to owe to a creature like her. She made no demands. I didn't know—none of us knew she felt the way she did about Beryl's alliance with Azrael. I mean, there's been some rumbling..."

"What kind of rumbling?" Isela tried to keep her voice pitched below Tariq's hearing. She'd heard the avarice and mistrust in the Alchemist's voice.

"It's nothing." Bebe shrugged. "I think. Witches are social, but we don't always agree or follow very well outside our individual circles. And we're not all the same in our practice. It's hard for us to operate under an umbrella even if that does offer us freedom and protection. There's some talk about Beryl being chosen to lead us."

First human resistance, now witches were unhappy with the alliance Azrael and Beryl had made. And the Alchemist, whatever she was, seemed to be on their side. She would have to warn Azrael, but her first concern was for her family's safety. If Beryl's position put her —or any of them in danger—Isela would not stop until she'd destroyed everything that threatened them. She'd promised her father, and if there was any comfort in this transformation, it was that she'd be able to do that in ways neither of them could have imagined. Bebe squeezed her again, bumping her with one hip.

"It's just talk," she said. "Everybody knows what we have here with Azrael is nothing short of miraculous. It's to be protected and defended. And temporary. We understand that."

Temporary. Was it? That had been Azrael's hope. That eventually others might follow his lead. But how long would that take? Witches could not attain the immortality of necromancers. Temporary could be a century or more. Necromancers had all the time in the world to decide whether or not to allow witches to exist in their territories. And Isela knew that kind of arrangement would grow stale.

Uneven ground forced them to split up. Isela fell a few steps behind, letting her thoughts turn over the possibility that Azrael might be threatened from within and from without. The god's continued silence troubled her.

Gold?

The response came after a long, heart-stopping minute. The voice sounded ragged and worn, as if from a great distance. And the pain shot into Isela's right eye.

I'm here, Issy.

She rubbed the bridge of her nose in a futile attempt to relieve the pressure.

Sorry, Issy. I'm still… recovering. She's very powerful.

Isela knew she should let the god rest, for both their sakes. But curiosity needled her. *Why did you resist her? She's so powerful, and she knows how to use it. She would have made a better host than I am, I assume.*

Warmth slid from her breastbone along her back, reminding her of the sensation of Bebe's arm wrapped around her in comfort and support.

She still hasn't given up trying to take things by force, no matter what she says. You're different, Issy. Even after what I've done, you treat me like… a friend. Now, let's talk again later if you want. I can't keep from hurting you right now, and we both need to rest.

Isela stumbled in a pit in the dirt, and when she looked up, they had rounded a bend where the farm road rejoined the main road. A familiar two-door coupe sat in the long shadows on the roadside about a quarter of a mile away. Bebe and Tariq were speaking about her. Their voices were pitched low but mostly counting on the assumption that she would not be paying attention.

"…and that has fallen to neither you or your sisters?" She could hear the frown in Tariq's voice.

Bebe said, "I've taught her a few things, but she's not a witch. We assumed Azrael…"

"He's assigned her combat training to his Aegis." Tariq shook his head.

"Combat?" Bebe gasped. "What does he expect she's going to have to fight?"

"The world is an unpredictable place," he said. "It would serve you all to learn to do more than just defend yourselves—"

"The pack will—"

"And your children," he finished firmly.

Bebe was silent. Isela could picture her lips pursed together in thought. Bebe was easygoing about everything but her children.

"Azrael...," Bebe said finally.

Tariq's head shook once, firmly. "As far as I can tell, nothing. He insists on protecting her himself, with his Aegis, and now us. She wasn't ready for what happened in there today, and she won't be. In truth, she's not a necromancer either."

"But someone...," Bebe said. "And she's capable of powerful geas. She must be taught. The codes at least. I'll talk to Beryl."

"That would be good," Tariq said.

The lights flashed, and the soft sound of the door locks releasing ended their conversation. Bebe opened the passenger door, but Isela slipped behind her to take the cramped back seat.

"Go ahead," she said, trying to keep the bitterness out of her voice. "I don't want to interrupt your conversation."

* * *

WHY DID it always come back to those fucking pigs? The Alchemist sighed. *Of all the things she'd done... everything she'd accomplished.*

When the car was well away, she whispered an incantation of the oldest kind, peering into the plastic tub of runoff repotting water. She waved her fingers over the still surface, and water rippled but remained dark. She tried again.

The image began at the outer edges and then dissolved. She swore. The god riding the dancer had been stronger than she expected for a little psychopomp, and the Alchemist had wasted too much energy trying to separate the two. A mistake—the dancer and her god were bound not just by pact. It went part of the way to explaining why the dancer survived the deity's presence. But even the Alchemist was not immune to a little greed. So much power for one so small. Who could blame her for trying? Even the promise of a stronger, more capable host had not lured the deity. Interesting.

The Alchemist knew she should have stopped when she'd gotten the dancer's full bloodline. When she'd been contacted—recruited, she realized fully—she'd thought it a dead end. All godsdancers were grace-blooded. It was why their dance had succeeded when language had failed—the gods heard the blood in their veins when the dancers moved, recognized it as their own , and came to give grace. This one's bloodline would be no different. That her mother was a witch was proof enough.

At the third attempt to open a connection with no success, the Alchemist reached for her phone. No doubt it would reveal her to Azrael's thugs, but by then it would be too late. She would be long gone.

"Our bargain," she announced when the procession of attendants gave way to a silk-clad voice on the other end.

"You dare question the vow of the Lioness of Petra?" Iron behind the silk for all that.

Kadijah's face, kohl-lined eyes and serene as a goddess sculpture, appeared in the water. She was smiling. A dangerous sign. But the Alchemist was old enough to remember when Kadijah was a young desert chief's daughter, cast out for calming a sandstorm and stoned nearly to death when the Alchemist found her.

"I have not stayed alive so long through blind trust, my precious one," the Alchemist announced. "And you threaten the woman who gave the cub water that she could survive to become the lioness."

Kadijah was too regal to look petulant, but the slight lowering of her eyebrows gave her away. "My sanctuary is yours, great Circe."

"Good. I grow weary of the cold and wet in this country." The Alchemist honored the use of her oldest name with a sniff, though her eyes cast mournfully around the sanctuary she had built for herself amid the hothouse flowers and green things. "I long for the lands of my youth."

"They are yours." Kadijah slipped into comfortable benevolence again though Circe recognized the edge to it. "Your home is prepared. Liwa awaits."

"You banish *me* to the desert?"

"The greatest oasis in the world," Kadijah said. "Deep in my territory, where my protection is complete. Your greenhouse is awaiting your touch... Mother."

"This barren womb is immune to your flattery, necromancer," Circe said dryly.

Kadijah's lashes lowered in supplication. "You just have to say the words to fulfill our vow."

Circe paused. She had no love of necromancers, though she had entertained Kadijah's affections for long enough to wonder if they might not be pure flattery. She thought of the young witch, Bebe, so like herself in her youth. Even with a litter of her own, she was fearless and impertinent, traits Circe admired in a woman of any age. No flattery there, even in her awe.

The image of the young witch's glare, cast over her shoulder as she supported the dancer out of the greenhouse, colored her vision for a moment, blotting out even Kadijah's immortal majesty. Done was done.

"I have the answer to the riddle of your dancer, and the tracking geas is in place." Circe sighed, sealing her exile with a brief pause. "But you will wait until the little witch is no longer in her presence, or your riddle will go the way of the Sphinx."

Kadijah's cheek twitched. A fidget. Circe wondered briefly what made her so eager to prick Azrael's ire. She certainly wasn't strong enough to face him alone. So she must have an ally then, and the confidence it gave her.

"Be careful, my beloved one," Circe murmured. "This game is too dangerous, and I fear you will become fodder in another's war."

"Mind your peace, old woman," Kadijah snapped, all semblance of deference gone. "This is my game to play."

Circe did not flinch. "I'll have your word."

The mask slipped for a brief moment. Beneath it, Circe recognized the same expression looking up from a naturally formed oubliette in red desert stone. Circe had expected pain and defeat in the child's battered face. But the blood in her bared teeth told a story of rage and a desire for vengeance.

Circe knew now—as she had understood then—that showing compassion or a lack of confidence would be deadly.

"I'll have your sanctuary and give you everything I have learned about the riddle of Azrael's dancer," Circe repeated firmly. "And his allies."

The mask returned in a wash of avarice. "I, Kadijah Nafisi, vow my protection to your body and soul." She paused. "And the safety of your witch."

A spark of jealousy there? Kadijah was too old not to see loyalty or affection. Both were, after all, powerful bargaining tools, or weapons. Perhaps Circe had endangered the young witch more than if she had trusted Tariq and Isela to protect her. Ah well, the die was cast and could not be withdrawn. Bebe was out of her hands now. And Circe must protect herself. Azrael's wrath was not to be played with.

"I was right then," Kadijah said. "The dancer is something special."

Circe sighed. "Yes and no." At Kadijah's upraised brows, she continued. "I will show you exactly what I mean."

Kadijah nodded. "Be ready. You will not have much time. And travel light, old woman."

Circe did not look at her plants. She would not have been able to hide the pain of their loss. She made her face careless and shrugged. "I am ready."

She closed the phone as the image disappeared from the water. She overturned the plastic tub, watching the rivulets make their way along the floor, leaving behind streaks of mud and potting detritus. So much built, to be lost. Her fingers trailed the soft petals and waxy leaves, nails scraping beds of moss and soil. She whispered her love and her grief as she went, feeling every year of her age weigh upon her like stones.

The door clattered against the frame behind her as she started up the hill toward the house. She would rebuild. She always did. That was the key to immortality—being able to start again no matter how many times you must. It would be a shame she wouldn't get to see that phoenix with her own eyes. But one also learned to live with disappointments, big and small, when one survived as long as she had.

Like Orpheus, she was unable to resist casting her gaze over her shoulder one more time. She imagined the horror and grief in his breast rising as it did in her own at the sight of the crumbling structure behind her, taking in the broken glass and mangled frame and the dried remains of abandoned plants and long-dead flowers. Her very own Eurydice, dissolving into the ether of the underworld. She turned her back to go.

* * *

SILENCE DOMINATED the car as Tariq pulled up in front of the building between the Vltava and Vyšehrad Park. The Vogel compound indeed, Isela thought as she peered through the triangular back glass. Tobias descended the front steps at a jog. His shoulders were tight with tension and his hands fisted at his hips. Markus followed more slowly but was no less threatening. Beryl and Evie crowded the doorway with matching expressions of exasperated concern.

Tariq opened the door and put a finger to his lips before either man could shout. "Peace, *vlkodlak*. Your lady is fine. But she's earned her rest."

At the sight of Bebe's sleeping face, Tobias hesitated. He opened the car door as Isela reached forward to unbuckle Bebe's seat belt. The look he gave her froze her in her seat. With more tenderness than she had ever seen her middle brother display, he scooped his sleeping wife out of the front seat so deftly she barely stirred, just shifted to a more comfortable position against his chest. Her fingers curled in the fabric of his shirt, and a little smile lifted her mouth. Isela hurried out of the back seat as Markus's trajectory continued around the front of the car toward Tariq.

"Mark," she said, placing herself between them. "Tariq is our ally."

"How dare you turn up with another one of Azrael's goons," her brother growled.

She glanced at Tariq for his response, but his expression remained implacable and even submissive. He made no move to come out from behind the door, keeping one foot in the car.

"Markus." Evie's voice floated across the distance. "He's made his vow."

Markus halted in his tracks, but Isela could almost see the hackles bristling on the back of his neck. Isela turned her attention to Tobias, jogging to keep up with him.

"She's just tired," she whispered. "It was a long day. I promise I wouldn't let anything bad happen to her."

Tobias turned on her with an expression that made her shrink away. "I love you, Issy, but if you ever drag my wife into one of your crazy necromancer errands again, I swear to whatever god is currently steering your wheel, I will—"

"Tobias Vogel, shut your damned mouth," Bebe whispered from his chin. "Right now."

He looked down, startled, at the woman in his arms. Bebe fought her way free until he was forced to release her or risk toppling them both, slipping to her feet and staring up at her husband.

"Don't you dare go alpha male on me now," she said. "I am not your possession."

Tobias blinked at her, then up at Beryl. "Mom should have—"

Bebe snapped, "You don't get to tell me where I can and cannot go. Issy is family. And if she needs me, I'm there." She sucked in a breath and calm, collected Bebe emerged in the space between exhalations. "You're in charge of bedtime tonight. I need a hot bath and a glass of wine. Night, Issy. Nice to meet you, Tariq."

Tariq did his best not to smile, but he bowed royally to her. "Mistress Barbara."

Bebe stomped up the steps and into Evie's arms. When Isela looked back, Tobias stared at her, his jaw clenched as the muscle jumped with tension. She fought the urge to capitulate. She wasn't as close to him as she was their youngest brother, Chris, but she had always looked up to him fiercely. She hated putting that look in his eyes.

At last, wordless, he turned and stalked up the stairs. Markus came last, not even bothering to look at her as he passed. Evelia went after him, murmuring something. Beryl paused on the doorstep.

"Bebe will talk to you about what happened," Isela told Beryl, doing her best to keep the emotion out of her voice. "I should probably... go."

Beryl didn't argue. Isela had never felt so cold, standing out in the snow alone. She had almost reached the car when Tariq tilted his chin to get her attention. She turned at footsteps behind her. Her youngest brother Chris hurried down the stairs with a paper bag, his wheat-colored hair bouncing into his face. He bounded forward, sweeping her up into a hug that parted her toes from the cobblestones.

"I almost missed you!" he said. "What the hell was all that about?"

"I put Bebe in mortal danger."

Chris sighed and set her down. "I doubt that. Tobias got all the worrywart genes from Dad. And Beebs has a knack for getting in over her head."

She introduced Chris and Tariq. Chris swept forward in a few huge strides and pumped Tariq's hand enthusiastically before hooking his thumbs in his jeans. He wore a T-shirt and work boots, as oblivious to the cold as he was undaunted by the presence of the centuries-old necromancer before him.

"I've been downstairs all day in the flat," he said. "Fi took the kids to the zoo with Evie and left me to do all the painting. I don't want her in there with that stuff now. Can't be good for her or the baby. She felt it move. Did she tell you? It's like all of a sudden we have a deadline. Like a real one. I think I can get the nursery done by the end of the week. But then we've got to get that master bathroom sorted, and

I'm still over my head in the kitchen. I wish Dad were here. He knew how to do everything."

She couldn't help but smile at her youngest brother's boisterous stream of consciousness. The baby wasn't due until June; they would be finished in plenty of time, even with Ofelia on reduced duty. She treasured how plainly he mentioned their father's absence. That was pure Chris, aching love and practical loss all rolled into simple fact. It wasn't about the kitchen—Markus was just as good as their father with his hands. With a couple of guys from his crew, he could have the work done in a week.

"I wish Dad were here too, baby bird," she said.

Chris flushed. Nobody had called him that in years; it had the desired effect of making him grin in that shy, adorable way that reminded her of their childhood.

"Anyway, Dad left me in charge," she said, "and I say you're doing great."

"The hell he did," Chris muttered, one lanky arm over her shoulder and giving her a squeeze that left her breathless. "He told *us* to look after *you*. You're the one too curious to stay out of trouble."

Chris had a way of making it sound like neither defect or fault but a quirky trait. Like a crooked tooth or a beauty mark. She hugged him back and felt his spine pop in places. He laughed, squeezing her bicep when they parted. "Look at you, all strong and stuff."

He handed off the bag and finished popping his back in two sinuous spinal twists. "Mom said you forgot this. Don't let the others get to you. They're still getting used to the new order of business. Give them time."

"I've got a lot of that now," she said ruefully as they parted.

"Hey, get my sister home safe, you got it?" Chris said in imitation of their older brothers before dropping the act. "Nice to meet you, man. I like your sword."

Isela's gaze whipped back and forth between them. "You can see?"

Chris shrugged. "We all can."

"I saw the one you helped the child carve," Tariq said. "Impressive."

Chris flushed and looked a bit like a kid himself. "I was wondering, could you teach me a few things… if you're going to be around for a while?"

Tariq bowed again. "It would be my pleasure, beloved kin of my mistress."

Chris grinned at Isela and wrinkled his nose. She didn't need to read his mind to know what his expression meant. She laughed. "Tariq's got a way with words. And you are my favorite... just don't tell Toby."

Chris bumped her shoulder as he passed, closing the distance to Tariq.

The two men clasped hands to seal a fresh agreement. Isela looked between them. Of course they would get along. The same way Gregor and Markus would when they finally decided not to kill each other.

She groaned, rolling her eyes as she sank into the car. "Let the bromance begin."

* * *

ISELA LEANED her head against the window and let out a long sigh as they pulled into traffic.

"Well, that was quite an adventure," Tariq said cheerily. "You know, I've never actually seen a were transition. I hear it's wondrous. Perhaps your brother will trust me enough one day. And your mother... In my day, women like her ruled empires and were more ruthless and just than any male. I like your family very much, Issy. They love each other a great deal."

"Yes." Isela closed her eyes. "They do love each other."

"I was including you in that statement."

She made a noncommittal sound. They cruised alongside the Vltava, and the unobstructed view of the castle struck her as it always did. Majestic and somewhat sinister, it overlooked everything. There was no escaping it.

"We need to talk about your training," he said. "And not with the blade."

Isela's phone buzzed. "Hang on."

"Issy, this cannot wait," Tariq murmured as she rooted in her coat for the device. "It is not right that you have no tutelage from either witch or necromancer..."

Tariq raised a brow at the image of the sunny smile from the dishwater blond on the screen.

"Kyle?" Isela picked up, ignoring Tariq's expression. "What's up?"

"Something is going down at the Academy." His brows were locked together. "I don't know if it's about Yana…"

Isela frowned. "What about Yana?"

"She asked me to watch Mischa for a couple of days, and it's been almost a week without a word. I just went to talk to Divya, but she won't see anyone."

A chill rolled over Isela. She waved at Tariq, pointing north.

"I'm on my way," Isela said, disconnecting.

CHAPTER THIRTEEN

Azrael drove and the others rode in silence as dawn crested the plateau behind them. The Land Cruiser climbed the rutted road into the foothills with a certain mulish capability, at last winding its way along broken pavement and into a small village. Villagers drifted through the sleepy, mist-laden scene like ghosts. A boy drove a herd of goats toward the fields. Old women in long skirts with elaborately embroidered handkerchiefs covering their gray braids moved slowly in groups, bearing baskets and buckets or wheeling carts behind them. If not for the abundance of rusted-out cars and peeling billboard advertising, he could have been looking at a scene from more than a hundred years ago.

A few eyes trailed them as they slowly made their way into the center of town, but most fell away immediately. These people were used to the supernatural. They felt it on their skin. They might not have known what the three in the Land Cruiser were, but they felt the unnaturalness of their presence and avoided it. Vanka had been here before him, and he knew by reputation that fear was well earned.

Guilt for not seeing to these border territories rose in him. They were his responsibility, his to protect, and he had abandoned them. Since he'd taken over the territory, he'd been stretched thin. He'd been ruthless, focused on the urban areas, taking care of those populations to strengthen his holdings. He'd left the outliers to their own devices, and this was what it had wrought.

Lysippe directed him through town to a ruined central square. They parked before the fragmented remains of a statue whose identity he could no longer recognize. More people were about—young men in groups, smoking cigarettes on corners and watching everything with mistrustful eyes; shopkeepers sweeping their stoops and cleaning their windows for the day.

He climbed out of the car slowly, allowing them to see him, to study him. He kept his hands in view and his face impassive.

They stared now, realizing that the passengers of the Cruiser were not Vanka's people and emboldened by curiosity. Their faces were a curious mixture of features—epicanthic folds and broad nose, high brows and cheekbones and the occasional tawny head of hair. More than a few redheads, he noted curiously, and the faces here had a general familiarity. He thought if he looked hard enough, he could see descendants of his mother's people, the nomadic steppe tribes that had once moved in long migrations from the Caspian Sea to the Caucasus Mountains and beyond.

"I've got to meet our guide," Lysippe said, pocketing her phone. "Service is shit here. I'll be back in ten."

Be careful, he almost said.

Climbing out of the car to stand at his flank in the position of guard, Gregor saw it on his face anyway. When she was gone, he shook his head, spreading the map out on the warm hood of the car and making a cursory pretense of examining it.

"She's the first of your Aegis," Gregor said. "Yet you treat her like a child."

Azrael bristled at the second mention of his treatment approaching paternalism. He spun but found his anger vanishing when Gregor wasn't even looking at him but after Lysippe's retreating form. "I made a promise."

"And it interferes with her oath to you." Gregor gazed back at his map. "She's stood for it long enough, but not forever."

Azrael gazed into the faces that stared back at him. "I'll have broken the vow I spoke to the woman without whom I might not be here now."

Gregor exhaled. "In the hold of a ship, when I decided to die, a man who was not a man told me, 'You're looking too far back when you should be looking forward.'"

"When have you ever taken my advice?" Azrael said wryly, a brow lifting.

"All I know is," Gregor said, "you have to trust that she's strong enough, that she's lasted this long, that she will survive without your guardianship." His voice was iron, confidence in every word. "Or you'll lose her."

Something in his tone drew Azrael's gaze back to him. Again, Azrael saw the battlefield sky in the blue of his eyes, the dark pupils filled with crooked pine trees and even darker soil. "Was that what happened to you?"

Gregor's gaze shuttered, and he folded the map meticulously. Their attention snapped to a small boy with a deeply freckled, sun-weathered face and a shock of auburn eyebrows. Gregor started forward, but Azrael held up a hand.

"Excuse, sir," he said in hesitant English to Azrael.

Azrael lowered to a crouch to bring himself to eye level. "How can I help you?"

"My grandmother," he said, placing each word carefully, "would like to invite you to tea."

* * *

THE FAMILY FLAT was above a grocery store that seemed to also sell hardware and the occasional stock animal. Azrael climbed the steps after the boy, quickly scanning the presences in the flat ahead. A young woman and her two children, a teenaged boy, and an older woman, the matriarch. The Grandmother of Invitation, he assumed.

All mortal. No trace of magic, though that could be disguised well enough. Still, there was something else here, a connection he was missing. After so long alive, he had knowledge buried deep enough to make it difficult to recall quickly. He waited for the tumblers to line up in his head with the information and paused at the top of the steps when the boy did.

The boy knocked on the door, calling out in the same dialect Lysippe had used.

Gregor hadn't liked him going alone, but an order was an order. And someone had to wait for Lysippe.

The door opened to the teenage boy, all sullen and angry with intense freckles and darker, almost brown hair. "Come in… sir."

An ancient woman's voice snapped and the boy flushed, his gaze on Azrael's shoes. "Please."

Azrael ducked, entering the small, smoky room that was living and family room for at least six people. For all the smoke, it was neatly kept, tidy, a small television in the corner showing Russian game shows. The two children played on the floor with Duplo blocks. A fine-boned young woman came around the corner from the cooking area, set her eyes on him, and retreated backward.

Ruling over her domain from the faded brown easy chair was the matriarch. She filled the chair, though it was impossible to tell how much was her and how much was the layers upon layers of old clothing. With braided wheat-colored hair faded to gray and silver coiled elegantly on her head, she seemed to be as eternal as the mountain and the village itself. She could have been anywhere from an aged 65 to a youthful 103. He scanned her for the kernel of death and found it, still small in the corner of her lung. He reckoned she had another hundred years or so, give or take.

"Welcome to my home, O lord of death," she said in clear, lightly accented English. "Forgive that I am not able to rise. My body is not what it was."

"Please." He shook his head and bowed instead. "You honor me with the invitation. I am not often granted such courtesies."

"Perhaps you understand why this is?" she said, a touch of humor in her craggy voice. She sucked from the pipe in one hand and glared at the staring boy who had been his guide. "Boy, a seat for the master."

The boy scrambled to drag a chair from the small dining table. Azrael resisted the urge to help him. The child placed it directly across from the matriarch, adjusted it slightly, and then stepped back like a soldier at parade rest. The matriarch's eyes fell on him, and though it wasn't clear how much she actually saw, it was enough for her to nod her prickly chin once in his direction. He seemed to sag with physical relief and retreated to a seat by the television.

"Please," the matriarch said. "Master."

"Azrael." He touched his chest, accepting the seat.

"Olesya." She imitated the gesture. "I studied in Odessa as a child. It is how I speak English so well."

Azrael scanned the others present in the room out of habit. When his eyes fell on the large, growing stain of black in one of the young children, it took discipline to school his face to stillness. Olesya's eyes were waiting for his when they returned to her face.

"So soon then," she said quietly.

He debated his answer. Most humans didn't want to know, not really, but the unflinching, rheumy eyes stared into him. "By the end of summer, if not sooner."

The rattle of a tea service brought his gaze up. He knew without being told that this was the mother. The young woman, balanced the tray delicately as she approached. She set it down on the small table between them, the rich aroma of soaking leaves blending with tobacco and whatever they used to keep the house meticulously clean. She kept her soft gray-green eyes on the tea as she poured, but they did not fill with tears.

"She has lost her father to the mines, two brothers, and finally her husband," Olesya explained, as though she were not there. "There is nothing else left in her to weep."

Azrael accepted his cup and thanked her in Ukrainian. It was a guess, but her startled and brief eye contact was his reward. When she asked if he took cream, he heard the tears in her voice that would be shed only in the cover of darkness while her own children slept.

"Will you take my life for the child's," Olesya asked.

The young woman looked up, startled. Now her eyes filled.

"That is not the way it works, I'm afraid," Azrael told them both. "It's not my power to grant."

The young woman clutched a fist to her narrow chest, fingers squeezing something at the end of a gold chain so tightly her knuckles went white as she looked at her mother-in-law with such raw, unfiltered emotion he had to look away.

"Go, I'm hungry, and you are burning my breakfast," Olesya barked gruffly, without any bite.

The woman scurried away, prematurely greying hair floating behind her like a cloak.

"I can delay," Azrael said when she was gone. "A year, maybe more. Would you ask that of me?"

"And what would you take from me in exchange?"

Azrael looked around. This family could afford to lose nothing, but he knew the code for such bargains. He would insult them with charity.

"This scarf." He fingered the delicately embroidered cloth that had been placed beneath the tea service. "It's finely made."

"For your lady," the woman said knowingly.

Azrael inclined his head.

"It is yours, master of night."

"Did you do this work?"

"With my own hand." She nodded. "Long ago, before my eyes— Now Julia, my daughter, does my work. But her hand is not as fine as mine, not yet."

The tumblers fell into place in his mind, and he knew the startling red hair, deep freckles, and green eyes. The height even, so much like the slouchy teenaged boy in the doorway—another son?

"Yes," the old woman said. "You know of him then?"

Azrael nodded.

"The one like you, the Red Death, came two months ago," she said. "She had a job that must be done in the mine. She offered riches, fortunes to any who did the work."

Her eyes unfocused, distant and aching with loss.

"The mine collapsed," she said. "All the men were killed. Except one."

"Your son," he supplied.

"He was damaged, breathing but empty," she said. "The Red Death took him. Said she would help him. We have not seen or heard from him since."

Azrael absorbed this knowledge. The phoenix, or the host body, had once been this woman's blood kin. He had no doubt that whatever remained of the young man was long gone.

"He is dead, isn't he," the woman said from the kitchen.

Azrael looked at her and then the matriarch. The older woman nodded.

"Yes."

The woman paled but held her ground. "But not dead."

"Yes."

To his shock it was the matron who began to wail, her voice rising in a long, sustained keen of grief.

"Mama!" the young woman collapsed at her knees, holding her hands away from her withered face.

Azrael removed the pipe before it could cause harm to them. The woman wailed about the dead who cannot rest and the curse of a life of loss. The young woman looked at him, eyes startled and afraid.

"Master, I am sorry," she said. "You must not hear these words."

He shook his head, reaching for the old woman's hands. He held the wrinkled, knobby fists in his own, loose but firm.

"He escaped her." He kept his eyes on the old woman, ignoring the gasp. "What he is now is not what he was. But he is under my protection, and no more harm will come to him."

She stared back at him out of eyes that were flat, empty. He didn't need to read her mind to see the thoughts on her face. What good was the promise of another necromancer? He was the same as Vanka in her eyes.

Who was the monster, he wondered—Vanka who bared her savagery openly—or him, who cloaked himself in manners?

He released the woman's hands when the fury went out of her. Gently he stepped away.

"I must go, but thank you for the tea," he said, unable to bear his own thoughts, circling toward one unassailable fact.

"Thank you," the young woman said, her voice shaking but her eyes dry. "For your mercy, master."

Azrael paused on his way to the door. He crouched near the twins, hearing the young woman's breath suck in deeply. They looked at him, curious and unafraid. Of course, they had nothing to fear—not yet.

He laid a hand on both curly heads, but the hand on the right traced a geas on the boy's temple. The stain retreated to a much smaller kernel. It took something out of him, pushing death back this way, but it was the least he could do.

Then he rose and went to the door. He showed himself out. Halfway to the square the boy caught up, breathing hard from running and clutching a fistful of crumpled fabric.

"Grandmother said you forgot this."

Azrael took the scarf, mutely nodding, and continued on his way. He held the scarf to his nose, thinking of Isela and how keenly she scented everything—not just the aroma but the sensations that went with it. What would she pick up from this—grief, anguish, the loss and hopelessness of a family that had fallen under the eye of a merciless power and been broken without regard?

Is this what he was? He had become part of it when he raised the hood of his cloak and stood with the rest of the Allegiance before humanity, declaring his intention to rule them. They had saved humanity. Only to set themselves above, as dictators benevolent and cruel, according to their temperament. When given limitless power, they became their worst, no better than the humans they claimed to surpass.

Electricity shot through him as his steps took up new purpose. How long had he simply been existing, coasting on his power and his status as something no longer human but more, and in doing so become something even worse? He'd admitted it to Isela—he was a monster. But when had his goal of keeping the humans in his territory safe justified the means?

They'd all become the monsters they claimed to want to stop, and now they were at each other's throats. There had to be another way for this to end. He thought of Lysippe's words and what a war among the Allegiance might mean.

CHAPTER FOURTEEN

Kyle had met them at the front door, and they'd taken over the student lounge. It hadn't been much of a takeover; the lounge was surprisingly empty for this late in the afternoon. Even the halls seemed mysteriously absent of loitering students. Kyle led them inside, and Tariq posted himself inside the closed door.

"Yana found out her grandpa was sick over a week ago." Kyle started to fill up the water kettle, but his hand shook so much water splashed everywhere.

Isela took over, planting him at the round table in the center of the room. He gave her a ghost of a smile when she squeezed his hands.

"The oligarch?" she said, filling the kettle and setting it on the base.

She retrieved mugs and picked through the assortment of teabags, wishing for her apartment kitchen and its well-stocked supply of ginger and lemon.

"The one and only." Kyle nodded, his fingers knitting together and unknitting.

"Yana said he was 'healthy as an old bear, going to live forever,'" Isela said in her best impression of their friend. She wished she hadn't as fresh tears sprang to Kyle's eyes.

Tariq moved away from the door long enough to slide a box of tissues across the table. Kyle looked up at him gratefully, and his jaw softened a little. He gave Isela a covetous look she knew well—*Is he for real?*

Before she could deflect, Tariq gave him a little smile and a wink. Isela stared openmouthed as Tariq retreated, but Kyle only gave a throaty little laugh and dabbed at his eyes.

"That's what she always said," Kyle went on after a moment. "I mean, he has more money than a god. He got in early with the Russian necromancer—the redheaded one you like so much—and he's been on the payroll since the beginning of time. But everybody dies, I guess. Present company excluded, of course."

Tariq's mouth quirked upward. The kettle binged, and Isela poured hot water. She offered a cup to Tariq, but he looked mortally offended at the presence of the teabag.

"Her parents sent for her," Kyle said as Isela sat down with two cups. "A deathbed-summoning thing."

He wrapped his hands around the mug but didn't appear to recognize it. Isela hooked her fingers over his wrist and squeezed.

"I promised to look after Mischa while she was gone," he said, hoarse. "It was just supposed to be a couple of days."

"Maybe it's taking him a while to kick the bucket."

He shook his head miserably. "That's what I thought. But Yana would have sent a text... if for nothing else than to check on Mischa. I looked online, and there's nothing in the feeds about it."

"Her family is pretty private...," Isela began.

Kyle nodded doggedly. "I called her parents. No response. I went to her dad's offices. They gave me the runaround, and when I wouldn't leave, her father sent his goons out to chase me off. Said it was family business and I had no part in it."

Isela felt a sick twist in the pit of her stomach. She gave up trying to reassure him. "What then?"

"I tracked down her flight information," he said. "She didn't get on the plane, Issy. She was booked on a commercial flight out to Moscow and never got on the plane."

His eyes were haunted, but he pressed on. "I have a friend at the private airfield, so I asked her to check the flight logs."

"Of course you do," Issy murmured fondly. Kyle knew *everyone.*

"The day Yana was scheduled to fly, a plane left for Russia," he said, tears springing fresh. "Her grandfather's. But it didn't go to Moscow. It flew to Saint Petersburg."

Dread kicked the air from her lungs, and Isela sat back in her chair. "Saint Petersburg," she whispered, her eyes finding Tariq's. The flirtation was gone. Now he looked outright dangerous.

Kyle looked between them. "What is it? What do you know?"

Tariq's eyes flared warning. Isela took a breath. "It might not be anything yet, Kyle. But you did the right thing, telling me."

"I didn't know what else to do." Kyle's shoulders slumped helplessly. "Her parents won't acknowledge she's gone. The police won't touch it because of her dad's connections…"

"You're very resourceful," Tariq said with a kind of gentle praise that made Isela like him a little more.

Kyle waved him off. "I read too many detective novels. I have some calls out to a friend in Moscow, but there's been no sign of her there."

"Maybe she met some old-country stud muffin and took off for some R & R." Isela forced the joke and a smile as her thoughts raced ahead.

He looked pained that she would even try such a paltry attempt to distract him. "Like she wouldn't call just to rub that in my face."

She squeezed his arm again, glad to see a bit of his sense of humor return.

"How's Mischa?"

"He was dying of loneliness in her apartment." He sniffed. "I brought him to ours. He's only clawed one of the chairs, and I think Jiří is finally getting used to having him around."

"Take care of him," Isela said. "It'll mean the world to Yana."

She rose from her chair. Kyle nodded, dabbed at his eyes and nose again before beaming up at Tariq. "So, who's the new bodyguard?"

"Tariq Yilmaz." He introduced himself. "At your service."

Kyle looked like he wanted to quip about what service that might entail, but Isela interrupted the thought before it could launch. "Does Divya know? Is that what this is all about?"

Kyle's brows grew together again. "That's what I can't figure out. I tried to get on her calendar, but she won't see me. Even Niles is silent. But I saw the tech guys come through here. And something is wrong. Classes were canceled this afternoon. I thought—what with you and Azrael—maybe you could…"

"We're going to take over from here," Isela said firmly. "I need you to stay out of it, Kyle."

He sputtered words of outrage.

"Isela is right." Tariq soothed him. "Even if she is just under the control of her family, they are dangerous people. Let us handle this."

"But Issy—"

"No buts, Detective Bradshaw," she said, teasing him gently. "Please. It's bad enough Yana's in trouble. If anything happened to you, I'd lose it. I promise you I will find her."

He sighed. "Okay. I'll go back to sitting on my thumbs and feeling helpless."

"You, helpless? Never." Isela looked to Tariq. "Let's go talk to Divya."

* * *

NILES MET them at the door to the director's office. Isela made a quick introduction, and he ushered them inside. "How did you know?"

"About Yana?" Isela asked. "Kyle called."

"I called Lord Azrael's security when the theft was discovered, but I hadn't heard back yet." Niles looked confused. "Yana?"

"You didn't know?" Isela paused.

Divya opened the inner door, deep in conversation with one of the techs. She looked surprised to see Isela, but grim. She dismissed the tech with a nod, waiting until he was gone to address Isela. "How did you find out?"

Niles and Isela shared the ghost of a smile.

Tariq sighed. "Perhaps, madame, we can all sit down somewhere and talk."

Divya gave him a long head-to-toe look. "Inside. I was just getting the report from the digital security team. We got them started as soon as we discovered the theft."

"Theft?" Isela followed.

"Your recordings were stolen from the archives." She paused. "Why are you here?"

"Yana's missing," Isela said. "Wait. *My* recordings were stolen?"

Under normal circumstances, rival schools and individual dancers often tried to steal or buy illegal footage of other dancers to imitate successful choreography. The Academy had benefited from Prague's status as a major global technology center with a security system that rivaled that of any major financial institution. All the godsdancing recordings for every dancer were stored on that system. After Isela had become the consort, there had been talk about destroying her recordings altogether. Until they knew exactly how she had channeled the god, the risk was too great that someone would duplicate her efforts.

They'd assumed the recordings would be safe until a decision was made. They hadn't moved quickly enough.

Niles spoke finally. "We thought it was a glitch in the system initially; it was made to look like a storage failure, but on investigation, it was a hack. The erasure wasn't random. And the files had been copied first."

"This Yana is also a dancer," Tariq asked.

"Yana is a principal in the Academy ballet," Divya said. "Not a godsdancer."

"The hack, do you know where it originated," Isela said quietly.

"Not yet," Niles said. "But they will find out."

"You think there's a connection," Divya murmured, looking between them.

It couldn't be a coincidence. Vanka's seat was in Saint Petersburg. According to Kyle, Yana was now in Saint Petersburg, likely against her will. A cold wave of terror washed over her. She thought of how vulnerable the human body was, fragile skin and bones. Vanka seemed the most savage of the Allegiance with the least regard for humanity.

But the pieces didn't quite fit. Yana was a ballerina. Even most godsdancers were not capable of the acrobatics and inversions Isela had mastered as part of her repertoire. Yana's only connection to Isela was their friendship. Maybe that was enough. Vanka didn't seem to be beyond pulling a petty trick like that just to stick it to Azrael.

Isela's breath paused as a memory caught up with her. Singing. The phoenix had been singing as he dragged her through the streets of Old Town. She'd caught only snatches of it on his breath, focusing on the where they were going and what he could possibly want.

"We need to go," Isela said, her eyes on Tariq. "Now."

Tariq rose with her. "Azrael's people will assist you. You will keep us updated."

Both Niles and Divya nodded. The director touched her arm. "Isela, what do you know?"

Isela hesitated, torn between comforting her dance family and keeping the secrets of the new life she now belonged to. But she was now a god, or part of one. And even a little one had more power in this world than any human being—and possibly many of its necromancers. She could do something. And she would.

She went to the school's director, knowing her eyes had gone gold and not caring. "We'll find her, Divya. I swear."

* * *

AT THE MAIN DOORS, Isela hesitated. "I need to check on something."

Tariq followed her up into the halls of the Academy. They climbed the stairs, but she took a left on the second floor instead of continuing up.

"We're not going to your apartment," he said slowly, "are we?"

"How did you guess?" She led him down a narrow, sunlit passage that connected the main building to an older stone structure.

"Well, your apartment's in the attic—"

"It was a rhetorical question." She cut him off as she opened one of the enormous doors.

The Powder Tower was one of thirteen original gateways to the city of Prague. In the fifteenth century, the Bohemian king restyled it as a welcoming entry point to the seat of his power, and for years it served as the gateway through which future royalty passed on their way to being crowned at Saint Vitus Cathedral. As the city expanded, its prominence declined until it earned its modern name by serving as a storage place for kegs of powder used in guns and explosives. Restored with the Municipal House for the Praha Dance Academy, it now served as home of the Academy library—the official and unofficial one.

Isela paused at the opposite end of the room before a small door guarding another set of stairs. "I don't suppose I can ask you to wait here for me."

Tariq crossed his arms over his chest, assessing quickly. "Only way out is through the door we came in, isn't it?"

"Or off the roof," she said with a smile. "And I haven't grown wings yet."

"Don't try today," he suggested. "Twenty minutes and I'm coming up."

Upstairs, Madeline was on her dais, a pair of thin gold-rimmed spectacles perched on the bridge of her nose. She peered into an enormous volume propped up on the desk by what looked like the top of an ornate wrought iron music stand. She blinked as Isela entered. A smile lit her face briefly before she frowned with concern.

"Bad business downstairs," she said by way of greeting.

Isela wasn't surprised she knew, but she did wonder briefly *how* Madeline always seemed to know what was going on though she hadn't so much as a telephone on her desk and no one had ever seen her outside the library walls. Madeline was the inner-library keeper, card catalog, and Isela had the strange impression, protector. Books lined the walls in a not-easily-discernible order that seemed to make perfect sense to Madeline. If the Academy had it, she knew where to find it.

Isela explained the bare bones of the incident. "The phoenix said I won't be the only one."

"And you think they're going to try to get Yana to replicate your success," Madeline finished.

The surprise must have shown on her face.

"This old girl didn't hatch out of an egg yesterday." Madeline smiled at her, flowing from behind her circular desk on the dais to the shelves. She muttered as she went, whether to herself or in conversation, Isela wasn't quite sure.

She emerged from the shelves in short order with four books of varying age judging by the layer of dust and the decay of their bindings.

"What you did was a conversation between you and your little gold friend. Can't just be copied like an old Xerox machine," she muttered, flipping through pages.

"What if they make her—force her—to try anyway?"

Madeline's humor faded, her expression grim. "Can't force a dancer. Not the way it works."

"But there're lots of ways to 'motivate' a dancer to try."

"Got to find her fast then." Madeline nodded, memories of times Isela had only heard of crossing her face with such immediacy that Isela wondered again exactly how old Madeline really was. She flipped pages of a book in an arcane language, found what she wanted, and moved to the next book. "Mirroring is a powerful tool."

That was how it began, wasn't it? The golden shadow appearing during her dances for Azrael, acting as a mirror to her every move.

Gradually their connection had gone from tenuous to direct. Eventually the golden shadow had been able to come to her outside the dance. "If she's using my choreography, can I track it somehow?"

Madeline looked pleased. "Now that is thinking outside of the box, girl. Good for you."

She turned her attention back to her books. Isela fought the urge to check the clock as she thought of Tariq's promise. She could always telepathically shout down at him, but knowing Tariq, he wouldn't be satisfied until he had eyes on her.

At last Madeline removed her spectacles, letting them dangle from the gold chain around her neck and onto her ample bosom. She closed her book, shaking her head.

"All godsdancers have something special, something that makes them different from any other dancers," she said firmly. "Trouble is nobody knows quite what it is. You can only train so far. It's why so many who begin fail to advance. And you, Isela Vogel, were the best of the best. A ballerina's going to need a little help to get anywhere near what you did. Whatever they give her to cross that bridge is going to kill her, if the god doesn't do it first."

Madeline watched her face. Seeing something that satisfied her, she began gathering her books.

"Better hurry, *ma chère*," Madeline called over her shoulder as she maneuvered into the stacks. "Lover boy is getting impatient downstairs."

* * *

"THE PHOENIX WAS SINGING in Russian when we ran through the streets," Isela said as Tariq whipped the car into traffic.

Premature winter darkness had settled while they were inside, leaving the city illuminated and shining in the reflected streetlamps and signage. He took a left, heading for the Štefanik Bridge.

"Yana, the recordings... I'll bet if they find the source of that hack, it's Vanka. And this all started with the phoenix. We've got to get him to talk."

Tariq paused at the red light. The flashing light from the tram crossing illuminated his face in the dim car. "But your friend is not a godsdancer."

"No, but she was an easy one to snatch because of her family's connections," Isela said, pounding the dashboard. "And she's connected *to me*."

Tariq opened his mouth to speak. The light changed, and he started across the bridge instead.

Headlights shone through his window. Isela's mind struggled to make sense of why a car would be coming at them from that direction as her throat constricted on a warning. Tariq jammed the brake and jerked the wheel, taking the brunt of the impact on the driver's side. The front tire and panel crumpled and the airbags went off at once, cocooning them in white.

The other car kept coming. They slid sideways. Unlike the stone bridges crossing the river near the oldest parts of town, the Štefánik barriers were metal and cable. The posts screamed with tension. Another smash and the door panel squeezed her into Tariq. Cables snapped. The car tangled briefly in the metal posts before being forced over the bridge.

They hit the surface upside down, floating briefly as water began to pour in through the smashed passenger-side door. Isela shook Tariq, limp in his seat belt. In the dim light, she could see blood pouring down his forehead and the shining bit of white that must be skull showing through. The car rocked as it sank. The display and lights flickered. Soon they would be in darkness.

Scrabbling through the glove box, she found a little hammer designed to break glass, exactly where Rory had promised it would be. The opposite end held a little blade under a hook, and she slipped it around her seat belt with a yank. The fabric gave, dumping her onto the roof of the car. She reached up, fingers slipping in the water, and fumbled for Tariq's. He fell out of his seat and into the accumulating water. It was icy—already she felt her body beginning to shudder.

Need heat, she thought, and immediately felt warmer. Her fingers scrabbled for the pulse at his throat, but he was already coming around. He groaned, a hand going to the bloody gash on his head.

Even with the airbags, the impact should have crushed bones. She felt the current tugging on the car; unbelievably, they hadn't hit the bottom yet. She batted the airbags out of the way to see through the windshield. The water pressed into her chest. Headlights illuminated the murky depths, which were thick with flotsam. The bumper hit something and the car spun, careening out of the main flow and into an eddy. Now might be their chance.

What she saw next froze her in place.

Illuminated as they were by faltering headlights, she first mistook them for misshapen people covered in mud. But that couldn't be. For one thing, they were all just standing motionless, oblivious to the current or the cold water.

Her mind instantly went to an image from a Chinese emperor's tomb full of a life-sized terra-cotta army. Hundreds of clay men and horses all lined up in rows like toy soldiers.

The car bumped into one, breaking off the head and arms. The broken limbs spun off in the current before dissolving into river muck. There had to be a hundred here. Perhaps more beyond the beams of the headlights. They didn't move or respond to the car or its occupants in the slightest, but she had the eerie sensation that they were somehow aware of her.

"What the fuck?" Tariq's words drew her attention back.

Isela'd never been so relieved to hear another voice. The water was up to their necks. The car appeared to be stopped now, snagged just off the field of mud men. Tariq stared out the windshield

"It's the creepiest shit I've ever seen." Isela tore her gaze away to check him. Already the cut on his head was no longer pouring blood. No need for stitches. "What if we woke them up?"

"I think we'd know by now. Time to go."

Isela shivered at the image of the silent, water-shrouded army. Drowning in the broken car sounded extraordinarily appealing compared to swimming through mud men. If she could drown.

"You're not afraid to get dirty, are you?" His words burbled as the water lapped his lips. Isela sealed her mouth shut and glared at him. Immortal or not, she was not taking any chances on the river water.

His mental voice filled her head. *One, two, three!*

They dove. The last of the air bubbles dissipated into the murky river. He pushed her out of the ruined car. His legs still weren't working properly, so she wrapped her arms around his chest, kicking as he stroked. She spared one more glance at the twisted metal folded among the ghostly shapes they left behind.

The mud men never moved, but she couldn't shake the sensation that they were being watched.

They broke the surface south of the bridge, halfway to the older Čech Bridge that crossed the river from the Jewish quarter to the bottom of Letná Park. In the distance, lights and the faint noise of the crowd gathering marked where they'd gone over the Štefanik. Here the cobblestone walkway was below street level, and the heavy shadows were broken irregularly by circles of light from the street above. She started swimming for the east side of the river. Tariq held her arm as they approached the shadowy hulls of the boats moored along the walkway below the street level. This time of evening there would be a few lovers strolling or tourists returning from a dinner cruise. Farther down, music poured from one of the boats that had been transformed into a bar, but here the dark was oppressive. Unable to shake the image of those motionless figures below the surface, Isela tugged free. She wanted out of the water.

At the bank she gripped the edge and dragged herself up onto the stone path. She turned to look back for Tariq. Something out of the corner of her eye flickered. Instinct drove her to roll as a blade passed through the air where she had been. It clattered onto the stone, sending up sparks. She cried out, but her body already fell into a counter, slipping the blade from the small of her back without thought. She rolled to her feet, skittering backward.

Gregor's voice came, embedded in her muscle memory. *Know your opponent. What they are will tell you how they fight. And how to fight them.*

Three men moved between her and the river, dressed in black with the telltale lack of breath and the scent that meant they were undead. She would have known right away if they had been Azrael's. These belonged to another necromancer. She scanned them, searching for some sign of whom they called master. Unlike the movies, Isela knew the last thing the zombies wanted was to eat her brains. The first thing seemed to be to see her dead. She put her back to the stone wall.

Her adversaries were utterly silent, their faces blank except for the grotesque expressions of delight. She knew the most useful zombies were the ones whose natural aptitude in life matched their service in death. From the way these moved, lightly on the balls of their feet and with no extraneous movement, they had been killers before being turned.

Isela flipped the blade in her palm. "Come on then, you ugly fucks."

A blade connected with her own as she blocked a strike, the vibration rattling up her arm with a high-pitched whine as she slipped sideways away from the second blow. He was strong, but she was faster.

Learn to feint, to give only enough to lure. Gregor again, a memory as familiar as the taste of her own adrenaline-tinged blood in the back of her throat. *Keep something in reserve.*

She dropped her shoulder, sliding backward. The wielder of the bladed staff fell for it, darting in. The weapon's reach could be deadly, but he overextended and she slid in close, jamming her short blade into the soft spot below his chin. She blocked his staff arm with her elbow and drove her second blade between his ribs. He jerked backward when she yanked both blades free, twitching as he collapsed to the cobblestones.

A glancing blow struck her shoulder, nothing compared to the ones that had knocked her to the sand of the sparring ring. She didn't flinch, following the strike and spinning to plant one blade in the second zombie's armpit, severing tendons and rendering the joint useless.

Two proved a challenge. She used them against each other, tangling them up as she avoided blows. She lost a blade, twisted in the rib cage of one of the two remaining zombies. She cursed her mistake—zombies didn't feel pain, and though they could be mechanically disabled by broken bones or severed tendons, the only way to really stop one was to silence the brain. Decapitation worked well. She suddenly understood the Aegis's preference for big bladed weapons.

Isela spun and planted her short blade in the second's eye. He twitched, rattling to stillness. She relieved him of his sword, taking his head in one long strike. The body stumbled into the last zombie. She took advantage of the traction, plunging the sword into his chest and aiming a kick at his jaw. The brittle snap of his neck vertebrae sent him to one knee.

Tariq staggered forward with the bladed staff and severed the zombie's head. He braced the blunt end of the staff against the cobblestones, leaning heavily on it.

"This is why I wanted you—," he panted, one hand on his ribs, "—to wait for the all clear."

Isela retrieved her blades but left them bared. "Can we skip the lecture?"

Her wet clothes and hair clung to her. They heaved, back-to-back in the reprise. If she concentrated, she could sense the spots that represented an absence of life. Zombies. She whirled her senses around them. Two more headed their direction from the north. And something else—something not human but not zombie either.

"Demon?"

"Maybe," he said, pleased. "We keep moving."

"Are they tracking us the same way?"

He shook his head. "Zombies can't. They work by smell. The other, perhaps. Let's go."

Tariq limped hard and his shoulder didn't quite sit right. She knew from experience that expedited healing didn't dull the pain. They ran straight into a second trio of zombies. Isela swore, dropping into a defensive stance.

Before she could engage, two went down, taken from behind. Gus moved like a gymnast, running up her opponents like obstacles on a course and riding them to their doom. The third spun too late. A long black braid whipped around as its owner cartwheeled, dropping the zombie with twin kicks before doing away with its head. She paused to glare at them both.

"Excellent timing." Tariq jerked his chin behind them. "We've got company."

"Get her to the Čech. The others will meet you there," Gus ordered, starting back the way they had come. Turquoise flares swirled between her fingertips and down to her slim, deadly blades to lick the pavement like waves. The river water churned against the bank as she passed. She glanced back once. "What are you standing there for? *Move!*"

Tariq dragged Isela toward the street level.

She resisted. "We can't leave her."

"That's exactly what we're doing," he said.

"That thing, coming—"

"Gus is more than capable of handling herself."

Isela resisted for a stride or two, then fell in, running beside him. The night was reduced to the cold air bristling in her lungs and the uneven cobblestones beneath her feet. They followed the easy curve of the riverbank south until the Čech Bridge loomed before them, narrow stairway rising toward the street level along the riverbank. Between them and the stairs a pair of zombies patrolled.

Tariq pushed her sideways into the shadows along the high stone wall. "Wait until I've engaged them, then get to the bridge."

Isela waited. Tariq limped cheerily toward the zombies, whistling.

When they were occupied, she ran. She glanced back once at the uneven footsteps behind her to see Tariq salute with a grin that resembled a rictus of pain.

Tariq careened around the stone pillar at the top of the steps and onto the bridge, almost crashing into Isela where she waited for him. It was empty. Tariq swayed on his feet. "You were supposed to run."

"And abandon the Dauntless?" Isela threw his arm over her shoulder. "Not a chance."

They started at a hobbling walk. Ahead in the darkness, the massive functioning metronome sculpture that crowned the hill in the center of the park kept pace in the shadows.

"I'm supposed to be protecting you," he said when an uneven step sent him into her side.

"You did," she said. "That move with the car before it hit… it should have been me who was smashed to bits."

"Well, I can take it," he said wryly.

She glanced back at the sense of something emerging from the shadows behind them. She gasped at the misshapen bodies not quite visible. "Demons."

Tariq nodded, moving faster. Ahead on the bridge, a squad of figures strode purposefully toward them. Isela tensed before she recognized the brothers. Dory grinned from the lead. Tariq sighed. "Cavalry's here."

On his left, Aleifr flipped his ax and drew a fat curved blade from his shoulder holster. Opposite, a spiky-haired Asian man seemed to disappear as they moved through a shadow, becoming indistinguishable to her eye before appearing at the edge of another shadow. This must be Azrael's head of intelligence, Ito. She knew him only by reputation, and though he was dwarfed by the bigger men, that stealth trick must be an enormous advantage. Bringing up the rear, Rory looked ready to chew cobblestones.

Tariq took his own weight and flipped his sword to the ready. "Go."

Isela jogged toward them, her mouth open to reply. She'd almost reached them when Dory dove for her, closing the distance in a blur. He snatched her up by the waist, spinning as he held her to his chest. The force of a knife's impact was dulled by the jerk of his body.

Isela's elbows slammed into the cobblestones beneath her as they fell, and the bright flare of pain blinded her for a moment. He landed half on top of her, his weight kicking the breath from her rib cage. Face-to-face on the cobblestones, she watched the last of a breath whistle past his lips, accompanied by the scent of fresh blood.

The corner of his mouth jerked with his order. "Stay down."

A keening protest she didn't recognize as her own voice formed a single word as she rolled him aside, blood splashing her palms. "Nononono."

The Aegis immediately fell into a guard position around them. Fully visible and solid now, the pack of demons left the shadows, circling. Isela pressed her hands around the blade protruding from Dory's chest. It burned with a curious, sucking sensation. She thought of Tariq's gift and wondered if something similar had been done to this blade to make it more powerful. Acting on instinct, she grabbed the hilt and pulled. The hilt bit into her hand, marking her, but now she could see it for what it was. The geas flared to life with her touch. She let the blade drop, clattering to the ground.

Soul eater, Gold said. *The geas to separate the soul from the body. This was meant for us, Isela.*

We have to save him.

He's bound by it now; it ties him to death.

Than we cut him free. Isela felt for the edges of that gray space.

An engine roared, and a familiar white Range Rover approached them from the bridge, swinging a wide circle. Isela couldn't breathe. All she could see was Dory's flat black eyes staring through her. The breath gurgled in his chest. Dory's hand fumbled up for hers, and blood stuck their fingers together.

Her fingers squeezed his hand.

His tightened briefly. "Go, Issy."

"Get her to the car," Rory shouted.

Tariq gripped her shoulders, but Isela fought him.

"I'm not leaving him here."

Tariq forced her gaze to his. "Don't let his sacrifice be for nothing."

"No sacrifices. Not for me." Isela dropped into the In Between. In that moment she was aware of all of them, yet apart. Outlined in the distance of the flat, sweeping darkness, she saw them on the bridge— Tariq blown back by her transition and picking himself up off the cobblestones. Azrael's Aegis, ready to fight—and die—for her. Gus, fighting in the dark alone against zombies and a thing made of night-mares and teeth.

She focused on the body under her hands. Dory was here too, but he had already gone solid, cold as marble. She searched around, the wind battering stray bits of her hair and sending them into her face. She swore, batting them away as she narrowed her eyes, extending her sight as far as it could go.

There. Gold sharpened her vision.

A bright pearl glow, almost unrecognizable for the sickly green binding that covered it from head to toe. Dory. It dragged him as he writhed against it. Isela sprang to her feet. Running. She needed a knife. What had Tariq said? When she reached for it, the hilt of the Damascus steel found her hand. The weight of it grounded her. It was real. She was real. This was real.

She caught Dory in a flying leap, not enough to stop the momentum of whatever had him, but now she had him too. She swung around him, ignoring the burn of the ropes where she touched them, searching for the source of the binding. Six or eight long tenta-cles closed around him. She sliced down. The first two fell away. She slashed and sawed until the last whipped away into the darkness.

Dory tumbled to the ground and she flipped, landing on her toes away from him. He writhed, weaker now. Working more carefully, she sliced the binding around his head. It fell away like smoke. Dory beneath was a luminescent glow, like the skin of a pearl.

Hurry. We won't be alone for long.

Isela glanced up. Around the edges of her vision, figures shuffled in the shadows, curious and wary. And hungry. She set to work on the binding. *Demons?*

They're called blights. Lost things. Untethered souls, malformed demons, summoning spells gone wrong. They don't have enough power to move on, so they're drawn to power that appears in the In Between. It feeds them.

Freed, Dory's soul lay still and glowing for a long moment. Then it began to fade. Isela grabbed at it, but her hands passed through.

What do I do?

You freed it from the spell, but the blade caught him in the heart. I'm not a necromancer, Isela. I don't know.

You brought me back.

Your body was intact.

Isela thrust her body backward, rolling to her feet and picking up speed.

What are you doing?

She leaped, legs kicking out in a grand jetè, and landed back in her body. The world spun until she forced herself to focus. The Aegis battled demons around her in slow motion, the growls and snarls and cries of combat an incoherent din. She turned to Dory. Crimson seeped between her fingertips to the cobblestones. She slid her fingers into the gaping wound, feeling for his heart. Bone scraped her knuckles until the tough muscle pushed back. *I've always been shit with a needle. Even when I danced en pointe, I traded favors to avoid having to stitch my own ribbons.*

Do your best. It's not real.

In her mind's eye, she placed a needle and thread and her own hands, stitching the ragged tear in a bright cloth patterned with luminous birds of paradise. She drove the needle, pulling diligently, with all the patience in the world. When it was done, she sat back, hands on Dory's closed chest. His eyes remained open, the flat black stare of his pupils empty.

"Come on, Dory," she murmured. "You're tougher than this."

Now call him back.

She thought of the shimmering soul on the ground in the In Between. She pushed herself there. This time it took effort to stagger to her feet.

What did one say to call a soul back into a body? She opened her mouth, closed it again.

Blights had begun to circle the fallen warrior, their hunger evident. What had Dante said? *Do not underestimate the power a word spoken on instinct with intention. All spells begin as such, and all beings of power understand that.*

Of course, he had ended with a warning. *Great things can be accomplished on impulse, but foolish, dangerous ones are more likely.*

Isela closed her eyes. She would have to take her chances. She thought of Dory's laugh and his bright smile, the small ways he made her feel welcome and at home in Azrael's world.

"I call you back to the life you've left behind you. To the brother who loves you. To the necromancer who trusts you beyond others. To me." Her hands stretched out of their own accord. "I call you to me. Come back. Please."

The sensation of power moving through her came from a great distance. She bowed into the strain of it, letting it flow through her. She closed her eyes and felt her balance give. Her senses shifted, vertigo hitting her as she fell too far from where she stood.

"I got you, Issy."

The scent of blood flooded her nostrils, stuck to her cheek. But where her ear pressed to his hastily stitched chest, a heartbeat pounded. It was the sweetest sound she'd ever heard.

Dory was on his feet, carrying her easily in one arm. Pain ricocheted through her skull and out to her extremities. She vomited.

Dory chuckled. "Well, we can't smell much worse."

The sound of fighting was a distant cacophony. Dory ran, his machete in one hand, her curled in the crook of his arm. He fought his way free and flung her into the back of the Range Rover. Her last sight was his face, beaming. She lunged at the door and he slammed it in her face. He hammered the roof of the car. In the driver's seat, Tyler hit the gas and swung the wheel, leaving the others behind.

Isela curled up on the back seat and surrendered to darkness.

CHAPTER FIFTEEN

P ain dragged her flailing back to consciousness.
I'm sorry, Issy, Gold whispered. *You pushed yourself too far. It's going to hurt for a while.*

Tenderness framed her joints in halos of ache. Icy fire raced through her as her extremities sent pain shooting into her spine and up to her skull. It roared through her, rendering her thoughtless. She clenched her teeth on a moan.

A hand closed over hers. "Welcome back, Issy."

Dory. She remembered his heart in her hands and sobbed. His voice came again, softly at first and then growing more steady. It was joined by its twin, even richer and more beautiful, if that was possible. What they carried between them was more chant than a song, but an unmistakable melody framed the words. It surrounded her, the origin of the voices lost in the darkness. She clung to the sound, dragging her awareness onto it like a raft on rough seas.

It's about a village, small but plentiful. Gold translated when she began to slide back into waves of pain. *With a gentle breeze and beautiful children, a long sea journey to find new land. A victorious return. Here... I think this won't be too hard on you, it's temporary.*

Isela felt something turn over in her mind, a slight sideways shift, and the words became clear. Not translated, but as though she had always known the language.

A little trick, that's all. Rest now. And listen.

She drowsed in the sound and the steady repeat of rhythm and melody. When she woke again, a sliver of light poked through the heavy curtains. She winced. She lay on the couch in the bedroom, a blanket thrown over her. The room was empty.

In the bathroom she squinted in the dim light until she was able to open the window shade. The clothes from the night before had stiffened. The stink of blood and sweat mixed with dried river water. Pain had been dialed down to a steady low-grade ache.

She knew pain. She had been twenty-four when her hip first began to ache after dances. Gradually the pain became her constant companion. She hid it well, but Divya saw her limp once and sent her to the Academy physician. Looking at the X-rays and going over MRI results, she'd compartmentalized the diagnosis. She told Divya the doctor was content with a short rest. Only Kyle knew the doctor advised her that surgery would be the only way to ensure she was able to walk, never mind dance, past her thirties. She'd set herself to learning her pain as fully as she had learned the moves required to make physical requests for gods. She learned its shape, its weight. Understood where it rooted in her brain and how to build a wall around it that barred it from most everything. She learned to hide the signs; to move slowly with controlled grace as a godsdancer of great renown. Let them believe she had bought her own hype, that she considered herself something better than the rest of them. As long as they didn't know the truth. She had a core group of friends she trusted and a family she supported with the money from the patrons she danced for. That was all that mattered.

But if sometimes, deep in the night, the wall came down and she lay hand in hand with pain, that was between her and the pillow soaked with tears by morning. That was the way of walls. They had a way of coming down at the most inconvenient times. And they all came down eventually.

She couldn't lie in bed all morning. Yana was in danger. Another necromancer had violated Azrael's territory. A phoenix lay dying in the aedis. And there had been no word from Azrael. She hadn't viscerally understood of what kind of danger he might be going into, other than in the abstract sense she always had when Vanka was part of the conversation. But last night had brought it home in a tangible way.

She shuddered. She peeled everything off and ran the hottest bath she could stand, sinking into the tub. She combed the worst of the tangles out of her hair, arms shaking with even that small effort. In the closet she found one of Azrael's T-shirts, pressing it to her nose for a long moment. She froze at the sight of the row of button-down shirts, the slacks on hangers, and tried to breathe. Fear dropped her to her knees. She hadn't even said goodbye.

Azrael, where are you? Please just be too busy to answer me.

She remembered how Gregor's words had guided her as she fought. She had no doubt that if she had acquitted herself well at all the night before it was because of his teaching. He had Azrael's back. And Lysippe, descended from Amazons, was Azrael's daughter in all but blood. They would protect him, and as she had seen firsthand, they would die for him. She had to hope that would be enough.

Come back to me. I don't care how long it takes or in what condition. Just come back.

She dressed slowly in baggy leggings and a butter-soft sweater. Even the cloth rubbed her skin raw. Hunger sawed into her stomach, and it took her a moment to realize it'd been triggered by the scent of food. As she came down the stairs, she heard movement in the kitchen.

She rounded the corner and paused. "Rory?"

The more solemn of the brothers moved around Azrael's immaculate, underutilized chef's kitchen. Saliva pooled in her mouth as the scent of bacon frying flooded her nostrils. His face did not lighten, not exactly, but he looked less... thunderous. The big red apron emblazoned with a palm leaf and a stylized island over the words DA ROCK helped.

"Please sit."

Her place had been set. She took a long drink of orange juice, wondering at the pulp that clung to her teeth. How long had it been since she'd had fresh-squeezed orange juice? She nibbled at some fruit, wildly out of season and all the more delicious for that. He came by with a pan, scraping a pile of eggs beaten into a fluffy yellow scramble onto her plate and setting down a paper bag that sent out the amazing aroma of freshly baked croissant.

"For me?" she said dumbly.

"Eat," he ordered. "I've seen stronger-looking sticks."

"Thanks," she said wryly but reached for the jam and a knife. "I think."

Her stomach grumbled. Between hastily chewed bites, she asked, "How's Dory?"

"I sent him home to rest." Rory returned with pan-fried slices of ham and a bowl of oatmeal. "He's alive."

Isela wondered where she would put it all, but the thought didn't stop her from trying. When he returned with his own plate and a cup of coffee, he grunted, pleased at the sight of the decimation of her eggs and bread.

"More eggs?"

"No way," she said. "I'm saving that spot for pig. Is everyone else okay after last night?"

He grunted again and took a few bites from his own plate. They ate in companionable silence, and Isela felt a bit of herself return with every bite. Along with a sense of wonder at what had happened the night before. She'd brought a man back from death. Stolen him back from a spell intended to rip his soul from his body.

That was very brave of you, Isela, Gold said. *And foolish. So many things could have happened.*

But they hadn't.

You're learning how to use my presence, Gold said, satisfied. *That's good.*

"I was seventeen when I met Azrael," Rory said. "My parents wanted me to follow in my father's footsteps, to lead. But I hungered for more, the desire to go further. And here comes this strange man who looked young but was so much older. We fought together, he and I. And when he asked me to join him, to become... what I am, I had only one condition."

Isela's attention on her plate drifted. She set down her fork.

"Dory and I shared our mother's womb." His voice cracked slightly. "He was born first, but in every way I was the elder. He was my shadow, but he also lit my way. Our names mean the moon that follows the sun and the sun that trails the moon. I would not leave him behind. For four hundred years, I have looked after him, and he after me. And together we protect Azrael. Last night..." His voice fell away, overcome with emotion.

Tears sprang to her eyes and she blinked furiously. "You think I don't know..." She shook her head as she struggled for words. "How *little* I deserve either of you and the sacrifice you are willing to make? How could I not do everything to save him?"

"Please." He palmed away the wetness on his cheeks and met her eyes. "I have not been kind to you. I have not trusted you or your influence on Azrael. But last night... what you did... for my brother. I have never seen courage like that. I am ashamed. I can never repay you."

Isela broke, her face in her hands. When Rory touched her shoulder, she folded into him. It wasn't so much an embrace as being swallowed whole by a mountain. He smelled of bacon and eggs, and beneath that the clean ocean and white sand and driftwood.

"Thought I was going to miss you guys hugging it out, eh?"

Rory jumped up and managed to carefully deposit Isela in her own chair before barking something in Samoan as his brother closed the door in his wake, strolling to the table.

"Sit down, man." Dory grinned, and to Isela muttered, "He takes this older-brother thing way too seriously."

Isela gaped. He looked as though the night before had been nothing more than business as usual. If she hadn't known better... If she hadn't *felt*— Wait, what was it she was feeling? She explored the thread that tugged gently on her as he grew closer. His smile softened and he tugged a chair into place before her.

"Hey, Issy. Can't thank you enough. For what you did."

He winced as he sat, and sensation tugged her again, as if a thread connected directly to the heartbeat in her chest.

Oh no.

Oh no what? Isela snapped, trying not to panic.

She could feel him breathing. She touched the slight, distant pain on her pectoral. It felt like a thin line, tight and itching faintly as it healed. He tried to catch her hands, but she shook him off. His fingers fell away as she split the fabric over his left pectoral, revealing a long ragged line of healing flesh that bore the marks of hasty, skill-less stitching.

She hesitated, but he covered her hand with his own, pressing down. She felt the pressure on the ache of her own chest.

"It will take a bit longer to heal than the rest of me." Dory shrugged casually. "Because the blade was spelled."

Shit. Isela jerked her hand away. *What did you do?*

Me? Gold laughed. *You insisted on going after him. I didn't do anything. You spoke the words to bring him back. To Azrael, and to his brother too. And to you... at the very end. You said "to me."*

The door opened, Tariq shrugging guiltily at Rory's glare as if to say *I tried.* Gus stalked in behind him before she ascended, catlike, into the chair at the head of the table. Dante detoured to the coffee machine and returned with two cups, sliding one to Gus before making himself comfortable and opening his notebook.

Rory rose to his feet and stormed into the kitchen after Tariq. "I told you to keep him—"

"Short of chopping off his legs, how did you think I was going to stop him?" Tariq muttered. "He's avowed. You don't keep them apart now unless *she* commands it."

Isela stared, touching the spot on her chest that ached dully.

Dory looked chagrined. "I'm sorry to cause you pain, Issy."

"Oh shit."

Dante cleared his throat. "That's not the traditional response."

"It's not the end of the world," Tariq said. "How about a plate of eggs for me?"

Rory slammed a pan down on the stove. "Eggs are gone; shame you don't eat ham."

Tariq grimaced. "Unclean beasts, pigs."

Rory grunted. "More for me. Isela?"

"Please." Isela cleared her throat with juice as Tariq made himself comfortable at the table. "You look like normal."

"Is that a compliment?" Tariq plucked half a croissant off her plate. "Are you finishing that?"

"Well, last night you had a flap of skin hanging off your skull." Isela gestured at her eyebrow. "Your shoulder looked broken. And yes, I was going to eat that. But you should help yourself."

He had the grace to look surprised when Rory set a plate of eggs and fruit down in front of him.

"Dislocated," he said, digging in. "I'm tough to kill. Though I do miss the days when it was just horses and carriages. I think I ruptured my spleen. Again."

"Azrael's going to freak out." Isela buried her face in her hands.

Tariq paused between mouthfuls to shrug. "Azrael has what... nine now? A bit excessive if you ask me."

Isela didn't have words. She could feel Dory's heartbeat, a counterpoint to her own and aching as it healed. "What if I say no?"

They all looked at her.

Gus sighed. "Apparently she turned Azrael down at first too. What is it with these mortals? Back in the old days, they begged for our favor."

"Issy, you began the bond when you brought him back," Dante said, patting her arm for silence. "That may have been the mechanism by which you were successful. Though it's traditional for the contract to be declared *before* the binding."

"It's not that I'm not grateful." Isela pointed her words at Gus before returning her attention to Dory and that lingering ache. "I don't want to take your will, your choices. You chose Azrael."

"My brother chose Azrael." Dory shrugged. "I choose you. Strength and shield. The strength when you cannot strike the blow. The shield to break so that you may live."

"Think of it like an exchange," Dante said. "He gets your protection as well. You become a battery for him, and you will feel his pain. And the rest of the vow is yours to make."

It would be good to have an ally, Isela. Someone loyal to us first.

"Do we have to do this?" Isela whispered to Dory. Her voice trembled.

"Don't be afraid, Issy," he murmured back. He placed his hand over his heart. "I owe you my life. I have my strength and my speed. That's enough. I give my service freely."

"How long will he serve," Dante prompted quietly.

"As long as he wants to and not a day more," Isela said automatically. Even Dory looked disappointed in her. Isela sighed. "Fifty years with the option to renew. Take it or leave it."

"Done," Dory said.

"I give you my protection. And the ability to draw on my power to fuel your gift. Deal?" She stuck out her hand.

"Jesus Cristo," Gus muttered.

"Blood exchanges aren't done anymore, Gus," Dante whispered. "Archaic if you ask me. Never mind unhygienic."

"It's her Aegis." Tariq shrugged, pushing his empty plate aside. "When you pick your first, you can bleed them like a goat if it pleases you."

Dory's hand swallowed hers to the wrist.

That was it. She couldn't exactly name the moment, it came and passed, breaking over her like a wave as the heart that had, a beat ago, seemed like a discordant rhythm, synced with her own. The ache subsided somewhat, and she could feel the exchange of energy moving toward him. Even when released, it was there like a single thread connecting them over space and time. Dory leaned forward, and she knew his movement instinctively. She tilted to meet him, closing her eyes as their foreheads touched. He spoke again, and now the distinct musicality of the language was as familiar as her own. He gave her his lineage, his place in his bloodline, and his name and, at last, claiming her as his family. She locked it in her heart with blurry eyes as he sat back, smiling.

"Don't cry, *tuafafine*," Dory said. "I always wanted a little sister."

Rory pushed a dishcloth to her side of the table. "Truth."

"Yes, but…" Isela laughed shakily, wiping her face. "What the hell am I going to do with another brother?"

Dory laughed so hard he planted his elbows on his knees and braced himself. Rory shook his head, patting his brother on the shoulder. "She's a funny one." He gave Isela's shoulder a squeeze. "He's all yours now, little sister. Take care of him."

"With everything I have," Isela said.

"Touching," Gus said wryly, crossing an ankle over her knee and setting a parcel down on the table. "Now that everyone's here, this is an Allegiance weapon. Guesses?"

Even beneath the wrapping and layered in carefully applied containment wards, Isela could feel the malignancy of its power. Soul Eater. They'd cleaned it, but she could feel the psychic impression of Dory's blood.

Isela reached out to the parcel.

"Careful, lady," Dante said. "It is a very potent instrument."

Isela flipped her palm over. Fading gray lines crisscrossed her palms, a few wrapping around her wrist and starting up her forearm. Tariq winced.

She studied them impassively for a moment. "These happened in the In Between, cutting Dory free from whatever spell that knife contains."

"What happens there is reflected here," Dante said. "It is the price we pay for journeying into a place living things don't belong."

She returned to the knife, using her fork to peel away the wrapping. It looked so ordinary, a finely made but simple blade, made for throwing, not display. The voices of the others faded. A rush of desert heat and the sea and a stand of temples in the rocks. She looked up, meeting Gus's eyes, repeating her vision.

Gus didn't smile, but satisfaction softened her glare. "Petra."

Tariq corrected her. "Raqmu."

"Kadijah fancies herself a god," Dante supplied. "She made the old city her seat."

"Reports claim she has spent much time lately in the north," Rory said. "On the Caspian Sea."

Tariq smiled. "The Kazar."

"Close to Vanka's borders," Gus concluded. "Ito's looking into it now."

"Kadijah prefers to keep her hands clean." Tariq shook his head. "She's too close to Azrael and not powerful enough alone to risk his ire."

"And yet." Gus gestured to the knife.

"Where does rest of the Allegiance stand?" Tariq asked.

"The Nightfeather claims Paolo came sniffing around for an alliance," Rory said. "Raymond was unwilling to be persuaded to breach Azrael's vow, but undoubtedly Paolo will have tried to recruit others to his cause."

"When did Azrael talk to Raymond?" Isela said.

Eyes slid away from her.

"Takumi has closed his borders," Rory said of the necromancer who held the greater part of the Asian coast and islands. "And Emma was never a friend of Paolo. Oceania will not interfere."

"Gola *is* a friend of Kadijah," Tariq said.

Gola, the kindly grandmother-looking necromancer from the African subcontinent. The one who liked to let her zombies mummify a bit before reactivating them. Isela had never spoken more than a word to her, but the thought of the woman made her skin crawl.

"It appears the Lionesses no longer run together." Rory filled in the silence. "It may be a territorial dispute, but Gola reinforced her borders. No one crosses."

"Effectively cutting her off from land routes," Dante said. "She needs those routes for exports. That must have been a helluva dispute."

"Gola's shipping and naval force is unparalleled," Tariq drawled. "She'll survive."

"Still." Rory absently nudged a discarded rind of melon around his plate with his knife. "It will be a costly break for both of them. And considering how close they've been for two hundred years, it's worth curiosity. Azrael's been gathering intelligence on the potential of Gola as an ally."

"An ally?" Isela barked, sitting back. First Raymond, now "mama mummy"? "From the Allegiance? They showed up here—"

"Most of them bowed to pressure from Vanka," Rory said.

"Or persuasion from Paolo," Tariq added.

Gus sucked her teeth bitterly. "Which makes them cowards at best, and at worst opportunists."

For once, Isela found herself agreeing with Gus.

"You must understand, Isela." Tariq spread his palms on the table as if to indicate the expansiveness of a subject so large he didn't know where to begin. "Our lot has always been solitary. As we grow more powerful, it can be difficult for us to be in proximity to one another, which breeds secrecy and paranoia. In olden days there were many more, but they destroyed themselves, overreaching their power—"

"Or were killed off by one another," Gus added darkly.

"Thanks, Gus." Tariq sighed. "With the codes and registry requirements the Allegiance put in place when it ascended, we've learned that there are fewer and fewer necromancers being discovered every year. And none born after the wall between gods and humans was erected."

"Inadvertently proving the theory that necromancers are the offspring of gods and humans," Dante said.

Isela sat back in her chair. "No gods dancing with humans. No new necromancers. And you can't have children… the old-fashioned way." She looked around the table. "But you're immortal. Some of you. All of you. Are you?"

"Only the most powerful," Tariq said. "It was not arbitrary that there are only eight in the Allegiance. Eight capable of creating the barrier between gods and this world. Only they will survive mortality."

"Unless they kill each other off." Gus shrugged. "The vow Azrael made was heard around the world. They're working against him, *and* they attacked his consort in his territory. It's on now. And about damn time if you ask me."

"A war between us serves no one," Tariq said.

"And you guys," Isela said, still fixated.

"Gus and Tariq likely will achieve immortality—unless, as Gus put it, they get themselves killed." Dante tipped an imaginary cap to her.

He held up a hand when Gus would have protested, two bright spots of emotion under her eyes. His face, serene with acceptance, rose in a smile. He patted her fisted hand gently until she loosened her fingers and he could circle them with his own. He murmured something to her, and she shook her head. When he looked back at Isela, his eyes held no fear.

"I am grateful that Azrael took me on—it's given me this much longer," he said. "I have no regrets."

Azrael might not have been able to father children, but he had created a family. These men and women weren't just his servants and protégés. He'd given them titles and roles and contracts and protected them until they were able to fend for themselves. But all that only served to codify the seeds he'd planted in them. They had grown together, first as allies and later to depend on one another in that bond that many claimed blood bestowed but in reality was rarer than that. None of it could have come had they not seen it, or been given it, first.

Azrael didn't crave dominion or power. He did what was needed to keep those he cared for safe—no matter the cost. The idea that necromancers couldn't love at all was laughable, she realized. The choice not to might be more concrete than a human could hope to make, but love was the only thing clear as dawn in this room of murky alliances and mysterious enemies. It began with Azrael and bloomed at this table. The loyalty of brothers beyond death, the two necromancers giving comfort with a simple touch, and her own heart, thumping against her rib cage in a rhythmic call of longing for him. Isela took a deep breath to steady herself.

Now she understood the fight before he left. It still burned. They were going to have a serious conversation about withholding information.

"The greenhouse?" Tariq asked.

"Empty," Gus grunted. "Áleifr, Chris, and I paid a visit after we got the bridge under control—"

"You took my brother?" Isela gasped.

"He was already assigned patrol with Aleifr," Gus said sensibly. "They're a good team."

Isela pressed her forehead into her hands, thinking of her youngest brother facing the Alchemist—whatever she was. "How dare you."

Gus's cold expression didn't budge. "Your family is better equipped to deal with this world than you are, consort. You might consider taking a lesson—"

Isela lunged, snarling, and Dory caught her arm. He lightly shook his head once.

"I'll see you in the ring anytime you'd like, señora," Gus promised without flinching.

Tariq eased over the arm of his chair into Isela's space. The feel of his power, crackling in defense around him as it neared her, made her aware of how much energy was leaking off her. "Infuriating little know-it-all, isn't she? Especially when she has a point."

Isela's control flexed with her next long inhale. Gus had already resumed her report and barely acknowledged the change in the room's atmosphere, though she kept her voice and her gaze respectfully low. "Whatever she is takes power. Place is in shambles—all weeds and broken glass. The neighbors say it's been abandoned since the war. Smart, pairing the wolves with patrols. Whatever we miss, their noses pick up. If it weren't for the consort's kin, we'd never have known she'd been there at all. He found this."

She dumped the warped remains of a mobile on the table. It clattered, and bits of old plastic flaked off as it skittered toward Isela before rocking twice and remaining still.

"I didn't pick anything up from it," Gus said, and Tariq's hopeful expression faded. "But Azrael's techs identified the time of the last call as shortly after you left."

"You think the Alchemist set us up?" Isela said.

Gus shrugged, sanguine. "If she truly is Circe, she's not grace-blooded, so it's impossible to know where her loyalty lies. She had to know betraying you would invoke Azrael's vow. So whoever put her up to it must have promised her a quick exit."

"And the phoenix was Vanka's pet before it escaped." Rory sat down at the table, all business now. "She's the only one of the Allegiance that gifted in alchemy. Though I'm not convinced he wasn't sent here. If he had destabilized in Old Town, it would have been quite a disruption to the human population."

"Azrael knew the phoenix belonged to Vanka?" Isela said.

Silence.

"This friend of Isela's, the ballerina," Tariq said, "has been taken, presumably by Vanka. And the recordings of her dances were stolen. Also likely Vanka."

Dante put down his pen. "When you lay it all out, it seems so obvious, doesn't it?"

Tariq threw a crumpled-up napkin at him. "Make any progress with the mud men?"

Isela was more certain that the phoenix was the key to everything. She had to get to him. She rose from the table, making her movement unsteady enough that Dory reached out for her hand. She pasted on her most gracious smile.

"This is all been very... educational," she said, adding an extra measure of hesitation to her voice. "But I'm afraid I'm not quite recovered from last night—"

Liar.

"Maybe you can continue your investigation without me," she said, slipping her phone off the counter on her way to the stairs. "But I should go... lie down."

Dory let her proceed when he was certain she could manage.

She turned her back on them, careful to make her step weighted with meaning. The room fell silent.

She was halfway up the stairs when Tariq's voice called, "I've been told that the deception of a woman of untold beauty will end my life. I'd prefer that not be you."

The non sequitur stopped her mid-step. She looked back to find everyone occupied with something else. Except Tariq—he stared at her, the intensity of his gaze making her struggle to resist a squirm. He broke his stare briefly to meet Rory's eyes. At some unspoken signal, Rory rose from his chair, giving his brother's shoulder a squeeze before hanging up his apron. The room was quiet until the door closed behind him.

"I have an addiction to fortune-tellers," Tariq said. "It's been the only prediction that never changes. At least among the ones who are truly gifted. So tell us how you plan to revive the phoenix without us."

Dory took his brother's seat, gnawing on a bit of leftover bacon.

She faced Tariq, letting the air of exhaustion fall away. "The Allegiance won't give us peace, and the gods are restless. A war is coming. It's time to stop being a passenger on this ride."

"And you plan to start with a phoenix," he said, whistling. "You certainly don't aim low."

"I need to find out what that phoenix knows."

"The Alchemist said…"

"That they can't be separated." She nodded. "I know. She also said the difference between me and it was choice. If I can get to them—the man and the phoenix—and help them see they can make a choice, maybe I can bring them back."

"And how and when do you plan to do this?" Tariq paused, considering.

She turned her face away, jaw locked.

Tariq sighed. "Isela, I—we—are not Azrael."

"You're his proxy," Isela said, glaring around the room. "All of you. And Azrael would gild the walls to keep this place from looking like a cage."

"He wants—"

"To protect me. I know."

"No." He sighed. "You're—"

"A weakness he can't afford to have."

"Look around the room." Tariq waited patiently as she surveyed their faces. Of Azrael's Aegis, only Dory remained and was the beginning of hers. "Who did we make our vow to in the hall?"

"You are Azrael's progeny," she bit out.

"And we served him in our tenure," Dante said. "That obligation ends when we leave the nest, so to speak. We came now to see if we could assist him as he faces his enemies."

"But we made no vow to *him*," Tariq finished. "He did not ask it, and we did not offer."

Isela stared at them, speechless. Dory chuckled and nearly knocked Tariq out of his chair with a companionable bump of his fist. "Very clever. You're smarter than you look, Dauntless."

"Ah thanks, you big lug."

Isela needed a moment to let that knowledge wash over her as the pieces of her world spun into correct place. At her unspoken question, Gus shrugged—agreement, annoyance and impatience in a single expression. Isela started down the stairs again.

"I have been doing some thinking," Dante said when she seemed to be grasping their offer. "What was done was done by a grace blood.

But perhaps with the necromancers and witches united, we can untangle the spell. Your mother's coven—"

Isela shook her head, thinking of her brother's face and Dory's. "If I make a mistake, no one else will pay the price. I won't risk another of Azrael's Aegis. Or his progeny. Or my family."

"That is not your decision to make, Isela." The door opened and Beryl Gilman-Vogel followed Tyler into the room.

Tyler announced, "Someone called for a coven and a pack?"

Isela smelled her brothers before she saw them—the distinctly warm, musky scent that was as familiar to her as her family home. The witches followed. Dante rose from his chair, and Ofelia slipped into it gratefully, a smile dimpling her cheeks as she cradled her belly. Isela searched the faces, and Tariq gestured with his thumb and pinkie to indicate a phone and winked at her.

"You called them here." Isela glared at Tariq, at the bottom of the stairs again. "You had no right."

"Don't be an idiot, Isela." Evie cut her off.

Gus smiled. She jerked her thumb at the taller blond woman. "I like this one."

Isela whirled on Gus, but Evie closed the distance first, hugging her. "All my dreams lately are of you getting into some trouble or other." A smile softened her words. "It feels good to be doing something for once. Chris and Bebe told us about the Alchemist—"

"Nobody messes with a Vogel," Bebe cut in.

Markus barked, his hackles flared as he paced the windowed wall. Christof circled Isela's calves and set his rump down on her feet.

Ofelia grinned resolutely. "My ankles are huge. I would love to get my feet back up on a couch ASAP. Can we get going?"

The pale wolf chuffed a lupine laugh. Bebe took her turn for a hug, batting him aside. Isela looked over her shoulder at Beryl. The older woman looked more energized than Isela had seen her in weeks.

She crossed her arms over her chest, taking in the Vogel brood with satisfied pride. She met Isela's eyes finally, and Isela blinked back tears at the emotion in them. "It's Sunday. If you won't come to us, we'll come to you."

Isela struggled to breathe over the emotion battling for dominance in her chest. "You mean to do this now?"

CHAPTER SIXTEEN

G regor took one look at the scarf clenched in Azrael's palm when he returned to the Land Cruiser and his brows rose. Lysippe drove. On the outskirts of town, a stocky Asian man in a fur cap tended four uniformly unremarkable brown horses working their way through piles of hay, their bellies barely clearing the sheep grazing among them.

Unremarkable, but strong and capable. Leave it to Lys to pick good horses. Gregor groaned at the sight of them. "You weren't joking."

The ride to the mine took them up a series of switchbacks and along winding goat tracks carved into the sheer faces of the rocks. Azrael gazed into the drop-offs, his fear of falling long ago silenced.

"Why aren't we taking the road, again?" Gregor inquired delicately when they stopped to water the horses.

"Booby trap," the guide pronounced proudly before rattling off the specifics in a language that only Lysippe understood with any fluency.

She looked at them. "Vanka left a few reminders of her presence on the road. To discourage any treasure seekers. After all, she paid the villagers a fortune. She didn't want them coming back to figure out what she was interested in."

"Which means she didn't find what she was looking for," Gregor said resolutely, batting at the horse's nose as it tried to use him for a scratching post.

"Or she hopes to come back for it," Azrael said, scratching his own nose idly. "Either way, she'll know we're here soon. I want to get in and out quickly."

Understanding the vibe if not the words, their guide tightened his own girth and swung astride. Lysippe joined him with enviable grace. Gregor did so with reluctant efficiency. Azrael came last. He'd grown up with horses, but as his power emerged, he found them increasingly skittish around him. He found it best if he moved slowly and didn't give them a reason to be startled. This one was a good, sensible beast. Still, it tossed its head when it caught scent of him and blew out sharply.

"Today is not your day, young fellow," he said affectionately as he swung astride. "You'll die an old man with your nose in the manger."

The horse bucked and loped after his fellows.

* * *

THE MINE SHAFT was every bit as foreboding as their guide had boasted. Feeling its energy, Azrael didn't wonder why the villagers feared it. This was the thinnest of places. Strangely, he felt his own power respond by flexing within him like a roused beast. His control strained. His horse reared, crow-hopping sideways. Azrael went flying, and the horse skittered away, eyes rolling in terror. Their guide scrambled to catch the animal. He stroked its sweaty shoulder, blowing in its wide nostrils until it calmed and stood beside his own mount.

Gregor and Lysippe watched him as their own mounts shied away, the former strangely, the latter with a knowing, worried gaze. His first and his last. They knew him best. He clenched hold of his control, bringing his quiet down over the flexing roar of power in him until the animals were all calm.

"What was that?" Gregor murmured as they shouldered their packs and headlamps.

"I don't know," Azrael said honestly.

"I don't want you bringing this place down on us—more than it is," Lysippe said.

"I'll control it."

They descended into darkness, leaving the guide staring after them with worried relief in his gaze as he muttered prayers to gods even Azrael didn't know. But his instructions had been good. Lysippe led them to a passage that hadn't fully collapsed, and deeper yet. The mines tapped a natural system of caverns. The cold and the dark both welcomed and set them on edge. Azrael scanned the rock around them, detecting the corpses of the miners left in the collapsed caverns.

"I fucking hate caves," Gregor said as an afterthought. "More than ships."

"You could have stayed with the horses." Lysippe laughed, fearless as always as she guided them along the tunnels.

The power swelled again in him and he had to pause, bent over double with his hand braced against the damp stone wall to gather himself.

Lysippe's light shone back on him, her face blocked by the brightness but her voice carrying the weight of her concern. "All right?"

"I will be," Azrael said.

A tug on the thread of gold that he'd come to associate with Isela thrummed through him. The icy shadow pushing back against his control raged at the idea that she was somehow threatened or in danger. He knew better. Thin places often had their own defenses against intrusion. Triggering his sense of wrongness and amplifying his connection with her might be the work of the cave itself.

"Here," he said as the passageway opened into a natural cavern. "Right here."

The unsettled sensation around his bond with Isela only grew as they pressed on.

Lysippe and Gregor spread out, sweeping the space with their beams.

"Something's coming," Gregor said, the hilt of his sword glowing at his back as he unholstered a short blade from his thigh.

Lysippe switched off her headlamp. A slim leather-wrapped bow appeared in her hand, quiver at her hip. "Lights out. No powers. Not in here."

Azrael let his labrys drop into his palms out of the ether from which he called it, the weight instantly heavy and comfortable in his hands. His eyes, preternaturally sharp in the darkness, made out the slightest flinch of movement in the shadows.

The attack came all at once. Slavering beasts made of claw and shadows, not demons but made of flesh that had once been human—

and animal. Lysippe grunted in disgust, emptying her quiver twice, and when the fight got too close sheathing her bow and switching to pair of short, sickle-shaped blades she wielded like the slashing claws of a big cat.

Gregor's blade was blacker than the darkness, a shorter, narrow weapon well suited for close-quarters skirmish. Azrael moved between them, the rhythmic swing and slash of the double-bladed ax growing more familiar with every pass. He'd missed the singing and pounding of the blood in his veins, the sweat and exertion of hand-to-hand.

There had been much more of it in the old days, and it had bonded them as vows never could. He caught a clawed strike intended for Lysippe, and she tipped her head in thanks before gutting the beast. Gregor's heel slipped on the floor and she spun, yanking him out of the way as she blocked his opponent. He recovered and stepped to guard her weak side instinctively. Azrael found himself apart from the others, dogged by twin scorpion-tailed monstrosities. He swung and dodged, but they had him on the retreat until his back brushed the stone wall.

"Down." Gregor barked a second before Lysippe cannonballed through the air. She spun as she flew, slicing the tips off both tails as she passed. Azrael rose again just in time to snag her in midair and assist her rebound off the wall. She landed in a crouch, teeth bared.

"I'd forgotten that trick." She laughed, rising and swiping her blades on her pants as they regrouped.

"Stay together," Gregor barked, glaring at Azrael. "And I'll see you in the training room when we get back to Prague."

They moved through the space, rotating their backs against each other as they took turns carving a path. On the opposite side of the cavern, Azrael urged Lysippe and Gregor ahead of him into a narrow passageway, then blew the cavern with a bolt of energy so powerful that the mountain rumbled around them.

In the ensuing silence after the thunder of rock coming down and the cries of the trapped and dying creatures, Gregor chuckled softly. "They heard that all the way in the village."

Lysippe leveled a long look at Azrael. "Do that again and we'll spend an eternity digging ourselves out from under a mountain."

Azrael couldn't help but look at his hands in stunned awe. He'd sent out what he thought was a controlled burst, meant to vaporize anything moving in the cavern. He hadn't intended to bring it down.

The mountain made an almost human sound, groaning as tremors moved through the walls. Was it the thin place wreaking havoc with him, or something else?

Lysippe led them, squeezing through the narrow rocks and sliding down a long talus slope. Azrael felt the cut of rocks and scrape of sharp edges, but he plunged after them with the heedlessness of one whom death could not touch.

He felt the power here now, something pulsing in the blackness beyond. The heart of the thin place. The air grew damp and full of a thickness that came with humidity. It was warmer here than it should have been.

They tumbled into a vast opening that was no less claustrophobic for the sense of space. Lysippe flicked on her light but nothing happened. Gregor tried. Azrael sent out what should have been a small ball of light but emerged a full-fledged beacon, illuminating the hollow they'd stumbled upon in the mountain. The glow bounced off walls thick with minerals that caught the light and shone like sparklers on a dark night.

In the center of the space, a stalactite glowed over a pool, a thin, viscous liquid coating it and the pool below. It took him a moment to realize the pool was still, reflecting nothing at all, and the water ran not from the stalactite down but from the pond *up,* sparkling droplets rising to the point of the rocky outcropping and sliding upward until they disappeared into the ceiling.

Lysippe thumped Gregor in the ribs. "Your flask."

He grumbled but drained it before handing it over. She reached out, turning the open end down and positioning it between droplets. They waited, one drop at a time, until at last the liquid spilled over the edge of the flask lip and rolled up toward the stalactite. She withdrew the flask, carefully screwing the cap on before turning it upright and offering it to Gregor.

"Don't sip on accident," she advised, brow raised.

He slipped it into his inner pocket. "No worries about that. Now we know what she came for."

The cavern cried out around them.

"Time to go," Azrael said, focused.

Lysippe had the instinct of a bird for the sky, guiding them ever up and out, and both men fell in behind her. They made their way higher, winding and crawling, scrabbling and dragging one another.

At last even Azrael could smell the fresh air. They stood at the base of a sheer cliff, the thinnest edge of light tricking over the top. Behind them, the mountain sighed and moaned like the restless sleep of an unrequited lover.

"Gregor," Lysippe said, panting with exertion.

Gregor dropped his empty pack and slid the coils of rope over his shoulder. He scrambled up, scaling the wall with enviable agility. When he got to the top, he disappeared over the edge. They waited. At last the rope sailed down, unspooling from the coil as it fell. Azrael gestured. Lysippe scaled the wall, gripping the rope hand over hand.

His chest still ached, and he rubbed it absently.

Isela? he thought before he could control himself. *Are you there? I feel you, what is—*

A tug of the golden thread snapped pain through him.

Distracted, the impact took him by surprise. Teeth sank into his arm, sending pain up his shoulder and into his neck. As the steel-trap muscles attached to those jaws clenched him hard, his feet left the ground. His body slammed into the walls. His bones broke and healed and splintered again. Hearing Lysippe's and Gregor's alarmed calls, he ordered them to hold their ground as the mountain rumbled again. He tried to make sense of his attacker—some kind of hybrid with too many teeth and slobber that burned his skin.

Azrael! Isela's shout was no illusion. She was hurt, in danger; she needed him.

Mine. Mine. Mine.

Then, suddenly, the teeth were gone. Gregor rode the unnatural's spine, his sword hilt deep in its neck. Lysippe's arrows sang their way to their target. Bristling with arrows and spending its lifeblood, the creature careened around the opening, bellowing.

Azrael wheezed as he dragged himself away, feeling his punctured lungs fill with blood and drain as his ribs retreated.

When it was dead, they were at his side. Gregor tried to put Azrael's arm over his shoulder. Lysippe had the rope ready. Azrael's knees refused to hold, but he did his best to shake Gregor away. The voice screamed now, telling him what to do, how it must be done, even if he didn't understand.

"Get out," Azrael said instead. "Collapsing."

"That's the plan," Lysippe said impatiently. "Let us help you—"

Azrael gave Gregor one last shove, the force sending both men stumbling apart as the ground shifted beneath them. "Isela is dying."

Gregor went still, his eyes the cold blue of battlefield sky that Azrael hadn't seen in two hundred years. Lysippe tried to push past him, reaching for Azrael, but he blocked her. His eyes sliced into Azrael, as sharp as the blade in his hand. "You can help her?"

Azrael closed his eyes, thinking of her face. "Get yourselves out *now*. I have to get to her."

"How—" Gregor began.

Azrael simply vanished.

CHAPTER SEVENTEEN

The fireproof room had been transformed. Vibrant tapestries of mythical creatures hung on the walls, obscuring the complex, layered sigils Azrael had burned into the concrete. A rich red-and-gold rug blocked the cold from the stone floor. The single bed was hidden behind a trifold screen painted with scenes of Cossack cavalrymen performing extraordinary feats of horsemanship. This room, clean and small but with walls thoroughly warded to protect against a massive expenditure of power, looked almost identical in the waking world. Except instead of it being crowded with witches and necromancers, Isela stood alone with a god and a man who was not a man.

Are we in the In Between? But Isela already knew the answer. There was no tug of power, no invisible wind or gray overlay seething around the edges with hungry blights. Gold stood beside her. Isela could feel their shared heartbeat, and when the god spoke, her voice was internal.

That's because we are in your mind, she said. *Sort of. Like sharing a dream. You gave him the room; he apparently did the decor. Be careful, Issy. There are certain assurances you must get from him before you agree to help.*

But he's dying. His vitals were poor, and in spite of intravenous fluids, he seemed to be wasting away at twice the speed of normal humans.

He's a creature of power, unwillingly trapped in human flesh, Gold said uneasily. *And we do not know where his loyalties truly lie.*

You think he'd help Vanka after all this? In the brief silence before the god replied, Isela studied the man.

I think the promise of a return to his true form, even if a lie, would be a powerful lure to get his compliance in any of her schemes.

Like getting inside Azrael's territory and finding out more about his allies.

Gold nodded.

A small wood writing desk stacked with a few books stood against the far wall, next to a hot plate and a pair of cups on a little table. A man sat at the little desk, shoulders hunched as he wrote in a small leather-bound book. Isela tapped on the nearest surface to get his attention. The figure's head jerked up—if he had been plumed, the feathers would have risen in warning or alarm.

Isela could appreciate the transformation as he rose carefully from his chair. Gone was the tattered drunk. In his place rose a lean man who appeared to be born of fire. His close-cropped copper hair and trimmed beard carried the threads of the red and gold that flickered in newly caught flames. Orange freckles stood out against pale cheeks, and when he turned those sea-glass-green eyes on her, she felt the shadow of what he had once been in his clear, piercing gaze.

"She told me that you would come back," he said anxiously, casting his glance about the room, as though he wanted to look anywhere but at her directly.

He could not look at Gold.

Can you turn it down?

Gold dimmed abruptly. He sighed and his shoulders lowered like feathers settling back into place.

"Tea?" he said, already moving to the electric kettle plugged in beside the sink and mirror.

He dragged the reading chair closer to the desk and offered it to her with flitting precision. Gold stayed behind Isela, just over her shoulder.

Go ahead. Time moves differently here than in the real world.

"Do you have a name?" She watched him arrange a small plate of crackers and candies from the tin stored in the shelves beneath the kettle. "I'm just not sure what to call you."

Again the startled bob of his head and the repeated blinking as he attempted to parse what to her seemed like a straightforward question.

"I had no need of a name. I simply was."

"Phoenixes are the holders of great wisdom," she said. "The memory of the world, all that ever was, has passed before your eyes."

It had sounded like beautiful poetry at the time. But looking into his face now, she wondered how much of the pain she saw had come from his capture and transformation and how much of it was the price he paid for an eternity of watching. Premature age carved lines into the face of the mortal the phoenix occupied.

"I was taken," he said. "For my *legendary* powers. But I was found wanting."

The words were spoken with an edge of mocking; an old wound continually prodded so that it would not heal.

"We'd like to help you."

"Is that what you want?" he whispered. "Or do you want to know what my maker is planning?"

His eyes were filled with the feral bitterness of a wild animal taken from its home and trained to the hand but never fully tamed. He opened his mouth, and when the voice came out, it was not the one she knew but the perfect mimicry of a raging woman that made the hair rise at the base of her neck. "What that witch-blooded bitch did is impossible."

A chill raced through her. That voice. She knew it in her nightmares still, and her brain went instinctively to the memory of the beautiful redhead who had once thrown a knife at her heart. Vanka. Isela fought the bile rising in her throat. The phoenix set down his cup, resting his long, elegant hands on his jean-clad knees.

Isela swallowed her revulsion. "You can imitate voices?"

"We have no voices of our own," he said. "It's a simple trick, but one that has caused more trouble than it's worth."

Simple or not, it makes them excellent spies, Gold warned.

"She's right." The phoenix sighed, glancing at the gold figure finally. "We have been used as such."

"You can hear her?"

His head rose and fell in that peculiar avian nod. "Everything magic in this world is of them, lady. Even the blood running through your veins is tainted with their presence in this world. It's all a matter of degrees."

"The gods."

"If you insist." He shrugged.

"What are they then?"

"This was their world first," he said. "They gave up their physical bodies to become one with the energy of the universe. You call it magic?" He nodded. "But some kept looking back at the world they'd left behind. They watched, first with curiosity and later envy, you primates learning to walk upright and master your environment. They saw too late that evolution is a one-way trip. So they contented them-selves with meddling in the lives of things that lived here."

He continued, "The human need to name things is stronger than the desire to truly understand them. When they appeared briefly in your lives with powers beyond your understanding, you called them gods and worshipped them. Their presence changed your blood when they bred with you. And then you learned to talk to them directly with your dancing. You thought you could simply ask and they would give without taking in return. You thought they wanted to help you become better."

Using dancers to draw power from the gods for petty human concerns and conflicts had almost destroyed humanity. Though it had only lasted a few weeks, the godswar would have ended in apocalypse if not for the intervention of the Allegiance of Necromancers. They had saved the world, but that too had come at a price.

Isela focused on the present. "And somehow you escaped?"

"I still have a bit of my old magic," he said before admitting, "Their undead are weak without the presence of their makers. I was able to overpower their command and run."

"Why did you find me?" Isela asked.

"She spoke of you enough. I thought... your god could help me. If I gave you information, what her plans are... perhaps. But I think I've run out of time. This body cannot sustain me."

"Is he still there, the man?"

He bobbed his head, pausing to blink at her. "What was before has been mostly burned away by what I am. He moves in the back of my mind like an old dream. All I have are these echoes." The phoenix rubbed his temple angrily, his lips moving in unspoken words.

"I think more than echoes," Isela said, pitying the mortal trapped within. "I think we can help you, both of you."

His nostrils flared as his chin rose, desire warring with fear.

"But first," Isela said, "we must have your assurances."

Gold nodded. *Good, Issy. You're learning.*

He looked between her and the god. Then his eyes hooded and he retreated into his chair, watching them both. "I give you my word that nothing we speak of will be repeated outside this room."

It was a start, but not enough. Isela swallowed her regret. "You must ask for sanctuary."

Sanctuary was not a concept native to humanity. She'd gone around and around on the topic with both Dante and Bebe before entering the phoenix's mind. They insisted formality was the only way to guarantee the phoenix's loyalty. But the fresh bond with Dory still made her uneasy, and now they wanted her to form another, less equitable one. A person offered a necromancer's sanctuary was a cross between a political refugee and an involuntarily committed ward of the state. The phoenix would belong to her.

His shoulders rose in a way that made her think of a bird ruffling its feathers warily. "You are prepared to offer it?"

"I will, as both the vessel of a god and Azrael's consort," she said formally. Then she rested her hands on the table and leaned forward. "But also as a friend. We *are* alike, you and I. I promise not to hurt you more than you've already been hurt and to do everything I can to restore you to who you were... before."

The great gold-and-green eyes of the phoenix rose to hers. He set down his teacup, folding his hands in his lap with a resigned air. At last he slipped from his chair to one knee.

"My lady." He clasped her hand. Nails were trimmed and clean, long fingers that of a teacher or a musician. He pressed her knuckles to his lips and then his forehead. She braced her other hand on his shoulder. For all his thinness, she felt the cords of muscles through his back. Muscles where once wings might have been. His head cocked as his eyes rolled to take in her fingers, his shoulder shivering slightly under her touch. He was like a human parrot.

He dropped his gaze again and took a hard breath. "I seek sanctuary. I swear devotion to your house. My life is yours."

"And my asylum is yours," Isela said thickly, speaking the words Bebe had drilled into her. "No other claim on you will be honored." She hesitated. "And it's Issy. Or Isela. Please, sit down."

The phoenix smiled for the first time, and her heart broke a little.

"How about Nix," she asked.

Be careful, Issy, Gold said. *To name something is to claim it.*

"It's just temporary," Isela said. "Phoenixes don't need names, remember?"

"Nix," he said.

She met the phoenix's eyes. "Are you ready?"

"What choice do I have?"

Isela felt herself smiling against all reason. "Someone once told me there is always a choice."

Gold nodded once. Isela reached out and took his hand in hers. This time she felt the power surge against her sternum. It was a peculiar fullness of opposites, like distant relations seeing themselves in one another.

That's the necromancers and witches working together, Gold said. *See how powerful they can be united? They are halves of a whole. It will take much to overcome what was done in the name of the Allegiance, but someday, Isela, they will need each other again. They will need us to be the conduit, see?*

Isela felt the edges of her own body being becoming a funnel. As the magic churned from necromancers and witches, it entered her. It took shape, and she focused on maintaining the edges, keeping it directed at the man in front of her. When she turned her gaze outward, there were two beings. A crumpled, emaciated human male, the shadow of the image she'd just spoken with, curled on the floor. On the chair rested a creature that would have put the most beautiful peacock to shame. A crest of fire and feathers sprang from the back of his head, and a savagely curved beak glittered.

It gazed down at the man, and its feathers shivered.

Isela remembered her first dancing lesson with Gold and how exhausted the god had been after the short time of being in control of a physical form. She crouched on the floor beside the man. Pale, thin skin marked with freckles stretched over his bones and frame.

"Why is he so emaciated here?" Isela asked Gold.

It was the phoenix that answered. She recognized the pattern of its speech but realized the tone and the voice she'd associated with it must belong to the man. The bird was musical and entirely inhuman. *This is all that is left of him, I'm afraid. It took me many weeks to learn to manage and care for his body. I've tried. But I failed.*

Isela stretched out a hand. The man on the floor started and stared up at her with wide, blinking eyes. Doubt crept into her. Their plan depended on her being able to negotiate between them, get a settlement that would allow both beings to share a body as she and Gold did. But looking into his vacant, blank gaze, she wondered if there was enough of a personality there to negotiate with. And how could she possibly help someone who didn't even seem to recognize another human face?

"Pretty." The word came out in a long slur, trailed by a line of spittle that rolled out of the corner of his mouth. "Sun and stars and pretty coins in the fountain."

Isela gasped as the hand reached out to her. No longer smooth, unblemished fingers, these were the coarse, work-roughened hands she remembered from the square. She kept her palm outstretched, and his settled into it. The grip was soft and unfocused, like his gaze.

"Can you hear me?" she asked.

A long sound, between a groan and a grunt. Tears softened her vision. This had been what she feared when Gold first offered their arrangement. To be left nothing but an empty, shambling shell of a human, a host of a parasitic power. Maybe it would be best if they failed and the phoenix died if it gave this man peace.

She snatched a cloth from the table and dabbed the spit from his lips. A wide, childlike smile stretched his mouth, and he snuggled his face into her hand. She glanced up at Gold and the phoenix. Both supernatural beings' expressions were impassive. Her anger flared.

How quickly you judge us for something that was not our doing, Gold said. *If you lose control of that power, you will do far more damage than either of us have done to that poor beast.*

Isela took a few long breaths, soothing the emotion that threatened to pluck the threads of her control loose. She needed to help if for no other reason than he suffered as she had managed to avoid through a twist of fate.

"Do you want to live? Do you want to be here?"

The phoenix squawked in agitation. *Your word.*

"I promised to try to help," she snapped. "Both of you. And if his suffering can't be eased, then I will not help you continue to use him as a body. I'd let you die first, no matter how powerful you are and what you know."

The phoenix flapped its wings, feathers flared as it screamed like nails on glass. Gold stepped between it and Isela. The god shook her head once in warning, and the bird settled onto its perch.

The man groaned again, voice a rasp in his throat.

She retrieved tea, placed the cup to his mouth and wiped the spilled liquid from his cheeks and lips. "I can help you. But you have to accept it. The bird, permanently. I don't think either of you will survive without each other. Do you understand?"

Great heaving noises broke from the man's chest as his eyes flickered up to the bird and the golden woman. Bubbles of snot flared under his nostrils as wet rivers fled his eyes. Isela maneuvered his head and chest into her lap as best she could, cradling him like a small child and rocking.

"I am like you," she whispered. "The gold one, she lives in me. And it's a life worth living. You'll find you can benefit one another. And most importantly, a part of you"—she paused, taking in the quiet beauty of the room around them—"a good part, will survive."

Isela, we should do this now, Gold said.

Not until he's ready, Isela insisted.

"It's not all terrible," Isela whispered to the man in her lap. "Maybe someday… if you have anyone left. Maybe someday you can find them. But it's your choice."

She glared at the phoenix.

I will not let your memory be lost, the phoenix offered finally. *I will… help you.*

The man groaned again, and after long moments of his relentless, broken sobs, he took a shuddering breath. He turned his face into her stomach, and his voice vibrated against her core. "Sanctuaaarrr."

"I'll take that as a yes." Isela sighed. She looked up, feeling the tears on her own face, and into the eyes of the god waiting patiently for her. *Now we do this.*

Gold nodded.

She reached out a hand and Nix alighted on her wrist. For a bird so large, it weighed nothing. With her other hand, she took the man's fingers. She remembered Dante's words. *It's a like a puzzle. Find the pieces that match one another. Make them fit.*

The power demanded her attention. It wanted entry, so she bade it, feeling Gold form a dense, protective shell around the flow. The two powers pooled and collected, swirling around each other until they were indistinguishable. A virtual chaos of beginning and ending on infinite repeat. As it gathered strength, it acquired a sound, like a chorus of disparate voices coming into harmony. It was rhythmic and continuous, alternating sound and silence. In the combination, she could hear the heart of the universe itself.

If she only listened a little harder, she was sure she could find the path that would lead her to its source.

Focus. Gold, calling her back.

Reluctantly Isela turned away from pursuit of the sound, felt her own heart crack at the loss of union with that mighty force. The merging forces had almost entirely filled the vessel she and Gold created. Pressing from within, it strained at the very seams of her, and for the first time she felt the beginnings of discomfort. Her instinct was to shut down the link.

But she must be an opening, a path from one to the other.

She returned to the image of the phoenix. She opened a channel to him through their linked hands, and immediately the commingling forces inside her found their work. The discomfort eased. The silk of something like feathers brushed her palms. She gasped with antici-pated joy. She opened the conduit a bit more, let the power flow more freely into him, hoping to speed the transition.

As the phoenix faded, the man began to resemble what she'd seen when she first entered the room. As they merged, both became less solid and more—a double image resolving before her eyes.

The vast, harmonic heartbeat returned, and she felt herself slip-ping, her attention wavering.

And then everything went wrong.

His physical body arched, rejecting the transformation. Influx from both the spellcasters and the resistance in Nix made her waver. Her body stretched taut. The power mingling inside her recoiled, doubling back like water expanding as it froze. She knew that it would not simply return to the space that once contained it.

She focused on holding herself together, knowing that if she gave up now, the feedback would hit the witches and necromancers. The necromancers might survive. Correction—Tariq might. But witches were subject to the laws of mortality.

Forced to her breaking point, she felt her ears ring as the sound of screaming reached them. It echoed off the walls—two voices, rising in distorted harmony echoing with pain. One sounded almost birdlike. The other was her own. The power began to leak from her skin, drawn off into the wards Azrael had imprinted on the walls. They brightened as they grew close to the point of saturation. She redoubled her effort, feeling Gold tighten around her.

She flung open her eyes. Bright blue light filled the room, mingling with green where Azrael's wards were aflame in their attempt to contain the outpouring of power. Dante had fallen. Gus was at his side, her mouth still moving with incantation and her eyes on the cracks forming in the walls. The witches were clustered and being brought down as if under an enormous weight. Tariq stood apart, arms and legs splayed. His whole body shook, and his eyes rolled white with effort.

The color of the light in the room was explained when she looked at Nix. He was engulfed in blue flames.

She had to hold it in. She would lose them all if she let it go. Her will was strong, but the rest of her lacked the training and the endurance she needed. She slipped, and a bolt of power shot across the wall, leaving a crack the size of her arm. She was going to fail.

Azrael!

PART III

CHAPTER EIGHTEEN

The truth was, an eternity could be awfully boring. Unless one knew how to occupy oneself.

A sudden jolt scattered his current distraction across a vast expanse of space, knocking two galaxies out of their regular orbits and sending a cascading burst of light and sparks as stars collided and masses skittered through dust like so many marbles.

He swore in languages older than both celestial formations and cast his gaze over the mess his little experiment had become. A rock skating through one of those misted star fields bobbed curiously. He paused to watch it gather dust and particles as it spun, forming a new orbit around a remaining dwarf star. He considered the distance from the star to the rock and the gathering particles and chunks of ice. Interesting. A few hundred thousand years and this might prove to be quite a happy accident indeed.

He turned his attention back to the sensation that had caused the distraction. *Hello?*

Like the tug of a fingertip on the string of an instrument, it thrummed through the fibers of his being.

That made it no less difficult to suss out. He'd been around so long there were parts of him all over—and not just in space. Time was its own miasma. He went still, calling the scattered bits of himself back, summoning and gathering himself as the sensation echoed through him. He was patient and he was old, and since time didn't matter that much, he waited.

Aha! His attention settled on a part of himself he'd released so long ago he'd forgotten. An old experiment. Back when he was still playing on a small scale. Curious.

The trouble was he'd expanded so much in the subsequent time that to go back required a certain reduction, a paring off of the most expansive versions of himself to something more manageable on a strictly physical, linear plane. It would make him vulnerable— becoming smaller always did. But when was the last time he'd taken any risk?

Nothing ventured, nothing gained. If any of his progeny had been successful, he'd imagined giving them that little nugget of wisdom. But of his many attempts, none had ever ascended to a level that would be worth his time, attention, and tutelage. None had ever shown such promise—*until now.*

It fit him like an old suit, this form. He stretched, rolling his awareness to the edges to remind himself of what this form was—and wasn't—capable of. It wasn't bad as these things went. For this time and place, he was quite powerful. A god. One of many. Older than most, and more powerful, but also more rarefied. That would be the vulnerability.

They would outnumber him—the younger, stupider gods—and given enough battering, even he could be felled. So that necessitated caution and stealth. He reduced himself even more to avoid them, still tracing the echo of the sensation.

He was drawn to the physical plane that they'd evolved from and the mammalian lives they still tied themselves to so dearly. Human. Ah yes, the memories came back to him, their tangible world and limited senses as enticing a challenge as he'd ever had.

The infinite bred ennui. Limits, borders, made everything more interesting.

Finally, deep in a cavern of the mountains on the edge of a vast steppe, he watched a many-mouthed creature writhe and spend the last of its life on the floor. On a ledge above, a man stood beside a woman. A thousand years or more of life separated them, but he had the sense in the way they stood together that they were kin. Partners-in-arms. Siblings of war. Dirt and sweat coated their skin—his pale, hers rich brown—but it was the matching wonder on their faces that drew him.

"He just… went," the woman said, unbelieving. She wasn't speaking of the creature.

Here he did not have command of time exactly, but he found that with focus he could move himself through it. He stepped backward. There were three originally. These two and one greater. Something more. Their maker and their leader. Watching them brave the deep caves and rally to fight off the attack, he studied their missing companion. The god froze himself in the moment before the monster attacked. He stalked around the third man—not a man, something more—with dawning recognition.

The spark of a god ran through the threads that bound this younger creature together. A laugh began to build in him, a full, belling thing that rippled through the air and sent the frozen tendrils of the man's dark hair flying. This one was his.

How could he have forgotten? He had tried for so long to breed himself into these animals. So many had failed—gone mad or destroyed themselves—he'd simply given up. And when the ungrateful little whelps had bound him from this tiny, forgotten world with the others, he'd turned his back on them and moved on. There were always newer experiments.

Now this. He sized up the dark, wavy hair, bronzed skin, high cheekbones, and full mouth. The slightly bowed nose and upturned eyes of silver. He too was old by the standards of this world. And judging by the ties he'd created to his companions, he was powerful.

Mine.

The god moved forward through time, stepping lightly out of the way as the man was attacked, thrown against the wall, recovering swiftly and fighting back. His warriors leaped to his defense, fearless and ruthless as only creatures on the verge of immortality could be. They barked conversation between them. A woman's name. Isela.

The monster fell, leaving the man facing his companions with a look of wild power building in his eyes. A look he well recognized. Then the man simply disappeared.

The god watched the moment the man vanished, recognizing it as the source of the tug that had called him back. This was his gift, his power, and one he had given up hope of ever seeing in these physical creatures.

He returned to the moment he had come, standing unseen beside the two warriors at the edge of the precipice. He admired their faces, the naked loyalty to each other and their master. It was impossible to think, after so long, that everything he'd hoped for was finally coming into being. The man and woman raced into the dawn, back to their own world.

Another human nugget of wisdom chided him. *Impossible only means it hasn't been done yet.* He smiled, and the force of it made the mountain tremble as caverns gave way under the weight of rock. *Indeed.*

CHAPTER NINETEEN

A rms closed around Isela. "Listen to my voice."
She was going to take out the castle, kill his progeny and
guard and her own family, and Azrael sounded almost calm. He
should be furious. Or at least concerned. He wasn't really here. This
must be a figment of her mind as it fractured under the pressure of
trying to keep it all together.

"Isela, stay with me. Breathe."

Agar. Toasted cinnamon. Molasses. His scent convinced her he
wasn't the delusion of a dying mind. She dragged her face away from
his neck, but his arms held her firm. Her mind made words when her
body could not. *How is this possible?*

"We're going to shut this down together," he informed her coolly.
"I need you to focus on your exhale." His left hand tangled in her hair,
fingers knotting in the loosened braid at the base of her skull. "Look
at me." Silver pools locked her gaze. "That's it."

She no longer felt the exquisite pain of impending rupture. The
power was being siphoned off her. And into him. His silver eyes
flared.

Incrementally the pressure eased. Her ears popped. She felt the
energy abating, safe enough now to return to its origin points without
threat of overwhelming them.

She sat half in his lap, half on the floor, her weight against his
chest. Bruises faded on his face as she watched. A long gash had been

opened from below his eye to his left jaw, and it bled sluggishly. His clothes were in tatters, exposing raw and broken flesh beneath. But his attention was on her. He cradled her face in his hands, stroking beads of sweat and tears that she hadn't known she'd shed. Around them, she could hear the others beginning to stir. In spite of everything, a tiny part of her that had tensed when he left released. He was all right. He was home.

* * *

THE EFFORT TO remain calm strained Azrael as they left the crowded confines of the fireproof room for his apartments. That the others inexplicably followed pushed him that much closer to the edge. When Gus flung herself onto a kitchen barstool with the temerity to joke, "at least we know the walls held," his restraint shattered.

"You risk my consort, my allies, and my progeny, and you laugh?"

Azrael had always found Gus's distinct lack of obsequiousness to anyone or anything amusing. With her teenaged appearance and insouciant gaze, most underestimated her. But he'd never, ever mistaken her for a child. She was too powerful for that. He had always known it would be Gus, not Tariq, to equal the strength of the members of the Allegiance first. Now it seemed his permissiveness to her innate sense that the world could be manipulated to her pleasure without responsibility for her actions had been his mistake.

Foolish, selfish, stupid girl. The words brushed the back of his mind like a snatch of overheard conversation. With them came a creeping chill, remarkable because he couldn't remember feeling the sensation of *cold* in a thousand years.

She seemed ready to say something else—likely flippant and glib, as was her way—but his look silenced her.

Gus straightened up from her slouch. Her eyes went from iris-less black to a completely obsidian sheen.

The quiet clattering and mental buzz of so many bodies in the space drew to an abrupt halt.

What risk she takes, mocking your beloved, the voice insisted against the back of his skull.

"I take responsibility," Tariq interjected.

The eldest ready—yet again—to shoulder blame. Azrael surveyed his progeny. Dante looked as if he'd gained another decade since the last time Azrael had seen him. Wiser, more mortal than the Dauntless and Gus, he would always be the weakest. It grieved Azrael that he'd never been able to bring Dante to enough power to halt the aging process. Whatever they had done in that room had cost him years.

Azrael had failed them. He'd brought them into their power, kept them alive during those critical years when the transition to the upper echelon of their kind killed the lesser among them. What grounding had he provided to keep them from trying to reweave the threads of nature to their own purposes?

Overconfidence and a blatant disregard for the lives of the mortals they endangered infuriated him. His consort had almost been ripped apart trying to protect her family. Had he not arrived in time, he would have lost her.

He wanted his progeny alone so he could exact the punishment deserved in all its force.

Mine. That hissing, stealthy voice vibrated against bone. *They threatened mine. Make them pay.*

Isela sat stiffly upright in the high-backed chair, doing her best to keep anyone from seeing how the use of power had drained her. Rory said she'd been senseless after she brought Dory back. Her voice was still raw from hours of screaming in pain. What had the attempt to restore the phoenix done to her? Azrael had tried to send Isela to their quarters to rest, but it seemed everyone else found an excuse to follow and busy themselves once they'd arrived.

The youngest witch made pots of tea, stepping lightly over the wolves sprawled on the floor to deliver cups to everyone. The high priestess and the blond witch attended to Dante. Rory took over the office, making arrangements to get Gregor and Lysippe back to the castle as quickly as possible, leaving Aleifr and Ito to take up casual sentry positions by the doors.

Azrael was, by turns, furious with all of them—that his allies insisted on staying when he'd given them permission to leave, that his Aegis lingered because the pack remained, that his own consort refused to take the rest she so clearly needed.

And now Gus challenged him. "You would have never permitted any of us to remain so ignorant and she's just as powerful."

"Isela is no necromancer," Azrael said.

From her place beside Dante, Beryl looked up for the first time. "Nor is she witch. But she must be taught. Who else but us?"

From their various seats around the room, her coven raised their eyes and nodded as one.

Gus snorted. "You keep a god like a pet. And you call her consort. You dishonor her."

Who are they to tell you how to protect what is yours? the voice taunted.

Aleifr took a step toward the younger necromancer threateningly.

Gus pushed off her barstool. The move angled her shoulder between him and the youngest witch in the kitchen. One hand slid to her hip—part attitude, part easier to get to the blade at the small of her back. Tariq stepped a little closer to the little curly-haired witch, Bebe, placing himself between her and Azrael's Aegis.

The irony struck Azrael. This moment might be the first time necromancers and witches had cast their lot together in recorded history, and it was against him.

Isela rose as Aleifr's palms went to the small of his back, pounding her hands on the table.

"This fighting among ourselves is wasting time." Her voice was so low every eye went to her. "We should be working together to figure out what Vanka and Paolo mean to do with an army of mud men at the bottom of the river. The phoenix was a test. They're trying to recreate my bond with the god. We have to stop them before it's too late."

At her shoulder, Dory stood a silent witness. His lips were sealed in a thin line, and Azrael knew he could feel the echo of Isela's pain. The link she'd created, breaking Dory's Aegis bond to Azrael, ended with the miracle that was Dory standing whole at her side. What she'd done, bringing him back, was impossible. No necromancer could truly resurrect the dead. Dory should have been a zombie now. Instead, they'd formed an Aegis contract. Her first, and unwillingly, as he'd been told.

And yet she sat erect, looking as magnificent as she had on a stage. His fireproof room had always been a theoretical precaution; thankfully he'd never needed to test it. At least now he knew it would withstand a phoenix's immolation. That wasn't a minor claim. The cracks in the walls could be sealed and the wards repaired.

The greater gain was that she had not failed, not completely. Azrael had never known an immortal creature to be bound by the sanctuary vow. Now a phoenix trapped in human flesh owed its existence to the woman at the table. According to Dr. Sato, its vitals were stronger than ever.

Only he saw the pain behind the grace, the slight tremble of her hand when she lifted it to stop Dory from helping her or following. She moved slowly but stood before Azrael with her shoulders back and her chin high. She placed her back to the room and her body between him and the others.

"What happened is my responsibility." Her gaze snapped to the room behind her, cutting off Tariq's protest. "They have my friend and my dance recordings. I wanted answers."

Azrael covered her hand on his chest with his own. Her cheek softened into his other hand at his touch. Her attention returned to him. His thumb tugged at the corner of her mouth, and she angled her head just enough to press her lips to his palm. The vibration of her, the light, tingling coolness of her power, thrummed against the shell of his fury. Like waves on a rocky shore, given time it would smooth even granite to sand.

"Come, Azrael." When gray eyes fissured with gold met his, he realized that Isela knew his struggle even if she didn't recognize the source. "When I met you, you would put a dozen mortal lives at risk to achieve your ends, the least of which was mine."

Azrael wondered how he'd ever doubted she would be capable of fulfilling the duties of his consort. The god, Dory, the phoenix. Three times the supernatural had pulled her past human experience, and with no training at all she had risen to each moment and conquered. There was power in threes. He'd failed her.

"I've been trying to shield you from the full duties and responsibilities of a consort," he said. "I wanted to give you time to get used to what you've become."

"I love you for wanting it." She touched the edge of his brow with her fingertips where the jagged wound was now a fading scar. "But you're preparing to defend us against the Allegiance. That's why your progeny have come home. And not taking advantage of what I am only makes the world more dangerous—for all of us."

That burgeoning ache in his ribs swelled at her words. She canted her eyebrow in question.

"That's the first time you've ever said that," he confessed.

Her lower lashes sparkled with liquid gold. She caught her own lips with her fingertips in surprise, but her eyes were sad. "Is it?"

He nodded slowly, not realizing how much he'd hungered for the sound of those words in her mouth. What had become of him that three words could create an ache and bloom in him stronger than any of his accumulated powers?

"I'm sorry." She paused, swallowing hard. "It should have been…"

Her voice trailed off and he started to protest. She pressed her fingertips to his lips with a small shake of her head. Their mingling energy crackled at the contact. When he cupped her fingers in his own, he felt the slight tremble of vibration. Shadows smudged the skin beneath her eyes, and her pupils were small as if even her eyes were bracing themselves against pain.

He brought his free hand back to her neck, rubbing the knotted muscles with his thumb. The tension there resisted, pain and weariness greater than her still vulnerable body could bear. She rested her forehead against his collarbone. He took her weight easily. His mouth brushed the edge of her ear when he bowed his head, and he felt her shiver at the fleeting contact.

"I have been a fool. I don't deserve you, Isela Vogel, daughter of wolves and witches, vessel of a god. But I am going to try."

He took in the room in a single sweep of his gaze. Let them watch, all the better. He needed them to see. Needed them all to witness what this was. Because if he lost control of the voice in the back of his head, he needed them all to recognize that he was lost and stand beside her.

"You're right. All of you. This ends today. I am sure between the witches and the necromancers, we will devise training suitable for a god."

I'll see about that, Gold said, an edge of humor in the gilded voice.

Azrael laughed. *I expect you will.*

"Do you forgive me, my lord?" Isela murmured, gazing up at him through a net of dark lashes.

The velvet waves of hair teased his fingers, earthy silk that begged to be tangled around his fingers.

She went up on her toes as his mouth obligingly descended. He unfurled a tendril of heat with the words that caressed her lips. "Don't 'my lord' me *now*, woman."

She shook her head slightly, the electricity of the almost skin-to-skin contact racing straight into his groin. He wanted to groan. Gods help him. A thousand years of training in self-discipline and he was helpless to resist her.

I am going to punish you for this later, you do understand that. It was not a question.

She could not keep the smile contained in her eyes. *I hope so. Very much. In the meantime—*

"You have some explaining to do," she said sternly.

And that was it. The tension went out of the room and the buzz of activity resumed. The youngest witch arrived with a cup blooming with the aroma of lemon and ginger. Azrael escorted Isela back to her chair, took the cup, and cradled Isela's hands around it as she spoke. "I didn't know necromancers could… materialize like that."

At his age, he expected his abilities to be stable. Changes caused increased and unpredictable surges in power—that was what made a young necromancer's transition to an immortal dangerous. Necromancers of power could project images of themselves halfway across the world or farther. But he knew of no other who had ever transported himself from one place to another, not from any distance. Even now he could feel this new ability in him. He feared it was connected to the voice that fed on his anger and spoke with cold, reptilian calculation. The whole room watched him, waiting. The time for secrets was gone.

He faced them all. "Neither did I."

CHAPTER TWENTY

I sela fought her way to consciousness. She inhaled the lingering scent of a home-cooked meal. After all the drama over the phoenix had settled, Beryl announced they would stay for dinner. It was Sunday after all. Evie and Mark headed home, ostensibly to take care of the kids, but Isela suspected her eldest brother still wasn't okay with her new boyfriend. That didn't stop Bebe, Tobias, Chris, and Ofelia from staying. Tyler joined them with amazed reports of the phoenix's continuing recovery. Ito had vanished on a mission for Azrael. She had closed her eyes for what she thought was a few moments and woken up as Azrael shook her gently and steered her to the table.

Food had helped ground her, solidify her. As had looking around the enormous table they'd drafted from another part of the castle at the faces she had begun to trust with her life. Stories were traded. Isela set down her fork as Azrael explained their adventure in the mine, and anxiety crawled its way up her throat. Only seeing him whole, seated across from her, kept her in her chair. Watching his jaw flex and clench at the story of their attack on the bridge, she thought he might have felt the same. But he didn't go into that steely, dead-eyed silence or confine her to the castle. He praised her bravery and her daring. When Tariq raised an eloquent toast to love, there was not a dry eye at the table.

At last the party wound down and they were alone. She remembered Azrael scooping her up and starting for the stairs. There was an amount of fevered kissing, and the heat of him against her and then nothing. She rolled into the empty pillow beside her own. At least this time the imprint of his body remained. The afternoon sun shot rose-gold arrows between the curtains. She ran her hands down her body, feeling the soft jersey tank top that was her sleep shirt. Most of the time that landed across the room. Her eyes felt dry and fuzzy.

"When I was a boy"—Azrael's voice preceded him up the stairs —"there was no such thing as coffee. Not in the world as I knew it anyway. I had my first taste of the stuff when I was just a little older than Gregor is now."

He appeared at the top, showered and dressed, two cups in his hands. His weight settled on the edge of the bed as she blinked and pushed the wild tangle of hair out of her eyes.

"Did you spell me to sleep?" she asked, yawning.

"I stumbled into this hermit's cave near the Dead Sea," he said, waiting until she had finished wiggling into a seated position before handing off her cup. "Nice old man. Batshit crazy, as you might say. He brewed me this awful-tasting stuff. I thought my heart was going to explode. It was a good thing I was in the middle of the desert—I turned sand to glass for over half a mile in all directions."

"It's good to see you've gained some control then," she said, wrapping her hands around the cup and closing her eyes. She opened them again at the unexpected aroma.

"It took a while, but that cured me of my ennui for another hundred years or so." He lifted his cup. "The kitchen seems to have underestimated the amount of ginger my consort requires. I hope this is an acceptable substitute for today."

"Did we, ah, last night?"

He cleared his throat and sipped from the mug in his hand. "Much better, this stuff. Cultivation has done wonders." He looked at her. "You seemed quite engaged for about two minutes. Then you began snoring."

She put her face in one hand and sighed. "I am so sorry."

"You did barely avoid being dissolved into your component molecules." He touched her forehead, smoothing her eyebrow with his thumb. "It seemed prudent to let you sleep. But I was beginning to wonder if my ability to burn down the bed had lost its appeal."

She smiled around a sip of coffee. He'd made it sweet and rich with cream. She could get used to this.

"Speaking of," she began.

"My ennui?" he joked.

"Control," she said finally. "That fireproof room. It's not just for ordinary fire, is it?"

"Growth spurts."

"Come again?"

He smiled. "When we are young and our powers are coming on, they can be somewhat unstable."

"So unstable you could spontaneously combust?"

"It's not unheard of," he said. "Fire is the most immediately dangerous of the elements. Though we once found the corpse of a water necromancer who had cut open her own chest in an attempt to keep herself from drowning in her lungs."

Isela stared.

Azrael seemed to realize how horrifying the anecdote was and pushed on. "There's a reason so few of the most powerful survive to maturity—it's not just infighting among us that poses a danger. Power is difficult to control."

He let that settle in.

"My adolescence was"—he searched for a word—"challenging. At best, I could have incinerated myself. At worst, I could have taken out a whole city, small as they were in those days."

"Is that what happened at Iram?" she whispered. "You lost control?"

The lightness left his face, and for a moment she regretted the question. But he didn't deflect. His voice grew somber. "No. That's not what happened at Iram."

She looked away first. "You have control now."

"We limit our use of power to the necessary." He nodded. "As you discovered, big spells gone awry can create unpredictable surges. But it appears you are the not only one who must learn to master new powers. And I have no idea what the dark side of my new ability will be or how it will affect my control."

He looked troubled for a moment, and she saw it again, the uncertainty. Something else moved behind his face, the flicker of a shadow. There was nothing uncertain about the expression it held. She shivered with the sudden urge to call him back even though he sat a few feet away. "And the fireproof room?"

"Would protect the city," he said. "Should my powers ever destabilize. But there is no guarantee the wards will hold long or disperse enough power to ameliorate the damage entirely. I'm counting on the castle to take the brunt of the it. If things get bad and I go into that room, it will be up to you to get everyone out of this building—out of the city if possible. If I survive, I will come to you. Now ask. Ask about the monster that destroyed the lost city."

She gnawed her lower lip. "The Alchemist said you turned it to glass."

His brows rose. "Circe is full of stories, but for this one she can claim only rumors." He contemplated her face with such intensity she found herself holding her breath. Still she met his gaze without flinching. "I would have nothing unknown between us, though you may not like what you hear. Would you have me tell the tale?"

She exhaled and nodded.

* * *

SOMETIME AROUND SUNSET, they'd moved downstairs. He watched her make popcorn in a heavy-bottomed skillet on the stove, intrigued. Then he took a handful of kernels in his cupped palms, shook them, and she hadn't been able to hide her delight at the sound of popping. He emptied the fluffy white kernels, indistinguishable from her own, into the bowl.

They ended up in the living room overlooking the garden. Sideways on the sofa, Isela faced the garden, her back molding to the side of his chest and shoulder, her knees drawn up to cradle the bowl in her lap. After the separation and the danger they'd faced, she found she craved the reassurance of physical contact. He seemed more than willing to meet that need. He stretched out his legs, crossing his bare feet at the ankles on the coffee table, and angled himself to comfortably drape an arm around her collarbones.

Another ordinary moment, a brief flash of what could be if it weren't for the necromancers trying to kill them and her own friend abducted.

Gregor and Lysippe were in transit back to the castle. Dante and her brothers were looking into the mud army in the river. Tariq and Gus stepped up patrols of the city with the rest of the Aegis, hunting for any signs of intrusion. Before returning to her coven, Beryl had insisted Isela recover, so Azrael apparently put himself in charge of making sure she remained in their quarters. She hadn't needed much persuasion. It was a rare moment of quiet, but she felt the storm coming in her bones.

If she had ever longed for normalcy, she might miss it. Instead, the rarity of these moments made them all the sweeter.

Outside, the first signs of spring showed in the trees. New buds protruded like tiny emerald spears from the mature, winter-darkened branches, braving the remaining weeks of cold for the promise of sun. They had months ahead of them, full of rain and wind, before the long days of summer. Yet they bloomed. That kind of faith took courage, she thought, and hope.

"Tell me," she said, feeling braver now that Iram was behind them, "about how you came to join the Allegiance."

Azrael traced her shoulder blade through the heavy black silk of her robe. "I had no interest in an alliance between us, though Róisín always spoke of a day when humans could no longer be trusted not to destroy us all and must be taken to hand. Paolo came first. Then Vanka."

Isela wiggled some distance away from him, and swung her legs onto his lap. His palm skimmed the bare shin revealed when the split panels of the robe parted up to her thighs. He paused, momentarily distracted by the expanse of skin on display in his immediate vicinity.

"You were her progeny." Isela opened her mouth and pointed for him to toss a popped kernel.

He obliged with a dubious toss. She caught it, barely, with a wry look of challenge.

"We had parted ways a millennia before," he said. "While I *appreciated* her tutelage, I was driven to pursue other aims."

"Wine, women, and song?" Isela grinned.

"I had no desire for a life acquiring power and the machinations of the others. Lysippe and I, and later Gregor and the rest, pursued the mysteries of our race."

"So you were like Indiana Jones." When his face remained blank, Isela sighed. "No time to see a movie in all that dashing around hunting out artifacts, eh? What brought you back?"

He tossed another kernel her way. "When they forged the wall binding the gods from humanity, Róisín called on me and I answered. That was the last time I saw her sane."

"But when the Allegiance declared itself, you stood with them."

"Many things happened very quickly after the war ended," he said, tossing her another kernel. "You are good at this game."

"I have three brothers—it was learn to catch or not get any popcorn on movie nights."

He let another kernel fly. "Humanity was at a tipping point. All the great strides of twentieth-century—art, technology, science were about to be lost to chaos. It needed to be stabilized and fast. It was Gola who reached out to me to fill Róisín's seat.

"The tension for control of Europe in her absence had already begun to split the Allegiance. Vanka wanted it all. Gola and Kadijah wouldn't have it. As Róisín's heir, it was my right to challenge. I did."

"You won." Isela felt the breath leave her in a wash of relief.

"A draw," he said, which killed a little bit of her joy. "And the others talked Vanka out of further pursuit on the matter. They needed my power. We fixed things—as much as we could—as quickly as possible. We were ruthless. I never believed Róisín had gone mad, but I had too much to do to spend much time on it."

"How did you find out?"

"Emma," he said, naming the necromancer who ruled the island region of Oceania. "She's a bit different."

That said a lot. Isela remembered the smoking woman with ropy twists of hair and eyes that were vacant one minute and soul rending the next.

"I think she wanted me to know the truth," he said idly. "Or she just wanted to see what would happen if I challenged Paolo and Vanka. Hard to tell with her. Her mind works differently."

Isela leaned forward, scooping up a handful of popped corn, and held a kernel up. Azrael missed his first three. He lunged at the last. Isela yelped in laughter. The bowl clattered to the floor, spilling popcorn everywhere. He opened his mouth, pointing at the fluffy kernel on his tongue.

"Dramatic, but effective," she said, licking the salt off his fingers. His pupils dilated and she smiled.

"You're right to fear them," he said, prowling toward her. "Gola and Emma most of all. They are our elders, and whatever was human in them is dust. We are the boogeymen—and women—Isela. The things that go bump in the night."

A little smile played at the corner of his mouth, and he traced a finger up her bare knee.

"I'm not afraid of you, necromancer," she said, fixing her eyes on his. "We have some unfinished business that I'd like to take care of."

The finger traced a lazy circle on the inside of her thigh. It took her a moment—too long—to recognize the geas in the motion. Her body went still an inhalation later. Her breath and heartbeat continued mostly as usual, quickening in alarm. But she could not so much as turn her head.

Dark lashes lowered over silver eyes. "Perhaps you should be."

"What is this?" She blinked.

Azrael smiled at her, showing teeth. "You endangered my consort by playing with spells. I warned you that a price would be paid. To get what you want, you'll have to break it."

He picked up her hand. She expected the arm to stay fixed, but it unfolded at his touch as if by command. He straightened her arm and pressed his lips to the inside of her elbow. She felt the graze of teeth. A shudder in this state was a peculiar sensation.

Isela struggled against panic at the state of frozenness. The glimmer of gold rose in back of her mind. An offer.

No, she commanded firmly. *I can handle this.*

Azrael wore the lazy smile of a satisfied conqueror. Broad, masculine hands settled at her knees, bronzed skin a few shades lighter than her own. His thumbs flexed against the sensitive skin at the inside of her thighs, and the impulse to open her legs away from the pressure drove another spasm of pleasure up her legs.

Just to prove he could, he parted her thighs without breaking eye contact.

She focused on what she could do. Swallow. Clear her throat. Speak?

"What did you do?" The distant gasp of her own voice, husky and trembling. "When you found out about Róisín?"

His fingers slid down her calves to the sensitive spot behind her heels. "I vowed to make them pay."

She wanted to throw back her head and sob when his mouth touched one instep and then the other. He worked a slow, wet path up her calf to the inner knee. Popcorn crunched as he slid off the couch and settled between her thighs.

"Do they know?" she whispered, fighting the sensation that threatened to overtake her as he licked the inside of her thigh.

"Salty," he said, a new tone in his voice. "I can smell your desire."

"About your vow," she insisted.

There had to be a way around this. She set her mind on the geas, untangling her thoughts from the physical response to sensation.

"They've always been uneasy with me," he admitted, sliding open the tie on her robe. "And they know I have a reason to hate them. But perhaps a vow for vengeance is no longer enough. Look at where it got Róisín."

He sat back on his heels for a long moment. Without the slightest urgency he roved her partially bared body with his gaze. Only once did he reach up to slide the black edge of the robe open. He did it with an intense carelessness, as a curator might make a slight adjustment to better display a piece of art. Then he rested again, simply watching. Awareness of his eyes on her skin brought a flush to the surface.

At one time Isela would have described his expression as cold. She thought of how she had first seen him—a ruthless power capable of terrible acts of violence to keep chaos from taking over his territory. She had questioned if he had ever been human.

Now she knew the small play of muscles and the tautness in the carved lines of his face. She knew the look in his eyes, the burning promise of ecstasy tightly reined with patience driven by purpose. He would wait an eternity for her to unravel this geas. The geas was a test and also a gift. Her first lesson in using her power, delivered in the arms of a man who would absorb a thousand blows to keep any harm from touching her.

The arms that had held her while she slept. The hands that stroked her body to passion she had never known. The eyes that claimed her with a simple glance no matter what trouble she managed to bring to his door.

Their door.

This magnificent, terrible being who had walked the earth for two thousand years had seen in her something that made him risk becoming a man again. And with one emotion came all the others.

Disregarding the physical, she experimented with sending out the curling essence of herself as she had so often felt him wrap around her to comfort, soothe, arouse. His eyes flared with surprise.

Connected like this, she truly felt him. Felt the rage that he had leashed for so long and the hunger for vengeance born of injustice. The sense of guilt for not having been able to stop what happened to

Róisín and his part in it. The loneliness of being the newest member to a body he could not afford to trust. And hurt at their betrayal. The certainty that he could no longer walk the path he had been placed on but hadn't found another way.

The room blurred in her vision. A single tear streaked down her cheek. Frustration—sexual blending with a desire to comfort—flared. Before she could check herself, the power surged. It hit him full force. The geas shattered.

She came back to herself with her arms around him, her face nestled in the space between his jaw and collar. Her breath escaped her in ragged gasps. She tried to push away from him, but his arms held her like a vise. She shoved, beating the heels of her hands against his chest. Fear that she had somehow hurt him clogged her throat. It was a moment before she felt his shoulders shaking. His breath hitched. With laughter.

Anger stiffened her limbs. Now she tried to get her legs between them, to push him away. He would have none of it. When he released her enough for her to see his face, she went still again.

"Come now." A smile of such lightness and beauty, echoed by silver eyes that were wet around the edges. She fought the urge to smile back. It was the first purely joyful expression she had seen on his face. He looked like a boy, all mischievousness and delight. "You just broke a geas that took me one hundred years to build, and you have nothing to say."

She scowled, crossing her arms. "Are you laughing at me?"

Shock took some of the joy out of his face. He clutched her close again. She tried to ignore her body's response to contact with the expanse of his chest and the ridged plane of his abdomen. His belt pressed into her thighs, and she wiggled a bit as cool leather and metal dug into the sensitive skin.

"I'd never laugh at you, Isela." The earnestness in his tone tugged at her as lifted her back onto the couch and then did his best to undo her braid.

"Then why are you laughing?" she said, swatting his hand as he continued to fuss with her hair. "I was worried I'd hurt you."

She could tell he was trying very hard not to smile.

"I had forgotten happiness," he said. "And you *may* have knocked out the power on the north end of the castle."

* * *

SHE SAT BACK on the couch with her arms folded over her chest, confusion and concern warring as tears dried on her face, and he'd never known a woman he wanted more. A sienna blush flamed in her face and, to his intrigue, her breasts. Her legs were still parted, the robe bunched around her hips and thighs. Her smell sang to him. His cock throbbed insistently even as his chest tightened against a surge of emotion he'd long ago thought he'd never feel for another living thing.

There was so much of her that was still human. It had taken him too long to see it as strength. The same part that made her vulnerable also made her power work in ways a necromancer would never expect.

"You did with compassion," he said, running a fingertip over the line of her mouth, "what most could not do with force."

She was mad at him, but it lacked any heat. Fighting for dominance on her face was wonder and surprise and love. He would do anything to have her look at him like that for the rest of their time on earth. It had been a long time since he'd believed in any divine power, but in that moment she was enough to make him thank whatever god had put her in his path.

He said the only thing he knew how to say, his hands settling on her hips. "Thank you, Isela Vogel."

Confusion won, turning her expression charmingly innocent. "For what?"

He yanked her hips to the edge of the cushion with a smooth jerk that made her gasp. "For seeing me," he said, looking up at her from beneath a fringe of tousled hair, "as I am. And for wanting me anyway."

Before the first tear could spill over her lashes, he lowered his mouth to taste her.

His name tangled with a sob and a shout in her throat. He smiled into the succulent flesh. When he glanced up again, her head was thrown back on the cushions, fingers fisting and releasing spasmodically at her sides. As tempting as it was to let those taut dancer's legs tighten around his shoulders while he brought her to her peak, he wanted more.

He pulled back. Before her eyes could open, he'd flipped her smoothly onto her knees, her chest resting on the back of the couch. She grunted with pleasure as her knees spread wider, preparing for his entry. But he pressed her forward, tilting her hips back so he could continue with his mouth at a new angle. He had to grip her hips to keep her from twisting away as release wrung her body of its pent-up desire. The wave of her surged against his lips, and he lingered to let her tremble and sigh as the last of her climax shuddered through her.

With one hand, he held her as the other made quick work of his belt and fly. She braced herself as he slid an arm around her waist, reaching to guide him. He wanted to go slow. But the touch of her swollen heat, the scent of her still lingering on his lips, rendered him senseless. She was going to be the death of him.

He felt the surge as he plunged into her. She opened, physically and energetically, taking him in. Sparks of gold danced on her skin as he quickened. Tightening again, she groaned, and he slid his fingers to a better position to help her. When he looked down at himself, his skin glowed, the emerald tangling with gold until she too shone. Her skin glittered. Denying himself final pleasure, he flipped her onto her back.

Passion heated her face, but the strands of gold in her hair and the irises of her eyes glowed with an energy all their own.

A gasp escaped her lips. "Don't stop."

He arched his body over hers, pinning her hips with his own. So much heat. Must protect her. Must claim her. Desire was in control now. All heat and fire with none of the reptilian coldness that had prowled his consciousness for an opening before. He slid home with a roar. There. Mine.

"Once more for me." Part plea, part command.

He thought she laughed, husky voice glittering around the edges. He felt his soul slipping free of its mooring, racing to catch the golden shape dancing ahead. His climax coiled low and building, painful now with urgency. He held it.

"I will have your surrender, goddess." His breath slid against her ear.

"Take it if you can, death dealer." The voice of his lover, coated in the gold of a god.

Stars bloomed behind his eyes when he caught the golden shape, and it was he who surrendered. Heat and power surged up through him in a roar of white noise. Blinded and deafened by his own release, he felt her begin to clutch him and let himself go completely. Her body formed a cradle. *This*, he thought in a language so old he'd not spoken it aloud in hundreds of years. *She is where I belong. This is my home.*

Then he realized where they were.

* * *

"DON'T MOVE." Azrael's voice caressed the shell of her ear.

A small, purring sound escaped her—all pleasure without a single thought that could be translated into language. She wasn't going anywhere. She could lie like this for days, just savoring the cool air on her back and his heat on her belly. Gold's giggle came languorously a heartbeat later. *Oh Isela, thank you.*

I suppose we are going to have to tell him about this. Eventually.

Pretty sure he figured it out.

A grin licked her lips, and she let her tongue dart out to taste the skin of his neck. Salty. "If this is how all of our lessons end, I think I'm going to like this training."

He shifted with a laugh that became a little growl of warning. Aftershocks throbbed inside her. The air caressed her back again.

Wait. That wasn't right.

Gold echoed. *Wait. Issy…*

Now she heard the slight edge in Azrael's voice. "Just don't—"

Her eyes flickered open and she blinked. The ceilings that had once housed the royal riding school and an armory before Azrael had converted them to his own personal quarters were twenty feet high in places. The exposed beams hovered before her. Her eyes caught on a little spider making its perilous way across the dark wood. Had her vision improved again?

The skin on her back puckered in the draft. A certain lightness in her own belly. As though she was floating.

She sucked in a hard breath and twisted her head to take in the room *below* them as Azrael called, "Wait!"

They fell. Azrael twisted in midair to land beneath her on the rug, but with her elbow trapped between them, she succeeded in knocking the breath from them both. They landed with a thump and a collective gasp for air. Azrael recovered first, rolling her from his chest to prop himself up on one hand.

He, of course, was laughing. Did nothing surprise this man?

Her first inhale came with the smell of charred leather and burned popcorn. He jerked his chin in the direction of the smoldering remains of the couch. A kernel sprang off the floor and landed a fluffy white ball.

A huff escaped her. "I liked that couch."

"I'll buy you a dozen more," he said, springing to his feet and pulling her up with him. "And we'll burn them all."

Her legs wobbled and he caught her, sweeping a forearm behind her knees.

"Did you do that?" she asked as Azrael bounded up the stairs to the bathroom. "The floaty thing?"

"No, little god…" He grinned, setting her down and hooking the robe from her shoulders with a finger as he passed. "You did."

Isela sat down hard. "I what?"

"Come, let me wash you." He herded her under the rainfall showerhead. "You reek of sex, and we're due in the training ring in a half hour."

"But I…" She reached for the soap but he was faster. "We?"

He slapped her hand away with a look of reproach. She supposed she'd had boyfriends with worse fixations. "Our master-at-arms was unsatisfied with my performance on our expedition. I've been ordered to report for a tune-up."

She gave herself over to the slow torment of his hands. "I thought powers were elemental."

He shook his head absently. "For necromancers. And witches. Gods have the laws of nature at their command."

Gods. That's what she was now, wasn't it? Not a witch, not a necromancer. For the first time it occurred to her that no one had tried to teach her because they didn't know *how* or even where to begin.

"That was why you had to work together," she said. "To stop the gods the first time."

He tapped the end of her nose. "We needed each other."

"And now?"

"Now we try to keep the peace between us." He turned off the water. "But the world as it is—necromancers over everything—this cannot hold."

"That's why the Allegiance was afraid of channeling a god." And why she was such a danger to them. And why they would want to strike now, while she was still mostly human and vulnerable. Even a small god would be more than a match for the Allegiance once she understood her power. She met Azrael's eyes as he handed her a towel. It took her a moment to recognize the expression in his—hope. "You're not worried."

He opened the glass door, gazing intently for a moment. "Watch carefully."

He traced a symbol in the condensation, ignoring the droplets that rolled away to create a sweeping, elegant dance of lines. It reminded her of calligraphy and hieroglyphics. She recognized it by the third stroke. The geas he'd used to immobilize her.

"You see?" he asked, waiting for her confirming nod before wiping his hand over the glass and erasing it. "Practice it until you can do it without hesitation. Then use it on Tyler or one of my Aegis. Someone I can release if it goes wrong. When you can safely undo it, try it on a human. It's useful to get information from a subject without truly harming them. Most people break quickly from fear and anticipation."

A thousand questions bubbled up.

Azrael shook his head before any of them could emerge. "You are right—a single project of focus will teach you much more than a stack of books. And Dante will handle the books in any case. Do you remember it?"

Isela thought back, surprised to find she could recall each stroke exactly.

"And now that you know how to break it and how it's formed, it can't be used against you again. *That* is the lesson."

A wedge of gratitude closed her throat. He finished with his towel and discarded it. Naked, he stalked to the counter, running the hot water and laying shaving implements on a clean towel.

She admired the dimples above his perfect ass and the corded strength of his legs before her eyes caught on the fading signs of his recent fight. She knew in a day or two they would be gone completely.

He had only three permanent scars, acquired before his healing ability had developed. She knew the story of each. He'd kept them to remind himself of the lessons they'd taught. The one on his back reminded him to be careful where he placed his trust. The broken lines on the knuckles of his left hand to remind him of the importance of hard work. The jagged tear at his throat to remind him of mortality. He'd placed her fingers over it in the dark so she could learn the ridges as he'd explained that it had begun to lose effectiveness. Until she came into his life.

She had taught him that fear and hope were sides of the same coin and that love was the prize for claiming one over the other. After, they'd made love with a fearsome gentleness, and when, at last, she slept, she did not dream of the dead.

He coughed lightly and she looked up. A little grin curled his mouth. "My eyes are up here."

She swallowed the emotion in her throat and focused on detangling her hair. "Quit strutting around like a peacock."

He laughed, giving a quick glance to assure himself all his tools were in order before examining the task at hand in the mirror. Trekking across remote plains and into abandoned mines didn't lend itself to personal grooming apparently. She'd never seen him with so much growth. It made him look feral and unpredictable.

"I realized something on the road," he said as he lathered. "The others run their territories like fiefdoms, and by turning a blind eye I have accomplished nothing. If I fall tomorrow, this will all go away."

Isela shivered. Only meeting the Allegiance had given her an indication that the world was not as stable as it seemed. The peace Azrael kept within his borders made his territory one of the most successful.

"There is only one solution," he said, taking the razor to his cheek.

She watched his strokes. Sure and steady, he razed the week's worth of growth in orderly passes, pausing occasionally to clean the blade. She was glad he hadn't asked her to do it. As intimate as it sounded, the fact that she had no idea what she was doing would have killed any growing arousal. She didn't want to test his immortality by accidentally slitting his throat. And now her hands were shaking at his words.

"You mean to take down the Allegiance." Isela sat down on the edge of the tub, the length of her hair forgotten over her shoulder.

His eyes met hers in the mirror. "One by one if I must."

"Why now?"

His words were simple, but she felt the conviction in them. "I wasn't strong enough before."

"Before what?"

"Before you."

Challenging the Allegiance. It sounded like lunacy. They would be two against seven, and she just learning how to use the power of the god.

He saw it in her face. "Not tomorrow, Isela. Not even in a year. But we can do it. Together."

Azrael focused on his reflection, gliding over his chin and along the skin of his neck. He scrutinized a bit of skin on his jawline, made a quick pass, and then set down his razor. A splash of water and the familiar face reappeared—controlled, unflappable. But now she knew what was there, beneath. She could see the untamed under the surface of his skin.

"My family," Isela said finally. "My friends."

He inclined his head. "We can try to wait it out, protect what is ours. It doesn't have to come to war. I've already begun to make allies in the Allegiance, perhaps we can persuade others to join us and dismantle it from within."

She thought of Yana. If they were bold enough to snatch her in the heart of Azrael's territory, was anyone she loved truly safe? Could she ever consider any of the others allies?

"You must promise me something," she said, proud of how calm her voice sounded as she managed to steady her fingers enough to make a braid.

A canted grin in the mirror. "You're learning how to deal with immortals."

"You will treat me as your consort. You will tell me everything, and you will include me in your plans and stratagems."

"And you've been reading the codes," he said admiringly.

"Dante is a good teacher."

"The best," he agreed. He paused thoughtfully. "There may be times that I must move fast, and I won't have time to talk it out. Can you trust me in those moments, that I do what is best for us and to explain later?"

Her heart thudded against her rib cage. Every beat now bore his name, as though it had always been so. "I can. Will you trust me to handle my goddess in the manner that I think best?"

Thank you, Isela. Gold chimed in. *You didn't forget me.*

As if you'd let me, Isela said wryly.

A rush of rose gold bloomed in her chest.

"I can," Azrael said.

Isela dried her hand and stretched it out. Azrael turned, crossing his arms over his chest and studying her. Isela kept her eyes north of his belly button. Mostly. He chewed at his lower lip, and every last thought fled her brain.

"For the gods' sakes, put on some pants," she muttered.

"Hard time concentrating?" he said, leaning back against the counter. "It's still worse when you prance about in one of those tiny leotards."

Isela's cheeks heated but she held his gaze. "Do we have a deal or not, O lord of death?"

His brow slid north. "One more thing."

She waited patiently.

"Your hair," he said. "Will you wear it down more? It favors you."

Isela snorted. "We're talking about taking down the most powerful seven necromancers in the world—"

"And their cronies."

"And their—cheese and crackers—we are in *way* over our heads," she muttered, glaring at him. "And you are worried about my hair?"

"I'm a simple man." He shrugged. "I enjoy the sight of my lover's hair and the feel of it free against my skin."

"Do you know how much conditioner that's going to take?" She sighed. "Fine. Don't run off into danger without telling me what's up. Hair down. Got it."

She extended her hand again expectantly. He clasped her palm in his own and drew her against the length of his chest, lowering his head to taste her mouth. She couldn't help herself, she drew her fingers along the smooth skin of his cheek, and arousal pressed into her core with pulsing heat. He lifted her easily so she could rest her knees on the countertop on either side of his hips. He stroked her cheeks with his freshly bare jawline and mouth until she purred.

"Is this how you seal all your deals?" She shivered when his fingers found her ready.

"With my consort," he said, sliding home. "Absolutely."

CHAPTER TWENTY-ONE

"How can an army—hundreds—of mud men just up and vanish overnight?" Isela shook her head.

Gregor shrugged with nonchalant grace. He'd whistled a jaunty version of "London Calling" in response to Isela's surprise on seeing him instead of Lysippe when they'd finally made it down to training. Being late hadn't put him in the best mood.

The only indication of his current focus was the speed at which he danced a toothpick over his knuckles. Its motion ceased abruptly, and Isela was able to see it wasn't an ordinary wooden toothpick. It looked to be made of some precious material with a slight iridescent sheen. Probably horn of a unicorn he'd hunted himself. And choked the life out of with his bare hands.

"All but one. Thanks to you." The toothpick resumed its steady path over his knuckles. She took a little satisfaction at the broken skin and the stiff movement of his wrist. She hadn't known it could be so much fun slinging a human body around by the thumb.

For fun, Isela concentrated on the levitation trick. The toothpick floated off his knuckles. He reached for it as she sent it spinning out of his grasp. But with one eye still swollen mostly shut her depth perception was off and she lost control of the spin. It clinked against the silver whiskey flask on the table and bounced off. Dante reached forward with the tip of his pen and slid the toothpick in Gregor's direction.

Her gaze lingered on the flask on the table. It fairly thrummed with latent power. She could smell it even with the container tightly capped—an impossible combination of midnight and old wine and dried flowers. Gregor and Tariq had immediately argued over whether to call it the Elixir of Life or *Amrita.* Dante corrected them both with *Soma* and a rather tedious explanation of that since etymologically even the word *ambrosia,* inaccurate as it was, had Indo-European roots, but it could apply. Soma was likely a more accurate name, though Soma was thought to be distilled from a plant, not found dripping from a subterranean rock. Or rising, as it were.

"Call it *manna* or the Peaches of Immortality for all I care," Gus barked.

"The peaches—" Dante began.

"Enough," Azrael said, calling their attention back to the matter at hand as he dabbed at the cotton in his nose. It had bled for an extraordinarily long time, but she supposed taking an ax eye to the face would do that. The swelling had gone down, but the bruising spread across his eyes like a mask still made her wince.

Isela resigned herself to understanding what exactly the liquid in the flask was capable of later. She shifted in her seat, the bruise on her backside making sitting uncomfortable. Gregor smirked.

"The one your car managed to damage, or the remains of it," Dante went on.

"In any case," Gus said, "it shows that they're willing to flirt with pushing not only the leeway Azrael gave them but the very code of engagement of conflict."

Isela frowned, muttering at Dante under her breath. "Is there a CliffsNotes version somewhere?"

Dante's eyebrows furrowed in question.

"Of these codes. I can't keep up."

His laugh slipped free before he could catch it. All eyes flashed to them as he tried to cover it with a dry cough.

"You've had a chance to examine it." Azrael's voice brought her back into the room. "Madame Witch?"

When Azrael had requested the presence of a witch to examine the creature from the bottom of the river, there had been some heated discussion among the coven. It was Bebe who cheerfully volunteered. She thought her sister-in-law rather enjoyed the hint of danger and independence from the others. Isela bit back a smile at the memory of

Bebe striding into the study regally with her four-legged guardian at her side.

She'd caught sight of Azrael and Isela and her brows shot up. "What the Grace happened to you two since yesterday?"

"Late to training." Isela glared at Azrael. He had the decency to look chagrined as he limped to his seat with a pointed look at Gregor's back.

Now Bebe's large dark eyes kept returning to the flask with the look of someone who had seen a miracle.

"They appear to be a kind of automaton, sir," Bebe said. Curled watchfully around her feet, Tobias flicked his ears at the sound of her voice

"Appear?" Gregor kept his face carefully blank.

Toby rose onto his forepaws, but his head stayed low, ears swiveled back as his lips curled in silent warning. Gregor's brows rose in return. Bebe settled a hand between her husband's ears.

"Golems," she said, meeting Gregor's eye. "Of a kind. We are in Prague, after all."

"Folktales," Gregor growled.

"I recall a particular American fancy about a headless horseman who may or may not have been Hessian by birth," Dante said.

Gregor sat back in his chair. "You know how I feel about horses. Loew's creation was benevolent And there was only the one."

"The golem was part of Jewish folklore long before Loew raised his man of clay from the Vltava, if the story is to be believed," Bebe said confidently. "The mechanics are the same. Created from mud or clay, impressed with the command of their master."

"It's a geas of some power," Dante filled in. "And a command for obedience. A necromancer's mark, which will activate them when called."

"Two guesses who." Isela sighed. "But where are the others? And what will activate them? And how do we deactivate them?"

"All excellent questions," Dante said. "Answers presently unknown."

"What they are tells us something of their purpose," Bebe interjected eagerly. "These are not complex creatures. They are stronger than humans or zombies, but they are not intelligent in any respect. Once activated, they do not deviate."

"If the Allegiance means to attack Azrael," Gregor said, "it could be that the golems are intended to divide his attention."

"The city," Isela murmured. "They could turn them loose on the city while Vanka makes her move to summon a god. Gold showed me a tear in the wall. Yana may be a ballerina, but she's also my friend." Her voice cracked. "And if Vanka found the ambrosia first... Well, could it make it easier for her to hold a god? Madeline said it would take something special—"

She found all eyes staring at her in the sticky silence that followed.

"Tell us about this Madeline," Azrael said quietly. His face had gone unreadable again.

Isela flushed. She wasn't sure *what* Madeline was, but after all she had seen, she was positive Madeline wasn't quite human. She was also sure that, until this moment, the librarian had managed to somehow remain below the radar of the necromancer.

Only Azrael's eyes never left Isela's. *Little wolf. We made a bargain.*

Isela tried to keep her face still as her mental voice strained with desperation. *She has been my friend and my guide.*

Then tell me what she is and how—

Isela sighed. *I don't know. But she's part of my family at the Academy. If we must involve her, please let me handle it. She trusts me.*

"Madeline is a librarian," she said aloud, spreading her palms to indicate the perceived harmlessness of the occupation. "For the Academy."

"She seems to know quite a lot," Dante murmured. "Perhaps, Azrael, I might have a conversation with her. Two old librarians might have a thing or two to talk about."

Gregor's nostrils flared. "I say we bring her here and extract the necessary information. No time for a palaver, old man."

"Isela will go." Azrael spoke to Dante, ignoring his second. "To earn her goodwill. Assure her that no harm will come to her if she cooperates."

"Master," Gregor growled.

"You will escort them," Azrael interrupted. "For the protection of my consort."

And if the woman does not comply... Isela barely needed to hear the finished sentence in her head. *You will bring her here for questioning.*

Gregor looked satisfied, if not entirely pleased. Dory objected to being left behind, but on that Azrael and Isela agreed.

"You're still healing," Azrael said. "And I don't want Isela distracted by your pain. Not until both of you are strong enough to manage it. The Academy is secure and the city is clean. Gregor will be fine."

Dory looked miserable, and Isela squeezed his forearm. "She's just a librarian. You won't miss anything exciting, I promise."

"Madame Barbara." Azrael's eyes turned to Bebe and she sat up.

"It's just Barbara, sir," she said. "Or Bebe—that's what everyone calls me."

Azrael nodded. "I have already taken much of your time, but I must ask one more favor before you rejoin your coven."

Toby pricked his ears, pressing his fur close to Bebe's thigh. Her hand slid to his back.

"And of your mate." Azrael inclined his head. "Will you also meet with this *librarian?*" He said the title with an edge of disbelief. "I would appreciate your expertise in assessing exactly what she is and her intentions in the city. If any information she provides is useful to the coven to determine how best to protect the city, that would also be appreciated."

To her credit, Bebe kept her usually animated face still. Mostly. Her brows ticked upward slightly.

"I'll do my best, sir."

"Azrael," he said, giving up on formality.

"Bebe." She corrected him with a smile.

* * *

WELL, *that could have gone worse,* Isela thought, crouching behind one of the overturned massive oak desks as another chair hurtled by.

Dante, crouched across the aisle behind another table with Toby and Bebe, peered around the table legs. He looked delighted. *I'm not sure how.*

"Maddie, I'm sorry. I had no choice," Isela repeated in the lull between the librarian's attacks.

"There is always a choice, Isela!"

Isela barely recognized the voice coming from the other side of the room. The musical patois of her accent had been replaced by what sounded like a choir of angry old ladies.

They'd taken Madeline by surprise, which Isela had both hoped for and dreaded. The tightness in her own chest flared as she saw the amiable greeting fade from Madeline's face at the sight of Isela's company.

Gregor had been no help, striding in like he expected to find the place crawling with zombies. Isela would speak to Azrael about the wisdom of sending a machine gun on a diplomatic mission later. At the sight of him, Madeline had shrieked in unearthly sexagenarian harmony before leaping from behind her dais to the wall, scuttling upward in a blur of motion. Isela admitted to staring slack jawed before Dante yanked her out of the way.

"Fucking spider," Gregor swore, drawing his black blade and 9mm as he shadowed her progress on the wall.

"Arachnea—of course!" Dante straightened, forgetting his cover.

Isela tugged him back. "A what?" Isela's attention whipped back at the gunshots that drowned out Dante's explanation. "Don't hurt her!"

Madeline doubled back as Gregor hurried to cut her off. He kicked a rug out of the corner, revealing a trapdoor. "They always have a back way out."

Madeline screamed rage, scuttling back the way she'd come. Isela registered her familiar form, but Gold revealed something many-eyed and limbed beneath.

"Spider," she murmured, entranced as the librarian slung herself from the wall to the chandelier, a thin thread of silk glittering behind her.

Isela and Dante crossed the room to join Gregor. His eyes never left the woman who was now spinning thin strands of silk into a web from the chandelier.

"I never thought I'd actually see one." Dante sounded almost ecstatic, palms pressed together as he watched her work.

"I'd hoped I'd never see another." The corner of Gregor's mouth dragged downward. "Well, dancer?"

"We need her help."

The librarian looked up from her web, and Isela had the impression that there were far more eyes turned on her than she could actually see. She experimented with initiating Gold's vision, and rows of shiny black eyes surrounded by soft dark fur became visible.

Good job, Issy. You're learning.

"Ungrateful child," the choir voice chittered. "You bring this mercenary into my refuge."

The librarian dropped to the floor, startling Isela. Even at a distance, she seemed larger than before. Isela swallowed hard.

"We mean you no harm." Isela held up her palms. "But there are two necromancers planning—"

The nascent web trembled with the force of her rage. "My purpose is older than the children too foolish to use the grace in their blood for anything other than power struggles."

Isela dimly registered Gregor moving in the corner of her eye. Her attention was on the glittering white ball attached to thread arcing toward her. Didn't some spiders throw their webs at their prey, her brain wondered belatedly.

Gregor hit her a heartbeat before the web did. He flung Isela aside as it snared his arm, yanking him backward. She landed with an airless "oof" against the bookshelves. Gregor rebounded quickly, slicing the sticky web free from its tether. Madeline swung a chair at him. It struck a glancing blow as she scuttled away. He paused, trying to free himself from the remnants of the web.

Dante darted across the space to help Isela into a sitting position.

"They are only aggressive when threatened," he said, fixing his glasses. "But the web is problematic."

Gregor swore again as he backed into a defensive position between Madeline and the exits.

Whatever she was, Madeline still considered herself the keeper of priceless treasures. She never threw a single book. The furniture was fair game though. Isela and Dante turned the two tables closest to the dais on their sides to form a barricade against the assault of paperweights, chairs, and balls of sticky web.

Isela scanned their group—Toby and Bebe crouched behind the other table. Gregor freed himself from the last of the webbing, murder in his eyes. She had to do something.

"Wise Madeline, spinner of the webs of knowledge and history of the world, hear me." Bebe's voice rang out as she rose from behind the table.

"Bebe, get down," Isela hissed.

But Dante grabbed Isela's arm and pressed a finger to his lips for silence.

"I've no love for your kind, little witch." The angry choir chided. "Take your familiar and leave this place."

Toby's jaws snapped, but Bebe ignored him.

"The city you are sworn to protect needs your help," Bebe said. "She is in danger, and without you she may be lost."

Madeline appeared from the shelter of the dais, her gaze on the witch.

Bebe didn't move forward, but her arms spread wide and her focus was solely on the woman in front of her. Tendrils of Madeline's silver-gray hair had floated free around her face. Her small wire-rimmed glasses hung askew on the plump bosom that heaved wildly.

"You are guardian of her walls, as far as they extend, are you not?" Bebe said.

"Wise little one, you know your histories," Madeline said, but the venom had gone out of her voice. She sounded almost admiring. "Unusual for someone so young."

Bebe dipped her chin once in solemn acknowledgment of the compliment. "I am the scribe of my coven. I aspire to one day attain a glimmer of the greatness of your long memory and record keeping."

Smart, Dante thought beside her. *Like all old things, she responds well to respect from younger beings.*

"Ah, a daughter of the Word." Though Madeline had not physically transformed, her movement was almost human again. She adjusted her glasses on the chain around her neck, smoothing her blouse.

Isela's mouth canted up at the corner. *Bebe's always been a diplomat.*

Out of the corner of her eye, Isela glimpsed a ripple of black and the smoky afterimage of a blade near the wall. She scanned the table across the aisle in time to see a flash of gray fur tipped with black disappear into the stacks.

Bebe had drawn Madeline into the early bits of a conversation, an apparent exchange of arcane knowledge about bookbinding. Isela tuned the conversation out, searching with Gold's senses until she located Tobias and Gregor. They'd split up and were making their way around the perimeter of the room.

Don't do anything stupid—

Isela popped up from behind the table in time to see Tobias launch himself at what he assumed was the librarian's blind spot as Gregor lunged. Madeline screeched, flinging a ball of web behind her as she scuttled sideways, dodging Gregor's grab by inches.

The web hit Toby square in the muzzle, blinding him. He crashed into the dais, bounced off the polished wood, and skidded across the floor. Bebe shrieked, running toward the wolf.

Gregor faced Madeline, naked sword bared. Her second web ball snatched the gun from his hand. She flung web after web at him. He ducked most, batted away a few, and sliced through rest. Whatever effect the web had on living things, his blade seemed impervious.

Bebe crouched over the thrashing body of the wolf. Her fingers tore at the thick, sticky netting on his face but that only left her stuck to him. The wolf's movements grew more erratic. A horrible, pleading snarl stuck in his throat.

Isela snapped. Her palms flicked forward as the hair on her body rose, taking most everything that was not nailed to the floor with it. That included Gregor and Madeline. Two of the heavy chairs cartwheeled through the air. Madeline tried to move away, but without any purchase, she swam in place. The chairs struck the librarian and soldier square, pinning them to opposite walls under the seats.

"Issy!" Bebe screamed. "He can't breathe!"

Isela's skin crackled gold as she turned to the limp wolf. His paws twitched faintly as Bebe sobbed, her hands stuck to his muzzle and unable to either help or free herself.

"Change," Isela said, seeing the image of her brother in his human shape.

The wolf shape withdrew, the muzzle retracting to reveal human lips and a nose in the new gaps formed by the sagging web. Bebe shoved her hands between the sagging web and his skin to keep the passage open. After a terrifying moment of stillness, his rib cage expanded. Dante shed his jacket as he hurried over. He drew a handkerchief from his pocket.

He muttered words at the cloth square as he tossed the coat over Toby's hips before crouching at his head. Using the warded handkerchief, he plucked the web free of the unconscious man's face. The web slid off the cloth when he shook it out, and he handed passed it to Bebe so she could free her own hands.

Dante sat back on his haunches, surveying room and its tattered occupants. "That was exciting."

Isela had no humor left. She let the rest of the contents of the room return to the floor except her two captured combatants. Lights flickered, and she knew her eyes were flashing gold. She didn't care.

"That's enough from both of you," she said. "Gregor, you

disobeyed my order. Madeline, we need your help and we don't have time for... palaver."

She ignored their furious stares, drawing on the greater power of the god to keep them both pinned like insects to a board.

"Madeline, whatever you are, I will protect you—" She paused at Dante's gasp. She wasn't a fool. "From Azrael if needed." She drowned out Gregor's strangled protest by slapping an open book across his face. "*If* you swear to answer every question we ask completely and do *everything* in your power to help us protect this city when we call on you."

Madeline's stillness was not due to being pinned. In a glimpse, Isela saw the spider in the web, waiting.

"How long?" she asked finally.

"As long as Azrael is keeper of the city and I am his consort. I'm sure to one as old as you, that is reasonable."

The old spider hissed. "Necromancers come and go. I remain."

Insist on her loyalty, Dante threw in. *She can help no other but you.*

"You will assist none against us, grace-blooded or otherwise."

Madeline's entire form shuddered a bit, and Isela had the impression of many legs moving in quick succession. She prepared to reinforce the restraint in case her bargain failed. She'd bind Madeline up herself and drop her in Azrael's aedis for that stunt with Toby.

"I don't really have a choice, do I?" Madeline said, speaking now to the god.

"There is always a choice, weaver." Isela heard the words come from her mouth.

"Upstart godling." Madeline muttered after a tense second. "Agreed."

Isela removed the book from Gregor's face and glared a silent command. He liberated one shoulder enough to give a half shrug. When she floated them both to the floor, he sheathed his blade and straightened his lapels, running a palm over his hair.

Toby moaned softly, his head in Bebe's lap as she stroked the hair away from his face. Her own expression was a mix of tenderness and irritation when she spoke. "I had it, you overprotective idiot."

At least he had the decency to look chagrined. Dante helped him to a sitting position. Bebe drew a pair of black-rimmed glasses from her coat pocket and handed them over. He met Isela's eyes as he adjusted them on the bridge of his nose, his expression so much like a puppy caught chewing something he shouldn't that it banished her irritation.

The main door opened, and Niles appeared bearing a silver tray with a tea service. If he noticed the disarray of the room or its occupants, his face revealed nothing.

"I see our timing is perfect," Divya said as she stepped from his shadow.

Isela sighed, flipping one of the heavy oak tables upright with one hand and making a shooing gesture with the other that chased eight chairs into place around it. As a final thought, she closed the door behind Niles with a twitch of her fingertips.

"Tea would do us all some good." Dante clapped his hands together, delighted as he approached the head of the table. He slid the chair back, his eyes only for the librarian straightening her hair and clothes. "Madame. Dante Abraham, at your service."

To Isela's shock, the faintest smile lifted the librarian's cheeks as she smoothed her skirt back into place and took the offered seat.

Bebe's shoulder brushed Isela's as they sat down with a grin. "Stranger than fiction."

* * *

"PROTECT THE CITY." Madeline chuckled, sipping delicately from the cup before her.

She set it down so lightly the china barely clinked with the contact. She'd replaced her glasses and now peered down the table at all of them.

Madeline confirmed their fears that the army of golems would be stronger than men and driven by whatever command they had been tasked with. The only way to stop them en masse was the verbal kill switch programmed by their creator; otherwise, severing the heads individually *might* slow them down.

"Rabbi Loew used the name of his god," she explained. "But he also was wise enough to create his creature with a kind of morality that ensured it would live in service. I have no doubt that these will not be so generously ordered."

Not if Vanka or Paolo had anything to do with it.

"So the golem is—was—real," Bebe said.

Madeline blinked at her. "Good man, that one. It's a shame…"

Everyone paused for the end of a story that seemed to be coming. But Madeline shook her head, her face returning from reminiscence with a sharpness of her gaze.

"You won't need to protect this city," she said, smiling. "Prague wasn't the first place a golem was attempted, but it certainly was the most successful. Don't you want to know why, I suspect?"

This time it was Dante who lit up. "Of course. Many places have their own defenses that lend themselves to a particular manifestation. If Prague's is animating the inanimate..."

Gregor leaned against the wall, looking bored enough to kill something. Isela, for once, agreed. They didn't need a history lesson. They needed to know what to do. Before she could push, Madeline held up a hand.

"A moment," she said. "Can I trust your guard not to try to take a piece of me?"

"If I can trust you not to attempt an escape," Gregor said dryly.

"I gave my word to your mistress," Madeline said, petulant now.

"You're safe," Isela said, if only to end the round of sparring before it began. "But we don't know when the army will strike, and since we can't stop them outright, we have to be ready to meet them as soon as possible."

The librarian moved with preternatural speed, scaling the wall. She went to one of the stone gargoyles inside the room. All female, the figures represented various stages of a woman's life.

The librarian stroked one, and Isela thought she heard the murmur of a geas. Obediently the gargoyle folded back into the wall, revealing a hollow just wide enough for a hand. Isela shuddered at the thought of putting her hand into a dark, unknown hole, but Madeline didn't hesitate. She emerged with an old scroll and murmured to the gargoyle. Isela blinked, hearing Toby beside her inhale as the gargoyle appeared to nod in acknowledgment and speak quietly back. She snuck a glance at Divya, wondering what she was making of all this. The director sipped her tea.

Madeline returned to the table. Dante looked optimistic, but it was Bebe she slid the scroll to.

She cut off any protest. "Activating the city's defenses is a spell of creation. It doesn't belong in the hands of death dealers. Understand?"

Her gaze was for Isela only.

Isela waited until her sister-in-law had unrolled the scroll. "Bebe?"

Bebe's mouth moved over the words, committing it to memory. "We can do this and will protect it as you wish, madame."

Madeline inclined her head. Dante chafed, but Isela put a hand on his arm in warning. Bebe rolled the scroll and returned it.

"I need to get back home," Bebe said. "We need time to prepare for this."

Toby stood at some unspoken communication between them. Niles had found a robe that fit him. Clear of the table, he lowered his head and shook briskly. The air quivered, blurring around him as the robe flared and then settled at the paws of an enormous wolf. Bebe caught his glasses in midair, folding them and tucking them into her pocket. She did her best to shake the long hairs out the robe, folding it neatly over the chair back with a smile of thanks for Niles.

Isela dropped to her knees to put her arms around Tobias's neck. She breathed in the faintest hint of the human brother she recognized under the animal musk and smiled. "No more taking orders from Gregor."

He chuffed, humor or agreement she wasn't sure.

"Kiss the kiddos for me," she said, patting him once before facing Bebe.

"I'll get the girls working on this. It's not complicated, but it will take some focus. And we'll need help to broadcast the signal to the whole city since we aren't really a full coven, no matter what your mother says."

It couldn't be helped that she had inherited from the wolf not the witch, but she felt a tinge of guilt that she could not have completed her mother's coven as she intended. Bebe seemed to read her thoughts, or the trouble in them, and laid a hand on her arm.

"That was a neat trick with the chairs." She winked. "Way cool. I bet you're strong enough to help us… you and your little friend."

Isela felt Gold's pleasure in her breastbone. *We can, Issy.*

Isela took in the wreckage as Divya and Niles waited patiently. "Sorry about the library."

Divya waved her off. "Any news on Yana?" At Isela's expression, she sighed. "Any news you can share?"

Isela paused. "We'll bring her home. I promise."

Dante hesitated as the group started for the door. He took a few steps toward Madeline, and she lifted her head warily.

"Madame, forgive me if this is too bold," he said with a new formality. "May I call on you again? When this trouble has passed, of course."

Madeline looked taken aback for a breath. Slowly she nodded but did not speak. That was enough to send Dante cheerily out the door whistling.

Isela bit back a smile. She met Madeline's eyes. "I'm sorry I brought this to your door."

"It was not to be helped." Madeline sighed, chucking her under the chin with a knuckle. "Godling."

Isela smiled ruefully. "I'm not sure what to call you anymore."

"Same as always," Madeline said. "I'm the librarian."

* * *

Gus minced no words. "What the hell happened to you?"

Gregor snapped something uncharitable on his way to the liquor cabinet. As he poured, the tear in his suit jacket revealed the smudged white shirt beneath. Tariq stifled a grin as Isela blew rebellious stray hairs from her eyelashes before tucking them behind one ear.

Her eyes were only for Azrael and the freshly-minted-silver gaze burning into her.

"I take it you had success," Azrael said, and a chair slid into place for her beside his own.

Seated, he kept his hand lightly on the back of her neck. She leaned into it. When she looked away, she found Gus staring, a little grin on her face. Tariq occupied himself with a book.

"Madeline's a spider," Isela said.

"Arachnea." Dante hurried to his seat and withdrew his notebook and set to work.

"And you have the spell," Gus said when Isela finished the story.

"Not exactly."

Gus stomped her foot. "*Entonces ¿Dónde está el pinche araña?*"

"*Madeline* is in her library," Isela said. "She's sworn to help us. And she did. The witches are prepping the spell now. I'm going to help them broadcast it over the city. All you guys have to do is stop Vanka and Paolo."

Azrael sat back in his chair. Gus looked at him as though waiting for the explosion. Instead, a slow smile curled his lips and his eyes never left Isela.

"All we have to do, indeed." The words left him in a soft chuckle. "Well, since my consort appears to have the protection of the city under control, let's turn our attention to where it's most needed. Finding the mortal they plan to use."

Emboldened, Isela lifted her fingertips. "Ah, I may be able to help with that too."

Azrael sat back in his chair, resting his elbows on the arms and folding his hands.

"Gold, the god, communicated with me the first time through dance," Isela explained. "She mirrored my movements. That's how she found me. If they're making Yana replicate my choreography, then I—we, Gold and I—can mirror them to find her."

Dante sat up, resting his notebook on his knee. Tariq closed his book with a snap.

"But once you find her, we have to get to her," Gus said slowly. "And there's no knowing how far they could be from here."

Isela shook her head. "The power weakens over distance—you have to be close to where you want to use it. It's why I went into the tomb with Azrael that night. No matter if they're powering the mud army or charging up, they won't be far."

"There are plenty of abandoned chateaus and farms outside the city," Gregor said. "Master, utilizing your contacts, I can begin searching the outlying areas—"

"We still have to travel to them, and if Isela makes a connection, they'll know it." Gus shook her head. "And they can be gone before we get there."

The room stilled. Tariq drummed his fingers impatiently. "Teams. If we divide up, then can the closest team get there and hold them until the others arrive?"

Azrael raised his fingers. "May I have a turn?"

All eyes went to him.

"My lady." He held out his hand to Isela. Without hesitation, she slipped her fingers onto his palm. His smile grew. "Exhale."

Isela's ears popped as the world spun out of view. She closed her eyes, and when she opened them again, they were in the garden of the Summer Palace by the fountain. The spring sunlight dappled through breaks in the clouds. Cool air raised the goose bumps on her exposed skin. She staggered and caught herself on the lip of the fountain. Icy water splashed her fingers. She inhaled damp wood and soft earth.

"What did you—"

"Testing a theory," he said gravely.

"You promised," she began.

"I'm explaining now. I didn't want to create doubt in you before I attempted it. And you were the only one I trusted to be strong enough. If something went wrong, I knew Gold would protect you. Now I know I can do it. And it was no more drain than simply taking myself."

He reached for her. "Close your eyes this time perhaps."

Isela recoiled, but by the time she struggled free, they were back in the study. Even Gregor looked speechless for once.

Azrael crossed his arms over his chest, smug as a cat. Isela sank into her chair and willed her head to stop spinning.

"That's how we get to them," Azrael said. "Once Isela finds the dancer."

CHAPTER TWENTY-TWO

Yana emerged from her cell, too weary to think of escaping the four guards that were her constant escort. They never spoke a word. She'd tried fighting, cajoling, pleading, even a brief and repulsive attempt at seduction that mercifully fell flat. They no longer bothered to lock her cell. The moment she emerged, one of four corpselike faces would look up from its assigned post and fix her in its blank gaze.

They weren't the worst of her imprisonment. That distinction belonged to the redheaded necromancer and her companion. She didn't need to be told Vanka was dangerous and unstable. On the runway in Saint Petersburg, Vanka had summoned an unearthly wind to scour the skin from the bones of the airline steward and the captain as the guards dragged Yana off the plane.

Her companion was no less frightening for all his smooth talk.

Won't you help us, carinho? he'd murmured in her ear, sweeping her hair out of her face as she vomited on the icy tarmac. *We can work together on this, can't we?*

Making it a question only served to prove how powerless she really was as he ran his long fingers up her arms, sending heatless crimson sparks dancing along her skin.

It hadn't done any good to tell them she wasn't trained as a godsdancer.

We know, the male said, his large, beautiful eyes mournful in a face too handsome to be human, *but your connection with the other one is important. You know which one we mean, don't you?*

Yana shook her head stubbornly, but the image of Isela came to her mind immediately. His eyes sparked with recognition.

And your late grandfather agreed that you should help us. You do want him to have his proper rest, do you not? So here's what you will do for us.

All that, spoken in her ear like the murmur of a lover, while the redhead looked on. Her facial expression vacillated from bored to irritated but never jealous. So he was the carrot and she was the stick.

Those lovely, mournful eyes settled on her again; their inhuman shine was knowing. As knowing as his fingers on her skin and the disrespectful words, cloaked in affection and seduction, that he used to address her.

She was certain that he could read her mind and was doing so. It didn't hurt like in the movies. She couldn't feel it, and that was the most insidious of all.

He smiled. *It doesn't need to hurt.*

"But it will," Vanka assured her without changing her position of disinterest as she leaned against a wall. "If you don't cooperate."

Yana wasn't stupid enough to think she could escape or that defiance would serve her in any other way than to get her tortured or killed. And if she didn't do what they wanted, who would they take next? Trinh? Kyle?

She gave them what they wanted—or tried to. That was the worst part. She did as they asked, day after day, for hours, laboring under the thinnest hope that if she succeeded they might set her free. She watched the videos until her eyes ached. She learned the choreography as best she could, and then she danced. There were moves she simply was not capable of achieving, and so she substituted them. She'd never respected godsdancers the way she did now. And Isela, her quiet American friend who had been swept up in the necromancer's machinations, was the best of all of them. She understood Isela's secret now. She'd watched the tapes long enough and knew enough about the godsdance technique to know the difference. There were 108 moves in godsdancing. Except when Isela danced. Then the number was infinite.

There were no days off, no rests. Yana wrenched her ankle badly. She danced on. When the pain moved to her knees and her hips, she kept dancing. She'd been a performer too long to show an audience her pain. She cared for her bloody, broken feet as best she could.

On this day she could not avoid limping as she walked to the dancing space. Her body hurt. She'd twisted her shoulder falling the day before, and now her arm was dead weight attached to a collection of needles pressing into her shoulder. Each twist drove the needles deeper.

I am never going to see the winter sun again, she realized as distant light flitted from the frosted skylight glass.

Something inside her, nameless and boneless, broke. All her life she thought she'd chosen the right path, the safe path, by becoming a ballerina. How ironic that it was her inability to godsdance that might get her killed, or worse.

Anger, deep defiant rage, boiled up from the place she thought had gone dormant when she'd bowed immediately to the necromancers' demands. The anger she could not take out on them now pumped blood into her extremities. A light sheen of sweat coated her brow.

The only thing she had left to attack was the one person who was responsible for all this. If not for her, Yana would be in her apartment with her cat and her latest lover. If not for her, there would be a career ahead of her; now, even if she survived, she knew her broken body would never recover. If not for her—

Isela, her brain stuttered out in its uncaring rage. *This is all your fault. I am going to die here, and it is all your fault. I hate you.*

Usually it was only one or the other necromancer present when she danced. For days it had been Vanka, and she feared she was closer to death than ever. But today Paolo's mournful eyes searched her face as she entered. The knowing look, the look she came to associate with her violation, crossed his face.

"Finally, the anger comes to you, *carinho,*" he said. "You realize who is responsible for all this? You will want to help us now?" He looked over his shoulder at the redhead in the shadows. "You have prepared the dosage?"

He took the cup. An ordinary mug, the interior stained with a dark ring of coffee, passed into her hands. But what was in the cup was not ordinary. It glowed with a faint sheen and sent off a distantly sweet aroma.

"It's not too strong?" Paolo called over his shoulder. "She is mortal. Too much and—"

"I know my work," the redhead snapped. "You doubt me, do it yourself."

Paolo sighed, taking in Yana with his liquid caramel eyes. "Drink up; it will give you strength."

Give her strength or kill her. She wished she were brave enough to wish for the latter. But she didn't deserve death, and the rage returned to her chest at the knowledge. She shouldn't be wishing for death. This was Isela's mess.

She drank the cup down. The liquid burned a hollow out of her insides, racing out to her fingers and toes. She no longer felt the pain of her limbs. She began to dance.

She gasped when a thick, powerful darkness, broiling with sparks like fireflies in a bottle, entered her. Everything she was strained to breaking. A scream rose in her but died immediately without anywhere to go.

"You called me." Her voice was no longer her own. "I came. What do you seek?"

"Master." The necromancer flopped to his knees, babbling in delight. "You grace us with your presence, O great lord of darkness and light. Ruler of life and death—"

"Enough." Her voice splintered as the presence within forced its way through. "This vessel is no longer suitable for my presence. If it is to be of use, it cannot be broken, and you have driven it too hard already. Speak quickly."

"It is us who extend effort for you." The redhead flung herself off the wall, ameliorating the defiance in her voice with a quickly added, "Great lord."

"For a price." Yana thought the voice inside her might have been laughing.

Vanka extended her arms, lowering her upper body in the approximation of a curtsy.

"We offer you the chance to take the betrayer," she said. "In exchange for your power, that we may bring the one who summoned her to heel."

The great mass inside her stilled. It was almost peace and quiet. Almost. The enormous presence strained, and a low, buzzing hum vibrated through her. It reminded her of a great cat, purring.

"You assume I am interested in the betrayer," Yana's voice rumbled finally. "Why would I care? I have this young, beautiful body and my freedom right now."

It gave Yana distinct pleasure to see Paolo look nervous. The great presence inside her was amused by her humor, and the straining ceased. She could have wept with relief.

"As you said, great lord…" Vanka never lost her cool. Not even once. "This body is weak. It will not last long with your presence, and you cannot exist on this plane without it."

Yana wanted to scream as the presence swelled angrily. "Arrogant git. You dare threaten me."

"I state only the obvious." Vanka inclined her head, but her eyes did not lower. "Great lord."

"I should rend your pretty head from your body," Yana's voice grumbled.

"Perhaps," Vanka murmured, nodding at Paolo.

Yana didn't recognize what he held in his hand, but it had the same crimson glow she recognized from his touch on her skin. When she looked back to Vanka, a gold-orange glow sparked from her fingertips. They were creating something between them. A wind picked up from nowhere, and the air smelled damp as if with rain. The presence inside her recognized it. For a moment it paused and seemed torn between rage and laughter. She prayed for laughter but sensed the rage and squirmed into as small a ball as possible inside herself.

"You threaten me?" the presence said, and Yana heard her own voice fall away. She wanted to warn them—they didn't know what they'd summoned up, what this thing was capable of. But what warning could she give, and why should she give it? She owed them nothing, and karma was a bitch.

Paolo spoke first. "Pardon, great lord. If it's a body you truly desire, consider the betrayer's host. She shows no sign of the deterioration. Perhaps she is different. Of use to you if you wish to continue on this plane."

And then the presence subsided. Paolo visibly exhaled, but Vanka smirked as the glow faded from her hands. Yana felt the quiet inside her, but it was not a peaceful one. A great humming stroked her, like a cat curling around a petting hand. But anyone who knew cats understood a moment of contentment could be ended by sharpened claws.

"You have a bargain," it said.

After a few moments of haggling over particulars that seemed strangely detail oriented to the dazed Yana, the bond was sealed by a melding of powers—sunset gold, crimson, and the firefly-in-a-bottle-tinged blackness that came from her own fingertips and left blistering burns. As the presence retreated, Yana felt it turn to her as if acknowledging her presence for the first time.

I will see you again, my beautiful one, and soon.

She shuddered at the promise before collapsing to the floor. She was too weak to protest the zombie hands that lifted her up, obeying Vanka's command to return her to her cell. She lay where they left her on the bed. She hadn't the strength to sit up, wash, or even feed herself. She didn't know if it was minutes or hours later that the door opened and Paolo entered.

It was all she could do to emit a strangled cry. Escaping him would be impossible.

"Relax, *carinho*," he murmured.

He stepped aside and three women entered. Wordlessly they undressed and washed her. They bandaged her blistered hands and combed her hair, dressing her in warm clothes and tucking her into the changed bed. She didn't even care that the watchful eye of Paolo never left her. He monitored every spoonful of soup they plied her with, snapped something in Portuguese when they fed her too fast and she vomited it all up.

When they were done, they stepped aside at the snap of his fingers, and he sat on the edge of her bed. Yana wanted to shrink from his touch, but it was surprisingly gentle. He brushed the hair away from her forehead. As she watched, the women patrolled the room, turning over every bit of furniture and cushion in the spare space. They removed anything sharp, she realized.

"You do not understand," he said, "how easy it is for us to disregard your fear after being so long without it ourselves."

"I hate you," Yana muttered between clenched teeth.

"Good," he said. "Hate is a powerful emotion. Use it. It will make what happens next more tolerable."

She felt the bile rising in her throat.

He laughed. "You think I would—? Ah no. You are not for me. Vanka, on the other hand—well, you are more useful to her in other ways. You should be proud of yourself—you succeeded in the task we gave you."

"That was a god?" she breathed.

He nodded. "You have been chosen by the god for the honor of possession. It will be a short-lived honor, but one that should not be taken lightly." He pointed up at the ceiling to the discreetly placed cameras. "You will be cared for very well to make sure no harm comes to you, our precious vessel. You must be at strength when the god calls on you again."

"I am going to die, aren't I?"

"Yes." He smiled broadly. "But everything dies in the end."

Yana lay back on the pillows. She'd known it the moment the presence had first entered her. Resignation weighted her body. "It isn't going to be your cat's-paw. It's more powerful than you know, and it doesn't care what you want."

Paolo watched her steadily. Once, his unblinking gaze had unnerved her. Now she met his eyes without fear. Paolo looked away first.

"Prepare her for transport," he said to her guards before addressing her. "Take comfort—at least you will be able to die in the city you love."

Yana laughed. She couldn't help it. It tore from her wildly with a trapped animal's desperation. She'd always hated Prague.

CHAPTER TWENTY-THREE

Isela rounded the corner to find Azrael standing in the doorway of the closet, buttoning his shirt. Navy blue today, tailored to fit him like a second skin. A black duster, with its impossible, alluring scent of reptile, saffron, and magic, was thrown over the reading chair. She paused a moment just to watch him. Each button complied with a quick twist of fingers, and a final sharp tug on the collar drew everything into place.

She'd caught a glimpse of Gus in the halls, her long hair braided tight to her skull in three thick rows and then together to a single plait down her back. A leather racing suit zipped to her chin and armored at the wrists, knees, and elbows covered her skin. Bristling with blades and wearing lug-soled boots that looked capable of liberating teeth from their sockets, Gus appeared to be about the business of murder and destruction. Azrael might have been going to a business lunch with a favored client.

Isela smiled anyway as Azrael fussed with the fold of his right sleeve. She crossed the room without a word and took the fabric in both hands, cuffing it neatly. She turned her attention to the second sleeve, tweaking the first cuff to match. She lingered, fingers stroking the skin of his arm beneath the shirt as she struggled to find a reason not to let him go.

"I would know your mind, consort."

"This should be armor," she chided, startled by the roughness of her own throat.

The bruising from his rounds with Gregor was gone. He looked as capable and deadly as Isela had ever seen him. "I have an Aegis. In the battle I fight, armor and blades will be useless."

"Yet still."

He swept the coat off the chair. She held the collar as he slid his arm in, then lifted the other sleeve. It was lighter than it looked, and up close the flat black appeared more like interlocked diamonds. Gold's sight revealed only an obfuscation geas to make the wearer blend in, chameleonlike, with the environment. But her senses said defenses against magic were embedded in every fold. On impulse, she leaned in and took a deep sniff of the material.

"What does your nose tell you, little wolf?"

"Well, it's not leather," Isela said, crossing her arms over her chest and standing back as he shrugged twice and the material settled into a familiar position around him.

"It is of a kind." A smile full of memory bloomed on his lips. "Wyvern."

Her brows rose. "You are wearing dragon skin?"

He shook his head. "Two legs, no fire. Though they are pretty much impervious to it. I found out the hard way."

"You slayed a dragon. Of course you did." She threw up her hands and stalked across the room.

"Wyvern," he said. "And I believe *slew* is the proper past tense."

She narrowed her eyes at him. "Not you too."

His mouth turned down quizzically. Isela fidgeted, bouncing from the balls of her feet to her toes.

Azrael sighed, sitting down. "And?"

"I thought you said we would do this together," Isela said, her words rushing out. "Take on the Allegiance. And you are leaving me behind again."

He spread his thighs and braced his elbows on either knee, opening his palms. Isela went like iron filings to a magnet. His cheek pressed against her belly through the fabric of her sweater.

"This isn't the Allegiance…," he began.

She coughed. "*Two. Allegiance. Necromancers.* I don't like those odds. And don't even mention Gus."

The thrum of his laughter against the skin of her belly woke desire even through her concern.

She buried her fingers in the thick waves of his hair and made a fist. Azrael's head drew away under pressure. "Are you jealous, consort?"

"Of your surly teenaged protégée?" Isela laughed, sobering quickly. "I know that you trust her—and Tariq and Dante—implicitly."

He squeezed her waist. "It is as I promised—I will explain whenever I can my decisions."

"Paolo and Gus have history," Isela filled in.

"You know about that?"

"Dante."

His brow furrowed. She waited until he was finished considering the quickest way to tell her. "It's true she has spent much of her life running from him. But it is also true that I have never seen a necromancer advance so fast since... Well, Vanka."

"But is she strong enough?"

"She's ascended, Isela," he murmured. "She's masking it well. Better she let him believe she is still weaker. But look at her eyes. Really look. Ask your little friend for help."

He tapped her breastbone with the folded knuckle of his index finger.

"She wants to end Paolo more than I do, I'd imagine," he said. "And that ravening desire is my dearest ally now. You need time, Isela. And training. One day we will stand shoulder to shoulder against the Allegiance. But today I need you to protect our city so that I can devote myself to the enemy. There is no one I trust more. Can you do that?"

Isela cradled his face in her hands, soaking in one more moment of those silver eyes, alight and earnest. "I will."

* * *

ISELA STOOD at the barre in the Academy godsdancing ring, doing her best to appear composed as she moved through a brief series of stretches to keep her muscles warm. When she'd reached out to Divya, she hadn't been prepared for the director to agree so willingly. Within a matter of hours, Divya had the schedule cleared—

clients be damned—and the school closed to students and public alike.

Isela took a long breath. She would *not* be nervous. *Tell it to my nerves.* So much rode on this, the least of which was Yana's life. If it worked, they might be able to stop an attack on the city and keep Paolo and Vanka from calling down a second god. If it failed, it might waste critical time they needed to figure out another plan. No pressure.

Gus strolled toward the mirror, resting on the barre close to Isela's hand. "You would have words with me, *señora?*"

Isela looked at her as Azrael had advised. Gold obliged, revealing Gus's irises under the carefully constructed geas. The obsidian now held a rainbow sheen, reflecting light like a spill of gasoline on asphalt. Isela withdrew in surprise.

Isela spoke after a moment's hesitation, "I hope you break Paolo into pieces."

Now Gus smiled, all teeth and fury. "May your words guide my hand, *señora.*" Gus touched her lips and bowed with less mockery than Isela expected.

Isela snugged her slippers and watched Gus rejoin the others. Azrael's Aegis wore the protection of their preference. Gregor chose the stripped-down armor of a modern-day black knight. Rory needed only the tattoo work under a leather holster for his massive, carved machete. Ito looked unarmed in the soft black cotton designed for stealth, but if she tilted her head just right, Gold revealed his well-hidden weaponsDory stood slightly apart, no longer counted among them. Only Azrael was a still presence in his midnight coat of wyvern skin.

The rest of the guard was stationed outside the Academy for her protection once Azrael and his team were away.

For her part, Isela had dressed modestly in a long-sleeved leotard and tights with leg warmers stretched over her knees and soft-soled canvas slippers on her feet. That didn't stop Azrael from drawing a breath when she skinned out of her warm-ups. When she faced the barre to get in a few last stretches, the wave of heat that made sweat bloom on her skin made her acutely aware that the leotard was backless.

It's standard practice clothes, Isela chided. The choice to look like a ballerina wasn't an accident. Nor was the place she'd chosen to dance.

She needed to tap into everything she and Yana had in common. *What any ballet dancer would wear to a company class.*

You are not any dancer. You are mine.

Tension and desire triggered a rush of warmth in her. Mine. Not my consort. Not god vessel. Not wolf kin. Mine.

That was all he needed to know. Speaking quietly to Divya, he might not have looked any different than a few days ago. But it was how he *felt* that had changed. Something restless in him had calmed, coiled deep and powerfully at the center of his being and gone quiet. She could feel the change; rather than straining at the tethers, it had heeled to him like an obedient hound. That their relationship could affect him so fundamentally shook her to the core.

She felt his gaze caress the long line of her spine to her bare neck. Her hair, braided and pinned to the top of her head, shivered as though stroked. She felt the pins loosen.

Ah ah ah, she tsk-tsked mentally, snugging the pins without lifting her hands.

He made a small mental sound of disappointment. *We had a deal.*

She looked back at Azrael and bit her tongue on unspoken words —be careful, don't take unnecessary risks, I love you. When she met his eyes, she saw he knew. *I'll come back to you, little wolf.*

She swallowed the fear that tried to choke her. *You'd better, death dealer.*

She moved to the center of the room, pointed her toe, and began to dance.

* * *

AZRAEL KNEW the mortals in the room could no longer focus on Isela. The light streaking from her fingers and toes was too bright, her movements too fast.

She moved through dances, seven or eight of the ones she thought the most likely Yana would use to replicate her. Her movements formed an inquiry, a call. She would repeat them, in sequence, until she got a response.

She had been through seven cycles, and nothing.

Gus murmured something dubious to Gregor. Azrael held up a hand before the doubt spread. A tingle snapped against his awareness. Her attention went up, her movements becoming directed, slowing down. He marked the repetition of the cycle and then the image her reflection wavered as the mirror lining the wall became a window. On the other side, another woman danced in darkness. As Isela matched the dancer step for step, he could see the tiny details on the other woman's face.

He felt Isela's heart leap with recognition, and the image wavered. *Steady, little wolf,* he said.

The image grew clearer. He took a big breath, extending his contact to the group around him. Gregor, Rory, Ito.

Gus reached for him eagerly. She'd cornered him the previous day as he reinforced his defensive wards in the aedis. *Sire, I would fight with you if you'll have me.*

She'd never feared him as Dante and Tariq had in their early days under his tutelage, but her ability to trust had been damaged by Paolo's vicious attack. Rebellion seemed to be her standard response to challenge, and defiance greeted his every command. He refused to adopt Róisín's way for his own progeny, though it was all he'd known. Learning to work with her had taught him more about patience and forgiveness than centuries among monks.

Quieres a Paolo, supongo. He spoke but kept his eyes on his spell-work. He'd always known there would come a day for this. A half dozen times over the centuries, she'd wanted to try. He'd advised patience.

She shifted on her feet. *Estoy listo, Azrael.*

¿Eres tú? When he met her eyes, the circle of metallic shine around her pupils was complete.

She lowered her chin once but her eyes never left his. *Es la hora.*

He remembered Gregor's words on the frozen plains and bit his tongue on words of concern. He nodded once.

The eagerness in her voice made it gritty. *I won't let you down, Az.*

She was halfway to the door when he was certain he could keep his voice light. *Hoy por ti, mañana por mí.*

Laughter shook her shoulders. *After this, I think you owe me one, old man.*

Once Isela made contact, he couldn't help but do a quick scan of her defenses. Her brow rose immediately—*checking my work?*—but he didn't care. Pride filled him. Her ward work was impeccable, focused and without a break. He reached for the mortal on the other side last.

Where was it? How far? He found he didn't need to know, only to focus his attention on that room, building the bridge with his mind.

NOW.

The power belled out from his core in a wave, sweeping over the small party and making the lights in the room explode into shards of glass and sparks. The director and her guard cried out. Dante's voice, shouting a ward to shield them, echoed in their wake.

He landed in the darkness, driven to one knee with the force of their arrival. The soft flapping of wings as startled pigeons alighted for the broken windows in the roof drew his eye. An abandoned building.

Azrael straightened his legs and tugged at the lapels of the coat that was both armor and a weapon.

"Everyone still alive," Gregor asked, rising and dusting off his pants.

Gus reached for her blades, casting an illusion geas around them. "They don't know what we are, but they know we're here."

"Where, exactly, is here?" Azrael scanned the dilapidated shell of a building. It had been grand once, the manor house of minor noble, but time and nature had taken their due. Moonlight spilled into the entryway from the buckled roof above. Birds called alarm as their wings beat air in hasty retreat from their shelter.

"Sudetenland, I'd guess," Gregor said, glancing at the weathered crest above the door. "That's a Habsburg unless memory fails."

Azrael doubted Gregor's memory was capable of such a terrific faux pas. "Is it one of the Teutonic Order's?"

Gregor scanned the room. "Unlikely. Paolo wouldn't have been able to use it for his purpose otherwise."

Azrael nodded. The order had been known for its protections against the supernatural. The last thing he needed was a centuries-old defensive booby trap to spring while he dealt with Paolo and Vanka. The old halls echoed with the sound of booted feet. Ito slipped into the shadows, and only Azrael's connection to him revealed his progress to the second floor and onto the roof.

"Incoming." Gus grinned, stepping forward in unison with Gregor.

Gus and Gregor made quick work of the undead. Azrael counted ten. At a junction in the corridor, Ito stepped from the shadow and jerked his head to the left before disappearing again. They entered a ballroom where an exhausted human dancer levitated above the floor.

The specter of death loomed large in this one, but she was still alive. Barely. And not possessed. Yet.

Between them and the dancer clustered a squad of undead, headed by a great shaggy brute of a warrior Azrael recognized as the head of Vanka's guard.

Rory recognized him too. He stepped forward. "Pietro is mine."

Gregor saluted.

Paolo's trio of tattooed brawlers dove from the balustrade above, and the fight became a melee.

Azrael slipped the double-headed ax free from his back and the leash from his rage. This time he didn't hold back his power, sending it away from him like a burning whip and cutting through anyone who stood in his path. Those unlucky enough to survive the blaze received the kiss of death from the sharp blade.

When he emerged on the other side of the room, gore splattered his coat, none of it his own. Gus slid to his side, leaving bloody trails beneath her lug-soled boots. Her eyes glittered as she spun a blade in her palm.

Vanka lounged in a chair by the cold fireplace. Paolo stood at the mantel.

"Welcome, Azrael," Paolo stepped forward. "And the lovely 'Gus.'" His voice was mocking. "An unexpected pleasure."

Gus bared her teeth. "I've come for your heart, deceiver."

Paolo laughed, patting his chest. "I offered it to you once, lady. And you declined."

"I'd rather take it myself." Gus snarled and the edge of her blade shone.

Paolo's sneered. "Come then, bitch. Try it."

For a moment, Azrael thought she would take the bait, but she held her countenance and issued her challenge formally. "I challenge you for your territory and all you hold within. I will take your soul tonight or you will take mine. There will be no interference. To the final death."

The remnants of charm fell away from Paolo. The predator beneath his playboy smile rose, ancient and inhuman as the eyes of any jungle reptile. "I am not here to answer to you, little girl."

"That's not how it works," Azrael said. "Answer or forfeit."

Paolo showed teeth, but Vanka cut him off. "You know the code, a challenge issued must be answered."

His furrowed brows betrayed uncertainty. Vanka met his gaze with a serene scowl and a little shrug. Azrael observed both, with dawning understanding. He'd assumed it was Paolo who pulled the strings, manipulating Vanka's rivalry with Azrael to his advantage. That had been a mistake. As Paolo and Gus dropped into the In Between, he focused his attention on the female necromancer who had once challenged for the territory he held.

CHAPTER TWENTY-FOUR

I sela sagged in the center of the ring, the scent of burned wiring wrinkling her nose. Divya and Niles crouched beside Dante, the faint blue glimmer of a dome fading around him. The bodyguard had stretched his coat over the director for good measure. The room was emptier without Azrael's team.

From across the room, Tariq grinned at her. "You did it."

The god swelled inside her with alarm, and Isela willed her legs into motion again. "They're here."

Outside, the threads of the witches' spell slid past her as they wove through the damp night air. The streetlights cut long swaths of light through the foggy darkness. She stepped into the center of the paving stones, framed by the Municipal House, the national ballet, the national bank building, and the Powder Tower.

This was the other reason she'd chosen to dance at the Academy—the Powder Tower was one of the original thirteen gates to the city.

"*Think of the old city walls and gates like ley lines,*" Bebe had explained the day before. She must have had the phone pinched between her cheek and shoulder because her voice was muffled and Isela had heard the rustle of pages turning as she spoke. "*They're natural conduits for power. Your mom didn't pick Vyšehrad by accident. The fortress and gates were the first time humans tapped into the ability of the city to protect itself. And Libuše herself saw the future of the city from Vyšehrad.*" That led to a half-hour history lesson that ended with how the American planes claimed a navigational mistake saved Prague from intense bombing suffered by other major European cities during World War II. *"Even the godswar left Prague untouched for the most part. Those necros picked the wrong city to fuck with."*

A thumping against the inside of Isela's skull, slimy as river mud, brought her back to the icy cobbles and the damp night. The wet aroma of composting mud was distant enough to be just her imagination, but she knew it signaled the invading army. She couldn't see it yet, but she could feel the golems as clearly as the bright, colorful threads of witch geas racing through the air around her and knitting between the buildings.

Isela went to one knee as Dory joined Aleifr and rest of the guard to form a defensive circle with her and Tariq as their center. The people passing slowed and stared at the sight of the warriors. A whispering went up, thick with unease.

Tariq began to murmur again, this time his geas a wordless whisper of suggestion. As one, the people began to take shelter in the surrounding buildings, moving with the slow, steady pace of compulsion. She could see them behind the glass doors as they sank to their knees, helping each other to the floors before curling up into fetal balls like puppies sharing each other's warmth. As the geas spread across the city, she could see the strain in Tariq's face, the sweat beading on his brow and rolling down his cheeks until his dark mane of hair was soaked and his shirt clung to him.

Isela closed her eyes, lowered her chin, and placed her hand on a single cobblestone beneath her.

She clutched the edges of the stone as though she might take it up as a weapon, but instead of drawing, she gave. She wrapped her intention in love, love for the only city she knew as home and the love of her man, who was no longer a man at all but something as elemental as the force that rose to her bidding. It spilled out of her and raced into the stones at her feet in uneven waves.

The crackle of gold sent sparks showering around her, bouncing off the figures and weapons of the guard that formed her circle. Not one pulled their gazes from the shadows surrounding them as she became a miniature sun at the center of their orbit.

Gold flowed into the colorful witch threads, strengthening and thickening them until a vast weaving overlaid the city.

The slimy sensation closed in. She could see the mud men now in the sweeping, impossible gaze of Gold's vision. They moved into the streets of her city, bringing the stench of rot and the strength of earth. Destruction followed in their wake, seeded in the thick mud of their limbs and gaping maws. They would pull the city apart, brick by brick, stone by stone, and not stop until it was reduced to river mud and waste. Such was their charge. The wordless, howling hunger of their approach battered her with silent dissonance.

For a moment, doubt clutched at her like the chill that crept into her from the stone. Who was she to protect a city? She was just a dancer. Her fingers gripped the smooth edges of the stone worn as much by time as by the original hand that'd carved it. Along with hundreds of others, just this size, made to fit in interlocking lines forming row upon row that paved the dirt beneath and turned it to a firm, even surface. It was one stone, but it was one of many. And so was she. Surrounded by warriors as good as immortal. Backed by a necromancer who could sing an entire city to sleep. Broadcasting the spell of a coven of witches that were both blood and family. Held above all others by the most powerful necromancer in the world. The vessel of a power so great it could only be thought of as a god. She stood at the center of it all.

She opened her mouth and roared back. The city roared with her.

Hundreds of years of human construction animated by something even older than the buildings or the name itself came to life at her call. The stone caryatids and atlantes beneath balconies and doorway columns; the etched sgraffito figures of satyrs and nymphs, warriors and goddesses; the statuary in gardens and fountains of parks, all rose from their places as if shaking off the same slumber that had claimed the human citizens moments ago.

It was as if the whole city splintered in two—the sleeping human one in shadows and the one now alight with the magic of an army of stone and mortar, myth and architecture. The dreamy art nouveau maidens with bowers of ginkgo leaves and reed baskets stood beside Renaissance ideal men amid the angular cubist proletariats wielding the weapons of industry. Stone lions shook their manes and roared, leading a menagerie of animals into the fight. Patron saints stretched their patinated limbs beside historical figures shaking off bird droppings in preparation for battle. Bronze horses rattled their bridles and breastplates, bugling in eagerness.

Horned imps leaned from rooflines and balustrades. Their cups spilled golden ichor that sizzled and burned the golems back to the brackish dirt from which they came. Gargoyle heads blasted golden flames into the attackers.

The mud army rose back. They dragged the fragile ornamentation down, burying them in thick, sucking mud. They swallowed the small birds and cherubs whole, crushing their golden bows in uneven stone teeth. Three dragged a proletariat to his knees, using his own massive hammer to pound him into the tracks of a tram.

In the sweeping gaze of Gold's vision, the massive figures of the Titans that did battle over the gates of the castle pounded the mud figures to bits. The great hill overlooking the east of the city and the central thoroughfare of Wenceslas Square stood empty; the mounted figures of one-eyed warrior Jan Žižka and the saint fighting side by side against a brackish wave of mud with hundreds of arms and sawing river-rock teeth.

The force of the defending spell stretched Isela taut and was glad she had gone to her knee as she braced her other hand on the cobblestones—this time as much for support as to feed power to the spell.

The god might have been able to withstand the demands made on her power. The part of Isela that remained yet human began to splinter. She called on it anyway. The trembling that had begun in her fingers and toes wracked her body now. She grit her teeth to keep them from chattering, bowing her head to hide the tension on her face as the hair shook loose from her braid.

As one, the golem army changed course. Now they had a new priority. She heard Aleifr's voice, a bellow calling his fellows to war, and then the clash of metal on wet earth. Her heart stuttered.

"Right here, Issy." Tariq called her back when she would have faltered. "Look in my eyes."

His gaze rooted her. He kept her grounded with eyes and geas, and gratitude swept her face. With every moment that passed, he looked less substantial. The wind picked up, no longer gentle but a howling gale; a sandstorm without the fine grains of sand was still a force to behold. For the first time she wondered what would happen if he lost control of his power. If Azrael was capable of destroying a city, what could his firstborn do unleashed?

"Stay with me," she said. "I'm not letting you go either."

"Let them come." A dangerous grin lit Tariq's face as the wind whipped his hair into a fury of streamers. All at once she understood what he meant to do.

She nodded. *Gold, I need a little more. And we have to protect the Aegis.*

The god did not answer, but Isela felt strength rise from a place she'd thought tapped dry. Tariq met her eyes once as the golem army closed over them, and then the light went out.

NOW.

A hazy drone of sound rose, muted by mud. As it grew, it became a sucking roar. She felt the pull on her skin and her hair, drawing her away from the street. Power domed over her, gold and shining, expanding to include the Aegis, and she looked up. Tariq stood with arms open wide and head thrown back. She could no longer hear him over the roar. A great tunnel of wind snaked above them. Beneath the translucent dome, she watched the surrounding golems battered by wind and breaking apart, sucked slowly into the funnel and blasted to their component parts.

At last the darkness lightened, and the tornado lifted into the roiling mass of cloud cover above. The rain began to fall, fat grimy drops of river mud and water. It quickened to warm sheets until faces became recognizable behind dirty masks and the mounds of muck washed through the streets and back to the river.

She turned her face up to the sky, hearing Aleifr's laugh emerge from beneath a coating of muck. Thunder boomed in response, and he lifted his ax and blade, calling challenge.

The weaving stretched taut one final time with a snap that brought the city's guardians back to their posts. Behind Aleifr, on the shadowed roof of the Municipal House, the last of the winged figures alighted, leaning casually on the hilt of his sword. He caught her eye and winked before he went still in a slouch as if he were suffering from a millennium of boredom. As the gold began to fade from the tapestry, the witch threads unraveled, withdrawing as they went.

At the sound of a gentle *whuff*, she looked back in time to see Tariq collapsing at her side. She grabbed for him as he went down, keeping his head from striking the stones. She dragged him onto her lap, wiped the mud from his face, and pressed her fingers to his throat. Dark lashes fluttered open to reveal dull topaz eyes as a soft gust of air like the desert at dusk caressed her cheek.

"Now that's a sight to bring a man back to his strength," he said groggily, eyebrows dancing as he dared to let his gaze drop to the rib cage heaving beside his cheek for a heartbeat before returning to her face.

"You swooned." She rolled him onto the cobblestones.

He grunted on impact, but he was laughing when he climbed to his hands and knees. "Nothing a few years' sleep won't fix."

The rain began to let up and the wind slacked off. Aleifr shook like a dog, spraying them all with water and dirt. Isela wrung out her hair and twisted it into a gritty bun at the back of her head. When she tried to stand, her slippers lost purchase in the mud and she landed on her butt hard enough to make her cry out. When she looked up, Dory stared down at her, laughter crinkling the corners of his eyes.

"Shut up," she said before the giggles got the best of her.

Tariq wheezed, hands on his knees. He scooped up a handful of mud and plopped it on her head. She gasped and threw a mudball. Her throw went wild and hit Aleifr square in the face. He paused, surprised, and hurtled a lump that glanced off her shoulder. And then they were all laughing and sliding in the mud, pelting each other like children.

You know those are golem guts, right? Gold sniffed.

This must be the hysteria of victory. It seemed perfectly normal... and better than pillaging and burning things, she decided. When the laughter was spent, a hand entered her line of vision.

She met Tariq's eyes. "Thank you."

His fingers closed over hers, drawing her to her feet, and for a second there was no wall between them. His thumb brushed the back of her hand. She dropped her eyes at the naked emotion on his face. Gently, she withdrew her palm.

"It is my pleasure, consort of my master." His words were cool and obedient. When he she met his eyes again, his gaze had shuttered.

Only it was as though with Gold's sight—now that she knew what was behind it, she could not avoid seeing it.

"Anything from Azrael," he asked.

"Not—" Isela began.

The earth jerked beneath them, leaving her grasping for Tariq to stay on her feet. The air crackled and snapped. The short hairs on her arms and neck rose to attention as a pungent sweetness stung her nostrils. She looked up, searching for the incoming storm, to see a roiling mass of gray streaked with lightning overhead, blotting out the moon where a moment before there had been only a gauzy winter sky.

Tariq put his shoulder between her and as much of the clouds as he could.

Isela. She had never before heard a note of panic in the god's voice. She felt her body tensing as though at a distance, reserves of strength she didn't know she had being called on. *We have to go.*

She tried as a great gale whipped up from the clouds. It pushed her back, driving against her straining body. Tariq reached for her, and the shouts of the guard surrounded her. But there was no one to fight. No attacker. Just this driving wind and the sudden lightness, as though gravity no longer applied. The ground fell away from her feet, or she was simply yanked upward. Lightning snapped and thunder roared in its wake. A second snap and a roar, and the stinging stink of ozone filled her nose. Tariq howled in pain, then silence. With the third, light blinded her and her senses fell away.

Thought you could escape?

CHAPTER TWENTY-FIVE

Azrael balanced his weight, ready for a fight, but Vanka remained in her reclined position, her cat eyes narrowed and a small smile teasing her mouth, as oblivious to the chair rotting beneath her as the battle being waged nearby.

Vanka waited, the fingers of her right hand sketching a symbol in the air at the end of the chair's arm. Nails the shade of a freshly opened artery danced through the air in quick, effective repetition. He deciphered the glyph before his eyes flickered to the ballroom to confirm what he suspected. He extended his awareness to feel the edges of the geas. The bubble was small—just enough to contain the two of them and make the battle appear to slow to a crawl around them. Time manipulation was a rare skill among necromancers.

"How easily you send your pawns into slaughter," he said, banking the bloodthirsty rage that coated his teeth and tongue in heat.

She gave Gus a long, speculative stare. "You are so sure of your training."

"I'm sure of my progeny," he said. "There's a difference."

She sniffed. If he knew Vanka, anything approaching power like Gus's would have been perceived as a threat. Had Róisín been any different in that regard? They'd spent almost two hundred years as mentor and pupil. When he'd ascended and betrayed his lack of interest in the highest echelon of necromancers, the relief in her face, mixed with wary consideration, stuck in his mind. He'd come when she found him again and obediently lent his strength to creating the wall that protected humans from the gods they wielded against one another. She hadn't trusted him even then.

Eventually you will try to take what is mine, goat boy. She'd smirked the final time he saw her fully sane. *They all do. But you will fail. Never forget a god is mine to command, and no progeny of mine, even one so great as you, can stand against that.*

By then he'd been seasoned with age and had progeny of his own, and he recognized the emotion behind the triumph in her face for what it was. Fear. She'd never stopped being afraid that someone would topple her from the throne she occupied in her own mind. She would never understand why he craved no power, but it was that lack of craving that eliminated the fear he held.

Of all the Allegiance, Vanka's rise had been the most swift, driven by a necromancer as cruel as he was powerful. They had that in common.

He said I would ascend or die, she mused once. *He forgot to consider what would happen to him if I survived.*

Azrael doubted he'd forgotten. More like he'd overestimated the effect centuries of terror and dominance had on her. He expected to retain control because she had feared him once. It was a lesson Azrael refused to ignore when he gathered his own progeny. But Vanka seemed to embrace her mentor's teaching even as she declared her own power. None of the progeny that she'd claimed had survived her tutelage.

He gestured to the second chair, curious now by her lack of hurry. Vanka nodded.

"Often they surprise you," he said, and the smile that rose with the words had barbs. "But you'd have to let them live long enough to find that out."

Vanka frowned. "Only the strongest survive, Azrael. Once, I would not have had to remind you of that. You've changed so much. I would have never had to go through so much effort just to get your attention."

She leaned against the arm of the chair, fingers of her far hand continuing their endless repetition. "You can stop this all now." Her voice was a tease, a siren lure lurking beneath the words. "Why should we be at war, Azrael?"

Azrael took in the dancer dangling in midair and the fighters. His eyes settled on Paolo and Gus, frozen in this plane. This time the rage came from a righteous heat. All this destruction. "I made you a promise."

"Your vow to anyone who threatens your precious pet?" Her brows rose as the end of her question tilted toward a laugh. "You deserve a consort worthy of your strength, not causing your weakness."

He paused, and she mistook his hesitation for him actually considering the offer. Her smile grew, and this time as she leaned in, her weight shifted, plumping her breasts beneath the cable-knit sweater.

"And who says we cannot master her together?" Judging by her blown pupils and the slight flush at the tip of her nose, the sexual nature of the thought and the accompanying arousal was genuine.

It left him cold. He blinked. He rose, moving slowly and hefting the labrys in his hand.

She sighed and sat back, drumming her free nails on the arm of the chair and twisting her mouth into a moue of disappointment. "No then? Well, it was worth a try."

Still she was calm. Her gaze went over this shoulder. That was when he saw it. Fear. When he glanced back to see what had caught her attention, the human dancer collapsed to the floor. Closer, Paolo folded in on himself with a grunt. The look on Vanka's face was his signal.

A second later, Rory confirmed the dancer was safe and away. He attacked.

Vanka rose unhurriedly, and he should have closed the distance between them, but it felt as if he were moving through water. His eyes caught on her fingers, still moving, even faster now. The bubble of altered time that once included him shrank, and she smiled slyly, edging around the striking ax. Her finger danced along the blade, but she pulled it away in surprise.

"First blood," she granted, flicking it.

The droplets moved too fast until they crossed into normal time, landing with a wet sound on his cheek and brow.

"To be finished another time," she said, backing toward the fireplace. Her other hand tripped a lever for a hidden door before she turned and vanished into the darkness of a secret passage.

By the time his ax came down, splintering her chair with the force of the blow, he knew there was no point in giving chase. She was already gone.

Gus came out of the In Between with a groan, staggering backward as Paolo sank to the ground. Azrael caught her, barely. Gregor was there in a heartbeat, sheathing his black blade.

Gus gasped, clutching ribs that split and bled before their eyes as the injuries she'd sustained in the In Between caught up to her physical body. She gagged on her own blood. "The body."

Paolo bled from hundreds of wounds that still fought to heal, but the pool forming below him was from the thick artery in his thigh, pumping darkest heart blood into the leaf-cluttered rug beneath.

"May I do the honors?" Azrael said.

"*Por favor.*"

The fire came easily, white-hot and contained in a sphere around the body. When he released it, there was only a gray-black pile of flake and ashes. Gus hocked a bloody tooth into the pile. "Rot in hell, bastard."

Gregor's brows rose. "Fought dirty?"

"Did he know any other way?" She angled her chin, the blood in her mouth turning her smile fearsome. The geas no longer hid her irises, and in the dim light the metallic shine glowed from within. "Too bad I fight even dirtier."

Gregor sniffed a laugh, and when her knees gave he was there, an arm around her waist to bear her weight. "Good."

Her face shuttered, and Azrael knew there would be no more talk about what she'd survived. Of all his progeny, Gus's past held the darkest shadows and the deepest wounds. He only hoped she found a way to release them before they bore her down.

Azrael surveyed the room. His Aegis was putting down the last of the undead. It was a mercy; without their masters, they would be trapped between the animated death and their afterlife. Robbed of the will of their maker, drooling and useless.

Most of Paolo's guard was dead or surrendered, Vanka's fled. Except Pietro. Her strongman was a barely recognizable pulp.

"The dancer?"

"Ito is securing a safe house for the ballerina," Rory said, cleaning his machete. "If she survives. Your surgeon will provide care."

With Vanka's escape, Yana would not be safe. He contemplated sending a warning to her family in Prague but remembered Isela's troubled face as she revealed they might have had a part in her capture. No, they would get what came to them.

Gregor surveyed the aftermath, and Azrael felt the itch of his judgment coming. "Master, this was wrong somehow."

Azrael nodded, the words labeling the feeling he'd had since they arrived. It wasn't just learning that Vanka been the pulling the strings.

"Where's Vanka?" Gus looked around for the first time as her senses began to return.

"Gone." Azrael shook his head distractedly, unable to connect the pieces.

"You let her—" Gus shouted, furious.

"Time." Azrael cut her off. "She's learned to manipulate time, at least close to her body."

"Time manipulation? That's—"

"Impossible?" Azrael met his progeny's eyes. "And teleportation isn't?"

If Vanka was counting on defending the city to take a toll on him, she hadn't seemed too concerned that he'd arrived at his full strength. Yet he'd seen fear on her face when the dancer collapsed.

They'd all assumed Vanka would use the summoned god against him. But what had Isela's god said? *If they come back, it will be for revenge.*

* * *

ISELA WAS no longer in control of her body. Just like the night in the tomb with Róisín, she was a passenger. *Where are we?*

Isela was no longer in control of her body. Just like the night in the tomb with Róisín, she was a passenger. *Where are we?*

"Remember the place I created to show you the wall?" Gold trembled. "This is something like that."

It resembled a circular tent. Beyond the main room, she could see breaks in the other walls where curtains hung as dividers. The walls themselves were hung with colorful weavings, and the packed-earth floor was covered with thick rugs. In one corner, children's toys clustered—simple carved figures and dolls made of stuffed cloth and tied leather thongs. Furniture was sparse but well made, carved wood low-slung chairs and a little table. The most impressive piece was a curule chair carved of dark wood and polished to a low shine with a seat of tanned hide. The arms were carved like running horses. Beside the chair was a wooden perch bearing the marks of a taloned bird.

The room looked well cared for but lived in, though it lacked any scent, which was a giveaway for Isela that something was wrong. Well, something besides the matter that a moment ago she had been standing in the middle of Prague.

"He's coming," Gold said, and their gaze swung wildly to the main flaps of the tent.

Let me drive, Isela insisted.

"What?"

Isela repeated herself, hoping her voice sounded as calm and certain as she felt. *You're terrified. Maybe I can negotiate—*

"There is no negotiating with him."

Then what harm is there in giving me a chance?

Isela abruptly felt the shape and weight of the form around her. It wasn't a body exactly, but when she lifted her arm, she saw the fingers rise out of the corner of her eye. Okay. She could work with this. She stepped back, away from the door, and looked for a weapon. She reached the small of her back and felt a familiar hilt in her hand. Tariq's blade. Of course. It would be with her everywhere. Even when she hadn't had it in the physical world. That was its geas.

"Put that down, young lady."

She took a step backward in surprise at the man who strode through the tent. She knew his face. Knew every line and angle down to the silver of his eyes. Azrael's double paused, registering her shock.

"Too disconcerting then?" He waved his hand. He aged before her eyes, growing leaner and grayer as Azrael never would. But his eyes flashed a liquid rainbow of power. "Better?" He paused in her silence, hands on hips as he stared around the room. "Please, have a seat."

"What do you want?"

His canted smile gave her vertigo. "I won't harm you. I have a certain affection for you."

"Me?"

"It is because of you that his evolution has begun."

"Who?" Isela knew, but she needed to hear it. Needed him to confirm everything Azrael had searched for, what it all meant.

"My son," he said, obliging her generously. "He has all the keys; now he must figure out how to use them. I figured you would be suitable motivation."

"This is a test?"

"Of his worthiness." The man smiled, wide and predatory. "He has shown an indication that he will succeed where all others have failed. But that doesn't mean I will make it easy for him. What's the fun in that?"

His laugh, light and pleased without an ounce of the sinister warning his eyes held, made her stomach squeeze with dread.

"Now, godling," he said, looking past Isela. "While we wait for *her* champion to arrive, let me you what will happen when your kind catch up to you."

CHAPTER TWENTY-SIX

Azrael materialized before the Municipal House in a rush of heat. The Aegis staggered back from the blast, their weapons and shoulders low.

Dory held Isela in his arms like an offering. Tariq was a broken heap on the cobblestones, full of a darkness that might as well have been death but crackled with crimson bursts and jagged streaks of light.

Rage spiraled seething energy up his body, seeking an outlet, a place to strike. This was the voice that whispered to him in the dark. Now, it screamed. It was all Azrael could do to keep himself from lashing out at anything—and everything—in his path. The howling rage battered his senses, demanding retribution.

Mine. Mine has been taken from me. Burn it to the ground.

The director and her bodyguard hesitated as they emerged from the Academy doors behind Dante. The bodyguard thrust her behind him at the sight of Azrael. Dante hurried into the gap between Azrael and the others, his fingers splayed in the building of a protection geas to those he stood before.

"Hey, old man, stand down," Dante said, his voice level. His compulsion geas was a fly on the flank of a bull. "You don't mean to do this."

Azrael forced himself to meet his progeny's eyes, wavering. Dante didn't flinch.

"We have the elixir," Dante said. "There's a chance."

A chance. Hope blossomed against the screaming tumult of the voice, and he used it to build a wall, drowning out the roaring fury. He managed a nod that did not contain the threat of violence. Dante stood down. Azrael took Isela, schooling himself to a gentleness that the rage did not want to allow.

Azrael did not speak. Instead, he closed his eyes again, felt for Dante's presence, and then triggered his new power.

* * *

THEY MATERIALIZED in the heart of Azrael's aedis. Dante dropped to one knee, his breath coming hard. "That was quite a ride."

The door opened and the phoenix fluttered in, trailed by Tyler. When his eyes settled on Isela, he gave an avian squawk of alarm. He was still thin but clean-shaven with close-cropped hair, his resemblance to the family Azrael had met in Stary clear.

Dante groped his way to a standing position before Azrael could unleash his fury. "I called him. He may be able to help."

Nix, Isela had named him, looked at him as though for the first time. The bird's eyes returned to Isela as he opened and closed his mouth without a sound. His mouth worked over words silently.

"She bears the one who betrayed them, no?" he blurted finally. "Ended their reign here. It's tied to *her* now."

"Then we sever the connection," Azrael said with the certainty that he would take Isela, god or no, damn the consequences. Mortality would be a small price to pay for her return. The voice inside was unleashed without her and gaining control. "Let the gods deal with their own."

The phoenix cocked this head, considering. "The thread that connects them is not so easily broken now."

"Azrael, she died that night." Dante shook his head slowly. "Without the god—"

The god had been the only thing that kept her from crossing over. How it had done it, none of them knew. The bird chittered to itself, shaking its shoulders and neck as though to ruffle feathers it no longer had. Irritated, Azrael was about to tell it to be still or ask Dante to take it away when it met his eyes and spoke again.

Nix lifted his head, scenting something, and nodded to Tyler. The undead man handed the flask gingerly to Dante.

The phoenix spoke. "I can help you bring her back."

Dante coaxed Azrael to release Isela. "You need to prepare. I have a feeling that where you're going, you'll leave your body behind."

He was right. And a soulless necromancer's body was a vulnerable, dangerous thing, even temporarily. He would need to prevent anything from trying to slip into him while he was absent. And plant the seed of destruction in the flesh if he did not return. It was a curious thing, he considered, the willingness to leave everything. How little it all meant in the end. He began to gather the materials to protect himself, and those around him, in his absence. Dante thumbed through a set of grimoires, discarding most and leaving open a few containing spells he might need. Azrael scanned quickly, already half forming geasa and intention as he went. He grafted one onto another, feeling the wards in the walls surge as he called power to him.

He needed to bind whatever opening the phoenix would create and keep anything from being drawn in or out. Salt would do. He laid Isela down on the floor. She would be cold. Tyler was there before he could ask with blankets. He wadded one up under her head, spreading the other over her body. Dancing had drained her again; she seemed thinner and washed out, her rich skin faded. Cracks had appeared in the facade of her skin, but instead of the veins of gold, the cracks revealed only darkness.

Azrael shook himself. He had to focus on his craft. It was the only way to save her. He laid out the circle in salt, then passed a hand over it, leaving bright yellow flames dancing in its wake as his wards carved lines in the solid line of white. Dante was there with the lapis and ash to mark the four directions. The phoenix stepped into the circle and sat cross-legged beside Isela. He chanted something that sounded like birdsong. Azrael recognized the words after a moment. It was the spell Róisín had created to tap into the vein the gods used to travel between worlds.

Dante joined Azrael with the flask. He looked troubled. "If the gods found a way through to claim her, it means the wall has been breached."

Azrael nodded.

"Tariq is not... able," Dante said quietly. "And Gus is still on her way." Dante hesitated. "The coven?"

Azrael shook his head. He would not risk Isela's family. They too would be drained from the spell to protect the city. He could bear it alone. "Hold the aedis, Dante. You can do that."

"Of course."

"If necessary." Azrael left the words unspoken. Dante was strong enough to trigger the self-destruction spell.

Dante nodded. "Good luck, old man."

"You and I know too much to believe in luck," Azrael said regretfully.

"Nevertheless."

"It should be soon," Nix murmured.

Azrael stepped into the circle. "Close it behind us."

Azrael sat on Isela's other side and unscrewed the cap of Gregor's whiskey flask. He offered it to Nix. The bird dripped three drops onto Isela's lips, then sipped before reluctantly handing the flask back to Azrael. Tears of joy slipped from his closed eyelids. Azrael drew a big pull, bracing himself. Dante caught the flask, spilling only a few drops as he hurried to cap it.

"Get out now."

The phoenix's eyes had gone to flame. Dante backed out, grabbing for the salt. Azrael laid a hand on Isela's. His other reached out. The phoenix clasped it. The bird inside the man arched. Feathers of light spread behind him, throwing off a rainbow of colors that coalesced to a bright white light that even Azrael cast his eyes away from.

A sucking wind pulled at Dante. He laid down the salt. The circle sealed at a single-word command, the wards etching themselves on the seal, and the wind vanished abruptly. The three bodies inside were still.

* * *

IT COULD HAVE BEEN hours or a few heartbeats. The god had left them, and the fire dimmed in the hearth, but the sense of timelessness struck Isela.

I turned my back on them all, Gold said. *I betrayed my kind when I helped yours.*

Isela tossed a bit of bark into the embers. It flared and burned without sound. *You saved my world.*

I'm a traitor. It was foolish to hope they'd forget about me in all this.

Gods don't forget. And they don't forgive. Memory hit Isela again in a wave. Had it only been a few days since Gold said something similar? It felt like a lifetime ago. And now.

I wanted to become a better dancer, Gold said.

Isela snorted. *I wanted you to kick Gregor's ass.*

Isela heard a god in her own laugh, and the warmth that spread through her replaced the absence of heat from the fireplace. *I just hate having it out of our hands. I don't trust the Old Lion.*

Gold agreed. *Any bargain he makes will favor him. And if there's a price, we'll pay it.*

One of the dying logs in the fire broke, sending showers of sparks dancing on the rug. A few threads of the rug smoked, but there was no scent.

You're thinking of your dad.

Isela started. *I forgot you could do that; read my mind.*

I tried not to, Gold said. *I know how much you value your privacy. You fought with Azrael over it. You think of your father every day. You miss him, but you still love him. You and your family. Even the young ones will grow up knowing his name.*

Isela would have wept if she had been in her own body. A breath later, rose-gold heat rushed to her eyes and the sensation of tears raced down her cheeks.

You do that too, Gold said. *Cry. It's beautiful. Gods don't mourn, Issy. When we're gone, it's as though we never existed. We don't tell stories of each other. They will crush me and I'll be forgotten. Nothing.*

Isela wiped her face out of habit, unsurprised to find her hands dry. *Nothing, or being hunted as long as there's an inkling of your consciousness in the universe, eh? Doesn't give us a lot of options.*

Gold's silence deepened to a stillness so great Isela wondered if she was still there. When she spoke at last, her voice trembled. *What if there was a way. What if there's no me to hunt? What if there's just... you?*

CHAPTER TWENTY-SEVEN

A zrael materialized with a weight on his shoulder that cast light over the darkness around him.

He could not look at it directly; the bright swirling light left flickering after burned at the corners of his eyes when he tried. "Nix?"

I am here. Follow the thread. Time is short.

Azrael turned his head and there it was—the thinnest twist of gold, no thicker than a strand of silk. He started running, and the weight launched from his shoulder, lighting the way over an uneven terrain as barren as an alien world. A bird the size of a peacock. He cast a glance over his shoulder to orient himself and stumbled in surprise.

The wall that bound the gods from humanity was not a physical thing in any sense of the word, but he knew each necromancer saw a different manifestation of it. To some it was the woven strands of a blanket, others saw a wall of spikes or blades. Perhaps it was the city he'd chosen as his home that made his vision of it a cobblestone wall, intricately patterned interlocking blocks of power. He recognized his own emerald squares, knit with blues and reds, turquoise, yellows, golds and browns. Except for a ragged hole where the squares had gone black with decay. The thread disappeared into that tear, and it felt like a threat and a promise.

The gods were not through—not yet. Their attention was occupied elsewhere. Azrael turned to the thread, wrapping it with both hands. "We don't have time for this."

Azrael—no. The phoenix's warning came too late. Azrael felt the snap of his body vanishing from one place, but without the corresponding pop of arrival in another.

Instead, he was suspended, whirling and thrashing weightlessly in space. He felt the bird beside him. It fared better, glowing wings flaring to hold it in place.

Out of the void came a deafening roar. Azrael would have covered his ears if a force stronger than his own will hadn't restrained him. The rage boiled again in him, and he felt himself roaring back. Soundless fury rolled off his skin in waves of power, only to be swallowed up by the void, leaving him spent against the encroaching force.

One moment nothing, then it was simply there. Like a thunderstorm without rain, it roiled before him.

The dark, swirling mass blinked at him with eyes of sparking embers. He could see brightness in it, contained like raging fireflies in a smoky bottle. It whirled, enormous and all-encompassing, the pulsing of a heartbeat of the universe itself.

My son.

* * *

"Come now," the man said as the air around them re-formed into a tent not unlike the one he had grown up in.

Azrael reached through time to memories long buried. Exactly like his foremother's tent. Though they had stopped being fully nomadic generations before, the home was designed to be broken down and easily transported—from the thick felted walls to the ornate rugs that could be rolled in a matter of moments. He knew every rug, every wall hanging, all the foldable tables and chairs, the drums and weapons and blankets.

The phoenix dropped out of the air onto a perch reserved for his eldest sister's hawk, its colors subdued to human visible shades of the rainbow. It fluffed and sleeked feathers in an ombré of shades from the deepest ember red to the hottest blue-white flame.

"A fitting companion for a son of mine," the voice said again. "Wings of destruction and promise. Death and life without break."

Azrael spun as the entity shaped as a man approached, his every move leonine and graceful and dreadfully familiar. An Old Lion.

Azrael cast his gaze around the room, looking for a weapon, and froze. A golden woman, the mirror image of Isela, sat in one of the chairs by the fire. An enormous pair of monarch wings cascaded down her back and lay in a crumpled mess on the floor behind her. Her hands dangled between her knees. She looked up, defeated. Azrael bristled and felt the power come cracking to his fingertips like the faithful, silky-coated hound that had followed him until its last breath. Azrael moved between the entity and his consort's god.

When I say run, go, follow the phoenix back—

"Stop, Azrael." Isela's voice halted him. She wasn't defeated; she was resigned. "We don't have time. They're coming for me. Her. Us. And you need to hear what he has to say."

The man inclined his head regally as he took a seat in the familiar chair that he had never occupied in Azrael's childhood. "She's right, of course. I am your ally in this."

"Who are you?"

"We have very little time for questions and answers, boy," the Old Lion said. "Best to skip the obvious ones."

Azrael's mind spun, dredging up old memories of his mother's face when she refused questions about his sire, her past. In the end he asked the only question that mattered. "Why?"

"Help you?" The old man's head angled. "Or why now?"

Azrael folded his arms over his chest. "Pick one. Two thousand years. *Now* you claim me?"

"Two *thousand* years," the Old Lion said mockingly. "I watched this universe be born, boy. Your years are a blink of my eye."

"My ally," Azrael snarled. "Prove it."

The flash of white teeth startled him.

"Now that is *my* son." The smile became a weapon, bladed and cruel. He paused, considering his answer. "That foolish redhead created an opening, baited her hook, and thought she could control the beast that came. There are others that would see your *bharya* torn into pieces and cast into the oblivion. What better way to keep her from getting into their hands than to take her myself?"

Azrael thought of the trickster. Older than the sun and the moon, life and death.

The man nodded, and Azrael had the distinctly discomfiting

feeling that for the first time in centuries, someone had read his mind. "The humans had their gods, and we took their forms. Or did the humans fashion their gods after us?"

"It's true then," Azrael said, hearing the tremor at the edge of his voice. "Necromancers and witches are your children…"

"So you call yourselves." The arched brow rose mockingly.

"What are we then?"

"An experiment."

At Azrael's silence, he went on. "Mortal life has always been enticing to us. Even the strongest of us must claim a human vessel to play in their world. But their flesh is so frail. It burns out quickly with the burden of carrying all that we are. Your kind—and the witches—came out of an attempt to breed with humans to create stronger vessels for ourselves. Witches diluted their blood through mixing with humans again. We put our hopes in your line. You had our longevity —when you survived your powers—and some of our strength. Yet our attempts to claim you failed. When we tried to force the matter— Well, the results were damned disappointing."

He crossed his arms and he took them in. "But your *bharya* is something of a conundrum, the first of our blood to successfully become a vessel. Twice now she's nearly burned out the human shell, and you have kept her alive, as it were. Perhaps we were wrong to give up on the witches' line."

Azrael thought himself old beyond time. But for the first time he glimpsed a larger playing field. The gods thought of humans as playthings and pets and had indulged them like children but without a parent's sense of preservation for their offspring. Was this callous disregard inevitable in necromancers as they aged? "An experiment."

He shrugged nonchalantly. "Others want what can be claimed now. I play the long game. It appears I still have pieces on the board."

"Pieces."

"Few of the original gods remain," he said. "My offspring, naturally, will not be like others. Your mother was outstanding among mortals. Blood of witches, no doubt. You are unique, the only one of my get to survive the gift I've given. You are the closest to becoming."

"Becoming what?"

Again the smile, this time sly. "That *is* the question, isn't it? I've an interest in seeing if you continue to survive my gift."

"Survive?"

"Your powers are growing, are they not?" Again the wicked look of knowing in the silver depths that mirrored his own.

Dread curled tendrils around his rib cage, creeping up his throat. He had told himself the voice wasn't real, that it wasn't part of him. But what if he was wrong? What if the voice inside, reptilian and cold, was not an invader but his own? No power came without price. He'd already grown attached to it, the ability to simply be wherever he wished to be. Could he give it up now, even if he wanted to? Would that be enough to stop it?

The Old Lion vanished, reappearing behind Isela. "And now we're back to your *bharya*. She has had a curious effect on you, hasn't she? Quieting the voice in your head, helping you regain control. I wonder if she will be able to save you from yourself."

"So you're helping us—"

"Because if I don't, neither of you have a chance. And we're back to the same old boring routine. I do hate to be bored. She can feel them," Old Lion said with a hint of menace. "Your gods. She knows their intent. Don't you, my girl?"

Gold eyes looked up at him and hatred slid away to cold fear.

"Isela had nothing to do with that," Azrael said.

"Collateral damage." The man shook his head. "It's the little one they're after."

"You... gods." He spat the word with mockery. "We're going to destroy the world. You had to be stopped."

"Humans and their dancing." The old man studied Azrael knowingly. "Can you blame us?"

Under the scrutiny of those eyes, the sense of familiarity nearly overwhelmed him. He did not back down, nor did he look away, even though that gaze burned through him with challenge.

"Ah, you are *her* son," he said, and Azrael had the image of his mother flash in his mind. "Even more than you are *mine*. For the moment."

Azrael's heart surged, but his head held firm to reason. The growing sense of dread banked. His mother's heart, the warrior, beat in his chest, even if it pumped the blood of this *thing* through his veins. He must always remember that. The phoenix made an impatient sound from its perch.

"I had been prepared to bargain with them," the Old Lion said. "Or attempt to, but your consort and her companion have come up with an interesting solution. A loophole. I'm curious to see if it works."

"Isela can't survive in her world without me." The god rose. "But nothing of either of us will survive in any world if they get their hands on me." A great shudder wracked her body. "Human grief has taught me that even the dead leave something behind."

She stepped close to Azrael, and he remembered the night in the garden. Gone was the reckless confidence of a deity. She reached up, touching her own face—Isela's face—as if it were a strange new territory.

He caught her wrist. "What do you mean to do, god? I would know the risk to my consort."

"The only risk to me is if you don't make it back." Isela's voice again. Curious how it changed between them. The voice itself was the same, but the tone, the cadence, gave it away. She dropped her voice to its lowest register. "Can you trust me in those moments, that I do what is best for us and to explain later?"

His own words. In spite of everything, a wry smile rose in response. Even through this, she was Isela—irreverent, unafraid, hopeful. He stepped closer to her, taking her face in his hands. The gold fingertips curled around his wrists, locking him in place. The gold was cool to his touch as Isela never would be. He wanted her back. Whatever it took. The phoenix flapped its wings and fixed him with a piercing look.

"I trust you, Isela," he murmured.

A great shudder wracked her body, and her eyes sealed shut. A sound escaped her that Azrael thought might have contained a clenched sob. "Kiss me."

Azrael's gaze flew from her face to the Old Lion.

The entity looked amused. "Forgotten how?"

The phoenix screamed and the humor left the god's face.

"Now or lose it all," the Old Lion said with dreadful certainty.

Azrael turned back to the face staring into his expectantly. He lowered his head. With his eyes shut, he could pretend, almost, that this was Isela. Her lips touched his with a tingle of power. Out of habit, he took her mouth with the soft, sucking pressure that usually made Isela melt into his chest. Instead, the god stiffened and the tingle became sharp, painful needles of energy.

"Don't let go, boy."

Azrael let the kiss linger even as the needles became pain. At the sudden release of pressure, he opened his mouth, stepping backward with a shout. Collapsed on the rug at his feet was the husk of the god. It folded on itself like shed skin. The once vibrant wings grew gray and brittle before his eyes. His ribs strained to contain the thing swelling in his chest, pressing outward painfully against his skin.

"She's there now." The Old Lion tapped the center of his chest. "What's left of her. And all of your mate. Now go. I will hold them for as long as I can."

The phoenix didn't need to be told twice. It launched itself skyward, and the tent dissolved around them. Azrael wanted to hesitate, sensing this would be the last time he ever laid eyes on the entity that claimed to have sired him. The Old Lion stood in the middle of the dissolving world and laughed.

The sound raised the hairs on Azrael's body.

He fled.

* * *

AZRAEL DIDN'T LOOK BACK until they were safely through the tear in the wall. In the void, explosions of light left bright spots on his retinas and booming noise sent concussive blasts through the distance.

The phoenix hovered, squawking a command. *We have to leave now,* he urged, fearful eyes glancing toward the ruckus in the distance.

Azrael shook his head. "I have to seal that tear."

Doubt rose in him. It had taken an entire allegiance to create that wall, and it had drained them all for months. The show for humanity had been just that—illusion intended to cow them into obedience. It had taken weeks before any of them could do more than simple zombifying. How much power had he spent coming here? Hadn't he told Isela just a few weeks ago that energy was not unlimited, that it could be tapped dry as any well. What then?

He steeled himself. He had Róisín's power, and ambrosia lighting up his veins. It was just a tear, not the entire wall. He would do this. Or he would expend himself here trying. "Go now."

The bird turned as if to obey. It looked up at the wall. Then it turned to Azrael with flames in its eyes.

"Go." Azrael barked.

The phoenix's wings snapped open with a pop of flame and a force that sent Azrael hurtling backward. Azrael instinctively curled himself into a ball to prepare for a hard landing that never came. He righted himself, floating to his feet.

She gave me her protection, the phoenix said, flying into the wall. *Tell her we are even.*

The scream of the phoenix, its long-arrested transformation finally released, dropped Azrael to his knees. He tumbled backward in the blast of energy that followed. When he could scrabble upright and open his eyes again, a gout of flame burst through the wall. As it subsided, the wall stood as it once had, a solid patchwork of cobbles in a rainbow of colors. Where the tear had been was a patch of iridescent gold, rippling with a wave of colors from the glowing red of deepest embers to the indigo blue of hot flame.

Nix was gone.

Azrael turned his back on the land of the gods.

CHAPTER TWENTY-EIGHT

"Hes back." Dante's voice broke the silence. Time stretched on after Azrael and the phoenix crossed over for Isela. Sometime during the night, the witches arrived without notice, coming to sit beside their mates, a larger circle around the necromancer's. The high priestess stationed herself at Azrael's head, as though she could will him her strength by proximity. She refused to listen to Dante's words of caution about what might go wrong.

The Aegis returned from the city first, taking up sentry positions. Gus and Gregor thundered in next, still reeking of undead. Gus swore and tried to broach the circle, but the salt and geas held.

"Old fool," she swore, blinking furiously.

"Perhaps you should see to our brother," Dante advised her sagely. "Tariq sustained great damage tonight."

They all gasped when the phoenix slumped to the floor with a burst of power. Wind and flames, iridescent lines of blue and violet whipped the air into a frenzy though it left the figures unharmed. The walls of the circle rose, visible now with the force of containing the maelstrom within.

The high priestess saw it too. "Phoenix fire."

At last, Azrael's fingers twitched. His eyelids bounced and rose. He rolled onto his side with the groan of an animal that had been run to the point of exhaustion. Other than the wind whipping her hair against her face and neck, Isela remained still. Azrael moved as if bearing a great weight, and when Dante closed his eyes again, he could *see* the enormous gathering of power in his chest. The glowing mass of golden embers pulsed with his heartbeat, shedding sparks and flames.

When he wavered, the room held its collective breath. Then he laid a hand on Isela's cheek, angling her face just so, and pressed his lips to hers. Dante closed his eyes again, watching the light shatter in his chest, flowing eagerly up his body and into Isela. Her back arched and her hands splayed with fingers wide. It was not comfortable, this kiss, but he held firm until the last bit of gold had faded from his chest. It moved through Isela, not gathering as it had in Azrael but spreading from her toes to her crown. The kernel of death vanished.

The salt broke, scattering as Azrael fell and the last of the phoenix fire washed the room in flickering shades of blue and orange. The high priestess caught his head before it could strike the floor.

When he looked up, she smiled. "Welcome back."

Isela stirred.

* * *

Isela rolled onto her elbows, her breath labored as she met his eyes.

Azrael propped them both upright, and for a moment there was just the warm feeling of her breath on his collar and the familiar, welcome scent of her sweat and hair. But he wasn't the only one who had been waiting. He let his arms fall enough so that she could see her family, knowing when she did she would be theirs.

"Mom? What are you doing here?"

The remains of the circle scattered under the force of their reunion. Gregor took one look at the flying tufts of wolf pelt and beat a hasty retreat.

"I'm fine," Isela assured Bebe, though her eyes found Azrael's and told a different story. "Yes, it's changed. I'm not sure yet how, or exactly what. But I feel it too."

Azrael turned his attention to Dante as he examined the phoenix.

Isela's hand slipped over his. "Is he—?"

"Not dead." Azrael shook his head, unable to find the kernel of death in him.

Dante sighed. "But not quite alive either. He's breathing, and his heart is pumping. But there doesn't appear to be anyone home."

"He sacrificed himself," she said, a note of grief in her voice.

Azrael slid an arm around her. "He was returning a favor."

"We'll look after him," Dante promised. "He may—Things may change in the next few days."

Wise, Azrael thought of Dante's amendment. Azrael vowed that the phoenix's physical form would not be kept indefinitely, languishing until it wasted away to nothing. He owed Nix and the old matriarch that.

Isela rested her cheek on his shoulder, and suddenly he wanted everyone to be gone so that he could have her all to himself. He was tired. So tired. The noise of the relieved, anxious minds in the room pressed on him, and his defenses were too spent to form a solid block. He wanted nothing more than to drag Isela to their bed and sleep for a year.

He looked away from Isela to see Bebe watching him. A knowing smile lifted the darkness from her eyes as she began to herd the rest of the coven toward the door. At her final glance back, Azrael thanked her with a little nod. Azrael checked in with Gregor for a report on the city, and Gus for Tariq's status. Gregor cheerfully informed him that Lysippe was on her way back, promising to brief her fully on her arrival. Isela sat in the chair beside Nix's gurney where she had been holding vigil. Someone had draped a blanket over her shoulders to ward off the aedis's natural chill. Azrael gathered her, blanket and all, in his arms and started walking.

He didn't stop until they were behind the doors of their bedroom and the world shut out behind them. When he set her down, she extended her arms above her head in one of those long, full-body stretches, allowing the blanket to slide off her and pool at her feet. The sight of her lean lines framed in the dim light banished his need to sleep.

She gasped when he cupped her breasts, rolling the peaks of her nipples between his fingers. The intake of breath became a purr when he touched his lips to the skin at the base of her neck. He bared his teeth, scraping lightly, and she shuddered hard enough to press her backside into his groin. The delicious pressure made sparks fly behind his closed eyelids and he groaned.

"You need sleep," he reminded himself.

"I know what will help me get there fast," she said huskily.

"Are you saying I put you to sleep?" His teeth closed over the muscle in her neck, pinching enough to make her whimper.

"Quit twisting my words and take off my clothes," she growled.

He laughed, loving the way goose bumps sprang up over her skin when his hand skimmed her arms, and complied. When their mouths met again, it was with the pleasant exchange of tongues and laughter. He launched her onto the bed, shedding his clothes on his way to join her. He slid his body onto hers, enjoying the way her legs parted to cradle him comfortably against her hips. He rocked his hips once, twice, to feel her response before seeking her mouth again. This time her fingers came between their lips.

When he looked into her eyes, gold irises flecked with the reflection of phoenix fire met his.

"Azrael," she breathed.

"Mmm?" He stroked the underside of her breast with his fingertip.

"When you…"

Unused to her hesitation, he slid an elbow under himself so that he could look down fully into her face.

"You kissed her."

Azrael wanted to laugh but bit it back with all his might. Was *that* what was on her mind? He curled a strand of hair behind her ear and feathered his mouth across her cheek. "It meant nothing. Just the Old Lion's way of screwing with us."

She relaxed her head against the pillow, but her eyes did not lose the intense expression. "I *know* that. Do you honestly think I'm jealous?"

Azrael let a chuckle escape, tapping her chin with his index finger. "She *is* a god, you know."

Isela let out a breath that could have been annoyance, a laugh, or a bit of both.

"Was." Azrael corrected her, sliding his nose against the skin below her ear until she shivered.

"She's gone," Isela said, her expression turning speculative. "I mean, I can't feel her like before. Like I was possessed."

She sounded sad. Azrael sighed and rolled onto his side, dragging her thigh over his hip to keep them locked together.

"She didn't give up everything," Azrael said, sliding a fingertip down the centerline of her chest to rest on her breastbone. "She's not gone."

He tapped his finger twice, lightly.

"Not entirely," she agreed. "But whatever was there that was her will, her desire, is missing."

"That troubles you," he surmised at the look on her face.

"I don't know why. I should be glad. No more voice in my head, no more strange pulls toward things that I can't explain."

He growled, nipped at the line of her jaw.

"I can explain *that* pull." She laughed, shifting her hips against his before her mood darkened again. "But it's just me now. No god."

Azrael flipped onto his back, dragging her on top of him. His fingers worked down the corded muscle along her spine, settled over the curve of her hips. At least if they were going to have this nonsense conversation, he could do it while making the most of their proximity.

She hesitated. "Are you sure that's going to be enough… for you?"

"More than enough," he muttered, squeezing the plump flesh.

She thumped him on the chest with a fist that packed a surprising punch. "Don't mock."

"I'm not," he said, kneading the long lines of her thighs. "I chose you before you chose her. I will always choose you, Isela. This is home."

"I chose her to come back to you." She stacked her palms on his chest over his heartbeat, settling her chin there with a long exhale.

His lips and breath caressed her brow when he spoke. "Now you have the powers. And the immortality. You have your own head back, all of it. I don't think it could be any more resolved."

Isela made a soft sound, resting her ear on the back of her stacked hands. Azrael sighed, threading his fingers through the hairs at the base of her neck. Resolutely he began removing the last of the pins from her hair, spreading the coils over her back and enjoying the way they sprang back at the first chance.

"She gave me a parting gift, you know," she said finally.

Azrael raised his head. The skin on his neck prickled with a prescience of trouble. "What gift?"

"She said it was a surprise." Isela frowned. "That I'd know… when it came. But the way she said it." She paused. "I don't like surprises."

It was Azrael's turn to let a thoughtful sound escape. He paused, stroking her hair for just a moment, thinking of the voice that had gone quiet since Isela and her god had become one. But for how long? "Whatever it is, we handle it, Isela. Together."

She looked at him finally, and the warmth in her eyes softened whatever tension had built in his chest. She stretched upward, dragging her skin along his in the most agonizing pleasure of his night so far. She planted a kiss on his lower lip. With the junction of her thighs resting treacherously close to the head of his cock, the temptation was excruciating. He waited.

"Do you think the Old Lion was telling the truth?" she asked, rocking away from him. "About who—what—he is to you."

Azrael interlaced his hands behind his head, letting his elbows splay wide. He released a breath before speaking. "My sire? Why lie? He has nothing to gain by claiming me after so long. It gives me every reason to hate him actually."

"Sire," she mused. "That sounds so—"

"We are their attempt to breed stronger bodies for themselves."

"It's not exactly parent-of-the-year stuff," she agreed.

"Calling him father seems a bit..."

"Silly?"

He stared down his nose at her. "An overstatement."

She sat up, straddling his hips. He thanked two thousand years for the ability to have a rational conversation in spite of the pressure building in his groin.

"You're the son of one of the oldest gods there is. At least according to Mr. Humble Brag 'I watched the universe be born.' And I'm the first successful vessel of a god. That's got to mean something."

"It means," Azrael drawled, "that the Allegiance is going to have every reason to want to destroy me, and the gods are going to have every reason to try to get to you. So. At least the next few hundred years won't be boring. What do you think about getting a dog?"

She blinked a few times, and then a small smile crept up her mouth. "A dog? With me? You want to get a dog with me?"

"Too domestic?" His brows furrowed.

She shook her head furiously. He loosened his fingers, sliding his hands from behind his head toward her waist, but she caught his wrists in a startlingly strong grip. He laughed, but she held firm.

"Did you want something?" She pinned his hands overhead,

nipping the corner of his mouth and sliding her body along his length.

She was wet. So wet. He groaned, arching his hips. "You know what I want."

"Tsk, tsk, tsk." She pulled back with a sly grin. "It's your turn to beg."

CHAPTER TWENTY-NINE

The gardens on the south hill of the castle provided her favorite view of the red-roofed Malá Strana district. On a clear day, the long stone walkway of the garden on the ramparts was the perfect place to watch the sparkle of the river winding its way through the center of the city. Today the sky was hazy with the kind of gauzy air that presaged rain. Pools of slate-gray clouds driven on a cold wind blanketed the horizon, dappling the sunlight over the city. The walkway led into the Garden of Eden, once the private retreat of an archduke. The gardens were also close to the buildings, an option she had taken into consideration when she accepted the invitation for a walk.

"I should have died," Nix said.

Isela paused as he navigated an uneven piece of pavement. She'd learned the hard way not to interfere. He'd recovered some weight and a good amount of muscle tone. He used a cane, but long walks took enormous effort. The physical therapist Isela had brought in from the Academy called his recovery nothing short of miraculous.

"Dante thinks it was the improper transformation into this body that may have saved me," he went on. "My link with it brought me back. Well, what's left of me."

Isela looked away, her eyes on the thawing city. The air held the damp promise of rain. She could not shake the guilt, the sense of wrongness that he was somehow forever trapped in this human body when he had once been so much more.

"I may not be what I once was, but enough of me remains to be of value. I have my memories, centuries of knowledge."

"Even if you didn't," Isela said firmly, "you would still be valuable. Just by being."

"You aren't like the others." He shook his head. "You are kind first. Your heart is soft."

Isela gave a wan half smile. "Gregor says it is my weakness."

"As you might say, it takes one to know one," Nix said. "Building armor is just one way to live with it."

"But not the only way."

"Not the only way," he echoed. "Another is to remain open."

"Vulnerable."

"A different kind of strength."

They paused before the tree Isela had named Her Majesty. At four hundred years old, the yew tree with its stately crown of evergreen branches earned a moment of respectful admiration. She let her eyes wander the twisted red bark. Her physical vulnerability had almost killed Dory, but the part of her that was still human-hearted had found a way to bring him back. Maybe there was truth to Nix's words. She considered the nascent connection to her new guard. It was like a healing wound, and the temptation to prod it was too great to resist.

Everything okay, Is?

Shoot, she had been too obvious. *Yeah, sorry. Don't mind me.*

His mental laugh was as good as the real thing. *Then quit yanking my string, lady.*

She smiled.

"So what will you do next," she asked, changing the subject.

"Azrael no longer sees the kernel of death in me," he said. "But what magic I have left is a shadow. In my true form, I was hunted every day of my life. Now I am valueless to those who would try to use me. It will be strange not to have to hide."

"Your bond of sanctuary has been absolved." She'd done that as soon as Dante confirmed there was no threat to him. "Where will you go?"

Nix hesitated for the first time. He drew himself up to his full height, and she had to look up to see the solemn, determined expression on his face.

"I'm told that you have begun the formation of your own Aegis."

Isela laughed, rubbing the phantom ache in her ribs. "That was an accident. I'm still trying to talk Dory out of it. I am no necromancer, Nix."

"The power of gods runs in your veins."

His face looked so hopeful it broke her heart. The first drops of rain darkened the ground at their feet. She shook the loose folds of the wrap around her shoulders, drawing the resulting hood over her head. It was a useless effort. They were a ten-minute shuffle from the doors to the castle at Nix's pace. They would be drenched in a few moments.

"I could be an asset to you," he said in a long rush. "You need an ally—information, history, background—I can provide it. Azrael's libraries are a resource, but it will take centuries to learn how to access them fully. And with Dante accompanying Gus to Suramérica for the time being... Well, I can help you."

She couldn't speak.

His words tapered off, and his gaze drifted to his feet. "I understand. What would you want with the embers of a once-great creature?"

She put her hand over his on the grip of his cane, squeezing lightly. "Nix, you are still a great creature."

Defeat creased his brow. "Thank you for not laughing at me."

"What could I offer you that's better than freedom?"

"I want only to be of service. And the books— access to the books."

Isela rubbed her forehead. A phoenix. "You have that. Azrael would let you stay if you asked."

"Necromancers respect those who serve. They don't suffer hangers-on."

"You can hardly stand up," Isela said after a moment. "Let's get you inside."

She started for the door, *Dory, a little help here?*

She looked back when she realized he wasn't following her. "It's not a no. It's just... a maybe."

Dory scooped up the recovering man in one arm, threw a blanket over her head, and they fled the incoming storm.

* * *

ISELA FOUND Azrael in the study. She shook the rain from her hood and dropped it back over her shoulders. Thunder made the stone walls tremble. Nix hadn't stopped talking until she dropped him off at his new quarters in the castle. He *was* a fount of information. That could be incredibly useful.

But create an Aegis of her own? Neither witch nor necromancer, she was in some ways greater, in others less. Gus had already taught her a few small combat geasa, and she spent three days a week with one of the coven. Could she make undead? She shuddered.

She slowed at the sound of voices. Azrael wasn't alone. She should have checked. Just another way she'd failed to use the powers she understood in the simplest ways. How was she ever going to learn how to use ones she hadn't yet tapped?

She started back the way she came on tiptoe when she heard her name. "This concerns you. You should stay."

She made one more attempt to dust the rain from her shoulders before walking into the circle of firelight illuminated by the enormous hearth and lamps. She understood why he had forgone electricity as soon as she saw his companion.

She hadn't seen Tariq since the night of the city's defense. When she'd asked, Azrael assured her he recovered. The niggling worry that Azrael might be keeping them apart for other reasons came in her quiet moments, but she refused to humor it. What had the Aegis told him of the moment in the square?

Tariq sat in the chair on the other side of Azrael's great desk. He looked as if he'd aged twenty years. Deep lines around his mouth and eyes carved fissures in his sun-bleached ochre skin. Streaks of silver raced from his temples into the dark length of his hair. But even more troubling was what lay beneath the surface. Energy roiled, fractured and bruised in places like rotted fruit. Something powerful had touched him—corrupted him.

"Tariq—"

She did her best to hide her shock, but his eyes fell away from her first. She looked to Azrael, unable to contain the alarm she felt.

Was this from defending the city?

Azrael's careful pause chilled her. *No, Isela.*

"Light of my master's eye." The melodious resonance of his voice was now a ragged scratch. "I beg your forgiveness."

The formality where there had once been none was a painful

distance between them. Isela's next thought made her stomach turn. *Did you... punish him?*

How little you think of me.

She wanted to cry but wasn't sure whether from knowing she still doubted her lover or the sight of her broken friend. Azrael the lover. Azrael the monster. Every time she thought she could accept the dichotomy, something happened to unseat her understanding of the world. It raised the anxious tension in her chest that made her want to move, to dance, to run. She set her hand on Azrael's shoulder, holding her ground. *You told him to protect me and the god—*

Azrael shook his head, but he took a breath and she felt his calm wash over him, steadying her. He spoke to Tariq. "Since I can't disabuse you of the notion you've fixed in your stubborn head, I'm going to let her try. Tell her, Tariq."

The broken necromancer closed his eyes, bowing his head. "My master, please, I beg you."

Isela forced herself to stay at Azrael's side. Her fingers dug into his shoulder. He covered her hand with his own, and the rock lodged beneath her heart eased so she could breathe again.

His dull eyes climbed slowly. A roiling darkness splintered the bronze irises. Isela refused to look away from the pain in them. "When the god came, I failed my vow to you."

"Gods save me." Azrael slammed his fist down on the desk. Isela jumped. Tariq did not flinch. "That is not what I meant, you self-righteous fool."

Isela put her back to Tariq to stare her lover in the eye. What she saw startled her—grief. It slackened his cheeks, made his mouth weary and cold.

"You tell me then," she said quietly. "Since he cannot."

"That night, he put himself between my *sire*," Azrael said, "and you."

Isela's vision went dark as she was flooded by memory. The sensation of being ripped in two, split from her body and yanked away from the world. She sat down hard on the edge of the desk, recognizing the darkness in Tariq now. She'd seen it that night in the waves of clouds and sparking red light. Tariq had gone up against the Old Lion and he'd lost. Whatever the entity had done to him had corrupted his power.

"That *thing*... even my god feared it," she said, hearing the tears

roughing her own voice. At the last moment there had been a tug, a
tiny pull on her. She remembered seeing the thin gold line unspooling
behind them as the black mass dragged her out of the world. She
confronted Tariq when she could breathe again. "You made the
thread. So Azrael could follow."

Tariq would not look at her. Azrael confirmed it when his progeny
was silent. "Even as he was being torn apart from the inside out."

Isela flung herself off the edge of the desk, going to her knees
beside Tariq's chair. She took his hand in her own, holding it even
when he tried to pull away.

"You look at me," she commanded.

With effort he obeyed.

"You did what you could. It could have *destroyed* you."

He turned his face away from her. "It did not fail, lady."

"Then you must keep fighting," she said.

He shook his head once. "I failed."

She took his cheek in her hand, turning that grayed, gaunt face to
her. He closed his eyes, sank his cheek into her palm as if it were a
cool cloth. Isela's mind spun with the understanding that she was
losing him. As surely as he had watched her being ripped from the
world by Azrael's sire, he was now being pulled away from her. Slowly
and painfully.

What will happen if he cannot defeat it?

Azrael's face was grim, full of a desperation she had never seen. *I'll
destroy him myself before I see that happen.*

Isela's heart tripped unsteadily in its rhythm. *You have to help him.*

*Whatever Old Lion did to him will prey on what he cannot forgive in
himself. Tariq has always owned more than his share of responsibility. It's
what keeps him from ascending. In this, he must save himself.*

Isela tried anyway. "I forgive you, Tariq. But I would never have
forgiven myself if you had been lost that night. You and Gus and
Dante are Azrael's family. Do you know how much you mean to us?"

"I am not worthy of that honor, lady."

For a long moment there was nothing but this impasse, the sense
they were on an irrevocable course toward tragedy. At last Azrael rose
from his seat with a deep sigh.

"I refuse to forgive you," he said quietly. "And in failing in your
task, you owe me your life."

Tariq looked up, resolute. This was what he'd wanted all along—

permission to quit fighting and for Azrael to exact a final punishment. She started to speak, but Azrael gripped her hand for silence. She remembered the vows they had made to each other and held her tongue.

"I accept, my lord," Tariq said.

Azrael's eyes lit on Isela, the heat gone from the silver. Silver was the color of ice, she thought suddenly, and Azrael was as capable of as much coldness as heat. Still, she trusted him.

He spoke slowly. "My consort's defenses will need a captain. As her Aegis is... incomplete at best, Tariq Yilmaz, I am assigning the responsibility to you."

Isela's jaw fell.

Tariq sucked in a hard breath. "But master—"

"Is your life not mine to command?" Azrael boomed.

Tariq bowed his head.

"You will not fail me a second time. Understood?"

Tariq shifted his weight forward as if to stand. Isela went with him, reaching out a hand to lend support. Instead, he took her fingertips and slid down to one knee at her feet. "I am yours, lady. I will earn your grace again."

Isela met Azrael's eyes over the bowed head. The skin stretched taut over his cheeks, and his lips as pressed together in a tight line. The silver of his eyes shone with a fierce and desperate light.

"Gregor will see to your permanent quarters," Azrael said. "You are dismissed."

When he was gone Azrael turned to the fire. His back was to her. With the light behind him, she could only see the silhouette of his body, but she knew him well enough to understand what she saw.

"You'll call me cruel," he said after a long moment.

Isela took a hard breath. "You told me once you could be a monster. That you *would* be a monster to protect yours."

Azrael's head snapped up, and she felt his attention take the edge of a honed blade. She let the air leave her lungs, taking with it any resistance or reluctance.

"I think you'll do whatever it takes to keep him alive," she said firmly. "And I think you'll use what he feels for me to do it. No matter how much pain it causes him when he understands I can never be his."

She watched his shoulders rise with an enormous breath, skin crackling with heat.

"You'll save his life even if it breaks his heart," she said, crossing the room to stand at his back. She laid her hand between his shoulder blades, nestling left toward the beating of his heart.

Azrael exhaled. His head hung heavy and she slid her fingertips up his neck, threading through the short hairs at the base. She rested her forehead against his shoulder blade.

"And I will help you," she whispered. "Because I can't bear what it will do to you if you lose him. It appears I, too, can be a monster when needed."

His fingers slid down her free arm to her hand. He pulled it around his chest, drawing her to him. Pinned between his heart and his hand, her palm vibrated with their contact.

"Forgive me, consort," he murmured, "for underestimating you."

"Don't do it again," she said, feeling weary and overwhelmed. "Now, about this Aegis—"

"It's customary for a consort to have his or her own set of guardians and trusted advisors. As the consort is often another necromancer, the Aegis serves both purposes."

"But your Aegis—"

"Will provide you physical protection," he said, interlacing their fingers. "You will have much to learn as consort. It would not be bad to begin with a necromancer, a scientist, and what's left of a phoenix as your council."

She looked up, surprised he knew of Nix. "Wait, a scientist?"

"Dr. Sato attempted a circumspect inquiry regarding an adjustment to the terms of his contract yesterday," Azrael said. The smile crept into his voice at his next words. "I will warn you, he needs much work when it comes to following orders."

* * *

ISELA STEPPED out of Divya's inner office, shaking hands with the director before Divya pulled her into a hug.

"We're looking forward to seeing you at the start of the new term," Divya said. "Professor Vogel."

Niles met her at the door. "I'll see you out."

"No need," Isela said.

"It would be my pleasure."

The halls were full of dancers when they should have been clear. At Niles's stern expression a path opened, but murmurs of her name —excitement tinged with doubt and, in some cases, a little fear followed her.

"I wanted to thank you, Miss Vogel," he said quietly. "After the news, I'd never seen the director so—"

Isela knew the feeling. The necromancers would continue to provide some response to the petitions, but for all intents and purposes, godsdancing was dead. The academies would gradually transition to schools for formal dance traditions. Many wouldn't survive.

Isela suggested that some godsdancers might be trained for another purpose. Those with the blood of gods—not powerful enough to be witches or necromancers—might be able to use their talent as she had to find humans and Others in trouble. Part of her teaching at the Academy would be seeking those special dancers out. Gradually they would be introduced to the world of the Others. And then work with Azrael's Aegis to form teams, much like the pack had.

"We can't get our hopes up," she said. "It might not even work."

"It's a chance," Niles said. "And hope."

Maybe the greatest thing wasn't love after all, but simple, unassuming hope.

"Don't you dare sneak out of here without saying goodbye, Vogel." The lanky dishwater blond trotted down the stairs to wrap her in a bear hug. "Or should I say Madame Vogel?"

"How is she?" Isela murmured into his shoulder.

His exhale carried the weight of worry. "Healing. Thank your boyfriend for the safe house and the nurse. She can't go back to her family. And dancing isn't an option anymore."

Grief welled up in Isela's chest, a tangible pressure against her ribs. She'd thought she would have time to win Yana over, that she would one day lose her mistrust of the supernatural and go back to being Isela's friend. But that would never happen, not after all she had been through. Isela knew she should be happy that her friend had survived, but loss stuck in her throat.

"It's not your fault." His words lost themselves in her hair.

"I want to see her please."

He drew back, hands on her shoulders. "I'm sorry, Issy. She's not ready. Not yet."

It was a kind way of saying Yana was still refusing. Isela searched his face, seeing only new lines of regret and age where once there had been careless youth. He squeezed her arms. "You did a good job with the eyes. Almost the same as the old days."

The smile that snagged one corner of her mouth was a shadow.

"What you're doing," he said, tugging her gently. "What we're going to do here. She'll want to be part of that someday. I know it."

"Thanks for the pep talk, Professor Bradshaw."

"Anytime." He hugged her again. "I've got a class. Got to run."

Niles stood a few feet away, ensuring their privacy but ready when she turned to him.

"Your car is ready."

Outside, Liberty 2.0 waited on the curb. This model was a flat, smoky gray. The butterfly doors slid up when she approached, and the car greeted her with a chime. She slid inside, buckled the belt, and let the doors seal closed around her. She contemplated the building that had been her home for most of her adult life from behind the tinted glass. It was good to know part of her would always belong here. But she had changed, for better or for worse, and for always. She belonged somewhere else now, and that place no longer resembled a building.

"Let's go home, Libby."

The car slid away from the curb.

EPILOGUE

Isela's blade sang, missing a clean slice of Lysippe's jugular by millimeters.

Lysippe bounced back on the balls of her feet, an unexpected combination of a featherweight's deadly speed and a street fighter's efficient grace. She bared her teeth, grinning and touched her neck. Isela smelled the metallic tang when Lysippe lifted her fingers.

Dory's laughing voice rose over the shouts of the rest of the Aegis. "First blood!"

It was all she was going to get. But at least Lysippe was magnanimous after giving Isela her thrashing.

The older woman gave her a hand off the floor. "You're improving."

"I'm learning to stay alive," Isela said, thinking of Gus on her way to her new territory. "And to dance."

Lysippe gave her a curious look, but before Isela could explain, Azrael materialized in front of them. A roomful of warriors sprang into guard. Lysippe, who'd reached for her weapon before recognizing him, scowled when she relaxed her grip.

Isela pressed a hand to her rib cage. "I'm not sure, but a heart attack might still kill me."

Azrael's expression was a mixture of eagerness and youthful pleasure. Once rare, it was becoming increasingly familiar to her. Wher-

ever he'd come from, he smelled of damp wood and fresh drizzle. His
hair was definitely askew, and was that mud on his shins?

"Still perfecting the arrival," he said. "Are you finished, Lys?"

Lysippe dismissed her with a nod.

"Good." He stepped forward, wrapping an arm around Isela.
"Come. I have something to show you."

She thrust her hands against his chest the moment she realized
what he intended, but it was too late. A slap of air pressure and they'd
arrived at their destination. Isela stepped back, bracing her hands on
her knees as she tried to catch her breath. The world materialized
around her in shades of rain-darkened green and afternoon gold. For a
moment she focused on just breathing.

"I don't think I like this new power." She sealed her eyes shut as a
wave of dizziness swept her.

"Let's not keep her waiting."

"Her?" Isela straightened, taking in their surroundings. She
smelled a wood-burning stove.

They were in a garden recently reclaimed from a wood. The grassy
slope they'd appeared on was circled by a driveway leading out to a
gate both physically and magically guarded. The sounds and smells of
the city were muted from here. She could tell by the light they were
somewhere southeast of the castle. She turned after Azrael and took in
a breath.

On the other side of the driveway was a small villa bristling with
scaffolding and builder's materials. The rectangular, tile-roofed
building featured sgraffito borders of dancing nymphs and satyrs, gods
and goddesses running below the roofline on the walls. The grounds
were an arboretum of trees with breaks for paths and stretches of grass
that promised haven to patches of sunlight on warm days. Warm gold
lights spilled from the windows onto the gardens before it. On the
opposite side of the circular driveway, a carriage house was under
similar reconstruction.

Azrael circled her hand with his. When her eyes met his again, his
were alight. The joy in them stole her breath again. "Welcome home."

Surprise made her lag behind on the way to the broad oak doors
pitted with age and neglect. Her fingers slid over the cool, carved
wood. He pushed open the doors easily.

"It was the estate of an industrialist in the prewar days," Azrael
said, pulling her into the entryway. "It was mostly abandoned when I

remembered it. The family lost their fortune. I made them a generous offer."

Isela stared up at the vast ceiling. The whole place smelled forgotten, like damp leaves, old cigarettes, and unturned earth. Faded graffiti marked the walls, and burned places scored the warped floor. But it also smelled of paint and fresh materials. There were signs of construction everywhere—scaffolding and ladders, ropes and buckets. She turned a slow circle on the cracked tile floor, Azrael striding around her as he explained work planned to restore the house and the grounds.

"We'll need to make some improvements," he said, sniffing lightly.

Before she could ask, he dragged her on a tour.

"There's an industrial kitchen also, of course," he said, "should you like to entertain. But I thought this would suit for everyday use."

This kitchen was mostly complete; appliances and features draped in sheets of plastic to protect them from the ongoing work. Except, instead of the sleek, modern feel of his apartment in the castle, this one had an enormous cement farmer's sink and—

"Are those from my drawers?" Isela murmured, touching the familiar mismatched pulls on the wooden cabinets. Under plastic was her old dining table, ringed by the assortment of chairs she'd collected from antiques dealers and auction houses.

She spun on him. Emotions—surprise, delight, gratitude—battled their way up her chest into her throat, fighting for her voice.

"I was told by Director Sauvageau that you wanted to have everything thrown out," Azrael tsked, disapproving. "What a terrible waste that would have been. You have excellent taste for a young creature."

He broke the moment with that newly familiar reckless grin. "Not done yet." He grabbed her hand.

Away they went. Isela staggered away from him, gasping when they materialized at the top of the stairs on the second floor. "You. Have. To. Warn. Me."

Azrael's expression held a new feature. Mischief. "The stairs aren't quite stable yet."

"I think I'm going to hurl."

"You can see the rest at your leisure," he said idly. "You'll have plenty of time, after all, to make it your own. But *this* is for you."

He spun her around and pushed open a door.

Bright hardwood floors greeted her. She let her fingers trail along the barre on the nearest wall. Three walls lined with mirrors, the windows overlooking the trees and a ruined vineyard. She raced to the middle of the floor to plant her hands and press into a handstand, wiggling her toes in delight. Upside down by the door where she'd left him, Azrael looked beside himself with satisfaction. When she returned to him, she couldn't keep the grin off her own face.

"What... when... how did you... *why...*" She broke off.

"I need to present a face to the city, to be a presence. The castle suited me for a while. But it's been centuries since I've had a home. It's close to Vyšehrad and your family. But far enough that we won't endanger them with our proximity. I thought... Well, I didn't think. I just gave orders." He shrugged. "It's an old habit. And when the director's office called about your belongings... Well, it just seemed natural that they should be here. With you. Us. Also, this was recovered from the car."

He let his voice drift into the silence of the room as she followed his gaze to the plastic bag hanging from the door and the box beneath it. She froze, fingertips pressed to her lips before she bounded across the floor and slid to her knees. She looked back at him as she withdrew a second zippered plastic bag.

"The bag held up well," he said. "But in case it still smells too much like the river, I asked Bebe to send over another box. She says the children are working on another gift; next time they'd like to give it to you in person."

Isela couldn't see through her tears. The bag tore easily with her strength, and she pressed her face into the faded black threads. A little muddy, but beneath that, everything she remembered. She laid it down on the box, rising before launching herself at him.

He staggered backward with the force of her crashing into him. Laughter rocked his chest as he tried to catch her, keep his footing, and meet the kiss all at once. Her feet left the floor, and he settled her on the barre. The hand in her hair squeezed, tipping her head back so he could explore her mouth more thoroughly. She locked her legs around his hips. From downstairs came a crash and he looked up with a little sigh. "Ah, one more thing. Are you ready?"

"In more ways than one." She leaned forward, but he took her hand and a step away.

"I thought we'd take the back stairs," he said, leading the way. "I don't want to scare her."

Isela let herself be pulled along. "You should know I'm not into threesomes."

He cast a look over his shoulder, one brow arched, and she felt the tips of her ears growing warm.

"Well, just the once."

Off the kitchen, in a small washroom with a door that opened to the back garden, a small pen had been set up. A young dog the color of ripe wheat pressed against the fence, her tasseled ears and tail shivering as she yipped her excitement at his arrival.

At the sight of Isela, the pup went silent. Isela held her breath, afraid to hope. She'd wanted a dog as a child, but her mother always managed to find a good reason they couldn't have one. The one time she had brought home a stray, the poor dog had wet itself at the first sight of her brothers and run away. Now she understood why. Some dogs rolled onto their back and cowered with tails planted firmly between their legs and could not be roused from an almost stuporous terror. Others started barking and refused to stop.

The pup cocked its ears forward, tilting its head and taking a long series of deep inhales. Its eyes never left her.

"She is the descendant of a long line of dogs bred for companionship and hunting," Azrael said quietly as the two made up their minds. "When I was a boy, dogs like this were trusted among children and stock, though they were known to take down bears and wolves, in packs. They know no fear. Let her scent you. She will know that you are her pack."

When the pup didn't come unglued, Isela crouched down, offering her hand. The pup ambled forward. Oversized paws planted themselves firmly on the ground before Isela, and the long neck craned forward as her nose wrinkled and twitched. The warm gusts of air tickled Isela's fingers. She wanted to smile but didn't dare.

At last the pup took two cautious steps, close enough to touch, and slipped her tongue against Isela's knuckles. Content, she closed the distance, coming up on her hind legs to plant her forepaws on Isela's knee. Her silky, plumed tail wagged fiercely.

"What's her name?" Isela breathed finally, trying a smile.

The pup rolled her eyes at the sight but did not back away. Good sign.

"We will have to think of something," Azrael said.

Isela stood, ignoring the paws dancing at her knees. "She's going to be big."

Azrael cocked his eyebrow in question.

"Big feet." Isela laughed. "You should have seen Markus as a teenager."

"The wolves," Azrael began, then corrected himself. "Your brothers. Your family will always be welcome here. They should come by soon so she grows accustomed to their scent and presence. If this went well, I'd hoped we could add others in time. She belongs in a pack."

"Gregor will love that." She laughed to keep from crying.

His hand found the back of her neck, kneading warmth gently into the muscles on either side of bone. She focused on the puppy. Her fingers traced long lines in the silky coat.

"I know you don't like surprises…" Azrael's voice rumbled against her back like distant thunder as he slid his arms around her.

An incredulous laugh tangled with the emotion in her throat and she coughed. "*This* is not a surprise. This is unbelievable. Pinch me."

"Why would I do that?" He was so earnest and concerned that she smiled.

"This must be a dream."

She leaned her weight back into him, and he brought them to a seat on the dusty floor. Seeing her opening, the puppy leaped into Isela's lap, licking furiously at her throat. Azrael pushed the tasseled head down and away with a chiding noise in the back of his throat. His free hand found Isela's cheek, pausing at the wetness he found there.

"On second thought, don't," Isela said, voice thick. "Wake me, I mean. If this is a dream, just let me stay here."

"Only if I can stay in it with you," Azrael murmured against the shell of her ear.

"Always."

ACKNOWLEDGMENTS

An author writes a book alone but never without help. This book would not be complete without a grateful acknowledgement of:

Nina, Izzy, and Jamison Murphy, Kim Szczepanski and the Someone Just Pooped crew for welcoming us back to Prague.

Authors Camille Griep, Eva Moore, Beth Green and Ariel Meadow Stallings for inspiration, support and opportunities.

Supporting organizations GSRWA, SVRWA, Clarion West and the one and only Old School Romance Book Club.

My pit crew: Shelley Douma, Mark Cook, Jason Dittmer, Jo Bryant, Wes Green, Gita Krishnaswamy, and the incomparable Graham Family for providing essential provisions (food, coffee, and cocktails), opportunities to escape the writing cave, and lots of cheer-leading.

My husband, Oliver, who is still convinced I'm doing something amazing, and supports me in every way possible. My mom, who regularly morphs into the Best Grandma Ever so I can disappear into the cave without guilt.

Readers, reviewers and friends of Death's Dancer for giving me an excuse to do the happy dance on a regular basis.

My Mamas: Jen, Silvia, Megan, Kyrie, Jill, Nina, Lucie, Caroline, and the whole crew at The Inc. I had no idea what to expect when I joined the village, and your love and support have kept me afloat.

And last but not least, the people that make the book in your hands look good: Chrissy, Alisha and the team of Damonza, and Victory Editing.

ABOUT THE AUTHOR

Jasmine Silvera grew up sneaking kissing books between comics and fantasy movies. She's been striving for the perfect balance of romance, fantasy and adventure in her writing ever since. A semi-retired yoga teacher and an amateur dancer, she lives in the Pacific Northwest with her partner-in-crime and their small, opinionated, human charge.

THANKS FOR READING

Reviews help other readers find their next favorite book. Please consider leaving a review on Amazon, Goodreads or your favorite source for book recommendations.

* * *

Interested in more from Isela, Azrael and company? Be the first to find out about new releases by subscribing to the mailing list at www.jasminesilvera.com where you can also find deleted scenes, extras, and other goodies!

CPSIA information can be obtained
at www.ICGtesting.com
Printed in the USA
FFOW02n1731200418
46290032-47786FF